Medea

Books by Kerry Greenwood

Out of the Black Land
Medea

The Phryne Fisher Series
Cocaine Blues
Flying Too High
Murder on the Ballarat Train
Death at Victoria Dock
The Green Mill Murder
Blood and Circuses
Ruddy Gore
Urn Burial
Raisins and Almonds
Death Before Wicket
Away With the Fairies
Murder in Montparnasse
The Castlemaine Murders
Queen of the Flowers
Death by Water
Murder in the Dark
Murder on a Midsummer Night
Dead Man's Chest
Unnatural Habits

The Corinna Chapman Series
Earthly Delights
Heavenly Pleasures
Devil's Food
Trick or Treat
Forbidden Fruit
Cooking the Books

Short Story Anthology
A Question of Death:
An Illustrated Phryne Fisher Anthology

Medea

A Delphic Woman Novel

Kerry Greenwood

Poisoned Pen Press

#FiC 7-23-13

3 6000 00108 7285

Poisoned Pen Press
6962 E. First Ave., Ste. 103
Scottsdale, AZ 85251
www.poisonedpenpress.com
info@poisonedpenpress.com

Printed in the United States of America

Dedicated to Dennis Pryor

This book is dedicated to Dennis Pryor, a man of infinite patience and kindness, who politely pointed out my most obvious heresies and who exceeded my friend Stephen in the civilised constraint of his reactions to outrageous theories which skim lightly over his most profound understanding of the classics. The errors in this book are all my own work, and completely against his better judgment.

Placetne, Magister?

Acknowledgements

Most especial thanks to my delightful and exceptionally learned friend Stephen D'Arcy, amongst whose multifold talents is an ability to come up with, say, a recording of Ancient Greek lyre music or a video on the double-pipe used for setting the time for rowers—without even raising more than one eyebrow at the strangeness of the request.

Voici Estebe—a man of terrible learning.

The Cast

ARGONAUTS

Admetos	Jason's cousin
Akastos	Jason's half brother, son of Pelias
Alabande	friend of Ancaeas
Ancaeas	the Strong of Tegea, son of Poseidon
Argos	the shipwright
Atalante	of Calydon the hunter
Authalides	the herald
Clytios	the bowman and runner
Erginos	of the grey hair
Herakles	of Tiryns, lost after Hylas at Mysion
Hylas	beguiled by nymphs at Mysion
Idas	son of Aphareus, the boaster
Idmon	the seer, dies at Lycus
Jason	son of king Aison, rightful heir to the throne of Iolkos
Lynkeos	the Keen-Sighted, Idas' abashed twin brother
Melas	son of Argos
Meleagros	a strong rower
Nauplios	the narrator, son of Dictys
Nestor	the Honey-Voiced, (later in Trojan War, Homer)
Oileus	the Locrian, father of Ajax (Trojan War, Homer)

Perithous	a strong rower
Philammon	the Orphean, a bard
Telamon	father of the other Ajax (Trojan War, Homer)
Tiphys	the helmsman, dies at Lycus

Found Along the Way

Autolycus, Deileon & Phlogius Autolycus, the thief, grandfather of Odysseus, famous for offending gods; all three were lost from Herakles' expedition against the Amazons.

The **Argo** also collected the brothers **Argeus, Cytisoros, Phontis & Melanion**—who make common cause with Jason in retrieving the Golden Fleece, encouraged by the ghost of their father Phrixos. Their mother is Medea's sister **Chalkiope**.

Achaeans

Aison	father of Jason, true king of Iolkes
Amathaon	king of Pylus
Amycus	the boxer, a bandit
Autesion	little brother of Nauplios'
Daedalus	the architect, who flew from captivity in Crete
Dictys	the 'net-caster', father of Nauplios
Helle	sister of Phrixos, fell off the golden ram, and after whom the Hellespont is named
Hippolyte	queen of Amazons
Hypsipyle	queen of Lemnos
Iphinoe	woman of Lemnos, Nauplios' lover
Kleite	queen of the Doliones, suicided after Jason killed her husband Kyzicus, king of the Doliones
Pelias	the usurper king of Iolkos
Pheres	king of Pherae
Phineas	the prophet, a hermit in Thynia
Phrixos	flew the golden ram to Colchis, husband of Chalkiope

Polyxo	Queen Hypsipyle's adviser
Promeos	old man of the Doliones, killed by Jason
Telekles	old man of the Doliones, killed by Jason
Thoas	father of Hypsipyle, saved from massacre on Lemnos

COLCHIANS

Aegialeus	only son of Aetes, half brother of Medea. Later called Absyrtus, 'swept-down', because his limbs were scattered in the water by Jason.
Aetes	king of Colchis
Argeos	son Phrixos
Chalkiope	daughter of Aetes, half sister of Medea, wife of Phrixos
Cytisoros	eldest son of Phrixos
Eidyia	latest wife of Aetes
Eupolis	counselor of Colchis
Medea	'of good counsel', daughter of Aetes and Aerope
Melanion	youngest son of Phrixos
Phrontis	son of Phrixos
Trioda	Medea's nurse and tutor, priestess of Hekate
Tyche	priestess of Hekate

SCYTHS

Anemone	queen of the Scyths
Dianthys	a Scythian woman
Idanthyrsus	the Scythian king
Iole	a Scythian woman

CENTAURS

Cheiron	the wise one, to whom Jason, and later Achilles, were sent to be trained to be heroes
Hippos	a centaur priest
Philos	a centaur boy

Gods & Demigods

ACHAEAN

Aphrodite	goddess of erotic love
Apollo	god of the sun, learning and medicine
Ares	god of war
Artemis	virgin hunter, worshipped at Brauron as a bear
Ate	discord and also fate
Boreas	the north wind
Clio	muse of History
Europa	child who was borne on bull's back to what is now 'Europe'
Hades	or Pluton, the rich one—king of the underworld
Hekate	dark aspect of Gaia, the destroying mother
Hephaestos	the blacksmith
Hera	wife of Zeus
Herakles	the hero, later a god; in the sky as Ophiucus, the serpent bearer
Hermes	the divine messenger, also Psychopomp, the guide of souls
Hestia	goddess of the hearth and of hospitality
Ino	see Leukothea
Kadmon	or Kadmos, hero and husband of Omonia
Leukothea	Ino transformed into The White Goddess
Morpheus	'sleep'
Notos	the south wind
Omonia	'Harmony', wife of Kadmos
Poseidon	Earth-Shaker, god of the sea
Selene	aspect of Artemis, goddess of the moon
Semele	daughter of Kadmos, mother of Dionysos, lover of Zeus. She was destroyed by divine fire when she looked at him.
Talthybius	the divine herald
Thanatos	death, brother to Morpheus

| Zephyrus | the west wind |
| Zeus | 'thunderer; cloud-compeller,' father of the Olympians |

COLCHIAN

Ammon	god of the sun, 'hawk in the horizon,' shared with Achaeans and similar to Apollo
Hekate	black mother
Isis / Ishtar	goddess of love
Ophis	Megale 'great serpent,' guards the grove of the Golden Fleece

CENTAURIAN

| Hippia | the sacrificial mare, similar to the Celtic GODDESS EPONA |

DOGS

Argo	puppy given to King Phineas
Kore	'maiden,' Medea's hound
Scylla	'black bitch,' Medea's hound

Chapter One

Medea

My mother gave birth to me in the darkness under the earth and died in doing so. I loved the velvety blanket of night before my dazzled eyes ever encountered light. And when I did, they say I wept, and the people said, 'Here is a true daughter of Hekate!'

I am standing in the dark again, in the central room of my own place—no, of Hekate's temple, which was once mine, before I went with Jason. Jason the thief, the pirate, the betrayer. Jason the stranger. I have left my own gods, my own tongue, my own beliefs, for too long.

Now I will rejoin the Dark Mother, Scylla the Black Bitch. Hekate, Lady of Battles, Blood-drinker, she of the leather wings and coiled snakes, Mistress of Phantoms, come. Medea, once Princess of Colchis, calls. Your unfaithful daughter, fallen far from lordship and wisdom. She Who Is Met On The Way, Lady of Ghosts, I invoke you. Queen of the Dead, I invoke you. Mistress of the Triple Road, I invoke you.

The knife blade gleams, and I try the blade. I feel the sting as it slides along my thumb. It is very sharp.

I can hear the children laughing as they play.

How did I come to this?

◇◇◇

The first thing I remember was the darkness in the cavern and grove dedicated to our Lady, Hekate. I must have been three, perhaps, when they took me from the arms of the king my father and brought me naked into the lightless cave.

The priestess Trioda carried me in her arms. I was comfortable in her embrace. She was a tall, plump woman and used to children. I was my mother's murderer and my nurse was nervous of me, afraid of me, but Trioda knew what I was and held me firmly, so that I was not worried that she would drop me. She smelt of sweet scents like honey—some flower essence, perhaps—and the slightly sour smell of much-washed black garments dyed with the soot suspension the priestesses made. Her hair was already white and tickled my face.

It was interesting. The grove was composed of cypresses and pines, growing so thickly together that the sun never struck the forest floor, which was carpeted with generations of pine needles; our footsteps made no noise. The dark branches crisscrossed like a loom, precise and exclusive.

The deeper we went, the less I could hear. No birds lived or nested in the grove, and no small animals squeaked or scurried through the drift of needles. We passed into deeper and deeper shade, until we came to the mouth of the cavern. It was only visible as a blacker ellipse in the gloom.

'Are you afraid, little Princess?' asked Trioda.

'No,' I said. I could see nothing of which to be afraid, so far. I noticed, however, that Trioda was breathing faster. Was she afraid?

Into the black dark, blacker than any night on earth, I was carried. I could see nothing at all. For a moment, the weight of unlight pressed on my open eyes and I felt fear rise in me, but still nothing had happened to make me afraid, so I closed my eyes and immediately felt better.

Sound returned. I heard Trioda's feet on rock. Then we were climbing. I heard a spring trickling and Trioda's feet splashed through a small stream. I smelt cold water and rock and a flat, sour scent like the clay we used for making pots.

We came into a great space. There was a feeling of height, although I could see nothing except the strange red flowers that were blooming in front of my tight-shut or wide-open eyes. Trioda's footsteps resounded.

'You will come here, soon, on your own, little Princess,' she said, and echoes ran down stone walls from her voice, wounding the silence. I wriggled to be put down and she set me on the ground.

'This is the cavern of the lady Hekate,' she instructed me, holding my hand. 'No light comes here unless we bring it at great need. Touch the wall.'

I felt as she instructed and found gouges and marks carved into the stone.

'By these you will be able to find your way,' she said. 'Feel. Here are two fishes. Walk along one pace and you will feel three fishes.'

It was three paces for me, but she was right; though the marks were almost as high as I could stretch.

'Then four fishes, then five. Now, if you are lost, stand still, calm your mind, and trace the picture. The cavern is fifteen paces across. The night is the goddess' gift, Medea. The world of light is busy, confusing and loud. Here in the womb of the goddess it is always silent, always dark, so that you may hear your thoughts and strengthen your mind. In the night lies peace and wisdom, remember that.'

I nodded, realised that she could not see me, and said, 'Yes, Lady.'

'You are not afraid?'

'No, Lady,' I said truthfully. I thought that she gave a small laugh, though there was nothing to laugh at.

'Step away from me,' she said. 'This is what I brought you here to know, Medea. The goddess is here.'

I let go of her hand and took several steps into the middle of the cavern.

Then I felt what she meant. The darkness pressed on me, negating the sense I relied on—sight. I could see nothing at all. Fear flooded through me and I whimpered, feeling for her hand. There was no one there and I almost screamed with terror. The darkness might be thronged with ghosts, the beloved dead strangely transformed by death into fanged shadows, their clawed hands reaching for me, hungry for my blood, as my nurses' stories told. I listened for them and realised that I could not hear them if they were there—they were ghosts and ghosts move without sound. My skin crawled with anticipation of their contaminated touch. I put up both hands to cover my neck, where my blood beat close to the skin, and waited for the penetration of a tooth, the slimy grave-mired clutch as the phantoms seized their prey. I cried to Trioda and she did not answer. I was alone in the pit. As she had told me I must, I called on Hekate, mistress of phantoms.

> *Lady of the Crossroads,*
> *One who is met on the road,*
> *Evoe, Lady of Three Faces, aid me.*

> *Queen of the Lost,*
> *Queen of Dark Knowledge,*
> *She Who Turns, guide thy supplicant.*

> *Lady of Changes,*
> *Mistress of the Underworld,*
> *Help one who fears.*

The invocation echoed and boomed in the high cave and I heard a rush of wings, though I saw nothing at all.

Then, suddenly, I was calm. I was shaking and sobbing, but I was calm. I wiped my face with the hem of my tunic and took a deep breath. Then I took a step, then another, sweeping the air with my hands until I touched the wall and stretched up to find the carvings.

Two fish. I walked three paces along the wall and found three fish.

Even if Trioda had gone—even if Trioda had never existed, I could find my way out. I chuckled. The sound ran down the walls as if hundreds of ancestral Colchian princesses were pleased at my progress.

Then, my other senses sharpened, I heard Trioda breathing, smelt the black dye and flower scent, and took her hand. She lifted me into a close embrace. Her heart was beating hard under my cheek.

We walked along, tracing the fishes, until we came out of the cave into the grove. The light was strong and my eyes streamed tears.

Trioda did not speak until we were out of the trees and into the beech forest which lined the king's road to the palace, then she sat me down on a rock and said solemnly, 'Princess, you have done well. The goddess has accepted you. You will never in your life be so frightened again.'

I did not believe her, but I was glad that she was pleased.

We came out of the Black Land, or that is what they said— Colchis was, they told me, an island of civilisation amongst the warring clans of the barbarian Scyths. I only saw the Scythians when we held the four great markets of the year. They came in wagons or riding on their shaggy horses. I found them magnificent and exotic, the women riding knee-to-knee with the men, all dressed alike in trousers and tight, brightly embroidered jackets over linen shirts. I remember my sister Chalkiope, veiled against the sun to protect her white skin, watching from behind a potter's stall as they rode in. I had never seen such people. They were shaggy, jingling with gold ornaments, and they stank of horses and curdled milk. The men favoured massive moustaches and beards. They were strange to our eyes, as all our men are clean shaven and our priests entirely hairless, even to the eyebrows.

'Medea, stay here!' She grabbed unavailingly at the back of my tunic, but I evaded her easily. I had never seen such interesting people and I was used to Chalkiope's reflexes. Mine were faster.

I jumped out into the cobbled street almost under the hoofs of a mare and the rider, controlling the beast's start with easy grace, reached down and grabbed me. Her brown skin was glossy with oil. Her three long braids were decorated with little bronze bells and her face split into a grin, showing teeth like seeds in her red mouth.

'Well, little Colchian, didn't anyone tell you not to dive in front of a horse?'

She tilted my chin with her other hand, directing the horse with her knees.

'Yes, Lady, but I wasn't listening.'

She laughed louder, calling to the rider in front, 'Sister, here is a Scythian maid in Colchian clothing!'

'Who's your mother, little Scyth?' asked the other rider. She was broader in the beam than my captor, and her breasts were melons, ripe and heavy. She must have been nine months pregnant and her presence in public was remarkable. No Colchian woman would so expose her swollen belly to view. She would be called ugly, and jeered at. If she was poor and had to go out, she was closely swathed in a mantle which the women of Colchis called a belly-drape.

This Scythian's belly was dropped, a sign of imminent birth, and she had unlaced her leather corselet over her girth. But she did not seem ugly to me, just different, and she sat the horse as easily as if she was sitting on a chair, though she was so close to her time that milk had leaked from her breasts to stain her shirt.

'I am Medea, Aerope's child, but my mother is dead.'

'And who is the woman calling after you from the market?' asked the pregnant woman.

'My sister, Chalkiope,' I said dismissively. 'Where are you going? Take me with you.'

'Nay, we go to the women's mystery, which you cannot see until your first bleeding. My sister is in labour. By noon she will be delivered. Then you can find us, Little Scythian Medea, at our camp, at the side of the market away from the river, where the horse herds are penned. There you can come and visit and see the new child. For that is the Dark Mother's symbol, Scythling,' she touched the emblem around my neck. 'She cares for the newborn. Give my sister your blessing, Medea,' she urged.

I leaned over and placed my hand on the pregnant belly, copying my teacher, and intoned, 'Hekate guard you and guide you to a safe delivery.'

They smiled at me, and I jumped from the horse.

A moment later, my ears ringing from my Chalkiope's slap, I declared to my frantic sister, 'I will be a Scythian.'

At this pronouncement she marched me straight home and told my father, so that I was locked in the cellar for the night to teach me my place as a princess of Colchis.

I cried and struggled, largely as a matter of form. I quite liked the cellar. I was pleased with the dark now, and the strange visions I could induce by staring hard into it. I talked all night with the spirits, who agreed with me that life was exceptionally unfair. But the voices out of the whirling night purple flowers before my closed eyelids told me that I would not stay in Colchis forever, and that comforted me, so I slept.

When they came to release a penitent and tear-stained girl from durance, I walked past them with dry eyes and a straight back and went to the temple of Hekate. I saw one guard make a sign against the Dark behind my back, and was pleased.

They would not overbear Medea as easily as that.

Nauplios

Even Tiphys, the helmsman, can't see any land. We're rowing blind through sea fog. I'm colder than I've been since I was lost in a little boat off Skiathos for three days when that big fish broke my net and a wave carried away my oars. My hands are blistered and re-blistered so that each stroke makes the new sores break and bleed. I'm hungry and there's nothing to eat but thrice-baked, ash-cooked cakes as hard as wood, and I've run out of prayers to Poseidon.

I can't believe that we are going to find the Golden Fleece, though just now I would settle for any end to this journey apart from the salt water grave which is the final destination of all but the luckiest mariners. And as I swoop forward again to bring my oar back, to the rack of every muscle and the sobbing breath of each man on board *Argo*, I do not feel very lucky.

How did I come to this?

I was a child when he was a child—Jason, the great hero. Of course, he was a great hero even then, this son of Aison, King Pelias' brother, and rightful heir to Iolkos; while I was just Nauplios, the son of Dictys the fisherman. He was never afraid to say exactly what he meant, Jason. Punishment didn't deter him from truth.

Cheiron worried about him. 'Men use words to cloak truth in an acceptable dress,' he chided.

'But it is the truth,' insisted Jason. 'King Pelias has no claim to my father's throne.'

'Arguable,' said the centaur. 'As you get older, son of Aison, you will find that there are few truths graven in stone.'

'How, Master? Is not truth truth?'

'What colour is the sky?' asked the old man, settling back on his wooden bench and biting into an olive.

'Blue, Master.'

'And that is true?'

'Yes, Master.'

Master Cheiron spat out the stone and grinned, his old face wrinkling like a winter-stored apple. 'So if I said, "The sky is blue" that would be truth?'

'Certainly, Master,' said Jason.

'True for always?'

Jason thought about it. His brow furrowed as it always did when he thought deeply. He was a slim boy, already giving promise of great strength, with golden hair and bright eyes. I had been grooming one of Master Cheiron's small shaggy ponies, and put down the hoof I was cleaning to listen.

'No, Master, after dark the sky is not blue, and sometimes it is grey, and at sunset and dawn it is red and gold.'

'So it is true that the sky is blue, but it is also true that it is sometimes grey or golden or red or black.'

'Yes, Master.'

'So there you are,' replied the old man, reaching for another olive. 'It is also true,' he added, 'that horses have little patience with those who fail to attend them properly.'

The pony made a sideways plunge and I heard his hoof whistle past my head. I blushed and was recalled to my duty. But Jason sat on the green grass outside the centaur's cave, biting his lip, and pondering on the nature of truth.

They had brought me from the sea and my father's house to be a companion for Jason, son of Aison, brother of Pelias, who had usurped the kingdom of Iolkos.

Cheiron the centaur had demanded me of my father because the son of Aison required a companion. And I had found it all very strange when I had first ascended Pelion.

The centaurs are a small people—I was almost as tall as Master Cheiron when I was eight—and their ways secretive and strange. At first I missed my mother and I missed the sea, but Jason was glad that I had come, and comforted me as I wept for the sound of the tide and the taste of my mother's honey cakes.

'We will go back when we are grown,' he whispered into the close, horse-scented darkness. 'One day, Nauplios, we will go back to your beloved ocean, and then your mother will be proud of you.'

The best thing about the centaurs was their stories. They were of short stature, clannish and uncleanly, compared to the wide-talking, frequently washed men of my childhood. Cheiron's people oiled their skin rather than washed it, and the smell of a centaur settlement was noticeable at first—wood smoke, flesh, horses—but the nose quickly grew accustomed. The food was basic and not very pleasant—how I longed for my mother's honey cakes! I have seen a centaur plunge both hands into a steaming carcass, drag out the liver, and eat it raw.

I did the cooking for myself and the son Aison. I never learned to relish raw flesh, or raw fish, and I was not allowed to drink the fermented milk which made the old men drunk. In view of the way they all groaned in pain the next morning, this might have been a mercy.

We were sitting around the smoking dung fire one night when Cheiron took Jason's hand in his own. This was uncommon. They were not touching people, the centaurs. He lifted a brand from the fire and quite deliberately burned the hand he held, so that Jason winced and cried out.

'Why?'

'So that you will remember what I am about to tell you.'

I could never read those wrinkled faces. He was concentrating, intent, his shaggy brows shading the bright brown eyes.

'Whenever you see this scar, you will recall the tale of Phrixos and the Golden Fleece.'

'Master,' said Jason. I watched a red weal rise on the smooth surface of his wrist and winced in sympathy.

'It was a woman's doing, of course,' said the centaur, slowly, spitting into the fire. 'A wicked woman—a woman's lies. All women lie. Remember that.

'Phrixos, grandson of Minyas—that is why your kin are called Minyans, boy—and his sister Helle lived happily until their father married again,' Cheiron began.

A tall young man he was, this Phrixos, dark and beautiful, and the woman desired him. The woman wanted him for his curly hair and his hands—she watched him with the horses, saw how skilfully he touched them, imagined her own flesh so gentled and smoothed, and burned with lust.

Perhaps it was Ishtar, whom you call Aphrodite, who possessed her—I do not know. But she came to him in the stable, calling his name, offering him wine, then slipped close to him so that he could smell the scent of her femaleness, like a mare in season, and she said, 'I love thee, Phrixos. Lie with me here in the straw and thy father shall never know.'

He was shocked, and pushed her away. Then she tore her garment—deceitful bitch!- and ran from the stable, crying that the king's son had attempted violence on her honour.

The air was cold. I drew my goatskin cloak closer, and rubbed my hands over my face. The hatred in the old man's voice stung my ears. I knew no harm of women—how could I? My mother was a woman. But Jason was drinking in the voice, mouth open. The stars were blazing, close as lanterns.

They bound him and carried him up the mountain to the high altar—Phrixos, the king's son, betrayed by a cruel woman. His sister Helle followed him, keening for him as though he was already dead, tearing her hair. She was fair, they say, and she scattered strands of bright gold along the stone, and the priest took a bronze knife.

It was noon, hot and still. Even the birds were silent. It seemed that the world was holding its breath. The priest raised the knife over the defenceless throat, stretched like a beast's for sacrifice. Then...

He stopped speaking to swig from a wineskin. Jason and I held our breath, like the world. I could almost feel the heat of the midday sun, scent the crushed grass under the feet of the witnesses to this sacrifice. The pause lengthened, so that I could hardly bear it, but it was not my place to speak.

'Master?' asked Jason in a strained whisper.

Cheiron grinned and resumed the story.

There was a crunching in the scrub, something coming toward them along the mountain path. Something heavy and strong and determined. The knife poised in the air. Phrixos had not made a sound. Helle stilled her weeping, wild with sudden hope. The creature came to the brow of the hill.

It was a man. Not tall, but very strong; wearing a lion's skin and carrying a club. A young man he was then; ah, I remember, Herakles the Hero, when the world was young as well. He can't have been more than seventeen. His hair was tangled back from a broad brow, a wide nose, a generous mouth, now shut like a trap. There were burrs in his beard, and grass in his hair. But his shoulders later bore the weight of the whole earth, and even then he was scarred with many adventures.

'You woke me,' he complained. 'I thought at least the top of the mountain would be secluded. What do you here, men of Minyas, at this altar, with this most unholy of victims?'

'This is Phrixos, the king's son, who is guilty of rape, and we will sacrifice him to Zeus,' said the priest.

Herakles yawned, scratched his chest and then shook his head.

'No,' he said patiently. 'No, you won't do that. Zeus does not accept human sacrifices. You cannot elevate your own killing of this boy to a religious rite, Minyans. If you kill him, you kill him on your own, and on your own consciences must your deed lie.

'You do see that I can't allow you to do this, don't you? Such blasphemy will bring a curse on innocent ones, women and children, not just on you alone.'

He never boasted, that hero. His voice was even and gentle. But he was tapping a club made of the best part of an olive tree against his broad calloused palm as he spoke. And he wiped his brow. Battle fury came on that hero with a wave of heat.

'Remember that,' Cheiron warned. 'If you meet Herakles. Beware of him when he speaks gently and you see sweat break on his skin. Once his anger is loosed, no man or god can call it back—not even Herakles himself.' The centaur returned to his story.

The Minyans quailed—for they had heard of Herakles, of his strength and his battle madness—but they had orders from their

*own king. They gathered, spears raised. Helle threw herself at
her brother and untied his bonds, hoping for escape.*

*Then the gods, who are just and weigh all actions in the scale
of Themis, sent a winged golden ram from heaven. Hera
sent it, she who is the protector of Herakles and guardian of
families. Hermes made it, who is the messenger of the gods.
Phrixos and Helle climbed onto its back and flew away into
the air, above the astonished faces of the wicked Minyans.
Phrixos was saved.*

I couldn't stop myself from asking, 'Master, Master, what
about Herakles? Didn't the Minyans attack him?'

'He had great presence, even newly woken and dusty,' said
the centaur.

*There were only twenty Minyans there, and they knew that he
might overcome them. For Herakles could leap like a goat and
run like the wind; his eye was keen as a lance and his hands
were stronger than tree roots that can rip through stone. He
stared at them, and they at him, after they had watched the
golden ram bear the king's son away. Then, they say, he gave
a sigh, nodded to the heavens, hefted his club and walked
away, quite slowly, down the mountain. They did not dare
to follow or assail him. He was Herakles the hero.*

'Remember that, son Aison. Authority is a great shield.'

Jason nodded impatiently. 'And Phrixos?' he prompted.

The old man's voice was flat with displeasure—though he
allowed Jason to interrupt him more than he did me—but he
continued.

*As to Phrixos, he flew on the golden ram across Thrace, even in
the sky as no one but birds, gods and Daedalus, the architect,
and his sons have flown before. When passing over the strait,
his sister Helle lost her grip on his waist and fell. They call
that water the Hellespont now.*

Women are weak, and she was a tender maid, too young to leave her mother's house. Phrixos cried after her as she fell, but the blue closed over her and she was gone.

The ram flew on to Colchis, the white city on the River Phasis, which flows into the Euxine Sea, and there landed, safely, the royal son of Minyas. He immediately showed his piety by sacrificing the ram to Zeus, his deliverer.

'Hera sent it, not Zeus All-Father,' I interrupted, 'and why kill the ram? It would be wonderful to be able to fly.'

'The actions of heroes are not to be questioned by boys,' snarled Cheiron, and I closed my mouth.

'That is the Golden Fleece, Jason, which rests in the sacred grove at Colchis, guarded by a serpent. It is a holy treasure beyond price, the rightful property of the rightful king of Iolkos.

'Phrixos met a princess there: Chalkiope, daughter of the king Aetes. She saw him and loved him, the fair hero, and she lay with him and bore him four sons. But the king disliked these boys, having no son of his own, and when Phrixos died, he did not adopt them—or so they say.

'That king holds the Golden Fleece without right. Zeus punished him by taking his queen, though they say he took another woman. She only bore him another daughter, Medea, before she died too. The hand of the gods is heavy on blasphemers. That is the tale of Phrixos, cousin of Aison—your father, and Pelias—your uncle. Remember it when you come into your own.'

Jason was alight with the tale; he told it to me over and over again as we lay down in the goatskins, and as I drifted into sleep I heard him whispering in the darkness over the snores of the centaurs.

'Rightful property—the Golden Fleece is the rightful property of the descendants of Phrixos, who rode on the golden ram from Mount Laphystios to Colchis.'

With my last conscious thought, I still considered that sacrificing it at all, and especially to the wrong god, was very unfair on the ram.

Chapter Two

Medea

I could read and write—and how inkstained I got, and how Chalkiope scolded me for the black blotches on the clean white tunic worn by all princesses of the royal house!—so I must have been nine years old when Trioda summoned me one hot morning.

It was sizzling as I crossed the white marble pavement. The sun had heated the stone, so that even my hard bare feet were uncomfortably warm. I wondered where I had left my sandals when I went fishing with my half brother Aefialeus and my sister Chalkiope's sons: Cytisoros, the eldest and leader; Argeos, the bully; Phrontis, the trickster; and Melanion, my friend.

My sister was fifteen when I was born. She had lain with the foreigner, borne his children and wept over his grave while I was growing up. I remembered him, a tall man with a loud voice. He had died eight years ago and the stems of the ivy around his grave were as thick as hawsers. I thought my sister old, of course, old and stern. And she disapproved of me, though we could have been close. Both of our mothers had died at our births—and she certainly interfered in my life as much as any mother could have done. Trioda said that there was a curse on all women associated with my father, Aetes.

Chalkiope had been pretty, I vaguely remembered, though now her brow was furrowed and her lips pinched. She did not like my friendship with her children, though the youngest was the same age as me. Melanion had smooth skin and eyes like the most expensive Kriti honey, and I was another boy to him, a playmate, not a princess.

I could not marry. I knew that the priestesses of Hekate are always maidens. I did not see, however, that I could not be friends with Melanion because of that. He was my nephew. No one could object to amity amongst close kin, surely. Possibly, however, it might have been a good idea not to get quite so dirty while demonstrating this.

Trioda eyed me. She stood in her black garments like a crow in the brightness of the strong sunlight, her arm raised against the light. I surveyed myself.

I had skinned one knee on the edge of the landing stage, and I had fallen in—once my mistake and the second time because I was already wet and going to be scolded, and I liked the feel of the water. The shallow river pond where we harvest shellfish had been as warm as blood, and I had already dried on my run from the banks. My tunic was crumpled and stained with tar and altogether I was a spectacle—an object lesson in what a princess of the royal house of Colchis should not look like.

I raised my chin and waited for a slap, but she did not hit me, or even seem to notice my disheveled condition. Instead, she gave me a potion and watched as I choked it down. It was bitter. Then she took my hand and led me into the grove.

I had been feeling defiant; now all my courage drained away. There was something in that grove—something new. The wind in the cypresses sang loud and shrill, though the day outside was as still as death. My mud-stiff hair stirred at the back of my neck. I could smell, suddenly, a reek of strong perfume, rank and fascinating, like a mixture of incense and rotting flesh, and I coughed, pulling against Trioda's hand, not to retreat but to run into the scent, into whatever was forming in the darkness under the trees. Something was pulling me. Trioda grabbed me by the shoulders.

'Speak,' she ordered. 'Pray. Listen!'

'Lady of Darkness,' I began. My words were blown away in the rising wind. 'Lady of Forests, Protector of the Newborn, Lady of the Three Ways, hear me.' Then I was guided or prodded to add, 'I am Medea. You called me. I am here.'

All utterances directed to the lady Hekate must be tripartite, or she will not hear them. The wind rose to a howl and we stood in the calm centre of it, untouched, though the pine needles whipped past, hissing.

'Child,' said a voice. I fell to my knees, my mistress beside me. Trioda covered her face, but I stared into the pine needles, green and brown, as they began to form into…something.

A woman, ten cubits high, wreathed in snakes, flanked by two black hounds. Owls flew about her head. Her face was forming, dark eyes, black hair which fell below her waist and writhed and curled. The vegetable hands were open, she held out her arms, and an irresistible yearning drowsiness took me, folded me close and warm and safe.

She said 'Daughter,' and I fell asleep on her breast.

I woke in the dark. She was gone. The world was hollow, comfortless. I wept inconsolably. I cried for hours, refusing all attempts at reassurance by a shaken Trioda, until at the flux of the night, when Trioda says that the goddess Hekate is strongest, when the tide is ebbing and old men die, I heard it again.

A sweet voice, saying, 'Daughter.' It vibrated through my bones and I shivered with fear and delight.

I slept then, and did not weep. I was the daughter of the great goddess, and the next day two black hound bitches were beside my bed when I woke, and Trioda said that I was to be taught the lesser mysteries of Hekate.

They did not, at first, seem to be very intriguing. We searched through the beech woods for a certain fungus, scrabbled through endless grasses for a certain dark-leafed herb, and plucked little purple berries from a tall, fronded, meadow plant. These three things, fungus, leaf and berry, Trioda gathered into a basket made of ferns, which had taken me a whole day and considerable damage to my fingers and patience to construct. We did all this in silence. I was scratched and bored.

'Mistress,' I ventured, following her erect back along the path toward the palace. 'Mistress, what are we doing?'

'Tell me, Medea, what do you see in that basket?' she asked, her voice quite even, but with a strange undercurrent which I could not identify.

'Berries, Mistress, a flat red mushroom and a handful of dark green leaves.'

'That is what you see, is it, acolyte?'

There was some trick to the question, and I considered the things again. I strained my eyes, hoping for another vision, but all I could see was a badly made fern basket—my next one would be much better—and some wilting herbage.

'That is all I can see, Mistress,' I said crossly.

She knelt down so that she could look into my eyes. I will never be tall. I saw inside the hood she always wears in daylight. Trioda with her pale boney face, her beaked nose, her bright eyes and a straggle of coarse white hair. She was almost smiling. She smiled very seldom.

'Medea,' she said softly, 'these are the mysteries of Hekate, queen of phantoms. What you cannot see in that basket, my daughter, is death. You hold death in your hands. With what you carry, you could kill twenty strong men, even if they be heroes in the first flush of their manhood and strength. What you cannot see in that basket, little Princess, is power.'

I stared. Her face was soft, like a woman looking down at a newborn against her breast.

'It is like this, little daughter.' She motioned me to sit down, and I folded into the beechmast, smelling the sharp scent, appreciating the springy softness. 'Men rule the world, as was not the case in the beginning, when Hekate was the Triple Goddess, maiden, mother and crone. Men stole her, fragmented her, bent her worship to their purposes. Have you never wondered why the pine grove is called "Sacrifice Wood"?'

I had wondered, among many other things, and nodded. She shoved her hair carelessly back from her face, letting the hood fall.

'Once, when Hekate ruled and men were recognised for what they are—mere providers of the seed, useful for a space, but of no value in the nurture and feeding of the world—the Summer King walked into that wood every autumn, and there he met… someone. There he died, and his blood drained into the fertile ground. There he was buried, and a new king was found for the next spring. For we do not need men, little daughter, except for one purpose and for a short time.'

I was a little taken aback. I had often played in the Sacrifice Wood with Melanion. He did not like it, saying the wood was too dark and cold. I had always found it cool and soothing.

Trioda spoke quickly, as though she had a lot to tell me in a short time. 'But then men conquered us, Medea.'

'They conquered the goddess?' I gasped.

'No, no, She Who Meets cannot be conquered by men. She who was a Titan before the Cronos children came and there was war in heaven. Latecomer Zeus gives her all honour, and the ability to grant any wish, if she pleases. She is as powerful as ever, but we are not. Women were conquered here, by stronger arms, more brutal laws. Women belong to men, to dispose of as they please. They are our masters. They forbade the sacrifice of the summer king, took away Her worship, thinned our blood, bound our limbs. They break us, kill us, sell us like slaves. But this they cannot steal. They cannot take away our knowledge, Medea. This I will teach you, all that I learned from the priestess who was my mother. Which herbs will heal. Which herbs will kill.'

'But Mistress,' I caught at her sleeve, 'my father holds Colchis in right of Aerope, my mother, that is the Colchian succession. To be king, you must marry a woman who is next in line for the throne—that is, Chalkiope, when my father is dead.'

'And Chalkiope has no daughter,' said Trioda. 'Therefore if she is to confer the kingship, she must attempt conception again, with a stranger. She must bear a daughter, and that will be hard. She is old for child bearing, and the penetration of the male will hurt her.'

'It will hurt?' I gasped.

'Men are stronger, harder, cruel. She will accept it in hopes of bearing an heir, as all women do. Except the virgin acolytes of the goddess, most favoured of women, who need not endure the weight and the intrusion and the pain. You will never suffer it, Medea. Be joyful, and remember what I have told you.

'Now, this is called hemlock,' she touched the green leaves. 'It is deadly if it is made into an infusion—we will consider how such a death may be delivered. Mixed with wine it needs a lot of honey to disguise the taste. This is the red fungus, *Mycis Kokkinos*. Grind it to powder when it is dried, and sprinkle it over food. It numbs the mouth on contact, so you must serve it in a savoury sauce. This is nightshade. The whole plant is dangerous, but the berries are most poisonous. Mix them with bramble and other berries and they will not be noticed. Do you understand?' she asked in her usual voice.

I said, 'I understand.' I didn't, of course; but I resolved that I should.

◇◇◇

The palace of Aetes, my father, was spacious, made of white stone figured with frescoes and inlaid with tesserae. I lived in a small room off Chalkiope's chamber.

I had a fresco. It was of strange trees and brightly coloured flowers such as I had never seen, and in the centre coiled a golden serpent, bigger than life size, with green stones for eyes. I flung myself down on my bed and heard the leather straps squeak as they took my weight. It was tending toward autumn and the nights were cold.

Chalkiope called from her room, 'Is that you, Medea?'

I muttered something, and she appeared, wrapped in a fleecy cloak, her hair unbound and falling to her shoulders.

'What's the matter, Medea?' she asked.

'Trioda says…' I began, then stuck. I could not repeat to my sister, who was not a virgin, what the priestess had confided to me.

'What says Trioda?' asked Chalkiope, sitting down beside me. 'Come into my cloak, you're shivering.'

I was, I noticed. I allowed her to wrap the cloak around both of us and leaned my head against her shoulder.

'When Phrixos…' I felt my way toward a question, not knowing how she would react. She smelt lovely, of skin and sleep and perfumed oil. I sniffed appreciatively and she stroked my hair.

'When Phrixos?' she repeated.

'Did he hurt you? When you lost your maidenhead?'

'Hurt me? Of course, at first.' She felt me nod, and added, 'Only at first. I submitted to his desire, which is proper. And lying with a man is the only way to conceive, Medea.'

'I will never do that, never,' I said into her shoulder.

'Not if you follow the goddess,' she agreed. 'But you are too young to decide such matters, little sister. You are only nine. There is time for the Maiden and the Mother as well, you know.'

'No, there isn't,' I argued sleepily. 'Once virginity is lost, it is lost forever. So says my mistress.'

'And she is correct,' she laid me down in my bed and covered me with the luxuriant fleece. 'But we are women, sister. We have no voice in our own fate.'

'It's not fair,' I heard my voice trail away, lapped in warmth.

'No,' she said softly, taking the light away. 'But it is the way of the world.'

Nauplios

I was twelve and a man, according to the centaur method of counting. Jason had grown, all of a sudden, it seemed. He was tall, fair and beautiful. His hair curled golden down his back and his eyes were a light, strange colour, almost green, almost blue. Such eyes had not been seen among the centaurs. I remember when I was brought to Cheiron as a small child, staggering with weariness up the steep path from my father's house, he had asked me whether the son of Aison was blind. But Jason saw well from those liquid eyes. We ran every day, chasing the centaur's goats up and down the steep hills. Jason could run down a goat and pin it as I came panting behind with the rope to tie around the truant's neck.

I was never going to be as tall. I was stocky, even as a child, and young manhood had not given me more than a few spans' height on the centaurs. My hair, unlike the hero's, was black, neither curly nor straight and mostly tangled with burrs. I used to spend patient hours teasing them out of Jason's hair. They always came out with an ouch and a little knot of gold.

We saw a glint of light once in a tree by Cheiron's camp and climbed to trace it. I heard Jason laughing as wings beat around my head. 'What is it?' I panted. He waved an arm to frighten off a frantic mother bird, and pointed. A magpie had woven bright strands of Jason's hair into her nest. The squabs sat squawking in gold thread.

'A royal nurturing,' I said, and we climbed down.

And Jason never forgot his fate and his lineage, although the memories of my parents had faded so that I might not have known them across a marketplace. He knew of the prophecy which said that a one-sandalled man would come to depose Pelias from his fraudulent lordship. He whispered to me, as we lay clasped under the goatskins, that he prayed to Hera the Mother that he might be her agent; that he might limp into Iolkos and reclaim his father's kingdom.

We were twelve and then we were thirteen, and the centaurs' festival of Carnaiea had begun. Once a year, under a certain moon, the mares all come into season. It may be that there are magical ceremonies which bring this about, of course—I would not dare enquire into such mysteries. One of the things which precedes it is a boar hunt, for at this time the centaur men have connection with the centaur women, after a feast of boar flesh.

Previously we had been excluded from this hunt and Jason had chafed, wondering if it was because we were human children, not of the race of the small horsemen. 'Can we hunt with you for Carnaiea, Master?' he asked.

The dark eyes surveyed us. We were naked, as he was, and Cheiron handled us as though we were horses. A hard hand ran down to my loins, cupped my genitals, tested my pubic hair and the hair under my arms, tugging. Then a thumb ran across my chin where down was sprouting. He grunted, then treated Jason alike. Then he nodded toward the boar spears, and we ran to get one each.

'At last!' said Jason with satisfaction, choosing the longest spear and feeling the edge. I nodded, taking a shorter but thicker spear, and tried not to remember the terrible strength of the boar, the filthy tusks dripping with poisonous saliva, and the death of the centaur boy the year before—exactly a year. They had brought him into the camp, limp and dying, and as they laid him down beside Cheiron's house his guts had spilled onto the earth, a flash of curving blue and red intestines, uncoiling, and he had so died. I hoped I could die silently, as he had. I did not think it likely.

The centaurs did not approve of idle speech, considering it a valuable commodity to be used sparingly and for effect, so that every word was treasured and remembered. Jason and I, said our master, talked far too much, wasting precious words.

'A man has a measure of words, as he has a measure of semen,' Cheiron said. 'More will not be made if he has wasted his substance. Keep silent, humans, on this hunt at least. The boar can hear a hunter's footfall across the mountain forest. He can smell us from a hundred paces. No words, young men.'

We nodded, overwhelmed by the honour of graduating from children to young men. There would be no manhood ritual for us. The eldest priest cut the foreskins of the centaur boys, wounding their breasts with a bronze pin dipped in soot and rolling them in the skin of the sacrifice; the only horse ever killed by the horse people.

We would not mate as our first gift of seed with a young mare in her first season. She who receives all of the brotherhood into her body, symbolising their kinship with the goddess of horses, whom we Achaeans do not know. Then the queen mare is garlanded with flowers and led to the sacrifice, and all of her lovers eat of her flesh and drink of her blood, and thereafter are centaurs.

Jason and I were fosterlings, not centaurs. The boys our age had gone from us, joined the clan of men, and we were left with the children, unable to join our friends, cut off from the ones we had known. We had been feeling lonely, but now, it seemed, we were to be admitted to the life of the tribe, to be young men.

Jason and I had lain together since we were children. When we grew newly sensitive flesh, we had touched and caressed, fascinated with the gush of seed, the strange scent, the jolt of pleasure. Cheiron had caught us, beaten us and forbidden us to lie under the same covering, saying that we would waste our strength.

I did not believe it. It might have been so for the centaurs, but not for a human. The earth soaked up my seed every night in silence, and I muttered the only prayer I remembered from my mother's teaching. It was a prayer to Aphrodite, goddess of love, and my mother had told me to say it to my lover, the first woman I lay with:

> *Lady of Cyprus, delight your supplicant.*
> *Lady of Doves, receive my offering.*
> *Foam born, teach me thy mystery.*

I began not to burn, as the stories of lovers told grudgingly by Cheiron described—he did not approve of the Achaean fascination with love—but to thirst, as though there was something inside me parching for lack of water. I could not imagine where I would find a human woman to lie with me. Jason, doubtless, would be provided with a bride after he had achieved his destiny. Perhaps she might have a slave or a maiden sent with her who would be given to me.

I wondered what she would be like as I lay in my cold wrappings, apart from my bedmate. Not beautiful, that would be too much to expect. Old, perhaps, even crippled—Nauplios, the net-man Dictys' son, could command no beauty of face or body—but possessed of those parts which could enfold me, take me into her body, give me joy. Her arms would wrap me close, hold me to her breast—ah, her soft breast!—and I would lie in her arms all night.

Such musings usually ended with me turning my body into the soft earth. She always accepted my libation graciously.

That night I slept intermittently around the fire. I was afraid of the dawn. I was even more afraid of my own fear. I must not fail at this hunt.

As soon as the goddess whom we call Eos trailed a pink garment over the horizon we were awake. I had polished and oiled the stone head of the boar spear, had tended my feet, too, which were as hard as hoofs, and tightened the belt and loincloth which held my shrinking genitals in some kind of safety. For a cornered boar strikes for the fork of the biped which assails it, tusks and tears for the belly and the sex, to bring the insolent attacker to his knees to be savaged. From my belt hung a bronze knife, one of a pair which Jason had brought with him. It was as sharp as I could make it. I tied up my hair and joined my friend, who was leaning against the corner of a hut and looking irritatingly relaxed.

'Which way are we going?' I asked, not wanting to trust my tongue overmuch.

He pointed and touched his ear, hunter's talk for 'Listen!'

I listened. Far up the mountain I heard the baying of the hounds. They had found prey. The boar was moving, from the sound, down the valley between Centaurs' Mountain and the next, which they called Axe Head because of its shape. That was bad. That valley was thickly wooded, with deep undergrowth. Jason and I had penetrated there in search of a lost goat once, and it had taken hours to find our way out again—with the burden of a new kid and a very affronted mother, who had chosen, she thought, the safest place in the world for her delivery.

The thorned red vines which the centaurs call wolf's fruit, because of a resemblance to the berries of blood dripping from a predator's jaws, were high enough to cut off the sky. I had drawn a deep breath of relief as we had paused on Centaurs' Mountain as the goat suckled her kid and I sucked my scratches, under the benign gaze of heaven again.

But there was no fighting the dictates of Fate, so I hefted my spear and we joined the soft-footed hunters.

In twos and threes we drifted down the slope, over the grass and the flowers of Adonis, stepped across the stream at the bottom and began climbing the other side.

I was lost in the space of time in which a man drinks a cup of wine. Jason at my side was fighting his way through the scrub, and I could not speak to remind him that we were supposed to stand still, unwind the vine, and slide through the bushes, making little sound. This slowed the progress but reduced the damage to human skin. I stopped for the thousandth time to unwrap my thigh from the cruel embrace of thorns as sharp as daggers, and then I saw him.

The hounds bayed, higher up. The hunters whistled, calling in the dogs, and I heard a crash and a short bitten-off scream on the slope above my head. They were seeking him on their own level.

But out of the coiled tangle of undergrowth, the head was emerging. A high-shouldered king boar—tall as a colt, wide as a doorway, scarred with many encounters, ten years old and cunning as a serpent. His eyes were red with rage and dark with calculation.

I froze. I could not move or speak.

He shook himself, tossing his head. His tusks dripped with blood. He was hideous and proud, lord of his world, and we mere humans could not dent his arrogance. The stench of him encompassed me. Almost human, the scent of a boar. An unwashed human who reeks with maleness and blood—that is the smell.

Then Jason screamed a challenge aloud, and thrust a spear into the creature's side.

The boar turned quicker than sight; I heard his jaw snap closed on the boar spear, and the splinter of breaking wood.

Jason was shaken as the boar shook his heavy head and then, as the spear broke, my lord was thrown to one side.

I had to distract the attacker. I grounded my spear, braced it with my foot, and whistled. The boar spun again, moving like a snake, and pawed the ground, grunting with fury. I saw the red wound in his side, bleeding fresh red in gouts, not slowing his advance. I cried to Jason, who was caught in the thorns, 'Help!' and he felt for his knife, shaking his head.

Everything was moving very slowly. The boar gouged great furrows in the leaf mould with his front feet, challenging me. I braced the spear and myself for his rush, knowing that if I did not hold him he would run along the spear, that even spitted through the whole length of his gullet he could still tear me to pieces before he died. I needed Jason to cut the boar's throat, and he was still lying in the bushes, looking dazed.

'Jason! Help me!' I screamed, and the boar charged.

The spear entered his mouth, a wet red cavern, and the shock of his attack knocked me to the ground. I was lying on my back, the spear grounded deep in the earth, and the boar was between my legs.

I was so afraid that I ceased to be afraid. I thought how we must look, the huge beast and the boy, the fragile limbs vainly wrapping the barred sides as the tusks sank into the belly, tore and destroyed, the toss of the head as he flung up loops of guts like a domestic pig roosting in beechmast. I was dead, I was floating. I heard some noises as something tore through the thorns, and then someone cut the string which tied my soul to my body, and I floated away like a butterfly.

Chapter Three

Medea

I was still pondering the nature of the relations between men and women when I went into Colchis for the autumn festival.

My two black bitches, Scylla and Kore, were well trained, silent mouthed, and watchful. They were sometimes just hounds, of course, but they had the ability to receive the goddess; they could become avatars of She Who Meets, and speak with her voice. They never left me. The priestess of Hekate is known by her black garments, her pale skin, her dangerous gaze and her fanged escorts. I was eleven years old, still unwomaned, but the crowds made way as I walked through the streets, and men and boys avoided my eyes. Women gazed hopefully on me, presenting me with their squealing offspring to bless, and although I disliked their sour, milky smell, I always kissed them with Hekate's kiss, She of the Newborn. I had duties now, and power. I had seen the goddess and felt her influence.

And alone in my bed I still yearned for that safety, rocked in the arms of the Dark Mother, cradled against her cloudy breast.

Colchis was crowded with foreigners. It is a small but rich city, Colchis Phasinos. When they came from Egypt, our ancestors brought with them seeds, tinctures and skills, and they used them, making a small island of civilisation in an ocean of barbarians. Colchis was built in a square, protected against strong winds and assault by high walls of dark local stone in which there are four gates. Scythgate looks toward the south and the plains. Eastgate toward the curve of the river which embraces the town at Rivergate, and west is Mountaingate.

Very high and cold are the peaks we see from Mountaingate, and there is always snow on them. There men search for gold, Colchis' reason for existence, together with the poison and medicine and dye we produce from the yellow flower, colchida. The flower blooms in spring, making the sedge and the river banks golden. It is the preserve of Hekate the Triple One, and can only be culled by her priestesses. When we have stocked our own temples, we sell the remainder to the traders, who come from many lands to Poti at the delta and thence down the Phasis to the landing stages of Colchis, for it is a precious and sacred herb. Some parts of the plant will save those whose heart fails them. Some parts will dye cloth golden as sunshine. Some parts will flavor food with an unsurpassable savour; and some parts, correctly distilled, will kill a man with one drop in a bowl of wine.

Autumn brings the colchida harvest, and I was on my way home to the palace of my father, my tunic overflowing with the precious flowers, the Princess Medea's share. The mist was coming down, as it does, in the marshes which surround watery Colchis. The elderly priestesses were already eyeing the weather doubtfully and ordering stores moved up from the cellars and away from all riverbanks, even from small trickles which bear water only in winter. I was charged with informing the king that the winter would bring flood and exceptional cold, so I would have to request audience of him.

I very seldom saw my father, Aetes. He had never forgiven my mother for dying without giving him a male child, though I would have thought that the birth of my half brother, Aegialeus, would have mitigated his wrath. I had seen him only in state, never in private, though they said that he had held me when I was two days old, when Trioda showed me to Hekate and said, 'Lady, your priestess is born.'

The palace is the only building in Colchis made wholly of stone. Stone does not grow in the marshes. It must be brought with great labour from the mountains, floated on rafts. Only the palace is built of it and has stone floors and interlocking courtyards all of marble.

One reaches the audience chamber of King Aetes by passing through a great door, along a passage figured with little gold rams, under the lintel of bronze and the lowering ram's head in the centre, and into the main courtyard.

No women are allowed here but, as a priestess of the Great One, even a minor acolyte, I could pass anywhere. Hekate's priestesses are not women like other women. Through doors and corridors I went, standing straight under my burden of golden flowers, my hard bare feet slapping the marble. The guards looked away from me as though I had the eyes of Gorgon, which turned men to stone.

The courtyard was built for a previous king by an architect who came from the Black Land, and was so pleasing to the eye that I paused, rubbing one sole against the opposite shin where one of Colchis' myriad mosquitoes had bitten me. Kore sat down on one side of me, Scylla on the other, licking paws and panting. They were beasts today, not goddesses, and I liked their warmth and their doggish disdain for the majesty of the king to whom all men bowed. I spared a hand to stroke Kore's warm silky ears and she nuzzled my palm.

The courtyard was square and had four fountains. The water flowed from bronze ram's heads, made marvellously by an Achaean called Daedalus, who contrived that at festivals one ran with oil, another with wine and a third with honeyed milk. The fourth was always supplied with water which was warm when the Pleiades set, but at their rising in summer bubbled up as cold as ice, wonderfully refreshing. No woman could drink of it, but I was not a woman. I cupped a hand and sipped the warm water. Kore and Scylla rose on their hind legs and lapped at the basin.

Vines interlaced the sky in the courtyard of the king, heavy at this season with Colchian grapes, almost black. Into the silence came the sound of wings. A raven dropped from the heavens and landed on the basin, almost on my wet fingers. She was as black as the grapes, with a blue bloom on her feathers, and she dipped her beak and drank three times, heedless of the dogs and of me. Then she cocked her head, examining me with her marigold eye. Swift as a flash, she took wing, plucking three golden flowers from the harvest in my skirt.

Then she was gone, gaining height in a flapping rush.

'Surely you are favoured of Hekate,' said a man's voice.

I turned, spilling flowers. A man in bronze armour stood at the doorway to the audience chamber. The crown of Colchis was on his head and I knelt and the dogs sat down beside me.

'Father,' I said.

I heard him approach. His boots rang on the stone floor. I heard the creak of the harness and smelt him; leather and maleness, wine and oil. An old hand laden with the rings of kingship reached down and raised me to my feet, leaning the while upon my shoulder.

'Daughter,' he acknowledged. 'What have you been gathering?'

'Colchida, Lord, the princess' portion. I bring word to you, Father, from the women of wisdom in the temple of the Dark Mother.'

'What word?' he motioned me to sit down. He had one hand on the fountain coping and one on me. He was heavy. Now that I saw him closely, I noticed that he had aged. He had always seemed god like to me, strong and tall. He was still ten spans above my height, but deep lines cut into his face, and his hair was thin under the heavy crown. The hand which gripped me had a faint tremor. His slaves said that his temper had become ungovernable lately; that he was willing to strike and to order slain any who displeased him. What I had to say would not please a king, and I tried not to wince at the bite of the coronation rings on my shoulder.

But I was a priestess of the Triple Goddess. I took a deep breath.

'Master, they say that there will be floods this winter. They bid me to tell you that the cattle should be moved to higher ground, toward the mountains, and they that tend them should be warned to expect early snow and long enduring. The sinking of the Seven Sisters this year will bite hard on tenderlings.'

'I am old,' said my father. 'I have seen many hard winters, and we have weathered them. But there is a change coming, Medea. They call you Medea—*of good counsel*—do they not, daughter?'

'That is what they call me, Lord,' I agreed.

'Counsel me,' said the king.

I became alarmed. He seemed unsteady on his feet. Using all my strength, I lowered him to the ground, but he held my wrist in a hard grip and would not let me call his attendants.

'In what can I counsel you, Father?' I asked as evenly as I could. His face had become purple and breath wheezed through his lips.

'They are all plotting,' he whispered, dragging me close to the blubbering mouth. 'All plotting against me. The sons of Phrixos the Foreigner, they conspire to rob me of my throne. They must die.'

'Lord, I am sure that they do not so; and I must tend you. Kore, Scylla, guard,' I said, and spilled my flowers into a pile so that I could run.

Into the audience chamber I fled, but it was empty; no counsellors stood beside the bronze throne of Colchis. I skidded straight into the king's only son, Aegialeus. He was taller than me and stronger, a warrior, wearing armour and newly come, judging by the mud, from practise.

'Medea?' he asked, pushing me aside, so that I grabbed for a bench to regain my balance. 'Why are you here, Hekate's bitch?'

'Lord Brother, our father is ill, and I am seeking aid. Where are his men?'

'He sent them away, flogging them from his presence with a flail.'

'He needs them, summon them,' I said imperiously. The dark eyes laughed at me and I lost my terror and stared at him. He was considered beautiful, this only son of the king. I had heard women say so. He was rounded and smooth and his skin had the gloss of oil and exercise, but I found him abhorrent. He put back his hair and said casually, 'In due time, priestess.'

'In due time we will mourn the death of the king,' I snapped. 'Let me pass.'

'Then Colchis will celebrate the accession of a new king to the throne,' he continued smoothly.

'No, lord Brother, there is no daughter of Aetes for you to marry, to confer the kingship upon you.'

'Medea,' he said, his hand sliding down my breast and further down, 'there is you.' And then he smiled.

I was outraged. My flesh cringed away from his contaminated touch. Furious, I screamed, 'Scylla!' and heard the thud of pads as the hound raced to my side, teeth bared, hearing the fear in my voice. Her sharp bark dropped to a low growl, and the king's son stepped away from me.

'Summon the men, tell them to bring the herbs I need,' I shouted. Scylla snarled at him. His face frew white under the mud and he turned and ran from my presence.

I laid a hand on Scylla's neck where the hackles rose. I stood where I was until a gaggle of frightened slaves appeared, bearing—thanks be the Triple Goddess!—warm wine and a decoction of the correct herb. I carried it to where the king lay, Kore standing over him as I had bidden her. She was licking the sweat from his face. I lifted him on my arm and dripped the decoction through the drawn-back lips and he swallowed, which was a good sign.

'Time to wrap me in oxhide, daughter,' he whispered.

It is our custom to inter the bodies of men in an untanned hide, wrapped about with ropes, and suspend them in the willows at the river's edge, so that neither earth nor fire are contaminated with their death. They dessicate in the air as the oxhide shrinks, until only dry bones are left. Only women, givers of life, may lie again in the womb of the Mother.

'Not yet,' I replied. He tried to smile, I think. I supported his heavy head against my breast, feeling a gush of some emotion as I saw the decoction begin to take hold. His breathing deepened. Under my hand his heart, which had fluttered wildly, began to beat regularly, a slow, strong pulse. His flesh, however, felt loose and dry.

'The blessings of the Triple Goddess, Maiden, Mother and Crone, be upon you,' I said, as I had been taught. 'Not yet will you be buried in air, Lord. But your attendants should be about you, Father. Has this fit come upon you before?'

'It has,' he said, sitting up and wiping his brow with the edge of my peplos. 'That is why the potion was prepared and ready. Your mistress Trioda made it, little acolyte of Hekate.'

'My Lord!' wailed a voice. Sandals scuffed and a fragrant white arm jiggling with heavy bracelets displaced mine to support the king. Eidyia, the queen of Colchis, braving the courtyard where no woman might go, had come and I would not remain. I relinquished my father to her scented breast and knelt to gather my fallen harvest.

'My Lord, my Lord, you should not banish your attendants!' wailed the queen.

He grunted and shifted in her embrace and called to me, 'Medea!'

'Lord?' I had secured all my flowers and called my hounds.

'I thank you,' he said painfully, as the slaves lifted him to his feet. 'Come and speak with me again.'

'Father,' I agreed.

I resolved that before I ventured into the king's presence again I would have words with my half brother, the beautiful prince of Colchis.

Nauplios

I opened my eyes on a horse's face.

Hands were busy about me. A weight was on my body, a crushing weight which lifted and I felt myself groan, though I yet felt no pain. A spurt of warm liquid spattered my face, and I lifted a hand to wipe my eyes.

I still had hands, which meant that I still had a body and I was still breathing. I chuckled, pleased. The masked priest of the centaurs, Hippos, their holiest and most learned man, was feeling over my body for injuries. Suddenly, everything hurt. I felt as though I had been flattened in a wine press under the stone.

Tears came to my eyes, but I made no sound. To distract myself from the sharp stabs shooting through my bones at every touch—though Hippos was clever and gentle—I looked around.

I was lying in the clearing. Beside me lay a giant boar. It had taken four of the centaur hunters to lift and drag the corpse off me. I shivered at the memory of the ravening mouth, the brute strength of the beast, its murderous weight on my body. I shifted a little, biting my lip, to catch sight of the head. Its red eyes were open and glazed. It was, somehow, miraculously, dead.

And I was alive. Although all my limbs felt like they had been broken, I was not, by the feel of it, badly hurt. I looked for my lord. Jason, dyed with blood to the elbow, was cleaning his knife in the grass. He must have dived for the boar and cut its throat while I lost consciousness. I blushed, ashamed of my weakness. I had fainted.

The horse priest made a pleased sound, then struck me lightly on the chest three times with his horse-tail switch. 'Rise,' he commanded, and I rose, grunting with pain. Jason did not come to me to help me walk. Instead, Cheiron himself mounted me on his favourite horse, and I clung on with both hands as it paced down the slope and through the stream and then up the worn path to the camp.

There I was laid down in fern, while a steam bath was prepared. Beside me lay a centaur youth. It was always hard to read their dark faces, but he was sweating with agony. His shoulder had been dislocated, and his elbow, and although they had been replaced by the skill of Hippos, he was in considerable pain and could not speak without disgracing himself.

I wanted words, a friendly face, a friendly touch, but Jason did not come to me. I had been so close to the dark angel Thanatos, who is Death, brother of Sleep, that Morpheus took me unawares, and I slept.

I woke again in darkness. I smelt the pungent scent of the purifying herbs, hyssop and rosemary. I was lying in hot water in the caves of Dictes, the cave of never-failing hot springs. The centaurs had carved out a basin to catch the mineral-rich water, wide enough to hold three men and deep enough for me to float, steadied by someone's hand under my neck. On a ledge sat Hippos, in robes and mask; beside me lay the centaur youth whose name I did not know.

'You will lie here for one quarter of this night,' said Hippos. 'I will tell tales to you, young men, and this shall be your manhood ritual. Then you shall rise, being healed, and go to the meadow where the centaurs sport with their mares. There Jason waits for you, son of Dictys. He who hesitated long enough to kill you then acted fast enough to save your life. You will forgive him.'

'Horse priest, there is nothing to forgive,' I said. The warm water bathed my hurts. I could feel my bruised limbs slackening, relaxing, and almost cried with relief. I heard a sob beside me as the centaur boy experienced the same blessing.

Hippos was masked so I could not see his expression, but he made a tongue click which in the centaur's language means vexation. I wondered how I had offended him, but he said nothing more of the matter; instead beginning a story in the centaur's deep, rich voice, which could make the driest matter fascinating.

These caves belong to Hephaestos, smith of the gods, husband of Aphrodite. He is crippled by a fall, but he is the greatest metal worker that has ever been. His son is Talos, who made the bronze giant. When this part of the world was formed, Hephaestos forged the doorposts of the palace of the gods here, even for Zeus Cloud-Compeller's palace, that Zeus who is Lord of the Lightning. When the metal was quenched with a river, the rock melted, and steam caves were formed.

When he returned with the forging to heaven, he left this gift for the centaur people who were his friends. He left us healing waters to comfort our hurts and cleanse our spirits. On this holiest of nights, when the tribe embraces Hippia and our boys become young men, the waters have special virtue.

Hippos indicated the centaur boy. 'There lies beside you, son of Dictys, Philos, who is now your brother, for you have been healed together. He is the son of Cheiron.'

There were many sons of Cheiron—the centaurs keep no wife to themselves—but I smiled as best I could at Philos, and he smiled at me. There was no manhood tattoo on his chest, but he was already sprouting a beard.

'Semele, the moon, is riding high, watching over our ceremony,' Hippos said, and continued his story.

Under such a moon heroes have come to Cheiron; heroes and gods. Herakles came here. He is the son of Zeus, and Alkmene to whom he appeared in the shape of her husband. She lay with him unknowing—she was a faithful wife, most unusual among women—and conceived the hero. He was designed by the Father to suffer as men suffer, to gain special insight into the lives and minds of men, and when he dies Zeus will take him into his counsels, and he will advise the Caster of Thunderbolts on the ways and feelings of his subjects. And that hero suffers more than men suffer, because he is struck mad. In this madness he killed his sons, and was condemned to labour by Eurystheus of Mycenae, who would not otherwise cleanse him of blood guilt.'

I stirred in the water. My skin itched, as though a thousand ants were biting me.

Hippos stroked my forehead and said, 'It is the magic, Nauplios, lie still,' and I strove to obey him. My hand met the hand of the centaur Philos under the water, and clasped. It was the first time I had touched one of the centaur men in amity, and I was so surprised by the cordial grip that I sank a little and choked.

Hippos lifted my chin, reminding me that men breathed air, not water, and I laughed. Philos, my new brother, laughed too.

It was the girdle of Hippolyte, the Amazon queen, that was demanded of the hero, and he did not fail at his task. But the strength of a hero is not only in his body, young men, nor even in his loins—though it was Herakles who lay with the fifty daughters of a king in one night. It is in his mind that a hero needs strength. For muscle alone would not have won him this prize.

The Amazons are women, but not like other women. They are fighters, fierce and dangerous; sworn maidens and protected by their goddess, Hekate, Blood-Drinker, the Black Bitch. Flee such women, they are unnatural. They have no timidity of the flesh, no modesty, no fear.

Herakles could not have overcome them without battle, and he was one alone and they were many. He took men with him, but they were separated by the action of some malign god; and Herakles walked unprotected, his back bare of a brother; into the city of the Amazons.

They took him to the queen. There he could have done several things. He could have challenged her to single combat, shameful though that would be, for a man to challenge a woman. He could have tried to deceive her, pleading for her girdle as a token of love, which would be even more dishonourable than offering to duel with her.

Instead, they say, he sat down in familiar fashion at the foot of her throne and told her why he had come. He never had the sweet tongue of the singer, Herakles the hero. His words were blunt and flat.

'I am Herakles, son of Zeus, and I have come for your girdle,' he told her.

'Why do you seek my girdle, foreigner?'

'I have been set twelve tasks by Eurystheus of Mycenae before he will cleanse me of the blood of my children, whom I killed in a fit of madness, thinking they were bandits,' he replied. 'I am Herakles of Tiryns.'

'You have come alone,' she observed.

'I brought an army to assail you, but it is wrecked and astray.'

'So you came anyway.'

'Even as I am,' said the hero.

'And what will you do to accomplish this task?' she asked.

'Anything I have to,' he replied.

The queen of the Amazons was a good judge of fighters. She looked at the hero. He is not tall but he is broad, and his body is whipcord, tanned by the weather. His hair is long and tangled. He bears no edged weapon but carries a mighty club. He did not plead or threaten, but looked at the queen of Amazons for a long time. This queen stated no false woman's terms but, like a warrior or a king, made her bargain.

'I could ask you for anything,' she said. 'But I will take no advantage of a warrior under such a burden of guilt. I will ask you to lie in the act of love with some of my women, that they may bear strong daughters with your blood in their veins. And as a reward, Herakles of Tiryns, I will give you my girdle at the end of three days, and my fighters will escort you to the sea, where you may find a ship.'

'You do not ask me to lie with you,' Herakles said, for his heart inclined to her. She was beautiful they say.

The queen shook her head. 'I do not lie with men'.

At the end of three days, when such of the Amazon women who could bear the touch of man had all lain with Herakles, Hippolyte the queen gave him her golden girdle and he came

to the coast, where he found a ship trading out of Achaea,
which took him home.

Hippos paused, then added, 'Authority is the quality of the
king. Hippolyte had it, when she made and kept a bargain with
a hero. Herakles, had it, when his gaze was enough to warn the
queen that fighting him would be unwise. Now, young men,
rise from this water. You are healed.'

I turned over, grasping for the edge, and found that he was
right. Nothing hurt. I got one knee on the ledge where Hippos
was sitting, and my body moved as smoothly as oil. We were
dried and dressed in tunics, then Hippos led us down from the
cave to the meadow. Philos went ahead with the horse priest,
and I stood watching from the rocks that marked the edge of
the flat green space, now grey under the moon.

Someone was standing next to me. Jason, averting his eyes. I
went to him and reached out my hand, but he would not take it.

'My lord,' I begged. 'Take my hand.'

'I almost killed you, Nauplios,' he muttered.

'No, you saved me. You cut the boar's throat when he had
swallowed my spear and was about to swallow me,' I said, but
he would not smile.

'I attacked too soon and missed my mark,' he said.

'Yes,' I agreed.

'And when it felled you, I froze,' he confessed. 'I was afraid.'

'So was I. Hippos says I must forgive you, and I do, if you
need forgiveness.'

'You forgive me?' he said, looking into my face for the first
time. He was as pale as marble.

'I forgive you,' I said, kissing him on the brow in token of
this, as is the Achaean custom. He embraced me, and I felt him
draw a sharp breath.

Then we turned to watch the centaurs. For a while I could
not understand what I was seeing. The naked men were pursu-
ing small figures, masked with horse masks like the one which
Hippos wore. Belts around their waists held horse tails which

bobbed and wove in the warm air. Then one ran close enough for us to see the breasts of a young woman, the spangle of sweat on her belly and pubic hair. She was out of breath and collapsed to her knees right beside our rock.

There her pursuer caught her. He, too, was masked, but it was a young man, his tattoo still bleeding. He grabbed her by the shoulders and mounted her in one movement like a stallion mounts a mare, roughly and from behind. She cried lamentably, wincing away from the hard thrusts, but his weight was on her and she was mastered. It was over in moments. He pushed her away, so that she fell on knees which must have been bruised.

I was aroused and shocked. My phallus rose at her nakedness, but I was sorry for the maiden. She was a maiden no longer, wiping a hand over her insulted genitalia and sobbing at the sight of her own blood.

The centaur sighted us. He did not lift his mask, but I heard him say 'Brother' to Jason and me. It was Philos, who had held my hand gently as we lay in the healing waters. His groin was dabbled with the maiden's blood and I heard him laugh.

He seized the girl and pushed her to her knees again, presenting her to us as a cow is presented to a bull. Her buttocks were pale, her hair parted over the nape of her neck, and the horse's tail flowed between her legs. Jason looked at me. I said nothing as my lord knelt and took her, as he had a right to take what was offered; and I watched his face grow blank, like a carving, as his body moved against her and inside her. He groaned and stiffened in every muscle. When he withdrew from her he was also marked with her blood.

'It is not the custom of my father's people,' I said to Philos as he pushed me toward the girl, 'to mate in plain sight.'

I took the girl by the hand and helped her up. She followed me behind the rock into the shadow of the bushes. I let her down onto the moss and said, 'I will not hurt you.'

'You alone of all men,' she said softly. I removed the mask to see her face. She was very young. She was beautiful, even tear stained and shaking as she was.

'They will notice if you do not have my blood on you,' she said.

'Give me some, then,' I replied. She reached between her thighs and smeared me with blood. The phallus rose at her touch, so sweet a touch that I gasped.

'I would please you,' she said.

'I will not mate with you. You bleed enough for one festival.' I was still disgusted by the centaurs' mating, their violence to their women.

'Lie down,' she said, 'and I will please you without hurting myself.'

I lay down under the bushes, in the scent of sweat and smoke and blood, and the centaur woman caressed me with her mouth and her hands, her breasts soft against my thighs, and I felt a rush of fire, and cried aloud.

Chapter Four

Medea

My father was ill for many weeks. There was no immediate opportunity to inform him that his suspicions as to who was conspiring to take over his throne were directed entirely at the wrong quarter. Besides, he would not hear a word against Aegialeus, his only son.

When Aetes became king, the oracle of Ammon—the Achaeans call him Apollo—had spoken. Thus I had been told as a child, to explain why my father never came to see me or my sister. A bronze horn had blown without human breath and a great voice had said from the sanctuary:

Thanatos selects from Colchis' herd; his calves or his cows.

'It is hard to love something which must die,' said Trioda in explanation. I had stored both the oracle and the clarification for future reference, for Trioda seldom answered further questions. Now I understood. Although I had seen the queen's care for my father, although he lay in her arms, he could not afford to love her because he had understood the oracle: if his children should live then his wives would die; as Chalkiope's mother had died, as mine had died, bearing us. He could not love us, for we had killed his wives. The anniversaries of our births were days of mourning for our father.

'The seed of Aetes is black,' said Trioda, 'death bearing'.

I felt fortunate that I was a dedicated maiden, never to bear fruit, for the seed of Aetes was in me. Then again, my sister's children were strong and fine. Perhaps the seed of Phrixos the stranger, was strong enough to overcome the dark. I said as much to Trioda as we compounded yet another combination of heart-strengthening herbs. My father was responding to the medicines, although he flatly refused to allow us to sacrifice to Hekate on his behalf. The shaven, white-robed priests of Ammon visited every day and had interceded for Aetes of Colchis, slaying the bull who is the avatar of their god. I could smell burning flesh from the temple of the Sun as I ground foxglove in a mortar.

'The sons of Phrixos are healthy,' Trioda said, pouring one decoction into another. 'But death is everywhere.'

'Surely,' I agreed. This was a ritual statement.

'Closer than you might think, Princess,' she added. I stopped grinding.

'Mistress, do you mean that my father's illness is induced, and that the sons of Phrixos are plotting to take over, as he thinks?'

'Tssh, daughter, do not speak so plainly! I mean, maiden, that death is everywhere. Consider the situation, Medea.' She lowered her voice and I moved closer so that I could hear her. The scent of the herbs was making me giddy.

'There are only two daughters of Colchis who could be married to provide the right to the kingship. There is you, daughter, but you are a priestess of Hekate and maiden and She Who Meets would lay a powerful curse on any who took you to wife, willing or unwilling.'

I resumed pounding the herb so I did not have to look at her. It was time to tell Trioda of Aegialeus' plans, but I was hot with shame that I had endured his hands on my maiden body.

'I would never be willing. It is my half brother who wants this, he touched me, Trioda, when I went to the king. He wishes for Aetes' death, Mistress.'

'Yes, yes, it is against all nature,' she said dismissively, unshocked, as though she already knew of my brother's assault on me and his revolting proposal. 'The seed of Aetes is death to women, and his son is Thanatos' own cousin.

'But listen, Medea. There is your sister, Chalkiope. She is proved fertile, she is a widow, and she had four strong sons. A man who took her would be assured of heirs even if she bore no more children. He would have kinship and kingdom, according to the laws. But...'

'But?' The sun was streaming through the window of the little temple. It was a bare building, wooden, with a tree leaning on either side and leaf litter on the floor for the serpents of the mother. Kore and Scylla lay asleep on the broad steps in the autumn sunshine, twitching occasionally. Trioda and I were working at the big table. Bunches of herbs hung from the roof, and baskets contained other ingredients. The big bronze cauldron was simmering on a brazier, beside the copper pot in which we seethe the infusions which cause women to miscarry. No woman in Hekate's kingdom carries a child to term unwilling. Unlike Achaea, a child of rape will not live in Colchis, to give legitimacy to an unholy act.

Along the wall were shelves of scrolls, the accumulated wisdom of the priestesses. I hoped that one day I would write one myself, and the scroll 'Medea' would join the others to be read by a new priestess in a hundred years' time, who might use my compound of feverfew, foxglove and willow bark to save another king's life.

Trioda was looking at me quizzically. I collected my wits and repeated, 'But?'

'But the union which can bring this about is not to be considered.'

I puzzled the sentence out. 'You mean that brothers and sisters cannot marry.'

'In the Black Land, this was the case,' Trioda said, stirring the cauldron. I dropped into it my now very well-mashed foxglove. The decoction was green, for we had added willow bark for the pain.

'Brothers and sisters marry?'

'They do. The king marries his daughter, sometimes, and frequently Pharaoh marries his sister. They are matrilineal, daughter, as we are. The possession of the princess confers the kingship.'

'But the marriage confers no power on the princess,' I reasoned. She gave me the spoon and I took over the stirring. One stirs a decoction for good in a sunwise direction, a poison widdershens, against the sun. This was a healing brew, so I made sure that the spoon always moved to the right.

'No, daughter, that is true. Since the advent of men we have lost all power but knowledge. You have seen the way the people defer to the priestesses of Hekate. They fear us, and fear is the beginning of power. But kingship we have not; nor will we have it again until the world changes. Now, as to your half brother, avoid him. If he pursues you, daughter, remember your power. How many poisons do you know, Medea?'

'Fifty-three, Mistress,' I said proudly.

'And rituals?'

'The seven blessing and the seven cursing, Mistress. And you promised to teach me the Grove Path.'

'So I did. We will go there after this potion is completed, daughter. Make your heart hard, Medea. I fear some stroke of Ate. Even Hekate cannot always control Fate. We will go and ask the question of the serpent. It is time, in any case, that you met her. You will take over her care when Hekate gathers me to her bosom. I would not leave you unprovided, acolyte. Women have no place in the men's world, ruled by Ammon and the Sun. But in the dark, in secret places, we are more powerful.'

She tasted the brew, nodded, and we poured it into a pottery jar marked with the three-legged cross, the sign of Hekate. Then she collected a series of flasks and a jug of milk mingled with honey, and we left the temple.

Eidyia, the queen, caught us as we came into the women's quarters. She was slim and beautiful, the wife of my father. Her hair was a rich chestnut, for she came from the mountains toward the west, where women are fair and, unafraid of prophecy, men gather gold from the icy streams. Her father had given her to Aetes, the youngest daughter in a house of daughters, even though he knew of the oracle. He had many daughters and could afford to lose one to cement an alliance with Aetes of Colchis. We knew that she had lain with him, but she had not yet conceived. My father treated her well, if distantly. She was dressed in the finest woven wool, dyed bright red, and she was hung about with gold; a ram's head torc at her throat, a crown, bracelets, rings and an embossed belt. The queen of Colchis wore enough gold to ransom a prince. But her lower lip was caught between her teeth and her smooth brow was furrowed. She held Trioda's sleeve in her soft, perfumed hand. I smelt a waft of summer flowers from her garments and her hair.

'Hekate's maiden, he calls for me again,' she whispered.

Trioda hefted her burden on one bony hip and said, 'Does he so? And are you still resolved, daughter?'

'I want to live,' said the queen almost under her breath. Trioda smiled, rummaged in the basket and produced a tiny flask, like the one which Achaeans put on graves to hold tears. It was sealed with the double seal, which meant that it was poisonous. No priestess wants to put her hands on the wrong flask in the dark. Really lethal concoctions, snake venom or hemlock, have three seals. The queen snatched it and hid it in her cloak, so fast that only a really dedicated watcher would have seen the transaction.

'How is the king?' asked Trioda, easily.

'He is recovering,' replied Eidyia. 'The medicines are working. And, of course, the prayers of the temple of Ammon,' she added hastily.

'They are eating well while the king's illness continues,' said Trioda dryly. 'They sacrifice a bull daily and feast on beef after the god has eaten his portion. When he recovers, they will chafe at their diet of pulse and grain. Do not allow them to give him any potions, daughter and lady.'

The queen nodded. Her silky hair fell forward over her face. I think she was afraid of Trioda. I bent my head for her blessing, and gave it quickly, then was gone into the women's quarters in a swirl of scarlet.

I was pleased with that cloak. It had been my first attempt at dyeing a fine colour. One finds the galls on oak trees in which the insects are working, and sprinkles them with new wine to prevent the emergence of the moth—though one out of five must be marked for the goddess, or the tribe of worms will die out. Then one steeps the galls in boiling water, and extracts the dye. It is concentrated, and I coloured my hands red for half a moon before it wore off. But the cloak had held up well through washing, even though Trioda said I had used too much salt to fix it. Salt comes from Poti and is very expensive. What decoction, I asked myself, was the queen requiring of Hekate, and why? Was she poisoning my father?

I could not ask Trioda while we were in the palace. We went to the king's chamber, but were denied—the attendant said he was asleep. The slave had a black bruise across half his face, indicating that the king's temper had not improved. Trioda sat him down and applied allheal ointment to the hot swollen skin. I noticed how the boy relaxed under her hands—deft, sure, and drinking in his pain. When she let him rise again, he was relieved but wary, as though, perhaps, her treatment had stolen something from him.

We left our potion in the hands of the king's counsellor, Eupolis, an old man and trusted. It is the ancient law in Colchis that if the king dies in circumstances which could indicate poison or assassination, all his counsellors are executed by being stitched alive into an oxhide and hung in the willows. Eupolis would not dare meddle with the medicine, and would make sure that it was administered correctly.

Then we left the palace and came into the city, walking down the street which led us to Rivergate and the Grove of The Serpent, outside the walls.

I was apprehensive. Trioda spoke of the serpent as she, meaning that the creature was an avatar of Hekate, as were Kore and Scylla. But although my hounds were sacred, they were also dogs, prone to snap if startled and provided with strong teeth and haughty tempers. The serpent of the grove would also bear her original snaky nature when she was not possessed by Hekate. And women whispered that the serpent was as long as a riverboat and as wide as a door, that even to smell her breath was death, the guardian of the grove where hung the greatest treasure of Colchis, the Golden Fleece.

We took the path which wound through dripping marshes, where the dead men of Colchis hung in their oxhides. This was an eerie place, haunted by the piping of little unseen birds which, they said, were the voices of the dead, diminishing as the bodies rotted, until they were little but a squeaking in the reeds, which were once men and had men's voices.

It was also the haunt of midges and mosquitoes, eager to feast on human blood, and leeches as long as my finger, black with red stripes, which dropped from the willows and fastened in an eyeblink, plumping out on their stolen harvest in seconds. They did not, of course, harm us. We were redolent of an essence of white summer daisies, sunflowers dedicated to Ammon, and another oil derived from a certain fungus which belongs to the Dark Mother alone. If any insect were bold enough to ignore the repelling power of Ammon and bite us, it would instantly die.

'What was the potion, Mistress?' I asked Trioda, as we waded through the black water in the rising mist.

'Potion, daughter?'

'The queen required it of you,' I reminded her. 'Is she poisoning my father?'

'No,' said Trioda.

We walked a few paces. A year before I might not have persisted, but now I had more courage. I had saved my father's life and I was a woman of knowledge, about to meet the guardian of the serpent grove. Also I needed some words to break the silence as we walked amongst the bobbing dead in the stench of rotting flesh and marsh water, the mist flowing around us.

'Then what is the medicine, Mistress? Does the queen suffer from some shameful ailment?'

Women's illnesses are indications of the disfavour of the Triple Goddess, and to placate the goddess it is essential to examine the state of mind of the woman. If she cannot conceive, for instance, she may have desired her stepson or a priest of Ammon, may have lusted to follow her own appetite—although there may be other reasons. A woman whose womb will not hold the quickening child may have blasphemed the goddess, cursing by Hekate at some domestic misfortune. Sacrifice and fasting will usually mend the fault, and the medicines of the skilled women of the temple. However, no woman would admit to illness before a man, lest she be shamed.

'Not precisely,' said Trioda. She held a bush aside for me as we took the winding path, almost invisible to the eye, toward the ilex grove.

'I am your acolyte, Mistress, your daughter. Tell me.'

'The queen of Colchis wants to live,' said Trioda after a long pause. 'If she bears a child, she will die. She cannot disobey the commands of the king your father to lie down under him and receive his seed, the black seed of Aetes. Therefore Eidyia, every month when the moon is gone, takes one drop of a certain potion.'

'What potion?' I watched a leech curl dead from my forearm and plop into the dark water.

'It is compounded in copper of fireweed and fungus of rye,' she said. I thought about it. The purple fungus which infects rye which has been wet too often in growing, produces gangrene and mania, a dancing madness. A pregnant woman who tastes of it…

"She aborts the child,' I said, astonished at the queen's cunning.

'There may not be a child. That compound causes the womb to contract, loosing the tide of blood that follows the moon. Thus Eidyia risks all—discovery and disgrace—to avoid death in childbirth. And thus, child, Eidyia endangers her husband, who needs another daughter, so that the sons of Phrixos, through their mother, shall not rule his kingdom after he is dead.'

'Mistress, you have told me that dead men die and rot, that their spirits fly to the land of Ammon to dwell in the sun, as the spirits of women are carried in Hekate's arms to sleep in her bosom. What should the king care that some other man will take his kingdom after he is gone?'

'It is the duty of a king to care for his kingdom, to leave it in safe hands. And that is as strong as the duty laid on women to endure the man, suck in his seed, feed his children with her blood, bear them in agony and nurture them, though she suckles the sons who enslave her sisters and breeds her own captors. That is all I will say to you, Medea.'

She waded onto the path again, and I followed her in silence.

Nauplios

I thought often of the young centaur woman in the next year, though I did not see her. I might have gone wandering to the other side of the mountain, where the women lived, despite the danger of death if I was caught, for my heart was greatly inclined toward her, but I had no leisure. Jason and I were worked hard by our master.

Cheiron kept us at his side, trying to instil precepts of government and all his wisdom into our heads, so that we would not forget when we left.

For when Jason, son of Aison, was fifteen, he would descend the mountain and try and regain his kingdom.

'Pelias, brother of your father, is a proud and cunning man,' he instructed as we sat close around a horse-dung fire, shivering in the chill winds. 'You are too honest, young prince of Iolkos.'

'How can I be too honest, Master?' asked my lord. His eyes looked blue in the cooling darkness.

'Is not Herakles the greatest hero? Yet he has cunning. You must try to acquire it, Jason, and not die untimely, your quest unaccomplished. Men cling to power, so will Pelias. Men cling more closely to power which is stolen and majesty which is usurped. Use great formality with your uncle, boy. Show me your obeisance.'

Jason got up and made a graceful, sweeping bow, flourishing his goatskin rug like a cloak. Cheiron grunted in approval.

'And the words you will say?'

'Master, I can't remember,' confessed Jason. Cheiron swatted at his ears and repeated, 'I am Jason, son of Aison, and I am come to reclaim my father's right.'

Jason repeated it, again and again, under the centaur's patient teaching, and eventually both of us knew it by heart.

Time passed, as time does. The festival came and went again, but neither of us were allowed to take part. Philos, who had offered us his captive, had been sent to another mountain in disgrace for defiling the ceremony. I asked the old man about their custom. Would they not rather have wives to live with, as my father lived with my mother?

I could remember my parents talking quietly by the fire, while my brothers and I were lying almost asleep in our sheepskins. Their voices had soothed me, though they said no words of love, just commonplace matters—the health of the flock, the fishing, the mending of nets, the rising or setting of the Pleiades which ruled the seasons. I sometimes recalled little vivid pictures from my past before I had climbed the centaurs' mountain, and that was one of them. The quiet voices discussing the likely value of the clip, and the unaccountable ways of Poseidon's folk, the fish. And I remember waking early one morning and hearing them sacrificing to Aphrodite, goddess of love. My mother had moaned, her arms were around my father's neck and she was kissing him. She had seemed to enjoy his embrace. She was not pinned and hurt like the centaur maiden. And afterwards they had slept companionably together, her head on his shoulder.

'Indeed, Master,' Jason joined in. 'Is there not true love between man and woman?'

'There is not, however many sentimental Achaean songs say there is. There cannot be. For, tell me, young men'—his old brow furrowed and his voice dropped to an impressive whisper—'Tell me, Prince of Iolkos, what true allegiance can you give to a weak king?'

'None, Master,' answered Jason. His hair was long and he wound a lock around his hand as he listened.

'Then there can be no true love between a woman and a man. True love is for equals, or inferior and superior when there is proper respect. Women are foolish, powerless, enslaved for their good, for they are flighty and weak and there is no integrity in them. They cannot be trusted. One sniff of a man and they are gone, leaving hearth, home and honour, and they will move from man to man and husband to husband without grief, for they are lacking in courage and bold only in their vices. If you find a woman who looks up to you as little less than a god, Jason, then you may feel safe with her, for woman is also religious and superstitious. But marry a woman who is learned, as far as such witless things can have learning, and has her own will, then beware, for she will destroy you.'

'But,' began Jason, and the old man cut him off with a fierce gesture.

'We centaurs know this. We keep our women as we keep our horses; with gentleness and discipline, but knowing that they are brute beasts, without understanding. They live apart and manage their own affairs, except for the four festivals, when we have connection with them to breed new men. Women are only the vessel for the seed, and as unreliable as the earth herself. In them lies no trust, and thinking of them can only weaken a man's spirit, and his body.

'The Aechaeans are a strong people, but think how strong they would be if they did not accept these creatures into their houses, allow them to take over their lives, complaining and caressing and filling their heads—even the king's head—with domestic concerns, with children and petty matters. The breeding of children is their business, and they do it well enough. But they must have no place in government or even in consideration. Do not think overmuch of women, young men. They are a necessary evil.'

'But do you need to hurt them, Master Cheiron?' I asked. 'I saw the maiden weep under the phallus—surely that bodes badly for conception.'

'If once our women tasted the joys of making love as your Aphrodite would instruct, Nauplios—ah yes, I have travelled, and I know of such things, and they are sweet, sweet and foul— they would be forever corrupted, and so would our young men. We are a pure people, and have no taste for sensuality. We need to breed, so let us mate as horses mate, who leap the mares. Our maidens conceive readily enough, for once they have conceived they may not go to the sire again for three years—four, if they produce a boy.'

'But I am an Achaean and a prince and will need to marry, Master,' said Jason. 'Or am I to mate as the centaurs do?'

'It would be better for you if you did,' snarled Cheiron.

He would say nothing further on the matter. It was cold, down by his little fire. He told us stories of heroes and battles, and strange centaur stories about the *striga*, the seductive phantom, a woman with white skin and hair like fire, who came in the night and lay with young men, sucking their seed from them, weakening them, so that they grew pale and trembled, useless for hunting or herding, longing for the night. And when they died of exhaustion, she would steal their souls, so that they in turn became spirits who overlay and penetrated young women, sapping their energy from their household tasks, depriving their master of their labour, finally to conceive and bear monsters.

I lay and dreamed, and Jason dreamed the same dream. It was the last night on the mountain with the centaurs. The next day my lord and I would venture into Iolkos and claim his kingdom.

A woman of fascination, a woman with dark hair, not red, a *striga* with dusky skin and warm breath, dressed in black, came and kissed us and stroked us, her clever hands caressing and slid- ing, her breasts in our face, her mouth on ours, until we woke clasped together, wet with seed, still shuddering.

We said nothing about it. It was dawn, and we washed and dressed in our finest tunics. We were, at last, returning to the sea. We were going down from the mountain to claim Jason's kingdom.

Chapter Five

Medea

The grove was as black as pitch and I stood still, as I had been taught, with my eyes closed. Beside me, Trioda began to sing. I listened carefully.

It was a high, simple, strongly-accented tune, punctuated with palm strokes on the small drum, and I caught the melody quickly and joined in. We sang, on a rising pitch:

Ophis Megale, Ophis Megale, Ophis Megale kale

Then the same triple invocation on a dipping pitch, then the three words on a level. We repeated it.

The treasure of Colchis, the Golden Fleece, hung from the biggest tree. It is the skin of a curly fleeced ram, of considerable size, and it gleams, because it is filled with gold dust. Each tress has been soaked in water-borne gold, and it shines even in the darkness of the grove. In sunlight—though it must never leave the grove—it would be blinding. Achaeans believe that it is the skin of a magical beast on which Phrixos rode to Colchis.

It is actually the skin of the king of the Massagaetae's ram, laid in the stream to soak up gold; and Colchians still lived who had seen Phrixos the Foreigner arrive in a perfectly ordinary ship.

The ilex is not a friendly tree and few things like growing under it. The floor of the grove was, therefore, smooth, and deep in last year's prickly leaves. I could not hear my own footfall, but I could hear something else.

Something very heavy was coming through the leaf mould. I was not sure that I could cope with sight, so I listened and kept my eyes closed, singing along automatically to the tune and the drum. The grove was resounding with the shrill alarm calls of birds when Trioda nudged me and I looked to see a serpent of amazing size. She was as long as a boat and wide as a doorway; wide as a pithos, the big-bellied grain amphora, and taller than me. Her head was the size of a cow's, her eyes the size of my doubled fists, and she must have been very old—only a huge length of years allows the serpent kind to grow so gigantic.

I could not move. She slid closer, her belly rippling over the prickly ilex leaves, and then rose to more than Trioda's height, towering over us. Her mouth opened pink and she flicked a forked tongue as long as my forearm at Trioda and me.

She was patterned like a tortoiseshell, mottled and magnificent. I would have fallen to my knees except Trioda had cautioned me to make no sudden move, lest the guardian be startled. I was awed and terrified at the power of the great goddess, who kept such a creature in subjection to guard her grove.

Trioda opened her basket and produced a bowl, into which she poured milk as prosaically as any housewife. The great head dipped, the tongue flicked, and the guardian drank.

'You may touch her,' said Trioda. Trembling, I laid one hand on the smooth scales, and felt them not wet as I had expected from their sheen, but dry as a pinecone, slippery as enamel, and warm.

The custom of serpents is to sleep through the winter. They are creatures of two gods, belonging to both Ammon and the Mother. During the summer when Ammon is exalted, they worship him. During the winter they seek the warmth of the Mother's breast, in darkness under the ground. To see this creature awake and alive in the cold winds of autumn, when the leaves fall ragged into the river, the sky lowers and herdsmen bring in their flock, was as astonishing as her size.

'She is unique,' said Trioda softly, as the guardian drank delicately, flicking her grey tongue into the milk. 'There is no other serpent in the land of Colchis. She has grown, daughter, since last I saw her—yes, see? She has lately cast her skin.'

Hanging in rags between two close-grown holly trees was the serpent's cast cloak; complete, even to the scales over the eyes.

'Walk slowly, daughter, gather that skin, and bring it to me,' said my mistress, and I did as I was bid. The skin was dry, thicker than papyrus, and very light.

'Strip and don the skin, daughter,' ordered Trioda, and I did so. Against my own human skin the scales of Ophis dragged and scratched, like the glass paper which craftsmen use to burnish bronze. Yet it was smooth over my breasts and so cold that all my nerves flared, and I flushed and then shivered. I was desperately afraid.

But I was a priestess of Hekate, and she would protect me. If I was worthy.

It was darkening in the grove. Outside the moon would be rising, Selene, who is also a maiden. Trioda ordered me to lie down. Then my mistress knelt, very slowly, and thrust something against my mouth. It was alive, no more than a handful, and it was clammy and squirming. I knew what it was. A toad, companion of Hekate, a sacred creature. I forced myself to kiss its slimy back. My lips numbed instantly. I felt something very strange beginning to happen to me.

Ophis' discarded covering, which had been cold, warmed into life, wrapping me as securely as my own skin. The chill receded, and the fear grew. I felt the snakeskin curl and enfold me, so that my limbs were confined and then forgotten. For a moment, I rolled helplessly on the leaves. Then I found the muscles and nerves of Ophis. I moved as Ophis moved, by shifting my scales. I saw as she saw, through the strange lidless eyes which know no night.

The ilex grove reddened to blood, against which a bright figure glowed; Trioda the priestess of Hekate, burning brighter than a hearth fire. Little lights moved on the ground, and I leaned forward, counterbalancing my weight with my tail, flicking my tongue to taste the air, which was full, not of scents but of vibrations. The world sang.

In Ophis' ears we all had our own tone, our blood hummed through our veins, and our life felt warm or cold in the air. The toad which Trioda held burned cool, dependent on the temperature of the air; a greenish glow. In the branches of the trees were the points of light which were roosting birds. They were golden.

Then there was the bulk of the great serpent herself, turning to regard me. Ophis was a column of white fire, so hot I could hardly bear to look at her, and I could not close my serpent's eyes. I heard her shift over the crackling leaves, and her tongue flicked out at me, tasting my breath. I could not speak while in serpent form, but in my mind I chanted the invocation to the Goddess for protection, as a weight passed over my body, a monstrous weight. There was an instant of blind terror, then she twined herself around me.

Sweet, sweet! The touch of scale on scale thrilled through my nerves. The clasp was strong but not crushing, her touch was delicate and soft as water. She slid and I twined myself around her, and I burned too, as bright as the great serpent. I would have cried for joy but I had no tears. The inexorable embrace melted us together, one body, serpent and priestess.

This was the mystery of the grove, which Trioda had brought me to experience, and it was cruelly sweet. I wanted to lie with Ophis forever, on flesh, all skin, but then I was blinded by a starburst, and became Medea again, lying on the dead leaves, slick with sweat and weeping because the joy had departed, leaving me shaking and vomiting into the thorns.

Ophis withdrew from me. I heard her overturn the empty milk pot and slither away to the other side of the grove, deeper into darkness.

Trioda lifted me to my feet and wrapped my priestess' gown around me. It was dark. She led me into the marsh again, and gave me water in which *menthe* had been steeped. I immediately threw it up again. Trioda let me lean on her shoulder, something she seldom did, as I coughed.

'That was the mystery, Medea,' she said.

'Oh, lost,' I mourned, shuddering through all my body.

'Not lost forever,' she said calmly. 'You will join with her again, at the festival of the grove, at this time every year. For you are the guardian's chosen one. She has accepted you. Be happy, Princess! You are fortunate.'

I followed Trioda along the winding paths through the marsh. As my nausea retreated, a thought occurred to me.

'Mistress, if She Who Is A Serpent had not accepted me, what would have happened?'

'You would have died,' said Trioda. 'She would have killed you.'

◇◇◇

I bathed in warm water, as I had been instructed. The scales had made razor-thin cuts along my belly, back, breast and thighs and the outsides of my arms. They made the water pink and I sluiced until I was bleeding freely, lest any contamination from the floor of the grove had entered my blood. I was still cold, though the memory of the embrace of Ophis tingled along my nerves.

My body, to which I paid little attention, was changing. I had grown taller. There was a scribble of hair under my arms and between my thighs. My chest, which had been flat, was curving with breasts and the nipples rose under my touch.

I shuddered anew and extinguished my new body under a wide linen towel. I was approaching the first bleeding. Now I must watch the moon and, in her cycles, my blood would spring. I would become penetrable, able to conceive, and would need to be ever more vigilant. No more could Medea play innocent games with Melanion the son of Phrixos. I was the dedicated maiden of the Dark Mother, and no man must possess me.

I dried myself, lay down in my bed, and hugged Kore and Scylla, who lay either side of me. No rapist would get to Medea over my guardians. The serpent of the grove had accepted me, and no man would ever lie with me.

I knew I had wept in my sleep, because I woke with Scylla licking my face.

Two weeks later I was tending the sacred fire with slivers of fungus. The temple was cold. I wore two black tunics and a black gown and cloak and my feet were clad in leather boots, and I was still cold. I could not seem to get warm. Scylla lay across the threshold—she could never believe that humans could not see as well in the dark as she—and I heard Trioda stumble over her as she came in.

'Daughter, make a light. The old women were right. This will be a winter to freeze the heart.'

I lit the big oil lamp and the flame flared then settled, casting a pleasant orange light. My mistress cast off her own cloak, speckled with snow, and shut the door.

Trioda rubbed her elbows and commented, 'You look pale, daughter. Build up the hearth fire. Medea? Are you ill?'

'I'm cold,' I muttered, laying logs on the ever-burning hearth, then kneeling and spreading my cloak to catch the heat as it flowed out from the burning wood. Trioda sat down in her chair and I leaned on her knee.

'Where does it hurt, daughter?' It was so unlike her to show concern for me that I felt tears prick my eyelids.

'All over, Mistress.'

'Hmm. Sit by the fire, Princess.' She lifted me into her chair and inspected my eyes, tested my forehead for fever, felt down over my body, and then pushed a hand into the hollow of my stomach. Something cramped and I winced. Trioda smiled.

'Maiden, you are maiden indeed, and about to sacrifice to Selene. A very fortunate time indeed, past the dead of winter and the central mystery of Ammon. For the bull ploughing will coincide with your third bleeding, Medea, and that ties you to power.

'Come, maiden. I will make you an infusion and prepare cloths to absorb your blood. You share the fate of all women, Princess, do not weep.'

I could not explain why I was crying, except that I felt suddenly ordinary, not a princess or a priestess, just a common girl with a pain in her belly.

Trioda said sharply, 'A common fate is to be gloried in, daughter. All women share the body of the goddess, who is Hekate, the Dark Mother, She Who Meets. No woman is apart. That is the sin of men, who consider that they are superior to their own mortality. Kings in the glory of their pride fall prey to gripes, to fevers, to wounds. No woman could ever think that she was apart from her own body and cycle, disconnected from the earth and the moon.' She busied herself with making an infusion of the heat-inducing root which comes from Libya, and I sat by the fire and stared into the flames, feeling the pain gather in my back and belly and blood trickle warm between my thighs.

While I bled, I lay in the temple, on a pallet before the fire, and Trioda tended me. The dogs, grateful for the warmth of the fire, lay sleeping on either side of me, warm bodies sure of their integrity, which had deserted mine. Trioda instructed me while I lay slightly drugged and forbidden to touch anything.

'You are in a sacred state for the first three bleedings, Princess. The goddess' touch is tentative, at first, testing your strength. Therefore, as you will have noticed, daughter, you are weak, clumsy, pained and a little lost. But that will pass. In future, Medea, if you have dark spells to cast or poisons to compound, the week before your bleeding is the time to make them. Then women are full of black energy; ideally, a little of the blood should be mingled with the poison. In the five days before the moon possesses us, we are moon powerful, crackling with power. Then, however, healing spells will be weak and may even be harmful.

'Compound your healing brews after the blood has gone. For you are cyclical now, daughter, not steadfast like a child. Your moods will flow with the moon.'

'What if I need to make a healing potion, and I am in the wrong cycle?' I asked drearily from my nest of sheepskins by the fire.

'Then you must concentrate, daughter, and if you need to change your state for some very urgent reason, and not just a desire to be relieved of the goddess' blessing, then you may take this.'

'What is it?' I asked, eyeing the flask marked with the triple seal.

'It is made of certain berries, which I will show you, and the urine of pregnant women. It mimics in its action the moon's cycle, and can alter your state; but it is very venomous. Use it only at great need. It will stop the flow of blood, dry up the fountains of the goddess. It can prevent conception.'

'This is the potion used by the queen?'

'It is. We would use it, perhaps, if a great plague struck Colchis—do you remember the plague at Poti, when the priestesses went down the river to treat the stricken? You were five, I think.'

I remembered seeing the river barges loaded with black-clad women, and hearing the wailing which followed them. Each temple of Hekate is tended by two or three women; there are many in the city of Colchis. The women in their sable garments, I remembered them, like a flock of crows. I nodded.

'It was haemorrhagic fever, Medea, which came from the sea, like all evil things. We went, all of us, to tend the fallen, bury the dead, comfort the dying. We carried with us all the herbs that we knew would be of use, though an unknown fever is the most alarming thing a healer can face. Each one of us risked death and the goddess' disfavour by taking the potion before we left, so that we should heal, not curse. Ah, I remember, little Medea, I left you with Chalkiope and you cried after me.'

I did not tell her that I had cried not because Trioda was leaving but because I did not want to stay with Chalkiope.

'How did we defeat the fever?' I asked.

She settled back in her chair and looked into the fire.

'We tried all the usual compounds—feverfew, marsh leaf, and then allheal and the Libyan herbs. Nothing worked. The fever burned them away, skin and bone they were after the third day, and so they died. Then we tried sun-herbs—but that was not successful. The pirates had brought it, the Achaean pirates trading for gold. Your father ordered the river closed with chains, so that no boat would bring death down Phasis to slay in his own city. We despaired and called on the Black Mother to relieve us of our lives, for we were weary. The priests of Ammon smoked the streets with their offerings. When I think of that time, all I can smell is burning bull's flesh and the stink of death.'

'Mistress, what happened? Did we find a cure?'

'No cure, daughter, but as I meditated in the temple of the Mother I recalled that some herbs can stop digestion altogether, and that would be a boon, for the sufferer's guts ran fluid and they could retain no food or even water. So I compounded the Egyptian poppy with henbane and fed it to the plague struck, and although it did not destroy the fever, it stopped the flux. With careful nursing, the stricken lived. When more lived than died I lay down in the temple and slept for the first time in a week.'

'A great feat, Mistress,' I said with respect. 'Did you find the cause of the fever?'

'Poti has too much contact with the outside. It is on the sea and many strangers come there. The people had left their faith, seduced by foreign ways, and thus had earned the enmity of our gods. Ammon sent the burning fever, and Hekate the watery humour. After the city had been cleansed of foreigners—they all died, for we did not tend them—then the gods smiled on Poti once more, content with their warning. No strange ships' crews can leave the narrow strip of houses and taverns along the sea, now. They are confined in their influence, and Poti is healthy. How do you feel now, daughter?'

'Strange. But better.' I leaned up on one elbow. Kore complained briefly, scratched an itchy ear, and lay down again—she was serving as my pillow.

'Good.' Most unusually, she stroked my forehead. With my moon bleed, a softness had come to my mistress, who had always been distant with me.

'Tell me a tale,' I dared to ak, as Scylla wriggled closer into my arms, her warm back pressing pleasantly into my sore stomach. The snow flowed down outside the temple, muffling her voice,

and the fire burned up hot and bright. We had a great store of
fuel, cut by sweating labourers in the forests and hauled into the
heat and Trioda's voice underlay my quietness.

*There was a great queen, Cerlithe of the Fortunate Island,
a place many day's journey distant, at the back of the north
wind. She is the mother of Ishtar, Isis, whom the Achaeans
call Aphrodite; the old woman, the crone, Hekate our own
Dark Mother. But in those places they call her Cerlithe.*

*She was a woman of knowledge and sorcery. She began
a powerful working for the sake of her son, for whom she
would risk sanity and life, to make a potion of inspiration
for him, so that the gods would breathe wisdom and power
into his mouth.*

The fire flickered. I closed my eyes. The pain in my back
and belly had ebbed under her influence. Her voice was even
and low, blending with the hiss of falling snow outside, until it
seemed to be part of the darkness.

*Many days Cerlithe gathered and distilled herbs. Many days
she laboured, first making the clay mould and then smelting
the metal. She called upon many gods, pleading for their
help, and the gods gave their help, because she was a woman
skilled and commanding. The cauldron was made, a bronze
cauldron such as we, too, know how to construct. Such a*
krater *can do many things—with the help of the gods. It can
make potent remedies to heal the sick and soothe wounds. It
can make poisons of such venom that they must be handled
through five layers of leather. It can make the acid that bites
a design into metal.*

And there is one other thing that such a cauldron can do.

*But in the making she had exhausted her energy. For a
priestess puts some of herself, her own essence, into everything
she makes, and the cauldron was a mighty task, even for
such as she. So she bade a child stir the cauldron while she*

slept, and keep the fire stoked; and thus was her ruin and a strange making.

I was almost asleep, lapped in warmth, but something of Trioda's horror crept into my mind. I looked up at her, lying still so as not to disturb the hounds.

'What ruin, Mistress?'

While the priestess slept, three drops flew from the cauldron and fell on the child's finger, scalding the skin. He sucked his finger. Thus her year's work was wasted, and the inspiration she had designed for her son stolen, gone into another.

She woke, and in her rage, transformed, as you, daughter, were transformed into Ophis. The boy was so terrified that he used his stolen gift to fly from her just rage, and turned into a hare and ran for his life.

'And Cerlithe?'

She turned into a hound and hunted him. They say the chase lasted for days. He turned into a fish, and she dived after him as an otter. He flew up from the water as a starling, and she swooped on him as a hawk. As a frog he hid beneath a lily leaf; as a heron her beak stabbed for him, seeking his life. He flew as a hawk; she pursued him as an eagle. Whatever he did, he could not escape her.

'What happened in the end, Mistress?' I asked, imagining the sleek flash of scale and fur, the blend of claws and hands and paws, flowing like water in the green meadow beyond the north wind.

'He fell from a tree into a heap of wheat as an ear of wheat, and thought himself safe.'

'So he escaped with his stolen blessings?' I was outraged.

'No, daughter,' Trioda's voice was rich with satisfaction. 'She transformed herself into the shape of a hen, clawed through the heaped grain, caught him and swallowed him.'

'So he was dead?'

'No, Medea. She carried him for nine moons and bore him in her own image; the rebel and thief reborn as poet and singer. They called him Radiant, the priest of Apollo, son of Orpheus, the sweet singer.'

'And her own child, Mistress, for whom she brewed the miraculous potion?'

'His fate was hard. All fates are ruled, not by Zeus or Hekate but by Ate, and she is unaccountable. But, daughter, your lesson is this. Women's magic cannot be avoided, for it is made of the earth and the fire, of sky and water. The thief could not survive his theft unchanged, and finally she incorporated him as her acolyte.'

'Mistress,' I acknowledged.

'And that cauldron has this property. Renewal. If a great priestess and blessed of Hekate is willing to put her whole being into the spell, then a dead creature can be resurrected, and an old woman become young again.'

'Then why have we not done this?' I asked, sleepily.

'The price of Hekate's gift of life is death, daughter. It would require something very important—something so imperative that the priestess would challenge Fate and Time to defy them—to make it. Few human objectives are that important, daughter. Now sleep, Medea. I hope that in your life you will never have to make such a choice. For to make the cauldron of renewal needs skill and wit, and most of a woman's life force, and Hekate may need you for other purposes.'

I slipped into a drowse, pondering on Cerlithe and the thief. One method of conquering a man, it seemed, was to take him whole inside one's body, and bear him again anew.

Kore snuffled me, and we settled into sleep.

Chapter Six

Nauplios

On the day that we at last came down from the mountain, I lost Jason.

Dressed in our best tunics, with plaited horsehair bands confining our hair and supple sandals of sacred horsehide on our feet, we walked down through the flower-bearing bushes onto the ridge which led down to the city of Pelias the Usurper.

Then a mist bloomed, it seemed, out of the earth. It blanketed sight and damped sound. Jason, who had been ten paces ahead of me, vanished in the time it takes to blink an eye. I stood still, as I had been instructed. These sudden mists are not unknown on the heights, though they were not usually met with so far down the mountain and at the beginning of spring. A truism of mountain ways is that one does not walk where one cannot see. I crouched down, pulling my cloak over my head, and called, 'My lord?' but heard no reply.

There was nothing I could do and it might be fatal to wander. I could not see any path. So I sat still, picking flowers and weaving a garland. It was not cold, and I knew the mist would pass as soon as the sun rose higher. And I knew my way down the mountain to Iolkos, for had I not come that way so many years ago?

But I had lost Jason. When the rays of Apollo burned off the haze, he was nowhere in sight. I donned my garland and walked, feeling free for the first time. Free of the centaurs' domination, free of teaching or command, free to wander whither I would, although my feet were taking me ever downward, downward, and when I reached the ridge and saw the bright gleam and smelt salt, I sat down and burst into tears.

For seawater is in the blood of Dictys' sons, the net men of Iolkos. In all my time with Cheiron I had never forgotten the sea.

'*Thalassa, thalassa!*' I called, stretching out my arms to the immensity of the salt river Ocean, which spans the watery globe of the world. Horizons, constrained among the mountains by the next ridge or valley, had been abolished. There was only the arc of the sky and the sea, Poseidon's kingdom, azure, pellucid, and I swore never to leave it again, reckless of my lord and my teaching.

I ran and leapt, taking no care, from out-thrust rock to boulder to grass, down a path which only a goat might enjoy traversing, and I never stumbled. There in front of me was the immensity of Ocean, eager to embrace me. Down a sheer side I climbed like a squirrel. I reached the edge, stripped off my tunic, cloak and sandals, ran for the water, and dived full length into the arms of the Nereids.

The water was cool and salt, and Poseidon bore me up on his bosom. I ducked my garlanded head and left the circle of flowers floating in homage to the Earth-Shaker. My salt tears blended with the salt wave, and I surfaced and laughed and turned over on my back to float, secure as a babe in his mother's arms. The Master of Horses had forgiven me, most faithless of Oceanos' children, for leaving him for so long.

Then I was recalled to my duty. A long wave lifted me and deposited me in the shallows, and I rose from the sand and reclothed myself, for something was happening in the city of Iolkos, just across the bay. A crowd was gathering, and voices were raised.

It seemed that Jason had arrived.

As I walked around the rocky edge and climbed up the steps from the sand to the landing stage, I heard raised voices. Iolkos was in festival. It was the most solemn day of the year. With the centaurs I had forgotten the calendar of life amongst the Achaeans. We had come—perhaps by chance, perhaps guided by a god—to Iolkos on the feast of Poseidon, when a bull was sacrificed to the Earth-Shaker. All the neighbouring kings and princes would be there. I could see them, a gleam of gold and bronze, a glint of light off bracer and necklace and helmet.

A crowd of common people were gathered on the sea side of the marketplace. I whispered to an old woman who was standing in front of me, leaning on a creel, 'Mother, tell me what is happening in Iolkos?'

'Young stranger, it is a prodigy,' she replied in a cracked undertone. Her garments and her hair smelt of fish, once a familiar smell.

'Surely the omen has been fulfilled,' she said. 'Here is come one with only one sandal—the one-sandalled man is come! See, there is Pelias, the Usurper.' She began pointing out each noble.

Pelias was staring in horror at someone I could not see. He was a tall man, carrying a considerable belly, dressed in the purple gown of a king. He was hung with jewellery and crowned with a golden crown, figured with bulls.

'There is Pheres, king of Pherae, a prosperous place, they say; him, in the rose-coloured tunic,' said my informant, stabbing the air with her kelp brown finger. Pheres was big, with a beard like a brown bush. He reminded me strongly of a bear.

'The slender one is Amathaon, a young man for the kingship of Pylus, but a good king, they say. He fought off the Corinthian pirates, wading into the sea to board their vessel. Killed them all, and took the ship.' Amathaon was slim and young, wearing very little ornament, and had long dark hair tied back under a plaited gold band. His legs and arms were bare and sinewy, and his expression was guarded, giving nothing away.

'Mother, what are they all staring at?' I asked.

'You look lithe, young man. Climb to a height and you'll see. But I tell you, it's the omen. He's the *monosandalos*. They don't make prophecies without meaning, you know.'

I scaled the landing stage, perched on a pile of fish-smelling baskets and saw what Pelias was staring at.

In the marketplace of Iolkos stood my lord Jason, son of Aison. He was still dressed in tunic and cloak, but one sandal was indeed missing. His brown foot was bare on the well-laid stone, and he was muddy to the hips. He was looking at Pelias, straight in the eyes, and the older man shifted uneasily under his blue green gaze.

'Who are you, foreigner?' he demanded roughly.

'I am Jason, son of Aison,' said my lord evenly. 'I am come to claim my father's right.'

The commonality shifted and muttered. Such nobility and beauty was revealed in Jason, that Pelias made a gesture which sent back his household warriors. They retreated, sheathing their half-drawn swords. The kings looked at each other, but did not speak at once.

'If you are indeed the son of Aison, then you are unwelcome to me,' said Pelias. Perhaps he had once had a deep voice, but age had thinned it, and it was high and tremulous. 'Why have you come to this city?'

'I have told you why I have come,' said Jason, faintly puzzled.

'And what do you claim is your father's right?'

Jason had been well rehearsed in this matter and answered easily. 'You my lord are the son of Poseidon, and Tyro the queen. My father Aison was the son of Kreutheus the king, and Queen Tyro. Your father was not the king of Iolkos but the god, and therefore, my lord Pelias, I claim my kingdom in my father's right, as the only son of the king of this city.'

There was a stunned silence. Jason spoke gently, as he had been instructed. 'I ask only what is mine, my lord.'

Pelias did not reply. His son Akastos, standing by his father's side, stared at the stranger. There was a tense silence. I bit my fingernails.

'How did you lose your sandal?' asked Amathaon. Jason shook himself like a dog, flinging drops across the hot stone. He put back his golden hair.

'I lost my companion in the mist,' he replied civilly. 'Then as I came to the Enipeus River, an old woman asked me to help her to the other side. I picked her up—she seemed a light burden, being old and bent—but as I crossed her weight increased at every step, and I could hardly carry her. I turned my foot on a slippery stone and wrenched off my sandal—a pity, for it was made by the centaurs from sacred horsehide—but I staggered to the brink and put her down safely. Then I turned to search for my sandal, but it had been swept away. The stream is in spate. When I looked again for the crone, she was gone.'

At this the crowd shifted, enough to knock my baskets out of true. I jumped down and shoved through the crowd, hearing them mutter 'a prodigy!' and 'the omen,' as I elbowed my way through to the accompaniment of abstracted curses from the people whose feet were trodden or ribs bruised. I finally managed to thrust myself into the space between Jason and Pelias.

Intercepting the glance of that king sent a chill through my spine. He meant death to my lord. I stepped back to stand behind Jason's right shoulder, to show that he had a battle friend, if only a fisherman.

'You have been fortunate,' said the bearlike king. 'You have met a goddess, for who else would have contrived that you should enter the city of Iolkos, in front of so many witnesses, with but one sandal, as the oracle foretold? Welcome, Jason, son of Aison,' said Pheres, and Jason bowed, the same graceful bow he had been taught by Cheiron.

'I acknowledge that you are Jason.' Pelias' words were forced through clenched teeth. 'What would you do, son of Aison, if you were king, and a stranger appeared who was destined to kill you?'

'I'd send him on a journey,' said Jason. 'To prove his rightful claim. I'd send him…' he paused for thought. I held my breath and so did the watchers. 'I'd send him to recover the Golden Fleece.'

'Done,' snapped Pelias.

I bit back a cry. That journey was perilous beyond belief. There was very little chance that the son of Aison, much less a net man's son, could accomplish it, and we could never manage it alone.

'I will give you a ship, made by Argos, the best shipwright in Achaea, who stands beside you. I will give you a crew if you cannot find your own,' said Pelias. 'There is something I want you to do for me, and for Iolkos.'

'Uncle?' asked Jason, innocently, and I heard Pelias' breath hiss as this stranger claimed kinship with him.

'There is a curse,' began the Usurper.

The man beside me, knotted like an old tree by hard labour, nodded sagely and muttered, 'Ah, he's going to ask about the ghost.'

'Ghost?' I whispered.

The man had time to reply, 'Ay, boy, the ghost of Phrixos,' before Pelias announced, 'There have been apparitions of late.'

'Phrixos, my glorious ancestor, died in far Colchis, and does not rest. Eight nights I have seen him, still in his bronze armour. He mouths but cannot speak. He wishes for burial in the land of his own birth. You shall fetch me not only the Golden Fleece but the bones of Phrixos. Then, young man, I will give you the throne, for I am old and the crown is a burden to my head.'

The crowd cheered. The kings laughed and agreed that it was a good judgement. Even the sacrificial bull dipped his head and lowed. Jason smiled his heart-stopping smile and the procession formed up for Poseidon's temple, with the fate of the disturbing and ominous *monosandalos* settled.

I felt ill. I walked along the quay and up into the town, listening to Jason talk about his ship to the gnarled man, Argos, the best shipbuilder in the whole of Achaea.

I did not think we could possibly succeed.

Then again, I cheered myself, the building would take months, long past the sailing season. We would be in Iolkos for some time. I could see my parents again, my brothers, and I could reacquaint myself with the skills of handling a small boat. Then I might be of some use to the hero on his quest, before I was lost in the endless ocean between Iolkos and Colchis, beyond the Hellespont.

I had underestimated the skill of Argos and his workers. I had also underestimated the fascination which the quest would hold for all the heroes who heard of it. As they were felling the trees to make *Argo's* hull, the word went out, and men of renown began riding into Iolkos, to lodge with Pelias at his expense and greatly to his displeasure. He did not dare object, as he had sworn before his neighbouring kings that he would pay for the cost of the expedition; but it did not make him like Jason any better.

We heard the fist comers before they appeared.

Iolkos' market is situated on and around the road, which passes through the middle. We have traders and sellers of every kind of food and drink—though, of course, we principally sell produce, seaweed for fires, murex shells for dye, fish for food. The excellence of Iolkos' fish and diversity of its produce bring many traders with bread, flour, oil and cloth to trade. The marketplace is always busy. There are women selling wine; men selling fish; net weavers; spinners; and a constant cast of truant boys called by their mothers for some undone domestic task; lounging youths who have escaped their lord for an hour or so, leering after the girls and making satirical remarks and rude songs; and restless fishermen who know that for another day they dare not venture to wet an oar, not even as far as Skiathos.

After which they join the others at the tavern and order wine to assuage their disappointment. I found my father at this tavern, and he embraced me. He felt strong, as he always had, though we were of height now. He stared into my eyes, kissed my forehead in token of welcome and ordered me some wine.

'Nauplios, my dear son, you've come back, and your lord is embarking on a lunatic expedition. I suppose that you have to go?' I nodded. It had never occurred to me that Jason might go on a quest without me.

'Then spend the time wisely, my son,' said my father. He filled my cup to the brim and bade me drink. 'Come out with the boats, boy, we could use your hands. Always were a neat child with a net, and a strong one. Ah, Nauplios, I don't want to lose you again. You've heard about your brothers?'

I nodded. My two brothers had been lost, drowned, taken by Poseidon, on the same day. They had died together as they had lived together, and they lay in the same grave, as a merciful current had brought the bodies ashore. They had been mourned, and the correct libations had been poured and nothing remained of them but two intertwined locks of hair which my mother wore in her breast. This tragedy was four years gone, though I had not heard of it at the time. My father had one other son, a child of three years old, conceived to comfort my mother.

My father was aging and did not want to lose me. I did not want to be lost. But I was going with Jason. I was bound by an oath I had sworn when I first came up the mountain. I swore that I would not leave him until he was king of Iolkos, and I would not break my word.

It was a relief when we were distracted by two voices: one loud, one soft but steely. Two riders came into the market, arguing. I put down my wine cup as I listened to them.

'And I say that with Idas on his side, the venture cannot fail!' shouted the first rider. He was of middle-sized, dressed in a leather hunting tunic and leggings.

'And I say that you are the most pompous, over-loud donkey in Achaea, and I am ashamed to be your brother,' said the other middle-sized rider, also clad in a leather tunic.

Both men had shocks of curly chestnut hair. They were twins, identical in every respect except that of temperament. A market woman directed them to the palace of Pelias.

The heroes were filtering through the countryside to join the crew of Argo. The next arrived in a group, such huge men that the market was amazed, until a fisherwoman called out, 'Look at the size of him! He'd have a phallus like an oar. I tell you, sisters; he's not putting that thing anywhere near me,' and they all laughed.

The heroes named themselves as: Oileus of Locris; Telamon, son of Aiakos; Ancaeas the Strong of Tegea, son of Poseidon; Erginos, with a knot of prematurely grey hair (the fisherwomen had a lot to say about which vices had bleached his hair so young); and Clytios, a bowman and runner, who looked like a child beside the bronze-clad Titans.

As the planks were cut and the keel of the Argo laid, I went fishing with my father, learning again the skill of managing a small boat. I had forgotten much. My mind did not remember, but sometimes my hands did. I was trying to tie a particular knot, one hot day as we lay on a sea which rocked like a cradle. The rope twisted in my grip and would not cooperate, so I closed my eyes and let my fingers work, and opened them to see the correct flat reef for securing the net.

My father said, 'Ah, Nauplios, Poseidon has not let you forget that you are a fisherman,' and embraced me.

Every day as we came in, dragging our heavy nets ashore, there were more heroes in Pelias' palace. Jason announced the names to me as I hefted a creel filled with shining shells through the loose sand. It was so heavy that I sank to the calf at every step.

'Tiphys has come to be our helmsman, Nauplios. They say he's the most beautiful man in Achaea. And Authalides to be our herald; the *famous* Authalides. Nestor, Honey-Voiced, rode in this morning. He will be very valuable—he can talk his way out of anything. Hermes gave him the gift of persuasion. My cousin Admetos is on his way, they say, and I think Akastos, the king's son, yearns for our adventure, though his father will never let him go. Meleagros and Perithous are coming, both strong rowers.'

I wrestled the basket onto the edge of the landing stage and leaned on it, out of breath. 'I don't know any of these people,' I objected. 'How many crewmen have you now?'

'I still need six more—no, five. Idmon the seer has agreed to come with us. Oh, Nauplios, don't look so worried!'

'I'm not worried, I'm out of breath,' I lied. 'Who's expected?'
'Alabande, he's a friend of Ancaeas, a quiet man, they say, but
strong. Poseidon Earth-Shaker! Who is that?'

I shaded my eyes. A slim girl dressed in a short tunic clasped at
the neck with a bronze brooch in the shape of a bear was walking
through the market with the confident, long-legged grace of a
deer. She bore a bow and a quiver. She had a rolled cloak at her
back and, unlike any but the boldest Achaean women, looked
every man she saw in the face. She seemed to be asking questions.

'She's looking for me,' declared Jason hopefully, springing
onto the landing stage and running into the centre of the square.
I followed him, dragging my shells into a safe place, and we
stopped in front of the girl and stared.

She was beautiful, but not desirable—by which I mean it
seemed wrong to think of her as a woman, as she patently didn't.
She had breasts, but she paid no attention to them…I am not
explaining this well. All I can say is that Atalante the Hunter,
favoured of Artemis, suckled by a she bear and raised by the
priestesses at Brauron, was no more a woman than I am. She
was a virgin and a comrade.

She became one as soon as she grinned at Jason and me and
said in her husky voice, 'I am Atalante of Calydon, and I wish
to join the quest for the Golden Fleece. I can row and sail, and
I can mostly hit a target with an arrow.'

I stared at her chest. Under the bear brooch, she wore only
one ornament. It was a necklace made of amber beads, strung
with two boar's tusks. It must have been a gigantic boar. The one
which had nearly killed me had tusks about a span long. This
monster had borne armament fully the span of both my hands.
The tusks had been polished and gleamed like ivory, extending
from Atalante's corded, muscular throat to her nipples. I had
heard of the hunt of Calydon. Atalante's arrow had killed that
boar. Her knife had cut its throat. I was full of admiration.

So was Jason. He held out his hand, palm slapped, then
Atalante the Hunter exchanged the kiss of brotherhood with

Jason and with me. We sat down and bought some wine and watched the ships coming in.

It was darkening. I heard the thud of wooden mallets from the shore, where Argos swore at his men who cut thousands of pegs which would be hammered into the planks of the ship. She was going to be beautiful, our ship. She was narrow, with a high poop and stern, as yet undecorated. The woodcarver—heedless of the insults flying around from the shipwrights, whose language would have curled Poseidon's hair—was chiselling out a bow-post for the ship, though I could not yet see what it was meant to be. A bull, perhaps, for Iolkos and Earth-Shaker?

Two men and four boys were stitching together our sail, patterned red and white as is the custom of Iolkos, from long strips of dense, perfect weaving. My mother had given me one length of bright red cloth, which she had been keeping for my wedding. I believed that she feared I would not return to be married to any fisherman's daughter.

'Have you the twenty-four?' asked Atalante, accepting a cup of wine and swallowing it in a gulp. She poured herself another.

I was fascinated with her. She looked female—her face would have been girlish if she had been a boy, but for a girl it was boyish. She had brown eyes and a complexion much damaged by the weather, not like any woman I had seen. She was a puzzle too complex for one of Dictys' sons to solve, so I sipped at my wine and watched the road.

We heard someone playing a stringed instrument. It was a sweet, trilling note, often repeated, as though the player was working on composing a tune. Without any announcement a man came into the market, head bent over his lyre, navigated his way to the tavern apparently by feel, and sat down with his back to us.

He was outlandish. His hair, instead of being of human colour, was as red as new copper wire. It curled over his forehead and flowed down his back, parting over his broad shoulders. He wore a green tunic, completely without decoration even in the weave, and there were no bracers on his wrists or rings on his fingers. He was utterly absorbed in his music. The tortoiseshell soundbox rested on his knee. One hand damped the strings from behind, the other plucked them from in front. His fingers were long and strong, the nails as hard as horn. I noticed that his well-shaped feet were bare as a beggar's, and he was as stained with travel as any farmer. But the music which he drew from the lyre had silenced all conversation in the market, and the people stopped packing up for the night and drew close, intent on the pure, plangent notes.

Atalante said, 'Stranger, your music is most welcome, but speak to us. Who delights Iolkos with such music?'

He lifted his head and smiled. 'Lady,' he said in reply. 'I am Philammon the bard, and I seek Jason, son of Aison, for I am ordered by my master to join this quest.'

'I am Jason,' said my lord eagerly, 'Greetings, Philammon. Who is your lord?'

'Ammon Apollo, of course, and through him Orpheus.' His voice was an instrument as thrilling in its way as his lyre. It was impossible not to listen to the voice of Philammon the bard, given the gift of song by Orpheus, the sweet singer. His smile was sweet, holding power.

I remembered that the cult of Orpheus had followers all over the Aegean—a religion of great mystery. I was about to offer him a cup of wine when Atalante said, 'I know that you may not drink wine or eat flesh, Philammon, but we have here spring water and wheat bread. Will you eat with us?'

He stared at each of us in turn. When his eyes met mine I felt that he knew all about me. It was most unpleasant. He held us all with his eyes—even Jason wriggled under his cool regard—then smiled again, picked up a flat loaf of bread, and broke it in four pieces.

'I will eat with you,' he said.

It was quite dark when we had finished our meal. The torches had been lit outside Pelias' palace. We could hear the sound of heroes feasting inside, the barking of their hunting dogs and occasional smash of crockery. Argos had taken his son Melas and one to his own house. The light caught the ribs of the uncompleted ship, which looked uncomfortably like bones.

But since the coming of Philammon my mood had improved. Just to be in his company was comfortable. He knew all about me. And he still liked me.

The marketplace was silent, the road empty. Then I heard the sound of weary footsteps. A heavy tread, and light feet pattering on ahead.

'Here, my lord,' said a boy into the darkness. 'This must be the town.'

'Is this Iolkos?' asked a quiet voice.

I called, 'This is Iolkos. Come and have some wine, if you come in peace.'

'I come in peace,' agreed the man, and he and his companion walked to our table across the empty market. The boy dropped a bundle of cloaks and cooking pots with a clatter and threw himself down next to Atalante, who clipped amiably at his ears for shoving.

The man sat down heavily and removed one boot, looking mournfully at a hole in the sole. He wiggled one finger through it, then dropped it and took the offered wine cup, draining it at one draught. He laid a silver piece on the table, and refilled his cup.

He was ragged and dusty and old. His tangled grey hair was receding away from a lined brow, and there was a bunch of blue flowers behind his ear. He had bright grey eyes, shaggy eyebrows, and some sort of cured skin over his shoulders. He was tanned by at least fifty years in the weather, and his thigh, next to mine, was iron hard and seemed to be made entirely of whipcord and bone. A long scar ran down his bare arm, and he wore an amulet of the Mother Hera around his neck.

The boy was pretty and knew it. His black curls were threaded with a silver band. His ears were pierced and ringed, and his slender body had never borne heavy weight; exercise, perhaps, but not hard work. I wondered what such a slip of the nobility should do, travelling with this old farmer.

The old man laid his gentian flowers on the table. 'Look,' he said, touching them reverently with the end of one work-worn forefinger. 'I picked them this morning on the slopes, but they will not last much longer. They smell cold. The mountain folk call them snowflowers.'

'Beautiful,' agreed the bard. He plucked a few strings in honour of the blossoms.

Jason was tired and did not want further company, especially not a pretty boy and his deluded lover. 'May we know, honoured lord, your name?' he asked with elaborate and ironic courtesy.

The boy began to giggle, then extinguished his laughter in Atalante's wine, for which she cuffed his ears again. The old man looked up from studying the blue flowers.

'My name? Oh, yes. You are Jason, son of Aison, are you not? I am pleased to meet a comrade.' He reached out a hand which engulfed Jason's palm and half his forearm. My lord was rather offended by this familiarity from a peasant, which made the old man's next words the more crushing.

'This is Hylas, my squire. I am Herakles of Tiryns,' he said. 'And for some reason, the goddess Hera, who is my mistress, wants me to embark with you on the quest for the Golden Fleece.'

Chapter Seven

Medea

My father owns the most ferocious bulls in the world. There are two of them, a matched pair of oxen. They stand almost sixteen hands high at the shoulder, and their horns and hoofs are shod with bronze. No woman may go near them or touch them, and every year the king yokes them and ploughs the first furrow, in honour of Ammon, the god of the sun, at the equinox when the year turns.

It had been as hard a winter as we had ever seen. Even the old women of Hekate's worship could not remember a time when the snow lay so long or so deep. I had piled all the wood we had onto the temple fire, and wrapped myself in so many layers that Trioda said I needed wheels, not feet, but even sleeping before the fire with a hound on either side, I had always been cold.

The goddess tried my body hard, making me into a woman fit for her purposes. My second bleeding came early and with much pain, and then the interval to the third was longer than a moon. But on the day that the priests proclaimed that the king would plough with the bulls, I felt the familiar trickle of blood, and bound my loins with pads of cloth, as is the custom of Colchis.

We stood in a row, the priestesses of Hekate, to one side of the field. I was shivering in my ceremonial mantle, figured purple on black with the three-legged cross of the Black Mother. The air was sullen and chill, with no signs of spring. Kore leaned on one side of me, Scylla on the other, panting. Their breath steamed in clouds. The surface of the River Phasis was as flat as a sheet of metal, unbroken even by ripples. The floods had passed, leaving rubbish and bodies caught in the willows. The sky was also grey, heavy with more rain. The plain of Ares looked desolate, untidy, and heavily cold. The ground was no longer stone hard with frost, but I doubted whether even the great bulls could turn a furrow.

The whole populace of Colchis was gathered to watch this magical ritual. Women with babies, such small children as had survived the icy nights, old people waiting hopefully for another spring—when, according to my knowledge of medicine, they would also let go of their grip on life—all the able bodied, farmers and traders and their women, even a group of Scyths, garish in their red, blue and green felt clothes and scandalous in their leather breeches. Everyone had been alarmed by the tenacity and cruelty of the winter. Everyone—even the Scyths—was relying on the ritual of the ploughing to restore the sun on his journey through the sky. I could see all faces, pinched by the cold, turned hopefully to the town, as trumpets announced the arrival of the king.

Aetes, my father, came, attended by many priests of Ammon. I reflected that they must be even colder than I was. At least I wore a hood. They were shaven and clad in one layer of thin saffron linen, and I could hear the chattering of their teeth half a *stadion* away. They carried the litter with the king—for his feet may not touch ground except before the bulls, lest his magic be lost—and he stepped down.

The plough was laid next to the beasts. It was of a strange metal, silver-coloured, and forged all in one piece. This being men's magic, I had never approached it, but I did wonder what it was made of. Hephaestos, the smith god, had given it to our ancestors. By the king's side stood my half brother, and behind a little to the left, the four sons of Phrixos. Should the king fail at this task, then his kingship would pass. His son would attempt and, if he failed, the next heirs, one after another, until some man could tame the bulls and plough the furrow which would ensure a good harvest. Trioda grunted that this was the last vestige of the good old custom of sacrificing the summer king. My father looked old. He coughed, wiped his mouth and walked heavily toward the bulls, who turned to survey him, horns down. I held my breath. If this did not work, if my father failed at the bulls and my half brother Aefialeus managed to tame them, then he would marry me by force, and I would have to kill him. And myself. No priestess of Hekate survives her own rape. The goddess has obviously withdrawn protection from her for some sin, or such a thing could not happen. Aegialeus, of course, would die first. And, if I had anything to do with it, painfully. Though perhaps She Who Meets would prevent it. I hoped so. My hand dropped to fondle Kore's ears and I felt better. While I had my guards, my half brother would only get to me after he had been thoroughly chewed.

The king approached the bulls. They seemed to wind him. I saw their muzzles lift. Nostrils flared. Aetes held out both hands, the ceremonial red and gold cloak billowing around him as a little breeze picked up.

The bulls snorted and plunged, backing away a step. I thought that my father looked puzzled. He wiped his hands on the ground and held them out again.

I saw Aegialeus smile, as though pleased. That boded ill.

At my side Trioda cursed by Hekate under her breath.

'What's the matter, Mistress?'

'Someone has changed the ointments,' she muttered.

'Ointments?'

'Prepared by us to allow the king to approach those great beasts. I haven't told you about it—but you shall learn how to compound it. Now what shall we do, daughter? Rescue the king, or let events take their course?'

'What will happen?'

'If he approaches those beasts unanointed, they will either stampede or trample him to death.'

I thought about it. I knew no great evil of my father—though no great good either—and I certainly distrusted my half brother Aegialeus. He might be the cause of my death. On the other hand, if we did rescue Aetes, he would kill whoever had made this substitution, and that would probably be my brother. Thus my brother would die if we rescued the king.

Better him than me. I said to my mistress, 'How shall we rescue the king my father?'

'Take this, daughter,' she handed me a small clay pot. 'When I distract them, run to the king and smear his hands. Then return fast—this must appear divine.'

The king was standing amazed. The bulls had sidled close to each other, heads lowered, dreadful bronze-sheathed horns lowered. Suddenly there was a bang and a bright flash and everyone turned.

I ran for the king. He had been looking at the flash and was blinded. I slathed the ointment onto his wrinkled hands and fled back to the crowd as the common people turned back to the field. The bulls sniffed deeply and ambled to the king, and he smiled as their soft muzzles nuzzled his hands.

They lowed, nudging him, as he laid the yoke across their backs—he had to stand on tiptoe to reach—and then they lumbered into a walk. I saw each red and white flank move as smoothly as a stone in a water mill as the bronze hoofs slogged through the mud. The plough leaned, then was righted, and the metal blade cut a wet, heavy furrow in the wake of the bulls.

Trioda said, 'Neatly done, daughter,' and I breathed out.

'Who changed the ointments, do you think?' I asked, knowing the answer.

'You have only to look at him,' spat Trioda with satisfaction. I looked. My half brother was crestfallen, his fine smile wiped away, and the beginnings of fear were crossing his face.

'One day a cock, the next day a fly whisk,' said Trioda, quoting a Colchian proverb.

'What will my father do to him?' I wondered aloud.

'We shall see,' said my mistress.

The furrow was completed. The king loosed the bulls, which wandered away to their pasture, and walked the furrow, dropping barley seeds behind him. The people cheered; he was carried, shoulder high into the city, and we followed at the end of the procession, curious to see to which doom he would put his betrayer.

A fine, sleety rain stung my skin as we walked through the narrow streets to the palace, where the men would feast. Sweating slaves had been preparing bread and roasting meat since early morning. Trioda placed the other papyrus packet into her sleeve. This was a mystery of the priestesses of Hekate; a combination of powders derived from mining, a yellow mineral, ground charcoal, dog dung, and a pale silvery powder would explode with a bang and a flash if they were lit and thrown. In such a way had the city been impressed with the power of Hekate when the common people had raided the shrines, some twenty years ago, after such a hard winter as this. It was the discovery of the priestess Althea, three generations ago, and she brought the secret from the Black Land with her. The ingredients were scarce and seldom found, and it was by the special intervention of the Lady that Trioda had been carrying a couple of them—or perhaps it was not. My mistress had a way of knowing most things. Now she was walking grimly beside me. I asked, 'What do you think will happen, Lady?' and she grunted.

'The king your father has no sense,' she said flatly. But she would not tell me what she feared.

The crowd had come into the precincts of the palace, where the feast was laid out. We walked through the throng of men, who were laughing and tearing chunks off fresh loaves, following the king into the inner palace and into the audience chamber. The noises of the feast faded behind us. My mouth watered. I seemed to be always hungry since the goddess made me a woman.

Aetes climbed out of his litter. A broad gesture dismissed the priests of Ammon, who scurried away. Facing the king as he sat down on his throne were the four sons of Phrixos and my half brother Aegialeus.

Aetes surveyed them in silence.

'Someone tried to kill me this morning,' he said. There was no reply from any of them.

'The man who did so must have had the ointment on him,' he said.

No one moved.

'Turn out your pouches,' roared the king. Kneeling, trembling, the five young men did as they were bid and the king searched through the contents. Knives, letters, a piece of bread—that would be Melanion, my old companion, who was always hungry—a sharpening stone, a lump of wax, an ivory comb.

No little pot of ointment which could tame the bulls.

'Confess!' screamed the king. He was purple, and Trioda whispered to a slave to prepare the draught for apoplexy. He was working himself into another fit.

'Lord, we did not plot your downfall,' said Cytisoros, the eldest son of Phrixos. 'Not I, and not my brother Argeos or my brother Phrontis or my little brother Melanion.'

'You are the sons of the stranger,' snarled the king. 'You are foreigners, bearing foreign seed.'

'Lord, we would not harm you,' said Argeos.

'Who, then?'

Cytisoros made a fatal error. He did not speak, but he looked aside at Aegialeus, and the king caught the look. I have never heard human voice rise to such a shriek.

'You dare to accuse my own son; the son of my loins?'

Cytisoros backed away from the incandescent king.

'No, Lord…' he stammered.

'Exile!' Aetes called for his counsellors, and they ran into the room, tablets at the ready. 'I cannot kill you, sons of the stranger, for you are my kin, after this my own son. But you shall leave my kingdom. I will give you a ship and you shall leave—all of you. Forever.'

'Lord, give us leave to say goodbye to our mother, your daughter,' begged Cytisoros. He was shocked, but he was still thinking.

I could not bear to look at the renewed smirk on the mouth of my despicable half brother. It was desperately unfair. The king was making the wrong decision. I stirred, but Trioda caught my wrist.

'The errors of men are not ours to mend, daughter of Hekate,' she instructed.

'But he's exiling the wrong ones!' I protested.

'He's a man,' said Trioda in a vicious undertone. 'Of course he's wrong.'

I was forced to stand and watch as Phrixos' sons, with whom I had played as a child, were marked with red paint to signify that they were exiles. Chalkiope, my sister, was brought in to receive their farewells. She wept painfully, crying out on my father that he was mad, so that he struck her across the face and the slaves carried her away.

Then my playmates were gone, and I could not avoid looking at Aegialeus. He was sitting at the king's feet. Aetes' old, veined hand rested on his curly black hair and he was as smooth and self-assured as a wolf.

He was smiling that smug smile, and I felt sick.

◇◇◇

It was just before dusk on the next day that Trioda announced that I was to travel with the Scythians for the spring and summer.

It was not unknown for Hekate's priestesses to travel with the nomadic, or royal, Scyths. They did not camp, except for the winter, and they travelled on many roads where the sacred places were unattended. Every ten years or so, one of the daughters of the Dark Mother would go along on the circuit with the tribes, to clean and re-sanctify the temples and altars, to advise on medicine and to learn, for a priestess is always learning, until Hekate gathers her to her bosom.

Trioda was sending me to keep me out of my half brother's grasp, and I was grateful.

I had no opportunity to speak with my father, and Chalkiope would not confide in me, even when I went to tend her bruised face. I gathered my belongings—precious few—and called Kore and Scylla. Trioda took me to the Scythian camp. We walked in amongst the noisy, colourful crowd and for the first time I felt different in my black robes.

'Little Scyth,' said a voice from above me. A woman sitting comfortably on a wagon tossed one plait back across her shoulder and grinned. I groped in my memory. I felt a strong hand, and remembered the street.

'Lady,' I replied. 'It is a long time since I ran under the hoofs of your horse!'

'You travel with us, priestess?' she asked, and I nodded.

'Excellent,' she said. 'Ride with me, if you can. My name is Anemone,' she added, as Trioda dragged me onward by the sleeve.

We bowed before a fat man, slouched on a pile of cushions in the corner of a sumptuous tent which stank of curdled milk. I had seen him before. He was the Scythian king, Idanthyrsus. His bulk did not preclude his excellent horsemanship, and he was reputed to have three wives—though that may have just been gossip. The Scythians were little known in Colchis, and out of ignorance comes fantasy. He was very dark of skin, with long hair arranged in two plaits, and was hung with gold jewellery. Like most Scyths, he had a broad face, with high, flat cheekbones, a wide nose, and eyes so black that their expression was impossible to read.

'Princess,' he nodded to me. 'Trioda. This is your acolyte?'

'Full priestess now, and very acute.' Trioda was even more short of speech than usual. 'You travel the usual way?'

'The usual way, yes. Unless you have some seeing for us?'

'Fair weather and good fortune,' said Trioda, spitting out the words as though she was cursing, not blessing. 'But if Medea returns unvirgin, then disaster and plague.'

'The women will care for her,' he said. 'She cannot take a man until she kills an enemy in battle—and that is not likely to happen. She will return to you as virgin as she is now. Come here, Princess.'

I approached him warily. His hand shot out and pinched my breast. It hurt. I struck the hand away. He chuckled, revealing rotten teeth in a cracked mouth.

'She's virgin enough,' he said. Trioda bristled.

'I wish to ride with Anemone,' I announced haughtily. The king raised his eyebrows.

'You have made a powerful friend in a short time, priestess,' he said, and made a sign which might have been to ward against evil. 'By all means, Princess Medea. If Anemone will have you, you may ride with her.'

The dogs accompanied me out of the tent. Once in the open, Trioda dusted me down with her hard hand, then gave me a bag of medicines.

'Remember your teaching,' she chided. 'Do nothing until you must, then act surely and swiftly. The goddess will aid you. Preserve your maidenhood against all force; rather die a maiden than live dishonoured. But in that case make sure that you take your attacker with you to Hekate's judgement. Speak politely to all women, they are your sisters, however strange their ways are. I will see you at the end of autumn, daughter.' She did not kiss me. She turned and walked away.

I stood clutching the leather bag, feeling a little at a loss—she could at least have told me that she wished me well—when a lazy voice at my elbow commented, 'Old witch. Come along, sister. Anemone sent me to guide you, guessing that Trioda would just leave you. This way,' said a young woman, taking my arm.

I was minded to resent her dismissal of my mistress like that, but she smiled at me. Her teeth were like seeds in her red mouth, and she had a wealth of beautiful chestnut hair. Kore and Scylla leapt up on her, licking her face. The dog's confidence decided me. Whoever she was, I liked her.

'I am Iole,' said the young woman, following a twisting path through a maze of caravans and tents. The Scyths live in wagons, which are drawn by oxen or horses. They are lofty, with wide axles, difficult to overturn. They stretch thick hides over high lattice work sides, making a kind of upturned basket. In them they travel long distances, taking their houses with them like snails. Each Scythian lives alone. The men have their own wagons, and the women theirs. The children live with whichever parent has time to look after them. They are a warlike people, and are much feared.

They are also averse to washing and not given to hygiene, possibly because water is scarce in the desert and they do not stay in one place for long. The camping ground was filthy with slops and droppings of animals and humans. I was glad we were leaving on the morrow. I gathered up my robe and picked my way through, trying to listen to what Iole was saying. Kore and Scylla, overawed by all the new smells, kept close to me and did not reply to challenges from the Scythian hunting dogs.

'The last priestess who came with us hated Scythian ways,' she said, avoiding a woman who was washing a recalcitrant child in a shallow dish.

'Indeed?' I said.

'She thought we were all barbarians. But Anemone says you are a Scyth in Colchian skin, so she is pleased that you are coming.' Iole turned the corner of a wagon and passed a naked man. He was sitting on the edge of his wagon and mending his breeches. Iole did not give him a second look and I tried not to stare. We skirted an uneasy mare who was suckling her foal.

'Who is Anemone?' I asked, recognising the painted wagon on which the woman had been perched when she had first hailed me. It was patterned with stripes and spots in various colours, mostly red and orange and yellow.

'She's the priestess of Ares, our own god, and the wife of the king,' said Iole.

I halted. When the woman appeared, I bowed. She waved her hand amiably and then extended it so that I could climb aboard. She was very casual, for a queen.

'Priestess,' she greeted me. 'Sling up that bundle, Iole. Good. Now, little Scyth, we shall have some drink, and you shall settle into Scythian ways which, as you will have seen, are more relaxed than the ways of the court of Aetes. How is he, by the way? Still having fits?'

'He has banished the sons of Phrixos,' I said, ducking under the woven hanging to come into the wagon.

It was dim inside. The hides which kept out the weather were not visible. The inside of the basket was hung with patterned cloth, cleverly painted with little horsemen and the animals they hunted: deer with elaborate antlers, oxen and boar. On the walls hung weapons, several bows and full quivers. A basket held clothes, and a pile of carpets and blankets made the queen's bed. It was close and comfortable, after the glare and the dust outside, and I sank down on the bed. Scylla and Kore flanked me, sitting close and nervous, ears back.

Anemone sat down opposite me. She was wearing breeches of light deerskin and a leather corselet over a linen tunic. Her feet were bare. Her necklace of gold coins chimed as she moved. She was very exotic to a princess who had worn black garments since the cradle.

'Drink,' she instructed, handing me a wooden cup. I sipped. It was strange but refreshing, tasting a little like fermented apple juice. 'That's kermiss,' she added, 'mare's milk. So, banished Chalkiope's sons, has he? Yet I would have said the threat came closer from his own heart.'

'Possibly,' I murmured. She gave me a sharp look.

'Wait until we know each other better, Princess,' she said and smiled. 'Meanwhile, we leave in the morning. I must go to the king directly, but I shall be back soon, and Iole will keep you company. She has no man yet—we really need a battle, or some of our young women will die maidens.'

I felt that travelling with the Scythians was going to be very interesting.

Chapter Eight

Nauplios

I wandered down with Herakles and Hylas to look at the ship.

I was tongue-tied with shame at not having recognised the hero about whom I had heard so many stories. In daylight, the cured skin across his broad shoulders was certainly a lion's hide, or what had once been a lion's hide. It had been slept on and dragged through thorns and wetted in both salt and river water many times since Herakles had stripped it from its owner's body. The golden mane was grey with dust.

The hero was also much weathered. He trod heavily, as though he were weary, but his eyes were alert and today he was delighted. One of the Iolkos chidren had raced up and shyly presented him with a miraculous shell, which the divers had found while hunting octopus. It was spiky, blue-green and iridescent, and Herakles carried it in his big hands as though it was a crown. By contrast Atalante, at his side, was full of the joy of youth. Her step was springy and light. Her feet seemed to float above the earth, and she moved like a dancer. Herakles seemed pleased to be with us, and Hylas was delighted. He shook his head, so that ringlets of ebony hair fell across his slim neck, and exclaimed 'Isn't she beautiful? Greetings, Argos! How long until she is seaworthy?'

'Soon enough,' grunted the old man. 'You'll be saying farewell to your breakfast soon enough, son of Dropion.'

Argo—swift—looked alarmingly fragile. The ribs stood up, half fleshed now as the shipwrights attached the pine planks fresh cut from the slopes of Centaurs' Mountain to the graceful bones of the vessel. But she seemed small, no longer than twenty paces from bow to stern, and perhaps five across. The keel had received its ram, which smooths the water as the ship moves, creating an area of calm on either side for the rowers. I stretched, flexing my hands, hoping my strength would be sufficient for the task ahead.

'Greetings,' said Lynkeos. He was brotherless. 'I've given Idas the slip—he's playing some drinking game. I don't think your uncle Pelias is very pleased at having us all in his palace,' he commented. 'Those heroes are hard on the crockery and furnishings. Idmon has come with me.'

He introduced a dark, thin, intense man, dressed in the saffron robes of a seer. He had the strangest eyes I have ever seen in a living man. They were perfectly blank. No emotion showed on Idmon's gaze. He bowed politely and we returned the courtesy. Hylas smiled his sweetest at Idmon, got no response, and pouted.

Idmon lifted one hand and whistled. It was a high, shrill, ugly sound, but it produced results. Out of the sky a huge white bird dropped, the one which the men of Iolkos call *Peregrinator*, Wanderer. Men see it sometimes—I had seen it myself—*stadia* out to sea, hovering over the pathless ocean. It is an omen of storms, but the fishermen say it brings the fortunate breeze, being a child of Zephyros, the west wind, most kindly of the four brothers. The wingspan of this bird was greater than the outstretched arms of a man, but it bent its regal head and wicked beak as though it was listening to what Idmon said as it sat on his shoulder, cruel talons gripping through the yellow cloth. I heard the word 'Colchis'. The bird flapped suddenly, as though alarmed, and nearly lifted the seer into the air, but it soon calmed, allowing him to caress its snowy head, and he finished his sentence. We could not understand the words. I do not speak, as Idmon did, the language of the bird people.

He lifted his hand and the *peregrinator* gained height, circling us twice before it flew out to sea. Argos, still clutching his adze, knelt down at Idmon's feet and asked in an awed whisper, 'Master, what omen for this my ship?'

Blood ran down the seer's breast from his wounded shoulder, but he did not seem to have noticed. 'A good omen for the ship, that she should go and return,' he said in a flat voice. 'She has great protection from heaven; a divine hand is over her.' He raised Argos and the old man was about to kiss his hand in thanks when the augur added, 'And for me, death. Yet I will not turn aside from Fate. Até cannot be avoided or controlled.'

He dipped one finger in his own blood and wrote a sign on the keel, a sacred sign, apparently, because the ship wrights knelt and bowed their heads to it. Then Idmon the seer went away.

My sense of unease was growing again.

But it was a fair day, tending toward hot, and there was nothing yet to fear. Herakles looked over the ship, grunted, and sat down in the shade, turning his shell to the light. I took one of the flasks of wine and water, cooling in the shallows for the refreshment of the labourers, and poured him a cup, kneeling down and holding it out at arm's length, as the centaur my master had instructed me.

He took the cup, saying, 'Seat yourself, son of Iolkos. Drink with me. How came you, an honest fisherman by the look of you, to be the close friend of Jason?'

I told him about the time with Cheiron. There was something about Herakles which invited confidences. I watched Jason, Atalante and Lynkeos walking the length of the Argo and, interspersed with the hero's comments on my tale, I listened to their conversation.

'But she is made of green wood,' objected Atalante. 'How can such fresh planks sustain the strain? She will warp and twist as the wood seasons.'

'You are a great hunter, or so men say,' retorted Argos, nettled. 'But you know nothing of my craft. The shipbuilders of Iolkos always use green timber. As she sails, she will settle. See, here, the boards are locked together, mortice and tenon. They cannot move. When she is launched, daughter of Calydon, you will hear her sing in the wave.'

Atalante agreed peaceably that she knew nothing about shipbuilding, and a mollified Argos took them forward, where the woodcarver was attaching the figurehead.

'It came to me in the night,' he said excitedly. He was a small man with curls of wood in his hair. 'I was going to carve the bull's head for Iolkos, when she came.'

'Who came?' asked Hylas, yawning.

'The goddess herself, boy. Hera, queen of heaven. She turned her head and smiled at me, a woman crowned with stars. She stayed with me long enough for me to draw her, and I have carved what I saw.'

Herakles and I looked. The bow-post was the torso and head of a woman of surpassing strength, not beauty. Her nose was a beak, her cheekbones high and shaped like the keel of a ship. Her mouth curved in a smile. I shivered. I did not like that smile.

Herakles patted my arm. 'She is not a goddess to be taken lightly,' he said. 'All my life she has guided me, from the challenge she set me when I was eight-months old and strangled her snakes in my cradle, to the deeds which made me a hero. Yet no man has endured such sorrow as mine. Battle rage takes me, and I slay all around, onlookers and innocents. She sent that rage, Hera, wife of Zeus Thunderer. The gods design fates for men, Nauplios, and there is no gainsaying them. But maybe you have been fated to return safely and marry here, and fish peacefully for the rest of your life. Be cheered. Have some more wine.'

'What think you of the crew, Lord?' I asked, daring to ask his opinion. He turned the blue green shell, and bright lights flashed across his broad face.

'I am glad that we have Idmon, even if he is doomed, and Philammon the bard with us,' he said slowly. 'Tiphys is a good helmsman, though far too vain of his own beauty. Lynkeos is keen sighted, and although his brother Idas is a boaster, he has great strength. I am glad to see Ancaeas the Strong, almost my match in strength, who can balance me at the centre oar. A modest man. Nestor will be valuable, though Authalides' skill as a herald has been overrated. He fell in love with the sound of his own voice many years ago, and cares not what effect he has on his own audience, and that is bad for a herald. Clytios and Atalante are very skilled with the bow. I hope that she can convince this crew to treat her as a comrade, as is right in a dedicated maiden and daughter of the She-Bear Artemis, goddess of hunters. They are both runners, so can be put ashore to search the land while the ship sails beside them. Admetos is a good fighter. Alabande does not brag, but is strong and skilful with an oar. As for Telamon, Perithous, Erginos with his grey hair, Meleagros and Oileus—well, Nauplios, strong men boast of their strength, not knowing that it comes from the gods. If Hera is with Jason and he can command his crew, then we may get to Colchis alive—though whether we can obtain the Golden Fleece is another matter. Very perilous, Colchis, or so the tales say. There are witches there who can charm the heart out of a man's body.'

'You must have met witches before, Herakles,' I suggested.

'Oh, yes, I have met with sorceresses,' he replied. 'I have defeated them, too, though I would always rather reach an agreement than do battle. For if I do fight, Nauplios, I win. I always win. Until my fate overtakes me, I cannot be bested. Not by men and not by monsters.'

'Lord, tell me—why is Hylas here? He seems—I mean, he looks unused to warfare.'

'He is also unused to travel,' said the hero, moving his shell into a better light. His voice was quite devoid of any expression. 'I killed his father in a quarrel. He tried to cheat me out of an oxen. The rage came on me and when I came back to my body there was Dropian, hacked to bits. Fortunately his son did not see this. I buried the pieces, made the libations, and went to tell the boy of his father's death. He demanded to accompany me, and I am bound to him by a blood debt. But he is joyful and witty,' said Herakles. 'He will get bored soon, and I will be discharged of this burden. I've been fighting off his suitors the length of the road to Iolkos, and he is likely to cause trouble among the crew if any find him comely. But there is no vice in him, man of Iolkos. He is a child.'

Hylas did not seem childlike to me. He was flirtatious and knowing. I wondered if he was the hero's lover, as well as his bond master. I really could not decide.

Then a shipwright called to me to come and tar the fathoms of closely woven rope which would manoeuvre our sail. I left Herakles to contemplate his shell and crouched down next to the tar pot, an expensive substance won from Libya, where black, evil-smelling oil bubbles in pools into the sand and shrouded men gather salt and bitumen with a basket on a pole, swiping across the surface. They sell it for its weight in bronze, which they need to make knives.

No one could really relish the smell of this oily water-proofing—I would stink of it for days, I knew, unless I washed all over with soap root and scrubbed my hands with volcano stone—but I soaked and coated the lines carefully, so that the salt would not penetrate and rot the ropes. Then I sniffed and leapt to my feet in alarm.

Argos had finished conducting his guests on a tour, and was attacking the side of the now planked ship with a flaming torch. Just as the wood was about to char and catch, he moved on, so the whole side of *Argo* was smoked and blackened.

'What are you doing?' cried Jason, summoned from the shore by the scent of burning wood. Argos snarled, 'The wood is fresh, lord, and wet. The slots cut for the tenons must be dried, or the vessel will part from her timbers in the grip of Ocean, and down will go all your famous crew into the cold embrace of the sea nymphs. Pegs,' he bellowed, and four men leapt to hammer in the tie-pins into the hull, securing the joints. Jason backed away and said nothing further, as the old man scorched the other side *Argo,* and I returned to my ropes and my tar pot.

'Never question a master on his trade,' my father had told me. It was good advice.

Jason seemed about to speak again, but decided against it and walked back to the palace as the marketplace began to fill.

Argo was completed just before the end of sailing season. The shipwrights worked late by torchlight, on Pelias' orders. The heroes were eating him out of palace and city, and he was anxious to be rid of us.

I was just as anxious to go. My mother wept over me every day. I tried to explain.

'I am bound to Jason by an oath,' I said for the fortieth time, as she wove blanket thread into a cloak for me. The sound I always associate with my mother is the clack of her loom as the heddle claps flat against the wall. 'I must go, Mother. But I'll come back, I swear.'

'Aie,' she wailed, weaving and weeping. Tears ran down her face. 'Come back, yes, Nauplios, you'll come back like your brothers. More likely you'll be lost in the sea near Colchis, and I'll never have a body to anoint. A curse on Phrixos! I wish he'd fallen into the Hellespont, along with his sister!'

'Don't curse, mother, don't curse.' I came behind her and she leaned her head into my shoulder. 'There's enough ill wishing on this voyage already.'

'Aie! I wish I had died giving birth to the first child, for there is nothing but sorrow for women. We bear in agony, suckle with our own milk, and then our children leave us. Oh, to be alive when my young sons are dead!'

'There is one son who will not leave you for many years yet,' I said, putting Autesion, my small brother, into her arms, and basely fleeing.

I found the crew assembling on the shore. The sail was sewn, the mast cut and planed smooth and the stores loaded. We had some trading silver, dried flesh and wine, and a quantity of meal. We would put in every night for water.

Around my waist I wore a belt made of bronze coins which my father had given me. I clinked a little as I moved. My mother's cloak was around my shoulders, for the wind was getting up, a fine breeze which might carry us out to sea without much rowing.

As we climbed aboard, I was amazed to see Argos the shipwright, in a black bull's-hide cloak, and Akastos, son of Pelias, hurrying through the marketplace. I knew that Akastos, at least, must be there against his father's wishes. He tossed a rolled bundle aboard *Argo* and sprang up to follow it.

'Akastos?' asked Jason, puzzled. 'You are coming on this venture?'

'I am, and I suggest we set off before my father sends men to retrieve me. I know some navigation, cousin. Phrixos is as much my ancestor as yours—and I tire of palaces. Come, are we all here?'

Herakles walked aboard carefully, his weight balanced by Ancaeas the Strong. They sat down on the benches amidships. Then came Telamon, Perithous, Erginos, Idas and Lynkeos—who sat down as far apart from each other as a small ship would allow. Tiphys took his place at the helm, with Atalante behind him, and Authalides and Idmon deferred to Philammon as to who should take the steerboard seat of honour. Nestor and Oileus concluded an argument on the respective merits of roast boar and boiled boar; Alabande returned Meleagros' dagger, with which he had been cleaning his nails; Hylas and Akastos were combing their hair; and Clytios was arranging a sheepskin to sit on. Everyone seemed to be present. Jason raised his hands.

Behind him, the sun was sinking. He was outlined black on a red, gold and purple sky—the colours of kingship.

'The ship is built,' said Jason. 'She is as beautiful as any vessel could be, and Argos, her shipwright, is coming with her on her first voyage. As soon as we can get a favourable wind, we can leave. Now, friends, we are all partners. You must choose a leader who will captain the ship to Colchis to retrieve the Golden Fleece. Choose carefully!'

He sat down. I closed my mouth only when I realised that I was gaping like a fish. Was Jason not to become captain of *Argo*? If not, what would happen to his destiny? And who would be leader? There was no doubt of the feelings of the rest of the crew. Beginning with Telamon, I heard them whisper, 'Herakles—Herakles the hero!' until Oileus stood up and proclaimed, 'We choose Herakles.'

I saw Jason's face at that moment. He was as white as a mortally wounded man who is watching his blood spurt into the sand.

But he said nothing.

Herakles stopped the outburst with a wave of his hand. He did not even rise from the rowing bench, but growled, 'I will not accept this honour.' He laid one hand on his club and added evenly. 'Nor will I allow any other man to accept it. The one who assembled this crew must lead it.'

'Jason, Jason!' yelled Authalides. He was doubtless an excellent herald, but dangerous to the eardrums in the confines of a vessel. 'Jason commands the expedition!'

'Now that Pelias has heard our news, now that all of Centaurs' Mountain has heard, I'd wager, let us out oars,' begged Akastos. 'I shall be caught if we don't leave soon!'

'Prepare the ship,' ordered Jason. 'We must dig a launching furrow for *Argo*, then sacrifice to Apollo of Embarkations. Then, as soon as the dawn brings a wind, we shall leave on our mission for the king—for the bones of our ancestor Phrixos and the Golden Fleece.'

He jumped down into the sand and we all followed. Herakles and Ancaeas began to dig the deep gouge along which the ship would slide into the sea. I marvelled at their casual strength. Taking turns with broad shovels, they heaved aside enough sand to bury me with each stroke, talking the while, not even slightly out of breath.

'This must remind you of Augeas' stables,' said Ancaeas, spitting out sand.

'This is a better shovel,' replied Herakles, lifting the spade. 'He was a strange man, that king.'

'He must have been,' said Ancaeas, digging in turn. 'To have never cleaned out his stables.'

'Yes, almost as though he liked dung. When the water washed through the byres, he cried aloud, like a man who has been robbed. Then later I saw him sitting on a trough, dabbling his feet in the water and giggling.'

I passed down the beach, watching Argos ordering two turns of stout rope to be wrapped about the ship, which he fixed at the sternpost. He hung his adze just under the image of Hera, for some reason. Every craft has its mysteries, and it does not do to enquire too closely into them.

I joined the heroes, who were carrying oars to the ship, and we busied ourselves with loading all the remaining stores, the mast and sail and a few extra water casks. It was almost dark. No one had come from the market or the town to see what we were doing.

The trench was complete. The sea washed in and encircled the little ship, and her keel lifted as she felt the touch of the ocean. We lined up on either side of her, my cheek against the smoky side. She felt like an animal, ribbed and fleshed, not a construction of soulless wood. I felt her rise and gasp as the water moved her, and as she began to slide forward, we heard her sing.

A high, breathy, delicate note. A woman's voice. A goddess' voice.

Then she was in the sea, and we backed her off with lines, or she would have run for Colchis on her own.

We fitted the oars, drew lots for the benches—though there was no doubt that amidships we would have Herakles and Ancaeas—and Tiphys was helmsman, Authalides herald, and Jason captain.

Leaving *Argo* rocking at her anchorage, we waded ashore and built an altar to Apollo out of driftwood and rocks. A slave brought a black and a white steer down from Pelias' stables. I wondered where everyone was. Did no one intend to farewell us? Were we to leave like robbers or pirates, unnoticed, in the dawn?

Hylas brought spring water for sprinkling, and Melas brought grains of barley—they were the youngest of our crew. Herakles and Ancaeas held the beasts on either side of the fire while Jason spoke.

'Hear me, Lord Apollo, who gave me this task: I look to you to guide us safe to Colchis and home. Accept this sacrifice, Archer-God, and give us success, accept these bulls as payment for our voyage out and our voyage home. Lord, bring us fair weather and gentle breezes to carry us across the sea.'

The beasts were sprinkled with water and barley grains. Herakles and Ancaeas struck, axe and club. The sacrifices dropped to their knees without a sound. Then the carcasses were quickly butchered, and the choice parts wrapped in fat and laid on the coals. Idmon eyed the smoke narrowly.

'Good,' he said in his low, clear voice. 'The smoke goes spiralling up to heaven. That is as it should be. You will return, Jason, decreed by Heaven to succeed, though countless trials await you on the voyage.'

There was a cheer. The sacrifices having been made, Oileus and Telamon cut up the rest of the beasts and set haunches to roast in the unsanctified fire. Several slaves brought down bread and wine from Pelias' palace. We settled down in the sand to feast and wait out the night. I ate hungrily of bull's flesh roasted on a skewer. Philammon, sitting near me, was drinking water and eating bread, as usual.

'Your pardon, Master,' I said, realising what a carnal spectacle I must appear, with blood and grease running down my face. 'I'll eat elsewhere.'

'No need,' he said affably. 'I've no objection to you eating flesh, Nauplios. I just don't do it myself.'

I took a gulp of unmixed wine, made a face, and reached for a water ewer to dilute it.

'Heroes drinking neat wine are prone to trouble,' said the bard. I did not catch the hint, but he pointedly stopped speaking and stared across the fire at Idas, who was drunk. He was calling to my lord, who was sitting on the other side of the fire.

I knew what Jason was doing. He was worrying. He always did, after he was committed to some enterprise. The night of the centaurs' boar hunt he had sat staring into the fire in just the same way. He was afraid of failing, my lord Jason. At such times I left him alone. He would gain resolution by morning, and make us a fine captain, I was sure. But Idas didn't know Jason like I did. He mistook this contemplation for fear.

'Jason!' he bellowed, 'What are these deep thoughts, eh? What's the matter? Scared already?' Idas staggered up, red faced. I saw his brother Lynkeos wince and turn his face away. 'Hear me swear an oath, then. By my spear, I swear that no disaster can befall you, not with Idas at your back. Not even a god can defeat you with a man like me at your side!'

'Idas, sit down, you're drunk,' yelled Lynkeos in an agony of embarrassment. Idas spun uncertainly round to abuse him, and came face to face with Idmon.

'It is unsafe to challenge the gods, Idas,' said the seer quietly.

'I don't care about gods!' blurted Idas.

'Your words are deadly, and you will suffer from them,' said Idmon. 'Haven't you heard what happens to the blasphemous?'

I thought that lecturing a drunken man on blasphemy was unwise, but could not see what I could do. Beside me, Philammon was unwrapping his lyre.

'No, what happens?' challenged Idas.

'They are struck down,' said Idmon.

'Beware, then, that you are not with me when my doom arrives,' sneered Idas. 'Or don't you believe in your own prophecies? We're going to live, Idmon, and according to your own words, you're going to die. Take care it isn't at my hands.'

'Enough,' said Philammon. He struck a chord on the lyre, and Idas sank down into the sand. Idmon returned to his place. The note was deep, thrilling, seeming to penetrate mere flesh into the bones. I could just see the bard, sitting up straight, the lyre on his knee, his red hair arrayed around his shoulders, so that in the firelight he was crowned with flame. And he sang of the beginning of the world while we sat, astounded and enthralled, on the sand on Iolkos beach, with *Argo* riding beside us like a tethered swan.

In the unlight undark,
In the void in the aeons,
Before the Gods, Destiny and
Unaging Time met where
There was no world. No Sun
No Moon, no day, no night.

Forms they took: winged horse,
Winged serpent. In the nothing,
In nonbeing they conjured
A shape that fell in love with
A shape. White-browed Destiny
Flung her arms around Unaging Time
And pressed him to her breast.

Not the hasty, fleeting, incomplete
Mating of humans and beasts,
But a melting, a fiery loving
Which melded the forms and shapes
Into one creature. In the music,
Male blended with female
And swelled with child.

Fruitful the body of Destiny
And Unaging Time: fruitful
The darkness before days. Out
Of the primeval waste, out of this mating
Came Light, came the World Egg,
Came Chaos, Order and Night.

As the Four Gods surveyed
This universe, the golden egg
Hatched: the shining shell split
And the Four hailed Phanes,
That which is revealed,
A glowing sphere, sky blue
And cloud white, balanced in space.

And Phanes cast his net
Over all that was made
Or will be made: and the
Earth Mother, spilling from her lap
Lizards and hyacinths,
Rivers, trees and horses, laughed
For joy at her creation:
The green earth her covering,
Woven with lions and bees.

And Themis, Order, to her children
Gave steadfastness, righteousness
Knowledge and peace. Her brother
Chaos gave chance, disorder,
Strange happenings and war. Day
Dawned and Ammon, who is the sun,
Ascended the sky in glory
Like a hawk in the horizon. While
Selene sailed silver in the night.

Lord of the Dance, Erikepaios,
Of flowering woods, Lord of Harvest,
Gather us with thy fruit; include
Us in thy vintage. Three hundred
Years, Lord of Light and Darkness
We will persist in many forms –
We will learn grasshopper lessons
In grasshopper body. As wolf we
Will prey on herds of our brother
Goats. As woman we will bear,
As man engender. In Phanes' net
And all the Gods, we will never die.

This is a song of beginnings,
Made by Philammon, bard of Orpheus,
At the shrine of Apollo Embarkios
On Jason's voyage to far Colchis

> *To reclaim the Golden Fleece*
> *And bring burial in earth and a new life*
> *To Phrixos, child of Minyas.*

After the last notes of the lyre had faded, we slept around the fire as though we had been dreaming of paradise. The images of the song persisted in my sleep, the winged bodies melting together, the Earth Mother laughing for joy.

The next morning, amid the weeping and wailing of women from the shore, we stepped the mast, shipped the oars, and *Argo* sailed out of Iolkos on the quest for the Golden Fleece.

Chapter Nine

Medea

I woke in a rocking cradle, my hounds like islands of heat on either side of me, deliciously comfortable and warm. For a moment, I did not know where I was, and I didn't care. For the first time since I became a woman, I wasn't shivering. Scylla opened her mouth and yawned, a huge yarn ending in a small absurd yelp, which she only did when she felt entirely full and safe. I put an arm around her and buried my face in her smooth black back and drowsed.

The basket hut smelled of femaleness, of dogs and grease and incense and some dark, smoky flavour which I did not recognise. When I opened my eyes again, a cold nose was in my ear and someone was laughing.

I sat up, shoving Kore aside. Anemone sat cross-legged next to me, rubbing her hands down the side of her breeches.

'No need to rouse, little Scyth,' she said. 'Iole is driving the horses, it's a chill day with a cold wind, and our next stop is half a day away. If you're hungry, here's some Colchis bread and Scythian cheese. If you want to piss, there's a hole in the wagon over there. Otherwise, we've nothing to do but tell tales or sleep.'

I shed the dogs, gathered up my robes, and availed myself of the hole in the wagon. I had never spent a day without duties before and I was at a loss. I knew many tales, but they were sacred—not to be told to an outsider, much less this Scythian queen.

The rocking of the wagon was seductive. I could hear the noises of the travelling Scyths, and I was inside the racket, not listening to it in the chill temple of Hekate as they went past. I heard dogs barking, men yelling abuse at recalcitrant beasts, women calling from wagon to wagon and someone singing to a hand drum. Further down, fainter, someone else was playing a most discordant trumpet, accompanied with a series of partially tuned bells. This was setting off a donkey, clearly a creature of delicate musical taste, who was braying in protest.

And together they formed a symphony with the sound of hoofs, cloven ox feet and solid horse feet, and the soft pad of the camels. The wagon chinked, groaned and chimed as it moved and the hanging tapestry swished. Scylla and Kore curled up again, making a warm rest for my back. Anemone smiled at me.

'Take some food.' She offered me bread and cheese. Scythian cheese is chalk white, soft and salty. It is made of mare's milk. I spread some on a lump of bread and bit into the crust. I was hungry.

'Lady, how came the Scythians to have such different customs from we of Colchis?' I asked. She unplaited her long hair, dropping little bells into her lap, and began to comb it out with a bone comb, teasing out each tress gently as she spoke.

'We are called the Sauromatae,' she said. Her voice was clear but not quick, and her accent was occasionally strange to me, so that I had to listen hard to puzzle out her meaning. I had learned Scythian and Achaean, of course, in order to read the scrolls and to speak to all who sought the goddess' help, but the Sauromatae dialect contained words I did not know.

'We are different from the ordinary Scyths because we were strangers here. Once a certain Achaean attacked the country of the Amazons, and took some of us captive. They loaded us on their ship and set sail, but we, of course, could not allow this to continue. Amazons do not live as captives. Once we had recovered a little, we attacked and killed all the sailors, but then we realised that this had been an error. We should have kept a couple of them, because we knew nothing of sailing. The ship was driven before the wind for two days, and we commended our souls to Ares, consoling ourselves with the knowledge that at least we would not die prisoners.'

The black hair bobbed as the comb ran freely through. There were streaks of white in it and I wondered how old she was.

'Then my ancestors saw land, managed to gain some control of the vessel, and ran it ashore in the territory of the Scyths. Ashore and safe, we found a mob of horses. Amazons and horses are sisters. We made friends with these mounts and, still having some of our weapons, which our captors had kept as prizes, we rode off to find food, for we were hungry. How puzzled the Scyths were as their herds were diminished, and how they hunted us over the hills! They found where we were camped, realised that we were women, and wanted us, but not as slaves. The Scyths value courage, and skill, and warlike valour. They wanted children of us—and we had no idea how to get home. Even now I do not know where the land of the Amazons lies.'

She drew her hair into a bunch then let it fall over her brightly clad shoulders. She beckoned me to turn my back and applied the comb to my hair. No one had tended me in that way since I was a child. The priestesses of Hekate are not encouraged to care for their own appearance. Anemone applied some sort of oil to my head—the dark smoky scent intensified—and began to comb. The movement was so soothing that I found myself leaning back into her shoulder. She was all muscle, sinewy and strong.

'So an equal number of young Scythian men camped within easy range of the Amazons, and offered us no insult. They moved when we moved, always at a distance, until we got used to them being there. It was a clever plan, whoever thought of it. Then a young woman came on a young Scyth alone in the bushes, and took her pleasure of him. The next day she returned with another woman, and two Scyths were waiting for them. The Amazons were pleased, the Scyths were pleased, and the two camps moved closer together until they were united. But we could not stay with them unless they agreed that we should not change our ways—we would not live in captivity. The Scythian women stay in their wagons and do not ride or fight. Our Scyths agreed that we should form another tribe and not give up our customs, so we collected as much of the stock as we could find and came here, to the shores and forests of Sauromata. We travel, as all Scyths do, in a great circle, following the seasons. We camp for the winter in Colchis on the Phasis, then set forth as soon as the king has ploughed the furrow. So here we are, little Scyth. Have you no sisters, Medea, to tend your hair? It is beautiful, such length and as black as ebony, but ill cared for.'

'I am Hekate's priestess,' I murmured, half-asleep under the strokes of the comb. Anemone laughed gently.

'The Dark Mother does not order you to be unkempt. That is Trioda, I guess, and her eternal maidenhood. A black and bitter woman, that priestess. I wonder that they gave you to her. Her last acolyte died of neglect. You are a strong maiden, Medea. So. Sit up, and I'll make you three plaits like the Scyth you are.'

She arranged my hair swiftly, pulling my head this way and that. It felt odd. Usually my hair hung in a mass across my back. Now it was tied up, my neck felt bare. I felt the plaits. The hair was smooth, not tangled, and smelt smoky.

'Good. Iole!' yelled Anemone.

A shout answered her from the outside of the wagon.

'Come in,' called Anemone. 'I'll teach our Scythian here how to drive the horses.'

Iole came in through the double curtain, saw me, and grinned. 'Sister Scyth!' she exclaimed, and hugged me. 'It's freezing out there,' she said to Anemone. 'She can't go out in those black rags.'

'Lend her your spare pair of breeches, then, and send her out when she's dressed,' said Anemone, and climbed through both curtains, letting in a scour of icy wind.

I was not used to being hugged, especially by a beautiful young woman in trousers. I was not used to being tended. I was not used to being considered. That probably explains why I sat down and burst into surprising and shameful tears.

Iole hugged me closer, wiped my face with a piece of my robe, and then rummaged in the basket, throwing out various garments until she found what she was looking for. She tugged at my black robe and I took it off. She offered me breeches, which I pulled on—a strange feeling, like wearing another skin. They fitted snugly over the cloth pads which caught my blood and hugged my belly and warmed my back. I replaced my own well-made leather boots, which came up to my shin. Then Iole gave me a linen tunic with sleeves, most odd, and laced over it a red and blue felt jerkin, figured with blocky women on horseback with spears.

'This doesn't fit me any more,' she commented. 'I've grown breasts. There, now put on my cloak.' She threw over my shoulders a fleecy sheepskin garment with the fur side inwards. She tied the ties and arrayed my plaits and kissed me lightly on the cheek.

'Go, little Scyth,' she said, sinking down into the blankets with Scylla and Kore. I stepped through the first curtain, allowed it to drop, and then pushed aside the horsehide cover and emerged into a fine, stinging rain. Anemone was lounging on the bench at the front of the wagon. Two large horses were plodding patiently, twitching their ears occasionally at the flying sleet.

'There is nothing to driving horses, at least, not our horses, who are Amazon trained,' commented Anemone, widening her eyes as she saw me in all my Scythian finery. 'Medea, I would not have known you. Sit down, child, and take the reins.'

I did as I was bid. The reins were thick straps of leather, connected in some way to the yoke over the patient beasts' shoulders. I could feel each tug and pull as the horses walked, and Anemone nodded in approval.

'They are your touchstone for the horses. You will be able to feel what they are doing, and after a while, what they are feeling, through the reins. Now, we are here only in case something happens. If a snake strikes one, if one shies, if the wagon wheel drops into a hole. Otherwise we leave them alone—they know their business best.'

'And what if a wheel does drop off? What do I do?'

'If one horse falls, it will take the other—they are bound by the yoke, so you must release it—I will show you how when we stop for the night. If the wheel is caught, you must halt them by pulling both reins as hard as you can. If you wish to turn them, pull the rein on the side you wish to turn. But these wagons are slow to respond to an order, and cannot manoeuvre easily. In any case, if anything happens, you can call me. I will send your dogs, little Scyth, to keep you company.'

She went back behind the horsehide curtain, and presently both Scylla and Kore nosed through and sat down, either side of me. I wondered how the Scythian woman had managed to order them, when she did not speak the language of Hekate and they were my hounds. I wondered if she had enchanted them, but they looked exactly as usual—Scylla leaning harder than Kore, noses up, drinking in the smells.

I was in charge of the wagon. The horses clopped at an even pace. I could feel their movements pulsing through the leather straps which bound them to servitude. I was warm in my shameless, primitive garb, which the cold wind could not penetrate. For the first time, I felt the icy tentacles of the wind flow around me, foiled by leather and felt and sheep's skin. I believe that I grinned.

A woman on the wagon next to me shouted, 'Welcome, little Scyth!' and I waved and laughed.

Looking back, I could see the trail of wagons and riders stretching back over *stadia*. We were following a flat road, made perhaps by these Scyths before the Amazons came. 'Well, maidens,' I said to my hounds, 'are you pleased with this change in our fortunes? This is better than Colchis and mud and plots and cold,' I said. Kore panted affably, and Scylla leaned painfully up onto my lap, digging her sharp elbows into my thigh, to kiss my ear with her warm wet tongue.

I had nothing to do but sit up high, not riding or walking but sitting at my ease, and watch the landscape fleeting past. I had never travelled in such luxury before. Priestesses of Hekate walk, or at the most, ride, though I had only rarely been allowed to mount Trioda's rickety horse. I would never, of course, be carried in a litter like a fine lady or a queen, but in a litter one is at the mercy of the carriers. That is like, I imagine, being a parcel, sent for and delivered by a panting slave.

Here I was in control of the wagon and the horses—as far as I could be—and if I chose I could direct them anywhere, and those huge patient beasts must do my bidding. It was utterly intoxicating. I did not care about the cold, because my garments and my delight kept me warm. I was not tired. I did not have to drag my heavy feet through mud, but sat dry-shod above the ground and watched the world go past.

I drove all day, until I observed that the lead wagons were turning off the path into a forest. It had lain on my left for the whole journey, thick, tall trees marching away from the lakeshore, of a type foreign to me. I shouted to Iole and she poked a sleepy head out through the curtains.

'Just follow the others,' she said, yawning. 'We'll be out to tend the beasts when we arrive.'

The wagon rocked as my two steeds turned without orders, carefully and slowly, and followed the king's wagon down a slope, picking up their heels as the wagon rumbled down a slope, picking up their heels as the wagon rumbled after, and across a small stream at the bottom. Then we paced through churned-up mud to what was obviously a well-known tree, and halted. I knotted the reins and jumped down. Iole and the Scythian queen joined me.

'Good time,' said Anemone, squinting at the sky and scratching her chest. 'Storm coming, I believe. Now, Iole, instruct our new Scyth as to the wagon, and I'll go and see the king.'

'The yoke lies here, across their shoulders,' said Iole, demonstrating how to lift it so that the horses could walk out from under, once the restraining straps were unbuckled. We lowered the yoke and the horses stood patiently, waiting for our attention. 'Then we rub down the beasts, and take them to water. Would you like to do that?'

'Oh, yes,' I said, as a nose snuffled me almost off my feet.

Iole handed me one brush and took another and we worked hard at the horses' coats, rubbing out the sweaty tidemarks and the dust. When they were shining, Iole bent and cupped her hands and I looked at her.

'Don't you want to ride?' she asked in surprise.

I allowed her to boost me up onto the black horse's back. He immediately began to walk toward a lake visible through the trees. I was high up, somewhat insecure, but pleased. The grey horse followed his stablemate as we came to the lake in the midst of a herd of other Scythian hoses. I was almost jostled off until an old woman grabbed my arm and dragged me upright.

'If you think you are going to fall, grip closer with your knees and sit up straighter,' she scolded. 'Didn't your mother tell you that, Scythling? You'll never get a husband if you ride like a sack!' I turned my head and she gaped. 'Goddess, have mercy, you're the priestess of Hekate! Pardon, Lady,' she said, deferentially. 'I took you for one of our own young women.'

'Never mind,' I said impatiently. 'Tell me again. Sit up straighter and…'

'Grip with your knees,' said the old woman, recovering her poise. 'As you see me doing, Hekate's maiden.'

Her old legs were withered but strong, and her knees pressed close into her horse's sides. I tried it. The movement was odd. My knees gripped all right but a flower of pain burst in my belly. I ignored it. The black horse, as I nudged him, moved obediently to the right and allowed the old woman's mount to reach the water.

'Good,' she approved. 'You have the beginnings of the skill. Now, Priestess, try and pull him up from the water and turn him. He's drunk his fill and is blocking the way for the thirsty ones behind.'

I wriggled a little, clenched some muscles which I had not used before, and the black's head came up. He gave me a mournful look over his shoulder, then backed a little, turned, and took the slope, followed by the grey.

I grinned at the old woman as I took my mounts away, back to the wagon. I had begun to master a new skill.

Five days later, I noticed Scylla licking at her hindquarters. There was an issue of a little blood. She was coming into season. While I was wondering what to do, Anemone woke from a drowse and asked, 'Did you bring some ointment for her?'

'No, Lady, I have not been allowed to compound ointments yet, not the sacred ones which control the bulls.'

Anemone grinned. 'They are not sacred, little Scyth. Unless all knowledge is sacred—which it is, of course. Have you ever thought how the world appears if you are a hound?'

'No,' I said, puzzled. 'How can I know what the world is like? I am a human.'

'Imagination, little Scyth, and reason. What sense do you most depend upon?'

I knew that one, having had to learn to do without it. 'Sight,' I replied.

'It is not the same with your hounds,' she said. 'How do they hunt?'

'By scent,' I replied. I had seen Kore trace a rabbit through all its twists and turns until she ran it down into the marshes and caught it.

'And if the world is a scent-map—if all important information is conveyed by scent—then finding a mate is a matter of the right smell, is that not so?'

'Indeed, I suppose so,' I agreed.

'So to fool the lustful dogs who will even now be massing, all eager to mate with Hekate's maiden hound—we will change her scent.'

She reached into a basket and drew forth a stoppered terracotta flask. In it was a dark oil. It smelled faintly medicinal to my nose, but Kore pricked up her ears immediately. Anemone dropped one drop onto Scylla's belly, and she immediately sneezed.

'What is it?' I asked, fascinated.

'Essence of male dog. It is made from semen and various other ingredients. The male smell will cancel out the female smell, and although the other dogs may be confused by Scylla for a few days, they will not mate with anyone who smells so strange. We live close to our animals, we Scyths. We have to know how important scent is to our sister horses and hounds, donkeys and camels. We apply the scent of various beasts to meet their need and ours. You shall learn more of this, Medea, if you wish. Iole's mare is to give birth soon. The mysteries of horses are much deeper than those of hounds. They need your full mind. So today we travel on, and tonight we shall see.'

I watched the other dog's reactions to Scylla during our journey. She was trotting in the wake of the wagon. Occasionally a dog would get a waft of her delicious perfume, rush up bristling, then retreat, foiled by his own scent. Some retreated so fast that they tumbled head over heels. It was very comic.

And instructive. The power of scent was not to be underestimated.

Iole's mare went into labour two nights later, as we camped by a marsh. The little lights which we call 'Hekate's eyes' were dancing over the chill surface, but it was not as cold as it would have been in Colchis Phasinos. The mare was tethered inside a shelter made of cloth, and only Iole was in attendance on her. Anemone and I stood outside.

'There must only be one person with the beast as she labours,' said Anemone. 'When the foal is born, watch Iole's hands. She has to be quick, or it will be lost.'

The nights deepened. I drew my sheepskin cloak around me and sat down on my heels. Anemone perched on a tree stump, continuing her instruction.

'There—see? There come the hoofs and the nose.' The mare groaned, shivered, and panted. Then she made an effort, and a foal was born in a flash of silver. I watched Iole. She parted the newborns' teeth and hooked something out of its mouth with one finger, which she shoved down the front of her bodice. Then she and the mare began to lick and massage the foal to its feet.

'Did you see it?' asked Anemone.

'She took something out of its mouth,' I said.

'*Hippocampos*,' said Anemone. 'The essence of infant horse. With that as her scent, Iole could approach the most ferocious stallion untouched. One has to be fast because ordinarily the foal just swallows it. Now, Iole will stay with the mare, gentling her and the new foal, and she will add three drops of first milk to the *hippocampos*, and then wrap it in oiled kidskin so that it will retain its scent. And that is the charm,' said the queen of the Scythians. 'Come along, priestess. There are secrets which Hekate does not know, even if she is Protector of the Newborn.'

I had to agree with her. This was a magic quite new to me, though Trioda evidently knew enough of it to tame the bulls. I said as much. Anemone sniffed.

'Yes, she knows, that dark woman. She would have been there when the bulls were born—it would not only be essence of calf, but their own scent, probably. But that ointment will lose its potency after a few years. I wonder what she intends to use after it is gone? They are a different breed, not your usual cattle. No ordinary calf scent will do for them. An interesting problem. Are there cows for the brazen-shod bulls?'

'Yes, three, I believe—they are men's magic and I have never seen them.'

'Men's magic, eh?' Anemone climbed up onto her wagon and I scaled it after her. We lifted the curtains and came into the darkness, scented with human smells and frankincense, the dark smoky oil which dressed the Scythian women's hair.

'I suppose she could prepare an oil which smelt of cow,' mused the Scythian queen, finding an oil lamp and lighting it from a coal in her brazier. As the light burned up, she added, 'But that could have all manner of unexpected results.'

I suddenly saw the king, my father, pursued by a lustful bull, and rolled on the rugs in laughter, clutching my sides.

Summer found us at the lake which the Scythians call Moeris. The season was hot; the grass was withering on the ordinary paths, but around the lake there was abundant pasture. The Scythian horses waded belly deep in buttercups, and we women had little to do but make baskets out of rushes and sleep in the warm darkness, telling stories and drinking kermiss. On such nights, those who had husbands went to submit to them. The others sat around the lake and talked.

'We need a battle,' said Iole. There was an edge to her voice which I could not account for.

'Why do we need a battle?' I asked. I had resumed my black garments, which were cooler than breeches in the heat, and I was lying on the dry lakeside.

'Because until I kill an enemy in battle, I cannot marry.'

'And do you wish to marry?' I asked in surprise. I could not see why free young women should voluntarily place themselves in subjection. I said so.

'Subjection?' asked Iole. 'Does our queen appear to be subject to our king?'

'She goes to him every night,' I said.

'To speak to him, to give and receive information,' said Iole. 'He complains that she wants him to mate with her too often, but he is an old man.'

'She wants him to mate with her?' I asked in complete astonishment.

I heard Iole lean up on one elbow. Her face was an oval in the twilight.

'Yes, of course. She is a lusty woman, our queen. And even if he's not potent, he pleases her. What has amazed you, Scythling Medea?'

'But…'

She came closer to me, wondering if I was ill. 'But?' she prompted.

'The female lies down under the male because she is required to,' I quoted. 'She receives the seed in pain and bears in agony, in order to breed new children for the goddess.'

It was Iole's turn to be astonished. 'So it may be amongst the people of Colchis—everyone knows that Colchis is a strange place—but not here,' she said, drawing me into an embrace.

'Here we mate as we please, and there is great pleasure in mating. Do the animals whimper when the bodies join? Do not the stallions leap the mares to their delight? The act of increase is an act of pleasure—so it was ordained by the goddess. I'll show you—if you will be silent.'

This was entirely new lore to me. Iola laid a finger to my lips, drawing me to my feet. I followed her, barefoot and quiet, to a red tent. I heard someone laughing inside.

Iola bent double and I crawled beside her until we could see inside through a flap cut in the wall. A lamp burned low. On scarlet cushions lay a young man, entirely naked, oiled and shining. I could not see his face, but his torso and loins were bare; and caressing hands ran over his skin, so that I heard the invisible mouth gasp. A woman with long dark hair kissed along the smooth chest up toward the throat. With a flash of muscular flanks, she mounted him like a horse, and the phallus vanished inside her. I heard him groan, heard the woman exclaim as if in triumph, as her round buttocks tensed and she began to ride him as though she was urging a horse into a gallop.

Iole was breathing as though she had been running. I felt something catch at my chest, and something clenched in my belly. This was not submission. Although I could not see her face, she was not in pain. She made cries like a bird, a rising tone, faster, faster, until she screamed and collapsed forward onto her lover's chest. His arms locked around her and we heard them murmur gently to each other, kissing softly. Iole touched my arm and led me away.

When we could walk upright and speak aloud, she asked, 'Did that look like pain?'

'No,' I said. 'But Scythians are different.'

'Thank the goddess,' said Iole.

Chapter Ten

Nauplios

A fair wind filled our sail. We sailed out of the bay of Iolkos into the blue distance. The grey green landscape flew past, dolphins danced before us, the children of Dionysos, and we skimmed out of the bay into the Ocean of Aegas like a bird.

There was no need to row, and we lounged at our ease. Herakles and Ancaeas, amidships, began to play knife, cloth, stone—a finger, palm and fist game known all over the Aegean. Hylas sat behind Herakles, combing the hero's hair and plaiting feathers into it. Idas crouched over his drum, discussing music with Philammon, demonstrating different percussion techniques with deft flicks of fingers and palm. Philammon took up a double pipe and began to play snatches of tunes to illustrate this point or that, and half the crew were listening and applauding. Lynkeos, who was cook, was cutting up loaves of bread, dividing a skin of cheese into portions and piling it into a basket with handfuls of black, winter-stored olives. Tiphys, the helmsman, was leaning on the steering oars, holding the ship on course, with the wind blowing through his hair. Atalante was whetting her long knife on a piece of mountain stone and whistling through her teeth.

'Unlucky,' said Telamon grumpily.

'What's unlucky?' asked Oileus, who was intensely superstitious.

'Whistling. And women. On board ship.'

Herakles did not look up, but I felt his attention. My oarmate, Clytios, was listening, and so was Jason. Nestor, three oars down, said, 'Now, Telamon. Now, my hero. We are shipmates and all, and must be, or we deserve to founder. This is no woman, but a maiden, and Artemis' maiden at that.'

Nestor was a thickset, strong man. His hair was cropped short around his head, and he had a short beard. He had a very pleasant tenor voice, to which it was a pleasure to listen. He also had a fund of the most scandalous gossip I had ever heard.

'Still,' objected Telamon. 'She's a female creature.'

'Your captain accepted me, Telamon,' said Atalante. 'Is it for you to complain of his choice?'

'If he'd taken you as his woman, that would be one thing,' said the big man stolidly. 'But as a comrade—that is another.'

'Let me see, how can I convince you that I'm worthy to sail in the company of such heroes as you?' mused Atalante. I tensed. I had heard that sweet delicate tone before. The last time was when she had been assaulted by some bully in Iolkos port, and she had not only broken his arm but made him recite a poem in Artemis' honour, with his blubbered face pressed to the tavern floor and his testicles in her hand. I had no doubt that she could do it to Telamon who, though very big, was slow. And, of course, stupid. She was right. If Jason had accepted Atalante, it was not for him to object. I hoped that the big man would accept Nestor's correction. How would he row with a broken arm?

'I don't like it. Toss her over the side, that's what I say,' said Telamon, and I tried to remember what healing herbs we had on board.

Quick as a bird, she swooped on the huge man before he could react. She caught him around the neck and bent him forward. Telamon's eyes bulged as a steely forearm moved up into a wrestling hold which cut off his breath. She was holding him easily, despite his struggles. Herakles nodded approvingly. Oileus, the wrestler, said, 'Nice headlock,' and Nestor put in,

'I'm sure that Telamon is now convinced that you are a valuable addition to the crew, Atalante.'

'Are you?' she asked in that sweet tone, which meant that she was still very angry. Telamon grunted something and she tightened the hold further, so that his face went as purple as the dye from murex shells.

'Are you sure I make a valuable comrade?' she asked again, and the huge hands signalled surrender. She loosed him, leaping back onto my rowing bench as he scythed round to grab her.

Telamon let out a roar of wounded pride, which made every Argonaut grin, then he groaned, 'All right. All right! She has Artemis' own strength and quickness, and that's the truth. Tell me, maiden,' he added, flexing his neck and shoulders, 'they tell me you killed the boar—are they the tusks you wear around your neck? I never credited it before, but now I'm prepared to believe it. No one ever played such a trick on Telamon before. You've got a grip like a god. Tell us about the hunt for the Calydonian boar.'

Atalante sat down next to me and said in her usual voice, 'I'll tell you and gladly, comrade, but it's a long tale and I observe that Lynkeos is bringing us food. There will be plenty of time for tales on this quest. And you must have seen some marvels, brother, on your journey from your home.'

And, to my amazement, the giant Telamon almost blushed and said in a modest tone, 'A few small things, perhaps, which might pass the time.'

Philammon and Idas had settled on a tune at last, and we sang along with it, a village dance which celebrated the wedding of Kadmon and Harmony.

Towards the evening, we had passed the rich Pelasgian lands and the rocky flanks of Pelion, where Jason and I had been nursed. *Argo* skirted Sepias, and saw Skiathos island, then, under the clear sky, Peiresiae and the coast of Magnesia. We had come a long way under the breath of Notos, the south wind, but now he deserted us. The wind veered around, our forward way was blocked, and Tiphys called that we should put in for the night on the nearest point of the coast.

We rowed a little, turning the ship to give her steering way, then the current dragged us straight for the shore as it was getting dark.

And there we stayed for two days. The sea ran fast and high, the heroes got bored. Herakles led Hylas, me, Atalante and Clytios in a search along the shore for a certain sort of weed which apparently grew there—we did not find it—and the rest spent their time fishing, lazing or wrestling.

I noticed that Telamon not only refrained from challenging Atalante again, but when she beat Clytios in a foot race and there was some argument about the starting point, boxed Oileus' ears amiably and roared, 'She won fair and square, brothers—let's not complain about it. She is a true daughter of Artemis and I'm not ashamed to admit it.'

He clearly had more intelligence than I had thought. The *Argo* was drawn up on the beach, and we were woken before dawn by Tiphys yelling, 'Get her into the water, the wind's turned!'

We heaved and shoved and *Argo* slid down sweetly into the sea. We rushed to climb aboard, flinging cloaks and skins and ourselves over the thwarts, scrambling to get her under way before the breeze dropped.

'If this doesn't hold we'll be rowing all the way to Athos' shadow,' grumbled Nestor, spitting on his palms and settling into his bench.

But Notos was faithful. We streamed past Meliboea, leaving the storm-racked beaches in our lee. We were half drenched from running into the sea to push *Argo* out, and sat back to dry our faces and attempt some repairs—in the case of Tiphys, at least—to our flowing locks. Jason had lost his worried look. Now that the voyage had begun he was confident.

'I hope we can make Lemnos before the wind fails,' he remarked.

'Lemnos?' asked Nestor in astonishment. 'Haven't you heard of the Lemnian deed?'

'I have, but I still intend to winter there,' said Jason, and grinned. I hadn't heard of this deed. Nor had my oarmate, or Akastos.

'What Lemnian deed?' asked the son of Pelias.

'The women of Lemnos have murdered all their men,' said Nestor impressively. 'The men were afflicted by some god and refused to go near their women, choosing Thracian concubines instead. The women, led by their queen, Hypsipyle, rose one night and murdered all the men on the island—with the exception of Thoas, Hypsipyle's father. She couldn't bear to kill him. She put him in an open boat. He washed up on Andros. Luckily it wasn't Lesbos, or they would have sacrificed him. He brought the news to the Achaeans. That is the Lemnian Deed, the worst that ever the Argives knew. And our captain is taking us there.'

'A whole island full of women with no men?' grinned Ancaeas. 'Sounds idyllic.'

'And do you want to wake up with a cut throat too?' asked Akastos.

'If you have a cut throat, you don't wake up,' Ancaeas pointed out reasonably.

'I think that we can make a deal with them,' said Jason. 'They are only women, after all. They can't really defend themselves against armed men.'

'You mean to rape a whole island? You've got an exaggerated idea of your potency, Jason!' said Oileus.

'And you're sailing under the protection of Hera,' said Herakles quietly. 'I don't think this is a good idea. And I don't think she'll think it's a good idea, either.'

'I think, however, that it is worth trying,' said Jason. 'If it doesn't seem expedient we can winter on another island, or in Thrace.'

We saw Olympus, home of the gods, loom up, white and forbidding, as we approached Euymanae. It was getting dark, but we ran all night before the wind. Notos blows only occasionally, and he seemed to be taking us to Lemnos, to whatever doom awaited us there. I slept badly. It was cold on the water, and there was nowhere to lie but on my rowing bench. It grew harder as the night darkened, developing unexpected splinters. I did not dare fall deeply asleep, because I was afraid of rolling off. So I lay and watched the stars wheel and rise.

It was full moon. The sea was rippling in our speed, piling up before the bow and the concealed ram. I walked to where Argos stood at the steering oars. From the little rear deck I could see the whole crew asleep or talking quietly, laid out like corpses. I was amazed that Ancaeas had somehow fitted himself into the space under the bench. I could see one arm and one leg, and hoped we would not have to disassemble *Argo* on the morrow to get him out again.

'Steady she goes,' said Argos. With his black beard and his lined face, he looked like Poseidon himself. His hands on the steering oars were light and sure.

'We'll make Lemnos tomorrow?' I asked.

'If the wind keeps blowing in this direction.'

'What do you think of this Lemnian Deed?' I asked, curiously.

'Nothing in particular, boy. News from the islands, that's what they call unreliable rumour in Iolkos—you know that saying, Nauplios. Either the women have killed their men or not. Either they want us there or not. If not, we can go somewhere else. With most problems, the thing is to divide them into little bits. Then you can solve the bits one at a time—and never borrow trouble. That's how I build boats, boy,' said Argos. 'And they're good boats, too.'

Obscurely comforted, I went back to my bench.

The wind failed in the midmorning, when Philammon was touching the strings, which meant that it was the hour of Aphrodite. He had a melody for each time span which related to how the planets, the wandering stars, moved. He had already explained the mathematical basis of this timekeeping, but I had not understood it, though I had tried hard enough to give me a headache. So now I just accepted the tinkling tune which accompanied some arcane mystery of which Philammon was master.

We were in sight of the island, so we out oars and began to row. The time was kept by the double pipe and the drum which Hylas played, sitting at Philammon's feet on the rocking deck. *Argo* moved smoothly under the swing and dip of the oars in a dead calm, and we slipped through the heads and into the harbour of Myrine, the principal town of Lemnos.

'I thought you said there were only women here?' shouted Akastos to Jason.

'So I believe,' said Jason.

'They don't look like women to me,' Akastos gestured at shore.

The quay was lined with bronze-clad warriors, in armour and helmets, holding spears and swords.

'Bring her in,' said Jason, and we bent to our oars again, manoeuvring the ship until we were within hail—and bow-shot—of the shore.

'Jason, son of Aison, in *Argo* out of Iolkos, sends greeting to Hypsipyle, queen of Lemnos,' he yelled. 'Will she receive our embassy?'

There was a stir amongst the armoured warriors. They exchanged glances. One gestured that we should back water and keep our place, and a messenger went running up the hill toward a large marble building which was probably the palace. I noticed that the messenger was definitely a young girl, and then began to examine the warriors. Were they broader of hip and perhaps a little shorter in stature than one would expect? Were they, in fact, all women?

They were. Once I knew, it was obvious. But although they were female, they were holding their weapons in a markedly professional manner, and after seeing Atalante in action I was not going to leap to any rash conclusions about the pacific nature of women.

We leaned on our oars as the current tried to pull us closer to the shore. Lynkeos stepped delicately the length of the ship to be, I hazarded, within gagging range of his brother Idas in case he was moved to make an unwise comment. This matter was poised on a knife's edge. Women or not, there were enough fighters on that quay to effectively oppose any landing we might try to make.

We waited for what seemed like a long time. The wind had ceased completely and the sea was as flat as a plate. If we were not allowed to land, it was going to be a long pull to the next landing place—which was probably somewhere in Thrace.

Philammon played the melody which told me that it was noon: Selene's music, a soft, Aeolian tune. Idas flirted on the drum, tapping out of time until Akastos begged him to stop. Being Idas, he continued until Ancaeas the Strong told him to choose between silence and death by drowning. Even then he gave a few more defiant taps before he shoved the drum under the bench.

Jason chewed his fingernails and so did I. The warriors on the quay stood to their arms, spears grounded. The sun was at his zenith and it was hot. We had no shelter in the open boat. Time passed.

Then a messenger came running—the same small girl, very self-important. She rushed up to the captain of the guard, pulling at her war tunic, and whispered something. The helmeted head inclined toward the child. Atalante and Clytios both bent their bows. It was so still that I heard the bowstrings creak.

'Welcome,' said the captain of the guard. It was a woman's voice. 'Queen Hypsipyle will receive the embassy of Jason, son of Aison, and three others from his ship *Argo*, out of Iolkos.'

Jason pointed to me, Authalides the herald, and Herakles. We allowed the guard to pull *Argo* close to the landing stage and clambered ashore.

Flanked by female soldiers, we were marched toward the palace.

Myrine is a pleasant, well-built town. The palace is of stone and so are most of the houses, whitewashed, with frescoes on some of the frontages. Each house has a vine growing over its portico, so that the town appears to be draped in green. I wondered how a madness had come on the inhabitants of so quiet and clean a place, and decided that it must have been from some god. I could see plenty of women and children at the windows and in the streets. They seemed well dressed and perfectly sane.

But the Lemnian women had massacred all the men on the island—in these nice clean streets, in those small tidy houses. I shivered and kept my eyes on Herakles and Jason, walking ahead. Authalides was muttering under his breath, rehearsing what he was going to say to the queen of Lemnos. The woman at my side was deep bosomed and strong, wearing a bronze breastplate and greaves and armoured sandals. She carried a spear as though she was born to it, but her face was not cruel. She turned to me a little, when she felt me looking at her, and gave a small smile. She did not look like a monster.

We came up the great stair, under the portico decorated with carved vines and grapes, and into the audience chamber of the queen of Lemnos. She was sitting on a white marble throne with a high back and carved arms. We paced to her feet and bowed, and our guards withdrew to the door.

The lady of Lemnos was tall and impressive. Her hair was black, her skin the colour of pale honey, and her eyes a most startling shade, almost green. She was robust and richly curved, a true woman in shape. She wore the purple robes of kinship which must have belonged to her father, and held his sceptre across her lap.

'You are Jason, son of Aison? Speak your embassy,' she said.

Authalides stepped forward, dropping to one knee, and began his argument.

'Lady of Lemnos, great Queen Hypsipyle, we beg leave to remain with you. For it is the end of the sailing season. Soon the cold winds will blow and the seas rise, and our gallant ship cannot live in such conditions. If you will not accept and harbour us, great Queen, we will have to fly this day for Thrace.'

'Why should I allow you to stay on this island, herald?' she asked. 'Are you not aware that no man lives any longer in my realm?'

'We are aware of your action, Lady, doubtless inspired by a god. But consider, great Queen. By killing all your men, you have condemned yourselves to extinction. No woman is immune to age, Lady. Soon—ten years, twenty years—you will be past childbearing, and those who are still children will wither untimely, until the Thracians come and settle this island afresh, making slaves of the old women remaining. Warriors you have, Lady, but warriors age, lose their skill and their aim and their sight, and you will have no small girl fighters to don your armour after you.'

'You have a remedy for this?' There was a thread of amusement in the queen's voice, though her face preserved its regal blankness, and I began to hope for a good outcome.

'Lady, we are heroes,' said Authalides without turning a hair at this boast. 'We have here all the best men in Achaea on a perilous quest to regain the bones of Phrixos and the Golden Fleece. Here we have seed not easily to be found elsewhere—the seed of heroes. Here we have Ancaeas the Strong, Clytios the runner, Alabande and Erginos, Idas and Lynkeos, Oileus, Telamon, Nestor, Argos the shipwright, Tiphys the helmsman and other crewmen—we have Philammon the bard to sing for your delight, and Idmon the seer for prophecy. Here is Jason, son of Aison, of the royal house of Iolkos; Admetos, his cousin; and Akastos, his half brother. From us you may breed heroes, Lady, and you shall have the raising of them, so you shall breed husbands to your pleasure.'

Authalides bowed his head, signifying that he had finished his speech. The queen looked aside to a woman in a plain tunic, who put back her veil, revealing an old wrinkled face.

'I say agree, Lady,' said the old woman. 'Put it to the vote, but we need children, or the Thracians will overcome us.'

'That is really your opinion, Polyxo?' asked the queen.

'It is. Better to give gifts than to be robbed. Let us take these Argonauts in for the winter. Let us choose which ones we want, let them lie with whom they will. The bard, and those who do not desire the flesh, may lodge in the temple of Artemis or Hera, and they will be fed. You women,' she called. We turned to behold a large gathering of women who had come in behind us and were standing quietly, listening to the queen and the old woman. 'What do you say? Shall we welcome them, or slay them now?'

'Welcome them,' said the woman in armour who had smiled at me.

'Welcome them,' said two maidens behind her, smiling at me.

'Welcome them,' said the queen, holding out her hand to Jason. He ascended the throne and cast his purple cloak around her shoulders.

What happened then is hard to remember.

I remember some of it very well—ah, very well. I remember being clasped to an armoured breast, sliding my hands to her sides to find the straps, and releasing the guard from her shell. And underneath she was smooth and soft, a strong woman with wide thighs and deep breasts which filled both my hands. I remember being danced through the streets of the town of Lemnos, someone shoving a cup of unmixed wine against my mouth, cutting my lip—though I never felt it—and the guard telling me her name was Iphinoe and that we were going to her house.

Then I lose some time. The next thing I remember was lying in Iphinoe's arms, kissing her breasts—such soft breasts, so wonderful, so smooth—and her hands moving over my body, pleasing me like the centaur maiden, except that before I reached a climax she shifted under me and I was inside her, into a liquid blood-heat sucking which melted my marrow and made me weep with joy.

And I remember waking up next to Iphinoe the next morning, sick but happy, and throwing up in the gutter outside her house next to my shipmate, Clytios, who was also drunk, vomiting, and covered in love bites and bruises.

'You look terrible,' he commented, squinting at me in the morning sun.

'So do you,' I replied. 'Clytios, did she…did they?'

'Absolutely and all night. If this lasts the winter, I'll be a very happy shell of my former self. Now I'm going back to sleep,' he dragged himself into a crouch, 'And so should you. It'll be another long night tonight.'

I never asked Iphinoe whether she had had a husband or a son and had killed him. I didn't know how to frame the question, and she was very good to me, very close and warm and loving, all that winter, which was cold, with many storms. I had often wondered what it would be like to lie with a woman all night, my head on her breast. It felt wonderful. I never went from woman to woman, as some of the others did—particularly the heroes. Iphinoe said that they had no talent for lovemaking, so they were sent on, all women hoping to share their seed but not much liking their company.

I was learning what pleased Iphinoe. She was older than me and had borne a child, so she was familiar with the ways of Aphrodite and the flesh. She loved to be stroked. She would lie down under my hands and almost shudder with delight, and I learned to touch the places which made her gasp, judging my success by the convulsive movement which clasped my phallus and brought me to the peak of delight.

I know I pleased her, but she told me nothing. I never heard what happened to convince the women of Lemnos to commit their dreadful deed. I never shared in their worship of some strange local deity, whose very name it was forbidden to mention. I slept and I ate and I made love in firelight while the storms raged outside, but I reflected sadly that if this was love, I would never be satisfied with it. I was not part of Iphinoe's life, and never could be.

So when Herakles called a meeting I was glad to go. He surveyed the staggering remnants of what had been a fine healthy crew and said coldly, 'It is time to leave. I have spoken to the queen and to Hera the goddess. We are not allowed to recolonise Lemnos. We have a task to do. Look at you! Drunk in the morning and drunk at night. We are leaving in two days. At least, I am leaving, and Jason with me. You can stay if you like—but the Lemnian women have not abandoned their ways, and you won't survive *Argo*'s sailing by very long.'

A sobering comment. Jason, who had lain all winter in the palace, was standing by Herakles. Behind him stood the Lemnian queen. Idmon, beside me, murmured, 'She's pregnant.'

Herakles had spent the winter in the temple of Hera. With him Hylas, unwilling and furious, had also stayed; as Herakles distrusted the women of Lemnos and Hylas was under his protection. Hylas had objected strenuously until Herakles threatened to send him home, after which he had followed the hero about all winter, helping with the carving and wood chopping and presenting a slightly suspicious picture of innocence. Philammon and Idmon had stayed together in the temple of Artemis with Atalante, who had not lacked for company amongst the priestesses of She Who Is A Bear.

The *Argo* was stored, cleaned, refitted and back in the water. As I lay with Iphinoe for the last night, I asked, 'Would you have killed me?' and she shrugged. She really didn't know, and neither did I.

The next day we set sail again on a fair wind for Samothrace and the Mysteries of Kadmon and Omania, which the bard said we needed in order to succeed.

Chapter Eleven

Medea

I heard the rustling as I paused at the edge of the sacred wood. The needles of many seasons made a thick carpet on the floor of the pine wood. The trees were strange to me. They were shaped like the spruce of upland thickets, but their needles were blue. In the strong sunlight they glowed, and the air was heavy with their distinctive, pungent scent. I had thought that nothing with a nose could live under them and had left Kore and Scylla in camp with Iole. Certainly nothing grew under them in that disinfectant smell. But there were some creatures alive in the pine needles. Bigger than insects.

I had with me water to sprinkle and my knife to let my own blood to re-sanctify the grove. The image of Hekate was ahead of me, a black pillar in the shape of a three-headed woman. It was so old that the carving had blurred. The forest litter had almost covered the icon.

I waded into the pine needles and the hissing was all around me. It was not the humming of summer insects. It was in the ground. I was walking through a thousand snakes. I heard the rustle as they moved and stopped as seven of them surrounded me, coiled to strike.

They were the black and red serpents called vipers. One was actually lying across my black hem, its venomous fangs bared, rising almost to thigh height next to my bare leg.

I stood still, as I had been taught. Although I felt that someone was emptying buckets of spring water down my back, I struggled to recollect that one who has twined with Ophis Megale is sister to all of the serpents. Now all I had to do was convince the snakes of that. If I panicked and ran I was dead. Very smoothly and slowly, I stretched out my arms and began to dance the snake dance as I had danced before Ophis in the sacred grove at Colchis. I sang the chant, the simple rising and falling tune: '*Ophis Megale, Ophis Megale, Ophis Megale kale,*' and saw their heads begin to follow my movement, back and forth. I watched them form a pattern of red and black; the snakes' heads, the white fangs, the bare brown skin of my legs, the curve of my fingers, the cloud of my hair following. I was divorcing my mind from fear, from the picture of those fangs striking home into my shuddering, vulnerable flesh, of the painful death of those who died of snakebite. The pine needles rustled under the lithe bodies as the serpents and I danced in the sunlight.

Then they lost interest in me and slid away on business of their own, leaving me exalted and breathless. I came to the image of the Mother and brushed away the litter, dusting spiderwebs off the Three-Headed One and pouring spring water at her feet. Then I cut my own thumb and sprinkled her with my blood, repeating the prayers to Hekate and dedicating the grove to her worship.

I met Iole at the fringe of the wood. She had Scylla and Kore with her and she stared at me in wonder.

'You are not bitten?' she asked anxiously.

'No, I am sister to Ophis, the great serpent of Colchis. The little ones will not strike me,' I replied, with the confidence of one who has managed to avoid death by one finger's width.

'Truly you are a priestess of She Who Meets,' she said with respect. 'Anemone sent me, Hekate's child. The Pardalatae are approaching, and we expect to meet them before evening. The queen bids you stay with the horses while we ride to battle.'

'Why are you fighting them?' I asked, as the hounds fell in on either side of me and we walked across the quiet, flower-strewn meadow toward the Scythian camp.

'They are the leopard men, those of the nomads who do not follow our ways,' she said, as we came in under the trees. 'They seek to steal Sauromatae women as wives. We seek to kill them so that we can take men of our own. But woe to any woman they catch! She will be confined in a wagon for the rest of her life to breed and sew; no riding out or hunting for the women of those Scyths. They venture their lives to steal us; we venture our freedom to kill them. Thus has it always been,' said Iole, and left me to puzzle over foreign customs, while she groomed her own horse and I sat on the wagon with my hounds, watching the Scythian maidens prepare for war.

Horses were being watered and bridles were being cleaned and cinched. The camp was quiet. The maidens of the Sauromatae were all dressed in breeches, boots and jerkins emblazoned with the green lizard which was their totem. They were not talking, arguing and laughing as usual. They were heavy with some religious purpose, like the devotees of some goddess on pilgrimage, awaiting a mystery.

Across the plain came a band of horsemen. A banner floated before them. It was the Pardalatae; their totem was the leopard, a spotted cat on a red field. No wagons accompanied them. I counted twenty fighters—young men seeking Sauromatae mates. Opposed to them were twenty Sauromatae maidens, seeking to kill so that they could marry. The rest of the tribe were spread around the meadow, cracking nuts and watching, and I heard Idanthyrsus bellowing a wager across the wagon to the man next to me, offering a bronze brooch on Iole for first kill.

'I hope that she wants to marry me,' grinned the Scyth, tossing back his long black hair. 'If she kills and chooses me, Majesty, I'll give you two bronze brooches—but I'll never bet against my ferocious Iole.'

Someone else took the wager, I believe. I was shocked. How could these fathers and brothers idle under the trees and watch their daughters and sisters risk their lives in some stupid ritual? And why would the women risk death or capture for the dubious joy of making love to a man, a process which, despite the evidence of the one encounter I had seen, I could not believe was anything but a duty?

They were about to meet in the middle of the green meadow, in the bright sunlight. I saw the leopard banner clash with the lead Sauromatae warrior, dip, and then recover as the young woman was thrown from the saddle. She clawed after her horse and remounted in an instant, to a cheer from the ranks. I looked for Iole. She was locked in a deadly dance, circling a young leopard man. His face was painted into the mask of a cat and his hair was clipped or tucked under his leather helmet. His horse trotted at his command and he and Iole were talking, were even laughing, as they circled, each with a long-bladed knife poised, looking for an opening. How could they talk and laugh and try to kill each other?

Kore whimpered and I let go of the ear which I had clutched and apologised to my hound. When I looked back at the fight, Iole had struck. The painted mask lolled over his horse's neck, and she was backing her steed, screaming, 'Mine!' In her fist was a leather helmet and a hank of black hair.

Her opponent's horse turned without command and cantered back to the eastern side of the meadow, where several older men were waiting. Horrified by Iole's bloody hands, I turned my gaze to the east. To my surprise, I saw Iole's opponent roll to the ground, wiping his face with both hands and apply a red cloth to the raw patch on his scalp. He was not dead. He was not, as far as I could judge, even badly injured.

But clearly he counted as a kill. Iole rode to the king, flourishing the scalp. He laughed aloud and tossed her a branch of the herb we call wormwood, herb of the reptile kind. She rode a little way along the audience, then threw it to the young man who had refused Idanthyrsus' bet. He leapt up behind her, clutching her around the waist, and she rode off the field with her new husband. As she passed the king, her chosen one dropped two bronze brooches into the monarch's waiting hands.

A shriek announced the loss of one Sauromatae maiden. She had miscalculated her blow, missed, and had been grabbed and bound by a leopard man and carried off the field, captive. Iole's friend Dianthys had her scalp, and chose her man. Now that I had digested my initial horror at these barbaric rites, I watched more carefully and realised that I was looking at a dance or a performance, not a war.

No one was trying to kill. Openings for lethal blows were passed over in favour of dramatic broadsides, narrow misses and displays of skilled horsemanship. In fact, the riders were assessing one another, changing partners until they found one whom they either liked or disliked enough to want to mate with or humiliate. The young men were risking injury and a shameful loss of hair and skin, which might possibly prove fatal if infected, but not otherwise. The young women were perfectly capable of fighting off unacceptable suitors, but were afforded the chance of leaving the Sauromatae if they wished and joining the Pardalatae, whose customs were different and might be more to their taste.

There are worse ways of finding a mate, I suppose. At least any woman who was taken by the other tribe had demonstrated her valour. And any Sauromatae male who minded to bully might recall that his bride had gained him through mortal—well, it could have been mortal—combat.

I began to enjoy watching them. The green jerkins clashed with the brown and white pattern of the cat people. The horses, obedient to the rider's least pressure, curvetted and ramped. The blur of weapons and riders was thinning. Eleven of the lizard women had gained scalps and chosen mates. Five of the leopard men had carried off lizard women. Now the last four pairs were circling, shouting abuse at each other, lunging for a hold, in a close dance loud with hoofs and the smell of crushed grass on the green meadow.

It ended suddenly. There was a flourish of banners and a flash of knives. Three women were dragged east as captives, one rode back to our lines with her handful of black hair. The Sauromatae raised a cheer, which was echoed by the riders of the Pardalatae. They withdrew a little into the woods and children raced into the centre of the meadow with armloads of wood to start a bonfire for the wedding feast.

Hunters had come back with deer, the old people had gathered various herbs and milked horses and goats. I contributed a large cauldron full of a brew compounded of various berries which had been fermenting for the whole season. It tasted of distilled autumn, a dark, luscious taste, new to the Scythians as their barley wine and kermiss were new to me. As dusk fell, the Cat People brought their captives back across the meadow, to gather their possessions and bid farewell to their kin. I tended the bruise on one girl's head as she folded her spare clothes.

'I won't need these again, Medea,' she said, putting down a pile of breeches and felt jackets. 'The Pardalatae dress their women in gowns. Take them, if you please. Ouch,' she added, as the ointment bit into the bruise.

'Are you sure that you want to leave us?' Iole asked curiously.

'I'm no fighter,' said the girl ruefully. 'Nor a rider. I'm not strong and I'm easily scared. I'm good at sewing and cooking and tending the sick. I'm no woman for the lizard people. But I'll breed fine sons for the leopard man who captured me.'

'You'd mate with a foreigner?' asked Iole, cleaning blood out of her fingernails with the tip of my knife.

'They're not all that foreign, the Pardalatae. He speaks my language. And I liked his smile, so I yielded,' she said. She pushed the garments into my arms. 'Farewell, Hekate's priestess. Give me a blessing,' she said. I gave the clothes to Iole and laid a hand on her belly. 'Hekate guard you. Hekate guide you. May the Three-Faced Goddess be with you forever,' I intoned. She bowed and was gone, her little bag of possessions swinging from one hand.

'She liked his smile,' said Iole disbelievingly. 'She liked his smile so she yielded, and abandoned all her sisters, her goddess, her customs and her kin.'

'Yes,' I said.

'I will never understand it.' Iole returned my knife, flipping it over to present it hilt first. 'Now, Hekate's maiden, I marry tonight. I must wash and prepare, will you help me? It is a sister's place, but I have no sister. My mother died bearing me.'

'So did mine.' I took Iole's hand. 'I will help you, sister.'

Preparations for marriage, it seemed, did not involve solemn instruction in the duties of a wife, as they did in Colchis, where maidens are told of the burden they are assuming to receive a man and bear his children. Amongst the Sauromatae, the bride (and presumably the man, amongst his brothers) takes a hot bath in a large bronze pot, fitter for cooking than bathing. She is scrubbed by her sister with soap root, paying particular attention to the genitals and the hair. When the bride is thoroughly clean, she is rinsed and dried with linen cloths which are then hung to dry in a tree, as they will cover her wagon, to show that she is married.

Anemone came to Iole's bath and sat down, talking about the customs of other tribes, while I laboured over Iole's filthy hair. Its condition had not been improved by being oiled and stuffed under a battle helmet.

'Consider yourself lucky, Scythling, that you are not attending a bride amongst the Melanchthani, the black-cloaked ones,' she commented, passing me a cup of kermiss to sweeten my labour. Washing a Scyth is hard work. I had shed all but a light tunic, and sweat was trickling down my body.

'Why? What are their customs?'

'They all lie with the bride, so she is prepared with an ointment that deadens all sensation,' said Anemone, and I shuddered. Even Iole looked surprised.

'But she would feel no pleasure,' she objected, her head jerked to one side as the comb hit another knot.

'Better no pleasure than real pain,' said the queen. 'Or, of course, the Androphagi.'

'Androphagi?' I drank a mouthful and passed the cup to Iole, teasing at the meaning. 'Man-eaters?'

'Yes. A tribe to the south. They have marriage feasts too, but the main course is…'

'Oh, Goddess, surely not, not even among barbarians!' I protested, dragging the comb at last through the shining black hair. 'Surely not human flesh!'

Anemone nodded. 'We always fight to kill when we meet them, for they do not take our women for brides, but for such cannibal feasts, and that cannot be borne. We have not clashed with the Androphagi for years, however. I believe they are avoiding us. Which shows some wisdom, even amongst man-eaters. Actually, in view of their omnivorous nature we ought to call them Anthropophagi.'

'Hekate's curse on them, whatever they are called,' I muttered. I wrung out the beautiful black hair over my wrist, and motioned Iole to stand up and be dried. The linen sheets were ready and I wrapped her in them. She was beautiful, deep breasted and round bellied.

'Lucky we met the Pardalatae before your wedding cloths grew moth holes,' commented Anemone. 'They have certainly settled into their creases, Iole.'

'And after tonight they may crease as they like,' said Iole, standing naked before the fire. Her hair fell around her hips, steaming in the head, and she was smiling. It was a smile of anticipated pleasure. I had seen a similar expression on the face of a hungry child being offered not just bread, but honeycomb, and I felt a strange pang of envy, which I hid by pouring out the cauldron into the ditch which surrounded the camp.

Anemone watched as I slicked perfumed oil across Iole's body; my palm, sliding across her breasts, made the nipples harden, and when I applied more to her thighs and genitalia, she gasped and moved with the touch, as though she liked my caress. Then I threw over her head the scarlet gown of the bride, tied at the waist with a golden belt.

I heard drums. An insistent throbbing of a hand drum, as fast as a heartbeat. First one voice and then another rose, men's voices calling, answered by women's voices, mocking, scathing.

'Come, come,' throbbed the drums and the men. 'Come, come to us.'

> *'Why?' demanded the women.*
> *'Why, why come to you?*
> *Is men's love so good?*
> *Are men's arms so strong*
> *That we should abandon the maidens?*
> *Abandon sister and mother?*
> *Why, why come to you?'*

> *'Here, here,'* sang the bass voices.
> *'Here is love, here is joy,*
> *Here is a man's love, come, come.'*

> *'There, there,'* screeched the sisters.
> *'There's a phallus spurting*
> *Over in a moment*
> *There's a snoring head*
> *On our restless pillow*
> *Why should we come to you?'*

> *'Come, come,'* throbbed the drums and the men.
> *'We'll love you all night,*
> *We'll make you pant and scream,*
> *Make the bird noises,*
> *Then sleep sound in our arms.'*

> *'How many heroes,'* sang the women,
> *'Does it take to complete us?*
> *How many men*
> *Have you got to please us?*
> *We don't come easily,*
> *If we come, come to you'*

The drums were joined by shrill pipes, which twittered and embroidered above and below the tune. Iole gathered her red robe about her. A procession was advancing through the camp.

I stepped back, but Anemone put an arm around my neck, drawing me close. 'Join us, Scythling,' she said. 'You came to learn about the Scythians, Hekate's priestess. This will teach you more about us than anything else. See, there, across the field, there are the Pardalatae holding their wedding feast. We will meet at the great fire. Aren't you hungry? I can smell roasting.'

Despite my misgivings, I accompanied the queen of the Scythians in the procession. Young men bore torches and the drums never stopped their throbbing which, after a while, entered my bones. The song had changed; it was still challenge and response, but the roles had reversed.

'Come, come,' sang the female voices.
'Come, come to us.'

'Why should we come?' growled the bass response.
'Is woman's love so good,
Are women's breasts so soft
That we should leave father and brothers
For the love of woman?'

'Come to us,' crooned the women.
'Come and lie in our arms,
And we will caress you
Until you weep with joy.
We will drink in your seed
Until you shiver with delight.'

'Women's love destroys,' said the men,
'Sucking out our life,
Drinking our blood
Until, dried and impotent,
She spits out the husk.
Why, why should we come to you?'

'*Women's love engenders,*' the women replied.
Children of your seed,
Small Scythlings nurtured
In Scythian wombs. Come,
Plant your seed inside us,
We will make you
Swoon with pleasure.'

We had passed the last wagon and were out in the darkened meadow. The moon was gone. It was Hekate's night, the Night of Hunted Things.

I felt I should object to this feast of unbridled licentiousness being held on such a night, but I was amongst strangers, however friendly, and held my peace.

The drums, the voices and the birdlike pipes carried the procession around the fire once, twice, three times. Now the voices sang together, strophe and antistrophe.

'*We will make you,*' sang the women
'*Swoon with pleasure,*' sang the men
'*In the burning*
Of our loving,
In the fire of our furnace,
In the heat of our phallus,
We will prove the love of men,
We will prove the love of women,
Tested in the fire,
Burning brightly.'

I was pulled down to sit next to Anemone, who surveyed the crowd with approval.

'We have mated well, I think. Iole shall have Idanthyrsus' cousin, a good young man of fine stock. Dianthys has taken the stranger—he of another tribe, the Geloni. We need new blood.'

'They're not horses, they're people,' I objected. She raised an eyebrow.

'Certainly they are people. Horses have a talent for choosing the best mate, but humans frequently desire weaklings, led astray by a smile or the rising of the blood. I was saying that most of the maidens have been sensible in their choices. They should have delight of their mates, and thus breed strong children. Badly-mated women bear, as all female creatures must, but their children are sickly and do not live. To engender the best babes, there must be pleasure.'

I had never heard this before. I accepted a chunk of roasted meat and a piece of the flat bread made by the Scyths, and extinguished my bewilderment in food.

And then, after we had eaten, the new brides began to dance.

I had never seen anything like it. Each wore a red garment which opened down the front. Their waists were confined with belts of gold coins which clinked as they moved, and they bore delicate chiming bracelets on each wrist and ankle. Their hair flowed behind them as they began to move to the beat of the drums and the piping of the flutes.

In front of my abashed eyes, the robes began to part and fall away. I was gazing at rounded flesh, bronzed by firelight, which twitched, pumped and flowed, turned in a flutter of red, then spun and slid across my sight. Knee and thigh and hip; mount of Aphrodite pearled with sweat, hands which curved and twisted and caressed the air.

It was so indecent that I could not look away. There was a shout, and the young men joined the dancers. They also wore a red robe caught in at the waist, and now as they also strutted like cocks, swirled and spun, I could see…I could see swollen flesh, hardening before my sight into the authentic phallus, like that which is worshipped every year in Colchis at the festival of Dionysos; where women are banned. Wooden phalluses are carried through the streets there; and I had seen one, once, while peering through a crack in a door. Trioda had caught me and beaten me, saying such sights were not for maidens.

And here were real phalluses of flesh and blood, attached to real men, dancing in the firelight, their robes billowing. The drums pounded faster and the dancers moved like puppets, jerking and twisting, until they came together in the cleared space before the fire, cleaving to each other so hard that I fancied I heard sinews crack.

The Scythians gnawed bones and drank more kermiss as I watched, fascinated. Iole lay sprawled on her back with a young man's face between her legs. I heard her moan with what must have been pleasure, then she pulled her lover into her arms, so that the phallus was extinguished inside her and the young man gasped as though he had been struck with an arrow, before his mouth met hers and he was silenced.

They were all mating, all the new married ones. Firelight gilded the bodies as they met, plunged and clung. Anemone drank more wine, offered me some bread, and commented in an approving tone, 'Such passion! Surely we shall have fine children by winter.'

I could not bear the pressure which was building up inside me. I did not know if I was about to rage or weep, but I had to get away.

I ran from the drums and the firelight and the flesh. I ran until I fell in a heap under a tree, and cried into Kore's patient back while Scylla licked my tears.

Chapter Twelve

Nauplios

Three days without food and I was no longer hungry.

They kept the initiates in the caves, under a hill in the island of Samothrace. I never knew its name. We were hungry at first, and some of the heroes complained, missing flesh and even bread. But the priests gave us a honeyed drink in which were mingled some strange and bitter herbs, and after the first day of inaction we did not wish to move. We became able to sit for a whole day, from sunrise to sunset, the passing of time marked only by the tinkling melodies of Philammon's lyre as we stared into the little ray of light which crossed the floor, from east to west.

The mysteries of Samothrace are the mysteries of Kadmos and Omonia—Harmony—and we were told the tale on the third day. The priests were preparing the ritual meal, which we would take in brotherhood before the Showing, the Revelation which is at the heart of all mysteries.

The head priest, an old, old man whose white hair flowed down his shoulders to mingle with his white beard, proclaimed in a voice which was still strong and compelling, 'There is no hero so beloved of gods and men as Kadmos. Zeus was his great-grandfather, Poseidon his grandfather, Ares and Aphrodite the parents of his wife. His daughter was Semele, the mother of Dionysos, and Ino, who became Leukothea, was his offspring also. We, the Kabeiroi, worship Kadmos and Omonia and also Hermes, for it was that marriage that begot the divine child.'

I was given a plate on which were phallic cakes. I took one. The cup which someone passed me was filled with cold water, which tasted of earth. The cake tasted musty, strangely fungal and oddly sweet. I was hollow. I ate all of it, licking up the crumbs from the palm of my hand.

'Kadmos searched the world for his lost sister, Europa, who rode the white bull into the sea. Here he came, after long wandering, and here the gods told him that he could not reclaim Europa. She had lain with Zeus, and was his wife. But they told him that a greater destiny was prepared for him. They told him to find and slay the dragon. They told him his strength was sufficient to kill the monster, and they gave him a sword.'

There seemed to be more light in the cave, seeping, perhaps, out of the walls. We heard a dragging noise, as of a scaly body being pulled along the sandly floor. Some cried out, and I drew closer to Jason, who was sitting next to me. A huge shadow was thrown on the wall. I saw a serpent shape bigger than a boat. Its monstrous head reared higher than a mast. The mouth opened and showed the shadows of teeth as long as daggers. I quailed. I felt Jason beside me, shuddering.

'He came to the den of the monster and cried a challenge,' said the old priest.

Now there was another shadow on the wall. A tall man in armour, his head protected by an old-fashioned boar's tusk helmet, armed with a long sword. The dragon turned its head, saw him and attacked.

The fight of Kadmos and the dragon lasted—I know not how long. The dragon feinted, struck, missed, and then tried to loop its length around the hero to crush him. We heard the snap of its teeth as they closed on air. We heard the sword whistle through the air as the hero danced and sparred, all in shadow on the white wall, while the light grew bright enough to hurt our eyes. Finally the dragon dived, stretching out to its greatest extent, and in that moment Kadmos leapt and struck and the sword cleaved its neck. The head dropped like stone, with a crash which shook the cave. We smelt the tang of blood in the air, and smoke from the priest's little fires. I heard every man exhale in relief that the monster was dead.

'Kadmos obeyed the gods and removed the dragon's teeth,' said the priest. We saw the hero sit down cross-legged and drag each tooth out of the monster's jaw, gathering them in his helmet. Then he stood and walked away, past the fallen body, and began to sow the teeth in a parody of a husbandman, broadcast from his helmet.

Time passed. I drank again from a cup of spring water, for my mouth was dry. Nothing appeared to be happening. Kadmos was sitting down, wearily leaning his head in his hands, looking at the ground. I wondered if we would sit here until spring, when some harvest might grow from the dragon's teeth, when I saw the shadow of a clod of earth move. It toppled and rolled. Kadmos had not seen it. A dark shape appeared from the ground, the bowl and crest of a helmet. Kadmos still hadn't moved. He was clearly exhausted from his battle with the dragon. More helmets were breaking the surface. I heard Oileus bellow, 'Kadmos! The earth-born men are rising!' and at last the hero appeared to have heard, and sprang to his feet.

Helmets and spear points broke through the ground. The earth-born men were armed and aggressive, shoving each other aside as they stepped free of the ground. The air was full of their snarling, incomprehensible conversations. Heads turned, seeking an enemy. There were far too many for one exhausted hero to fight. I despaired. Next to me, I saw tears course down Jason's face.

Then Kadmos lifted a rock, and flung it into their midst.

It was like a tavern fight. One, feeling the blow, struck the one next to him. That warrior flung out an arm and struck another, who retaliated by stabbing the man next to him. In falling, that one sliced the feet out from under the fourth. In a moment, all of the earth-born men were fighting, spears moving like reaping hooks. No blood flowed, for they were not living. Unliving, they died, falling one on top of the other, until there was no movement in the heap of dead.

And beside them Kadmos leaned on his spear, weak with relief. Then we all cried out and hid our eyes, for the light brightened to a dazzling ray. In the light came a golden woman and, when we could see again, the earth-born corpses were gone. Kadmos was transfigured, clothed in golden light, and a god was arraying him for his marriage. He was stripped naked, washed in a shower of light and combed and crowned with gold.

We were transfixed. I could hardly breathe. The golden woman, naked and lovely beyond belief, came to Kadmos as the god urged him forward. They met face to face in the middle of the cave. We sat in the scent of honey and flowers, abolishing the battle smell of smoke and blood. And there, as we watched, Kadmos' hand touched the maiden Omonia's hand. She stretched out her arms to him.

Without kiss or caress, moving as those who are fated, the bodies met and embraced. The phallus slid into the sheath, and Kadmos and Omonia were joined in a flash of light so bright that we covered our eyes. When we looked again, they were gone. Only golden after images danced in my sight, of golden body on golden body, of the divine marriage.

Such were the mysteries of Samothrace. We were conducted into an antechamber and allowed to sleep. I woke the next day with a headache and my stomach rebelled against me for two days—the first time in my life that I have ever been seasick.

But every member of the crew now wore around his neck the purple amulet of Samothrace, which guards against drowning. And in the light of my recent discoveries about the flesh, I wondered again about the nature of human love. I knew, now, all that I could know about women and their bodies and their sex. But I knew nothing of their mysteries. And it seemed that I was destined never to know more, because I could not imagine who would teach me.

But with any luck I was proof against drowning—something my father had prophesied also. His view, of course, was that I would die a 'dry death'—somewhere on this dangerous voyage.

We rowed out over the gulf of Melas, with the land of Thrace on the left and Imbros on the right. Just as the sun was setting and Philammon was playing his tune in honour of Apollo (or Ammon), we caught a wind at the headland of the Chersonese. We set the sail, leaving Argos to steer. The old man knew these waters well, and called out to us as we passed the landmarks, visible in starlight because of the pale cliffs.

'This is the Hellespont,' he said. 'If this god-provided wind lasts, friends, we will pass it without rowing, a special mark of favour, for I know of no ship which has managed that feat.'

Argo flew like a bird, dived like a dolphin, all that night. She would rise as the wave crested, then bury her nose in the sea, rising with a spout like a whale, then sliding down again. It was intoxicating after the long rowing we had endured coming out of the lee of Samothrace. I lay back on my bench, my head on Clytios' thigh. He was sitting with his back braced against the bulwark, talking to Atalante, who was plaiting flowers into Hylas' hair. Alabande was greasing his hands yet again, cursing the blisters which deformed all our palms. Herakles was asleep, breathing like a grampus. Oileus and Telamon, having settled some sort of argument about who was to sleep where, were lying head to foot on a board which had been laid over both their benches. Nestor was talking in a low voice with Authalides and Philammon—something about omens, to which Idmon was contributing a story about ravens which I could not quite follow. Idas was telling Lynkeos that he was too modest and Lynkeos was responding that any modesty, however self-effacing, was better than the arrant and shameful boasting of his brother, and that, modesty aside, he had lain with more than seventy Lemnian women, and happened to know that this was a total far higher than that of his proud brother. Idas responded that numbers were not important and that he had possessed the most beautiful of the Lemnian maidens. They had conducted this argument at least twelve times in my hearing, and it always ended with Lynkeos calling Idas a puffed-up braggart and Idas calling Lynkeos a chicken-hearted coward, so I stopped listening.

Jason was talking to Melas about being a hero. 'If your destiny is to be a hero, there is no use fighting it. The gods direct all the actions of men. You must allow them to move you, like a piece on a board.'

I hoped that the gods would take care of the minor and unimportant game piece called Nauplios and went to sleep.

I woke as Argos announced, 'We have passed Dardania, Abydos, Percote and Abarnis. We are through the Hellespont without touching an oar, and if you heroes will apply yourselves a little before we miss the harbour, we shall greet the dawn at Artarkis in the Propontis. To your oars,' he bellowed.

We jumped. There was a flurry of limbs, a heartfelt curse in two voices as Oileus and Telamon unbalanced each other and fell off their bed, some very rude comments from Ancaeas, who was attempting to untangle himself from his usual sleeping place under his bench—I still do not know how such a huge man managed to pack himself into such a small space while retaining the ability to breathe—and we were reacting to the drum.

Forward the oars swept, then backward they were hauled. *Argo* skimmed, turned, and dived for the harbour of Artarkis, the haven in Bear Island. We were, in truth, in the Propontis, the arm of the salt river ocean between the sea of Aegeas and Euxine Sea.

And people came to meet us on the beach as the sun rose. Three fishermen dropped the nets they were mending and approached, hands held out in token of peace.

'Hail, comers from afar,' they chorused, eyeing us narrowly.

'Hail,' replied Jason. 'Who is your king?'

'Kyzicus, and he is still at his wedding feast,' they replied. 'What name shall we report to him, Lord?'

'Jason out of Iolkos, on the quest for the Golden Fleece,' replied my lord. We dragged *Argo* up the pebbly beach as the fishermen withdrew to the town. To pass the time, we left three of the heroes on guard and made a small altar to Apollo of Landing, to thank him for his protection. Atalante was standing by the edge of the sea, looking fixedly up into the thickly wooded slopes of Bear Mountain.

'What is it?' I heard Herakles ask. She blinked, made a sight with her fingers' ends, then shook her head.

'I thought I saw something—several things—up on that ridge.'

Herakles looked along her line of sight.

'I see nothing there now, but your eyes are keener than mine, Artemis' maiden. What did they look like?'

'Bears, I suppose,' she said with decreasing confidence. 'They were as big as bears. But they seemed to have more arms than a bear. Six arms, in fact. No, I've been deceived—the distance must have confused my eyes.'

'I have never known you mistaken by distance,' said Herakles. 'We must keep a careful watch on Bear Mountain, about which I have heard some very strange tales.'

'What tales?' asked the young woman.

'About the savages,' said Herakles. 'Earth-born men, knowing no law, having no language, fierce and sullen. Poseidon, they say, keeps them from troubling the land of the Doliones, where we now stand. I think, perhaps, that they are afraid of the sea. They are supposed to have six arms, maiden, which is why I do not think your keen eyes were deceived. Two in the usual place, four around their waists. We shall see if this is true, if we are unlucky. Keep your weapons about you, Atalante. Here comes a nobleman. What welcome will we have from the Doliones, I wonder?'

It seemed to be all the same to Herakles if we were greeted with flung flowers or flung spears. Fighting did not trouble him, nor did adulation particularly please him. I admired him more than I could say. I was deeply honoured that he tolerated our company, even that of the boastful Idas and the brutish heroes— grey Erginos with his tales of slaughter and rape amongst the Amazons (whom I was convinced he had never seen), Oileus with his greasy beard, Telamon with his continual hearkening to the time when he felled a Cyclops with one blow, even Jason and his stories of the centaur way of mating. I was getting tired of heroes, but there was no way home for me but the long way, for I was bound by my oath and I would not be forsworn, and I had promised not to leave Jason until he was king of Iolkos.

Kyzicus had come down himself to greet us. He was the same age as Jason, and the same stature—fifteen years old, the down growing on his cheeks, a golden young man redolent of virtue and good fellowship. He took us all into his city, a small one but prosperous, and sat us down to dine with him. He had been married only the day before, and the Doliones' wedding feasts last for three days, until the husband professes himself pleased with his bride, can confirm that she has no private faults, and the dowry is delivered to her father.

To judge from the king's glowing delight, I would have said that the dowry was as good as paid.

As was proper for my lowly status, I sat at the end of the long table and talked to some old men who seemed, from their wrinkled eyes and worn hands, to be fishermen like me.

'We are sailing to Colchis,' I said, dropping automatically into the fishermen's dialect. 'Can you tell me anything about the route, Lords? For you are men long used to the ocean, or I miss my guess.'

'Long used to ocean, aye,' said one. 'You are a mariner's son also, young man.'

'I am called Nauplios. My father is Dictys, the net wielder of Iolkos, Lords, who laid me in the Nereid's arms when I was two hours old,' I confirmed. Three old heads nodded, bald polls together.

'Ah, so did I to my son, and my father to me, and my son's son after me,' agreed the first old man. 'That's the right way for the sons of Oceanos. Such being the case, Dictys' son, Nauplios of Iolkos, we can tell you a little as a sharer of our mystery. Your leader, I guess, is not.'

I unravelled the sentence and nodded. Jason belonged to the centaurs much more than he belonged to the Ocean, and his patron was Hera, not Poseidon Earth-Shaker.

'Beyond this island you will seek the coast of Mysia which, unless the wind is divinely inspired, you will have to reach by rowing. You must pass the mouth of the River Rhyndacus, which you will know because beside it is the barrow raised over Aegeas. Then you will find the harbour of Kius, under Mount Arganthon. Beyond that, Nauplios, other men must guide you. But there are fishermen there, my heart. You will always find a guide, as long as you can proclaim your name and kinship with Oceanos, our master.'

I thanked them for their counsel and they wandered off into telling stories, the endless talk of fishermen, punctuated with, 'That was the night that a tree fell on Didymum, felled by the lightning, and we saw the mountain burning as we came in from the sea,' or 'That was the day that Promeos caught that massive eel, that serpent—you remember, Telekles, he tied it to his boat and it took him and his two brothers to counterbalance the weight.' It is a soothing and fascinating speech, endless as the tide, and I could listen to it all day. It had run in my mother's blood and in my father's, and I had listened to it as I lay in the salty tides of my mother's womb. We ate largely of roasted flesh and fruits, and I drank two cups of grapey wine. Jason, at the high table, was flushed, as were most of the heroes. Herakles put down his cup. He never drank much. He hauled Ancaeas to his feet and said roughly, 'It is time for us to set forth.'

Ancaeas grabbed Oileus, who brought Telamon with him, and we swayed down to the shore again, laughing and singing snatches of exceptionally indecent songs. I was afraid that the heroes would overset the boat, but they were strong men, and we backed and rowed out of the harbour of the Doliones.

We had been resupplied with fresh water by Atalante, Hylas and Melas. Hylas was even more biddable than he had been before, and I felt that this boded no good. I saw Philammon looking hard at the graceful head, bent under the burden of a basket of bread donated from the feast, and exchanged a glance with him. Hylas was clearly planning something, though I could not imagine what it was. Herakles appeared to notice nothing amiss, and it was not our business to inform a hero that his protégé was up to no good—even though we were both sure that he was. Melas knew. The son of Argos was glowing with a secret. I wondered if his father would notice and force it from him, though boys have very high notions of honour and he might not have told, even under a beating.

However, it was time to pay attention to my oar and stop worrying about wayward children. Oileus, Erginos and Telamon were bellowing out a scandalous chorus as we left the haven and took to the sea again.

Then the storm struck.

It picked up *Argo* as though she were a splinter and whirled her around, until we lost all sense of direction. There was no wind which would help us, and every time we tried to row in any direction it was like forcing a cow up a mud bank. For every shoulder-cracking heave we made in one direction, the current dragged us back to where we had been. For one step forwards we made two steps backwards, but even backwards we did not continue for long. Another current under the sea would catch *Argo* and pull her. It was like being a rat shaken to death by a dog. We were sick instantly, vomiting mostly over the side all of the wine the hospitable Doliones had given us.

'Land!' yelled Argos, and we braced for a shock. The ship was picked up and flung onto a shelly slope, from which the sea retreated fastidiously, like a dog who has mouthed an unclean thing, spits it out and wipes its mouth on grass. We sat for a moment, breathless and sick and desperately glad to be on dry land which stayed where it was put. My head spun. We all looked at each other, wondering what to do next, so sudden had the blow been. Fortunately, we had a captain.

Jason took charge. 'We must find out where we are,' he said. 'Half of us will climb to the top of this mountain—we should be able to do that in daylight—and the rest stay here and mind the boat. Clytios, Atalante, Nauplios, with me. Idmon, can you divine any omens? Hylas, Melas, distribute some water. If we are in trouble we will light a fire. You light one down here and make some broth to settle your stomachs. Come along,' said my lord, and we climbed after him.

The slope of this mountain was thickly wooded but not too steep. We were heading for a ridge which we had seen from the beach, which seemed to give some command over the ocean, but we lost it instantly we began to climb. I had the path firmly in mind, however, and Atalante was not going to be at a loss in mountains, being born in Calydon of the forests. Clytios was familiar with woods and Jason and I had hunted Centaurs' Mountain. This was easier walking, and we came without undue difficulty up onto the cleared ridge.

'That way,' said Clytios. 'That must be the coast of Mysia—I suppose. I do not know this area. But clearly we are meant to continue east.'

'We are on one side of a large island,' said Atalante. 'I think tha…'

We never heard what she thought, for at that moment we were attacked.

It was gathering into dusk. Out of the trees came huge figures with six arms, wielding clubs. They cried no challenge but grunted, and when the first arrow from Atalante's bow struck one, they wailed, a high animal noise with nothing of the human in it. I was grabbed by Clytios, who was retreating, with Atalante as rearguard. We were not going to escape. The huge bodies were behind us on the path, and before us I saw gigantic naked, furred arms and chests breaking the bushes. Most eerie was the lack of voices. All men cry out on attacking, their own names and the reason for their war—all men. But not these monsters. The air was rank with their stench. I ducked under a thrown club and tried to pick it up out of the blackberries, but it was too heavy for me to lift.

Then I heard feet on the path below. A huge man was thrown aside and fell with a dreadful thud, then another, with his skull crushed. Something quite methodical and utterly ruthless was ploughing through the earth-born ones, striking, killing and casting aside. One fell close to me, and I saw that what I had thought were extra arms were the four paws of the bear, dangling from the skin fixed around his waist. I slipped aside as Herakles passed me, mowing the attackers. I looked at his face. He was not in a battle rage. He was quite calm. He was splashed with blood and brains but he himself was unhurt. Atalante, her last arrow still on the string, joined us in our bush and watched in astonishment. He killed all the attackers, seventeen of them, and their bodies rolled down the slope and lay like logs waiting for the shipwright, lined up on the beach. Then he wiped his club clean on the grass, took a handful of berries, and walked down to the ship, eating them.

We came down the mountain in the wake of Herakles and reported that we had to sail east. In view of the fallen bodies, no one seemed to want to stay, and we set sail in hope, which proved vain.

It was dark and we were spun like a top and flung like a toy. We were utterly confused, superlatively uncomfortable and in fear of our lives. Our mood was not improved by Philammon, who began to sing 'Descent Into Hades,' a song usually played at funerals. But even the heroes were too preoccupied with trying to bend *Argo* to our will, to hurl more than a request to play something else at the bard.

Herakles rowed methodically, as he did everything. The oars would not bite on the choppy water and we made no headway, slipping from forward to backward motion in sickening alternation, and in the dark of the moon, so that all sense of direction was utterly lost.

We beached, finally, somewhere. We pulled *Argo* out of the water and lay down on the shingle to sleep as best we could, on land which was cold and hard but immovable. Herakles lay down under the keel, watched over by the goddess Hera, fell instantly asleep and snored like a whale. I wandered a little aside to vomit again, then found a piece of beach that had more sand and less stones, and fell asleep as though I had been gathered to my fathers.

I woke in profound darkness to shrieks of pain, and the clash of weapons. I felt a body near me, but since I did not know if it was friend or foe I did not strike. Someone had no doubt, however, for they hit me so hard that I lost my wits, and wandered out of the world on the strange pathways of the initiate, to be welcomed by Kadman and Omonia enthroned. Just as the beautiful queen leaned down to lift me to my feet, I came back into daylight to a bit of pain, the smell of blood, and voices wailing like gulls.

'Lie still,' said Philammon. His coppery hair fell over his eyes, but he had been crying. I wondered what had happened and where I was.

'Lord, why do you weep?' I asked, raising a wobbly hand to touch his face. 'Are many slain of our company?'

'None of our company is slain,' he said. 'Someone has hit you rather hard on the forehead, Nauplios, but you can see and you seem to have all your wits. Did you kill anyone on this god-cursed beach?'

'Me? No. I woke and someone hit me,' I replied. 'Why, what happened? Did the earth-born men come upon us in the night?'

'The Doliones, who treated us so kindly, came upon us washed up on their shore again,' said Philammon in a dry, despairing tone. He allowed me to sit up against his knee. I saw bodies on the pebbly beach, and heard women keening in unutterable grief and loss. 'Herakles slept as though he was swooning—presumably Hera was protecting him. If he had been in battle rage we would all be dead, which might be for the better, considering what we have done. Our shipmates, Nauplios, uttering no challenge, speaking no word, fell upon the Doliones and slew; their king is dead. The noise you hear of women's voices are the maidens lamenting the suicide of Kleite, the bride, who could not live without Kyzicus, her husband. She hanged herself when the news was brought to her. And how we are to atone for this, I do not know.'

I saw double. My eyes failed me. I could not believe that we had done such a dreadful deed, but I could smell the blood, see the bier brought to carry the dead young man away; Kyzicus, who had been so sleek and virtuous, so full of joy, and with him two of the old men who had told me stories only two nights before, their white heads matted with blood, their wisdom spilled and wasted along with their blood, flowing in a sticky red stream among the pebbles.

I laid my head on the bard's knee and wept, and he wept with me.

Chapter Thirteen

Medea

We were returning to Colchis.

The Scyths turned their wagons when we came to a certain river and began their journey back. It was high summer and we travelled only in the cool of the morning, starting before dawn and stopping under the trees as soon as the day became hot. Then we lazed, talking, for no beast suitable for hunting was out and about in the fierce sunlight, and it was too hot to dance or even fight.

One morning I was walking, on foot and alone, to the shrine of Hekate, the oldest shrine in all the lands. It was in a cave about an hour's journey from the river where the Scyths would stay for three days, to water the stock and clean and re-dye all the winter garments. Only at this high point of the year was the sun hot enough to really dry the felt, of which they made most of their cloth.

At the Washing Place valley, they would dismantle the outer coverings of the wagons, turn out the bedding, and the whole tribe would descend into the river, to pound everything clean. The river, they said, would run discoloured for a day because of the amount of lye used in this operation, which must have been hard on the fish. Then the Scyths would peg and weight all the clean things out in Drying Meadow. This would abolish lice and fleas, which cannot stand strong sun. After that, large pots of dye would be brewed and the dry cloth would be painted and coloured, to be pegged out again until it was absolutely desiccated. The old women still talked about the year when it rained all summer, and how in winter fever had swept through the wagons, the god of the Scyths being affronted by their filth, smiting them with death for their disobedience. I remembered Trioda telling me of this epidemic, though she attributed it to the Scythians worshipping altogether the wrong pantheon, and being savages besides.

The dyeing sounded interesting, but I wanted to think, and Scylla and Kore were delighted to be out of the encampment, smelling new smells and rolling in the grass. I knew where the shrine of Hekate Oldest was. All I had to do was follow a tributary of the river and it would take me there.

The sun was hot. The grass on the slopes above the stream had burned almost white, and even the green of the trees had retreated from its fresh spring colour to the matte surface for summer. I was wearing my robes, as I was to visit the most important priestess of the Black Mother, and I was soon sweating.

I would not have done this in Colchis, but I stopped and removed my long black gown, rolling it up under my arm. I could replace it later, when I was close to the shrine. I threw a stick for Scylla, which was foolish of me, because she would be retrieving it and demanding that I throw it again for the whole journey. But I was feeling happy. I was singing a little Scythian song, one that they use to put children to sleep, as we walked along the bank and I picked up and tossed Scylla's stick.

Sleep, Scythling,
Thy mother is here.
Shalt be a rider,
Shalt be a fighter,
Shalt be a fine woman
When thou art grown.

It struck me that I had never been alone before. Not in all my life. I had been Trioda's charge since I had been a baby, and constantly in Scythian company since. Scylla pounded back along the path, dripping wet. My last throw must have landed in the water. She dropped the branch in front of me and stood panting, ears on alert, almost bouncing off the ground in her eagerness. She was comical and I embraced her. Kore, instantly jealous, lolloped over and washed my ear with her wet tongue, and I sat down abruptly, hugging the hounds and giggling.

I never did such a thing before. I had never been out of someone's supervision before. This struck me as so funny that I laughed until I cried, with both dogs squirming to get closer to my mirth and grinning and licking.

'Scythian, what do you here?' asked a soft, cold voice, and I sat up abruptly, spilling the dogs. They cowered down on either side of me.

The speaker was a small woman, no taller than a child. She was immeasurably old, her hair was thin and white, falling around her face. She was draped in the gown of Hekate's priestess, and leaned on a staff of black wood, carved and painted in the likeness of a serpent.

And there I was, sitting in a thin tunic on the grass and laughing. No wonder she thought I was a Scyth. Such behaviour was entirely unfitting for a priestess of the Dark Mother, but instead of being ashamed I was annoyed.

I stood up. I was taller than the old woman. I put back my hair and donned the robe, shaking it out carefully and smoothing it down. Then, one hand on each black furry hound's head, I stated my name and my allegiance, as was proper, in as cool and formal a voice as I could manage.

'I greet you, Hekate's Maiden. I am Medea, Princess of Colchis, Aetes' daughter, She Who Has Twined With The Great Serpent Of The Grove Which Guards The Golden Fleece. I am acolyte to Trioda and sister to Chalkiope. I travel for a time with the Scythians to tend the shrines.'

'And did Trioda teach you to walk alone through hostile country, wearing only a tunic, to be found lolling on a river bank and laughing?'

'No, Priestess,' I replied. 'But I am guarded, and I have learned that there is no harm in mirth.'

'If the Scyths have taught you that, then it was worth a journey,' she said unexpectedly. 'Why are you here?'

'The Scythians are at Washing Place and will be there for three days. I thought to visit the oldest shrine of Hekate and profit from the guardian's wisdom,' I said, still nettled.

'Then come this way, Medea, Princess of Colchis, and we shall see what profit lies in speech,' said the old woman. 'I am called Tyche. You show some courage, young woman,' she added, as we climbed the bank, the hounds following obediently behind.

I did not know what to say in reply, so I kept silent.

We came to the mouth of a cave and entered, stepping carefully over the warding spells traced on the threshold.

After the heat of the day, the interior of the cave was gratefully cool. I closed my eyes, as I had been taught, and stood still, facing the darkness, waiting for my eyes to get used to the dimness. This takes the time in which one can say the first four prayers to Hekate, so I said them; and when I looked again I could see, though I was careful not to glance back toward the cavern mouth, for a glimpse of the sun would ruin my night-sight and I would have to begin the process again before I could safely go on.

The old woman had padded on ahead of me, and I caught up with her by sound as she tapped her way slowly along the corridors, which were close to being utterly dark.

Scylla's nose bumped me from behind. She did not like the dark as well as Kore did. I grasped her collar as we came around another corner into a cavern which was lit with a strange greenish light.

The walls were glowing.

'Is this some mark of Hekate's special favour?' I asked.

Tyche leaned on her staff, inspecting me for what seemed like a long time. Then she made some sort of decision. She took my hand and scraped my nails along the wall. They left a dark smudge in the light, and my fingers were suddenly oily and shining.

'No, it is called phosphorescence. It's produced by a fungus. Doubtless it was fabricated by the goddess in the beginning but it grows here because it likes dark places with this amount of water in the air. And the temple was established here because it is far underground, hard to find. The Androphagi are not averse to roasted priestess if they can get her, but they are terrified of the dark. Actually I haven't seen them lately.'

'The Scyths kill them when they can,' I said. 'Anemone says that the Androphagi are avoiding the Scythians.'

'That might be so; a blessing on the Scythians, then. They may be savages but they are great fighters.'

'Priestess, I have brought you a small offering,' I said, remembering my bundle. 'Just a few honey cakes, and some kermiss. Trioda said that Hekate did not allow us such intoxicants, but Anemone told me to take it—I hope that you are not offended.'

Tyche unsealed the flask and sniffed.

'Anemone is correct, and Trioda was instilling in your head the correct precepts. We should not need any intoxicants, Medea. But that does not mean that we are not allowed them. Come, we shall sit down in my chamber, after we have made the offering.'

She poured a little of the kermiss into an *anagismos*, a death-altar, before a stone image of the goddess. Unlike a *bomos*, the hearth altar which is used for other gods, the altar of Hekate is shaped like a funnel, so that the blood of the sacrifice can pour down into the earth. Tyche added a piece of the honey cake, and bowed. She chanted the prayer for protection to Hekate in a dialect strange to me, though I could pick out most of the words.

'Now, daughter, through here,' she said, and I came into a cosy little cave. The priestess' bed was piled against one corner, a huge heap of Scythian blankets and fleeces. A broad hearth was laid with a good fire, which was burning brightly.

'The Scyths bring me wood,' said Tyche, sitting down in a carved chair and motioning me to a pile of cushions and rugs at her feet. The light, absolutely forbidden in any of the temples I had seen, washed over her wizened face. She was all wrinkles and hollows. She looked as old as time, but her eyes were alert, black and bright.

'They cut logs and roll them down into a valley which is almost at my back door. The builders of this temple knew that the priestess might be trapped underground, by a rockfall or by hostile tribes. So they made a bolt-hole. It is perfectly concealed, and comes out in the middle of a bramble thicket. So, daughter. Let us share these honey cakes and sip a little kermiss and you can tell me how things are in Colchis. I have not talked to any who came there for ten years, and not been there for…oh, Goddess, it must be forty years. Aetes was a child when I last walked through the mists of the Phasis to grove of the Golden Fleece.'

'Aetes was a child? Lady, Aetes the old is my father, a venerable king with a white beard,' I said, taking a crumb of the honey cake.

'Is he so? Is he so indeed? A long time, child, as I said,' she sighed. 'Tell me, then, of your mistress. Trioda, I believe? A strict teacher, or so I have heard.'

'Very strict, Lady, but she has taught me well.'

'Has she indeed? Tell me, then,' and she fired a series of questions at me, mixing doctrinal ones with recipes and spells and herbs and the geography of the king's domain, an examination of everything I might have been taught, from concoctions for treating staggers in sheep to methods of diagnosing which poison had been used on a corpse. From the best method to dye wool a fast scarlet to the various signs to be looked for that someone is lying. Then she asked, in various dialects and tongues, for information and directions in the cities of Colchis and Poti.

I managed quite well. I found that as long as I concentrated on one question at a time and did not allow her to rattle me, I knew most of the answers. But her last question floored me.

'Why are you a priestess of Hekate?' she snapped, and I didn't know. I gaped at her and she chuckled, patting Kore on the head.

'Aha,' said Tyche. 'And that is the important one, isn't it, maiden?'

'I never wondered about it,' I said stiffly. 'It is my destiny, from the time I was born. My mother died and my father gave me to Trioda, and the Mother had marked me.'

'Others are marked, Medea. Hekate wants women of their own will, not those who have never thought of any other life.'

'But the other life would be a terrible sin,' I whispered. I felt myself blushing.

'The love of men is not, of itself, sinful,' she said calmly.

'The reason why Trioda sent me away,' I whispered. 'The reason why I am with Anemone and the Scythians…'

'Well, daughter, out with it. I doubt you will shock me. It has been many years since I had even the pleasure of a surprise.' She smiled. Tyche had a very charming smile, a snake charmer's smile, which drew confidences out of me like serpents out of a basket in a marketplace.

'My half brother wants to marry me to give himself a right to the throne,' I said as flatly as I could. I was looking at her as I spoke, and she did not even blink.

'Oh, that again. There has always been trouble with the sons of the king if they had multiple wives, and of course Aetes' seed is deadly. What is the new queen like?'

'She is young and pretty and afraid,' I answered. 'And she takes measures not to conceive.'

'Wise, if she wants to save her life, but sometimes life is not that great a boon. So there will be no more players in this drama. There are the sons of Chalkiope, however. Strong boys, I was told.'

'Yes, but my father has banished them. He thought it was they who changed the ointment in the bull ploughing. Trioda and I managed to save the king and the ceremony by a fire flash and a trick, but it wasn't Phrixos' sons.'

'Who was it?' she asked, sipping kermiss, perfectly relaxed.

'Aegialeus. I saw his face.'

'Hmm. And he is the one who wants to marry you to cement his claim to the throne, once his father has been removed?'

I nodded. 'But Trioda says that the mistakes of men are not our concern,' I said.

'Not our concern?' Tyche snorted. 'They affect our fate, daughter, and must be our concern. Hmm. There has always been trouble because of the female succession in Colchis. In fact, Medea, by right of your mother, you and your sister are actually queens of Corinth in Achaea as well. Not that this is at all helpful at the moment. Helios, whom some call the sun (but do not let the priests of Ammon hear you say that), was your mother's grandfather. Corinth descends in the female line and you and Chalkiope carry the right to the kingship—though you would have to confer it on a man, of course. Such is the custom of Achaea. So, you suspect that your half brother will not relinquish his plan, hmm, little daughter?'

'I do suspect that. I do not know what will happen when I go back there, and the Scythian journey has already turned back. I am on the way home, and I fear to arrive.'

Kore and Scylla, sensing my nervousness, snuggled closer to me and I hugged them. Tyche was thinking. Her already sharp features had sharpened further. But what she said was not about Colchis.

'How have you found these Scyths? Have they treated you well?'

'Very well and kindly, Lady. But they have strange customs. They are primitive. And many things they say do not agree with what I was taught.'

'Such as?'

'Lady, they say that there is pleasure in lying with a man.'

'And with what other blasphemies have they defiled your maiden ears?' asked Tyche. She was laughing! I was astounded. The old woman laughed like a girl, an incongruous sound. I shifted away from her, affronted.

After a long time she conquered her merriment and told me, 'Of course there is pleasure in the love of men, Medea, if one

finds the right man and the right time. We priestesses sacrifice
the joy we might have felt and the children we might have borne
to the service of the Dark Woman, the Three-Headed One. It
would be no pleasure to Hekate to be served only by children
and bitter old crones, with veins full of black bile. She is, after
all, Guardian of the Newborn.

'Your Trioda is evidently just such a disappointed woman,
sour as wormwood. We decide to remain maidens as a free gift
to the goddess who loves us. There, Medea, I have shocked you,'
she said, without the least sign of penitence. 'Come. We will
cook the birds which my Scyths brought me yesterday, and you
will feel better after some food.'

We cooked the birds in a clay pot beneath her fire, wrapped
in the sliced smoked flesh of a wild pig, with the roots of a sharp
herb whose taste was new to me. It was a feast. Trioda did not
believe in pampering the appetite. With her I had never had
entirely enough to eat. But the Scyths ate well and I had been
urged to join in every feast, tasting strange roasted beasts and
new bulbs and drinking the milk of their goats, which also made
excellent cheese to lay on their flat bread. I had been introduced
to a strange thickened curd, *yourti*, which they flavoured with
berries or with wine. Since the spring I had gained flesh. My
hair had grown longer and thicker and my breasts now filled
my hands. Tyche did not scold me for my gluttony, but refilled
my plate.

'I like watching the young eat,' she said, putting down
her half-empty bowl for Scylla. Kore would get mine and the
remains of the feast. She knew this, but whined anyway, largely
as a matter of form.

'Why?' I asked, my mouth disgracefully full.

'They enjoy it. And that is a new savour, daughter, is it not? It
has been fifty years since I tasted a new taste. Although that is a
good method for cooking those birds, I have eaten it thousands
of times. But there, my life coming to an end. The goddess will
wrap her cloak around Tyche soon, and I will lie down in her
embrace with pleasure. You will stay tonight, daughter?'

'The Scyths will not look for me until late the day after tomorrow,' I said. I was about to wipe the last of the delicious gravy up with a piece of bread, but I felt Kore's imploring eyes on me. I sopped up the juice, gave her the bread and the bowl, and leaned back full and complacent. Tyche was right. Things did look more explicable after a meal.

'I will think about your half brother. You could, of course, kill him,' she said.

'I have thought of that, Lady. But if I kill him and Eidyia the queen bears no more children, then what will become of Colchis? I am a maiden and Aetes has banished the sons of Phrixos. My sister Chalkiope is getting too old to bear, and in any case the king will not allow her to marry again. There will be no heir, and there will be an end of the house of Aetes.'

Tyche stared into the fire and sighed. 'That is true. I will think about it. Ask the goddess to help, Medea. Now, take your hounds outside for a walk—I will not have them fouling my temple—and then, when you come back, we will talk again. Some demonstration will be needed, I think—something large and public.'

Her head dropped on her breast. She was asleep. I took the cooking pot and the licked-clean plates and retraced my steps through the glowing temple and the corridors. This was, of course, another test. I had to find my way out and back again alone.

It was no test, really. The hounds knew the way out—they always do, they are anyone's best guide in caverns. They sniff the air and find the current which leads to the open. Scylla and Kore bounded along joyfully, and we emerged into the sun.

It was late afternoon and the light was dimming, leaching out of the woods slowly, as though the sun was draining like water. But to my eyes it was dazzlingly bright, and I felt my way down to the stream and washed the dishes, filling the waterskin I had found in the temple.

The hounds barked and chased each other through the trees along the verge of the water. I waited until I was sure that they would not foul the temple floors, though they were well trained, and would have gone on their own through the tunnels rather than commit such blasphemy. I noticed some pale flowers growing by the foot of a tree. Aconite. Very poisonous, but the flowers were beautiful. I picked a handful. They were a suitable present for the priestess of the Queen of Phantoms, and I turned back into the darkness, following my own travel sense down to the glowing temple, and into the small chamber.

We slept in warm darkness, lit by the banked fire. I was very sleepy, and lay in the skins and blankets in such a profound slumber that I was only woken by Kore getting up and shaking herself. I realised that it was dawn and I was alone.

I made my ablutions over the drain in the corner, then dressed in my robe before I went into the temple. I found the old woman on her knees, her forehead against Hekate's icon.

'Yes, Lady,' she murmured. 'I will do as you say.'

I bowed to the image and helped Tyche to her feet.

'The goddess has spoken, which is fortunate, because I could not think of anything dramatic enough myself,' she said.

'What did she say?' I asked.

'The cauldron of renewal,' said Tyche.

'But Lady, does that not take most of a woman's life force, something she can only do once in a lifetime?' I objected.

'Indeed, to really make such a thing is a desperate endeavour and takes at least a year and even then may fail,' she replied. 'but this is not such a difficult matter. Now, we need to go up to the light, taking my big cauldron and that box and that bag, and a coal in the firepot,' she instructed.

Puzzled, I gathered all the things. Heavily laden, I struggled up through the caves and found the old woman leaning on her staff and contemplating a rabbit in a basket. It was not a healthy creature and I hoped that she was not thinking of eating it.

'This is a sick, old rabbit, is it not?' she demanded of me.

'Very sick,' I said. 'It won't last many more days.'

'Put the cauldron there, and light a small fire,' she said. I did as I was told. As I worked, Tyche instructed me.

'The cauldron of renewal is rarely made, because it is so difficult and because it has such a high chance of failure and the waste of at least a year's effort. I have never found it necessary to make it. However, the fact of it having once been made has entered the folktales of every tribe on the Euxine Sea. Even as far away as Achaea and Thrace they have heard of the witches of Colchis and their cauldron. Now, Trioda must have told you about belief. A patient who believes that she will die may well die, in spite of medicine and even if she has no disease. Yes?' The pin-sharp eyes were fixed o me. I shoved a log under the cauldron to steady it and agreed.

'And a patient who believes that she will get well often recover, even if she is grievously wounded or sick. Is that not so?'

'Yes,' I agreed.

'And a young man who is intending to blaspheme against Hekate by taking a maiden priestess unwillingly to wife may be frightened and outfaced,' she concluded.

'I suppose so,' I said.

'Watch,' she commanded.

The fire burned up around the cauldron. Into the flames she sprinkled a powder which gave off a thick white smoke. Then she reached into the basket and brought forth the old rabbit. It hung limply in her hand as her knife came down with a skilled stroke and severed its throat. Then she cut it into joints and dropped them into the bronze pot.

Then she began to chant. I did not know the words. It might have been any ancient language, no longer spoken by humans, or even the grunts and squeals of some savage tribe who know no gods. The smoke rose. It had a sweetish scent. I began to feel a little lightheaded. I watched Tyche as she paced around in a circle, chanting her strange words.

She stood up to her full height and made a broad, summoning gesture. Her arms in their wide black sleeves swept over the cauldron. She screamed like a hawk. Then she stood back, turned to me, and out of the bronze pot leapt…

A baby rabbit.

It was perhaps seven weeks old. It sat still for a moment, perfectly real. It licked its paws nervously, flicking its silky ears. I could see early sunlight on its fur.

Then it caught the scent of the dogs. The baby nose twitched, it leapt into the air, and it was gone. A white scut flashed for a moment in a patch of briars.

'And the only thing you must remember,' said Tyche, a little breathlessly, 'is not to allow anyone to look into the pot.'

I rose unsteadily and hauled the cauldron off the flames. It was burning hot to the touch, and from it arose a smell of unskinned, roasting, very old rabbit.

'It's simple,' explained Tyche. 'Fireweed produces a mildly hallucinogenic smoke. The baby rabbit was in my sleeve, but the robes are wide enough to conceal anything up to a kid or a lamb.'

'Why did it leap from the pot?' I asked stupidly.

'Because it scorched its feet,' she said.

'And the chant?'

'A Libyan taught it to me, but any words will do, as long as no one can understand them. You must not use a real invocation of the Three-Headed One for this sort of thing, you know.'

'That was terribly impressive—what were you saying?'

'It's a very rude song about the neighbouring tribe,' said Tyche.

I was so torn between weeping and laughter that I did both, and the old woman had to sit me down and douse me with spring water before I could stop.

Chapter Fourteen

Nauplios

Three of us were wounded. Erginos had a speared leg, Alabande had a bruised belly which made him vomit repeatedly, and I had double vision and growing pain in my head. We could not row, but it didn't matter, because *Argo* was staying just where she was, pulled up on the pebbled shore in the country of Doliones, at the foot of Mount Didymum.

We were cared for by Idmon, Melas, Philammon and Hylas. My head hurt all the time. I slept with a pain above my eyes and woke to the same pain. It was my punishment, just as the howling winds which made it impossible for us to leave the harbour were an expression of just how offended the gods were with the crew of the *Argo*.

I asked Philammon how many gods we had outraged by killing the Doliones. He brushed his copper hair back from his forehead and began a list. Apparently we had angered Hera, goddess of women (by occasioning the queen's suicide); and Hestia, goddess of the hearth, by outraging hospitality; Talthybius, the divine herald, by ignoring the usages of war, which had also defied Ares; and then Poseidon, by misusing the gifts of the sea and not trusting in him enough. By the time the bard reached Clio, the muse, who would be angry with us for not using words, I begged him to stop.

'Actually, son of Dictys, I can't think of an Olympian we haven't affronted,' he said mildly. 'We deserve whatever happens to us. How is your head?'

'It hurts,' I mumbled. Settling back into a comfortable position, he began to play a sweet, plangent tune and some of the pain seeped out of me.

I fell asleep, and woke to smell smoke. The Doliones were burning their dead. I heard Philammon's voice intoning the instructions to the departed. The Orpheans know where the soul must travel after death, and willingly impart this knowledge to the dying and to those who have already begun their journey. I heard his strong, clear voice chanting through the smoke and the stench of roasting. It made a pattern to my unfocused senses; the voice and the mountains and the darkening sky, the cold wind, the gritting of sand under me, the cup of watered wine which Hylas held to my lips. The sweet flowery scent of his ringleted hair and the salt smell of the sea were all part of the pattern, in which throbbing pain and the wailing of women and gulls were also mingled.

'Open your eyes,' sang the bard to the dead. 'You can see. You will see a dry valley with one dead tree. Rise to your feet and walk through it toward the stone wall. Let no shadow stay you, but walk and climb toward the sun. If any try to stop you, say, "I am the child of Phanes, thou knowst I have free passage of thy realm, Shadow," and the shadows will leave you alone.

'Do not fear shadows,' sang Philammon, amid the keening of the Doliones, weeping for the irreparable loss which we had caused. 'Do not turn back. Over the wall you will find a green meadow, and in it is a spring of clear water. There are guards on it. As you kneel to drink, cup water in your hands and say, "I am a child of Earth and Sky, of Heavenly Race and the universe's child; you know this well. I am parched with thirst, I perish. Therefore give me leave to drink of the spring of recollection."

'They will allow you to drink,' sang the bard to the writhing corpses, as the fire took on their limbs. 'The water will give you remembrance of the path, for you have been this way before;

for you are Phanes' creation and part of all things and worthy
to walk in light. Walk therefore to the right of the spring, and
thence into the light, where lies the land of heroes. Many wait
to greet thee there with joy and music.'

He sang this three times at the pyre of the Doliones. I drifted
out of consciousness and walked in dark ways, in agony and
despair, for many days.

The next time I came back to myself I could see clearly and
there was only one of everything. I was so pleased that I smiled
into Hylas' face, and saw my smile mirrored in his dark, almond-
shaped eyes.

'Nauplios, you are back,' he said, sliding an arm under my
shoulders and lifting my head with gentle skill. I lay back against
his slim bare chest and sipped from the cup he held to my lips.
He was a tender nurse. He could judge when to lift the cup away
and allow me to swallow, his strength was sufficient to hold me
and his dexterity admirable in touching without hurting. 'I'm
glad you are better,' said the boy. He stroked my hair back from
the healing scar on my forehead and asked, 'Does it hurt when
I press here? Or here?'

'Not much. Hylas, where did you learn to tend the injured?'

'My mother had great skill,' he answered. 'There. The bone
was broken—it was a heavy blow. It is knitting, and as long as
you are careful it will not cause any more trouble. I found some
of the herbs my mother uses, but the most powerful do not grow
here. I could not find wound-leaf, which dulls pain. I am sorry
that I could not find it.'

I vaguely remembered that I had drunk bitter concoctions.
I also remembered that it had been Hylas who had been there
when I called for my mother, for death, and it must have been
these slender arms which had embraced me when I cried with
the pain in my head, which had been worse than anything I had
ever suffered before. I was ashamed at having dismissed him so
easily as worthless, valuable only for his beautiful face. I finished
the soup and he laid me down again, tucking my cloak around

me, for the wind was cold. Then he rose effortlessly, with a flash of smooth thighs, and I touched his foot like a supplicant.

'Stay a little and talk to me,' I said haltingly. 'I thank you for your care, Hylas.'

He smiled again, so vulnerable and so young that I was freshly ashamed of my suspicions. He sat down, cross-legged, next to me, saying easily, 'Idmon has had a sign. A sea eagle came down to him and told him that the gods would be appeased if the Argonauts built a shrine to Rhea, goddess before the gods. Most of them have gone up to the top of the mountain. Can you hear the singing?'

Faintly, the noise of spear clashing on shield and deep voices chanting came to me on the wind.

'What brought you on this voyage, Hylas?' I asked.

'I came with the hero, Herakles,' he said. 'I came seeking adventure. I made him bring me, otherwise I would never have left my father's land. But I came in search of a dream.'

'What dream?'

'I saw her in my sleep, and now she comes almost every night. I thought she might be on Lemnos, but she was not there. I shall find her soon. She is the most beautiful maiden in the world.'

'A real maiden or a dream maiden?' I asked. For the first time since my injury, I was not in pain. Nothing hurt. The relief was so profound that I was falling asleep.

'A real maiden and a dream maiden,' said Hylas. I saw his grave and beautiful face, smooth and terribly young and solemn, as Morpheus gathered me into his arms, and it stayed with me until I woke again. Hylas was in love with a dream.

We set sail the next morning. The sea was as smooth as glass, and we sped through the water on whirlwind feet, like the horses of Poseidon, leaving the Doliones behind us with relief. We rowed well until the hour of Selene, when a breeze chopped the sea and rowing became difficult. The Mysian coast was in sight, we were weary, and the oars heaved *Argo* through the water, dropping from crest to trough. We passed Rhyndacus and the barrow of Aegeas, we were almost to Phrygia, when the oar in

Herakles' grasp stuck fast, it seemed in the sea itself, and with a creaking crunch, broke in half.

We stopped immediately. The hero sat on the bench opposite Ancaeas the Strong, glaring at the oar shaft still retained in those great hands.

'Snapped!' breathed Atalante in astonishment. 'Two spans thick pine wood and it's broken in half!'

'We'll need to stop,' said the hero. 'We can't get far without the amidship sweeps. You, Clytios, unstrap your oar and bring it here, and you, Lynkeos, stop rowing. The stern pair can have a rest for the present. There.' He pointed to the thickly forested shore. 'What do you think, Jason? Will that yield me a suitable tree?'

'I believe so,' agreed my lord.

At the time in which fishermen, possessed with longing for food and a dry bed, commonly turn their boats for home, we came to the Mysian shore. We made landfall without difficulty, and some shepherds brought us two sheep and a couple of skins of wine. We made camp. I was restless, possibly because I had spent such a long time asleep. Hylas, bearing a bronze ewer on his shapely shoulder, was going in search of water, and I wandered along after him and Herakles, who was looking for a suitable sapling to fell for the new oar.

It was a pine forest. The needles blanketed my footfalls. I was not trying to avoid being seen, but I did not want to talk, either. Herakles was touching trees as he passed, as though he could test their soundness by the feel of their bark. I watched as he grunted in approval, stopped, and raised his club.

Methodically and with great force he struck each root of the tree, on one side and the other, until it was loose in the ground. The earth rang under the blows of the olive club. Then he wrapped his arms around the tree, legs wide, seized the trunk low down, and lifted.

It was a pine tree, ten years old, straight as a poplar. I had frequently cut such trees down and it had taken a hundred blows of an axe and three men's strength to win the wood. This tree was strongly fixed in the ground. But it came up roots and all, shedding clods of earth, like a mast torn out against the wedges by a sudden squall of wind. Herakles was not even rendered breathless by this monstrous effort. I had never seen anything like it in my life.

He snapped off the branches between thumb and forefinger—branches as thick as my arm—then hefted the trunk over one shoulder and walked past me, heading for the shore where Argos was waiting to adze off the bark and smooth and shape the raw wood into a new oar. The favoured of Hera looked as he always looked, like an old peasant. Hylas had braided his hair and decorated it with feathers, but Herakles never looked like a hero.

Except that I had just watched him tear a ten-year tree up by the roots with the same ease as my mother pulled chickweed out of her herb garden.

A little amazed, I wandered on toward the river, hoping to meet Hylas. I had carved a small image out of the head bone of the big fish which we had speared the day before. I wanted to give it to him as a thank-offering for his care. I had tried to make a sea trout. It wasn't a very good sea trout, but I was pleased with the curve of its back and belly, which were almost lifelike, though the fins weren't quite right. Hylas liked decorations. I thought he might plait it into his beautiful, black hair, along with the shells and pearls.

But I did not find Hylas. The bronze ewer was lying by the side of the stream, empty. I called, but there was no answer.

Oileus and Atalante came in answer to my cry, and cast aside like hounds, looking for tracks.

'He came here,' said the young woman, her cheek on the mossy edge of the stream. 'See, comrade, here is his sandal print, and there…see?' She pinched something between finger and thumb and lifted it to Oileus' eyes. He squinted.

'Gull's feather,' he said.

'Yes. And what is a gull doing here in this pine wood, *stadia* from the sea? Hylas was here.'

'And is here no longer. Where can he be?' asked Jason, hastening out of the trees.

'He must be in the water,' said Atalante, reluctantly coming to a distasteful conclusion. She stepped down into the stream, taking Oileus' hand unselfconsciously to steady her against the current. The water foamed about her knees, making a collar of glass, and Oileus hauled as her feet were suddenly snatched from under her. He lifted Artemis' child out of the stream and set her upright as he would a man.

'If the boy fell into that,' Atalante exclaimed, 'he'll be over the waterfall by now! It's running very strongly, and it's as cold as death—it must be snow water.'

'I fear that it may be death,' said Jason, picking up the pitcher. It was wet inside, showing that Hylas had begun to fill it before whatever had happened to him had occurred. 'How do we tell Herakles?'

'Tell Herakles what?' asked the hero. He moved, as always, like a cat or a shadow, and we had not heard him approach. Jason held out the ewer and stammered our story.

'Did he die in the water?' he asked, quietly.

'It's possible, Lord,' said Atalante.

'He was under my protection,' said Herakles.

'He is gone, Lord,' said Jason.

Herakles changed. In front of my eyes, he seemed to alter form. His face darkened. He wiped at his brow as sweat poured down his face. I recalled the warnings about him and backed, grabbing for Jason, who collected Oileus who brought Atalante, and we all moved away from the hero, because we knew the battle fury was coming upon him, and he might slay us all without intention or mercy.

The fact that he would then have to spend another lifetime performing heroic deeds in expiation for our murder did not, at that moment, comfort me.

He opened his mouth and roared, 'Hylas!' with a volume no man has ever produced, before or since. I covered my ears. He called again and branches broke at the sound. Herakles tore, wild-eyed and witless, through the pine forest, smashing trees in his path, thundering always in that terrible voice for lost Hylas, and we turned and ran.

We fled down the valley path to the sea, shaking and terrified, to hear Tiphys calling 'Quick! A wind! Come now!' We were very afraid of the great voice bellowing like Poseidon's bulls behind us and that is the only way I can explain our actions. We ran to the ship, wading out into the water, and climbed aboard, and the wind carried us faster than a running horse can move out into the ocean.

Then of course, we realised what we had done.

'You've left Herakles behind?' yelled Telamon. 'How could you? We must turn back at once?'

'We can't. The wind is set and the current is strong,' said Clytios. 'It would take three day's rowing to get back to Mysia.'

'How could you leave the greatest hero in the world behind, yes, and Hylas too! He deserves better of you than this, Jason!' cried Alabande, the first time I had heard him speak out on anything.

Jason said nothing. He would not reply to such taunts. He sat in the bow and wrapped his cloak around him, crushed by this mischance. I could not explain why we had run away, but we had. The sea was running; Clytios was right. We could not turn back, not without losing days in possibly fruitless labour. Herakles was lost, and Hylas. I still had the bone fish which I had thought to give him, the beautiful, gentle boy.

While the others were all screaming at each other, I strung the little carving with a leather thong and hung it around my own neck, and breathed a prayer for Hylas and Herakles, thanking the gods for having allowed Dictys the fisherman's son to have been in their company, and commending them—as far as my own small worth could—to the divine attention of those who are most high.

'Hera,' I whispered, as Telamon yelled at Oileus and Oileus yelled back at Telamon. 'Your hero is mad again. Protect him, Lady Queen, and protect the boy if you will, for all things are in your gift and Herakles *Kallinikos*—Herakles Beautiful in

Victory—is your most faithful warrior, and surely you have tried his courage and his love as much as you need, Lady of the Heavens.'

I did not receive a reply. I ducked as Telamon dived over me to fasten his hands around Tiphys' comely neck.

'You may well loll there at your ease,' he exclaimed furiously, squeezing hard. 'You planned this so you could be the most famous in Achaea instead of Herakles. But I'm going back for him, and you are going to turn this ship around and we'll start rowing, and anyone who wants to go on to Colchis without Herakles can swim!'

Tiphys was quite purple, his feet kicking in the air a span off the deck, when Philammon struck all the strings of his lyre at once and cried, 'In the name of all the gods, Telamon. Stop!'

Telamon put Tiphys back on his sandals and loosened his grip a little.

'I have received a vision,' said Idmon, standing beside the bard. 'The last I shall ever receive, and I die soon, so listen to me. Release Tiphys, Telamon. The gods have spoken.'

Idmon was a dark shadow across the sun, a thin man pregnant with his doom, already mourning his lost life. Telamon pushed Tiphys so that he staggered back against a steering oar and the *Argo* staggered too, before she recovered and the wind filled her sail again. Idmon held out his hand, and three strange birds—I had never seen the species before—settled on his arm. They were snow white with blood red beaks, small and eerie in that they were quite silent. As I watched them I fancied that I could see sunlight through them. They may not have been really there at all.

Idmon, staring at the birds as though he were relaying a message, spoke. 'Thus say the gods: Why do you try to take Herakles to Colchis? He belongs in Argos, to which he must return to suffer his fate.' The first bird flew up and away, as though it had delivered its message.

Idmon continued, 'Do not mourn for Herakles, who will join the immortals after his worldly voyage is closed in flames.'

The second bird also left its perch. Idmon bent his head as if listening, then said quietly, 'Hylas has gone to the Naiads, who fell in love with his beauty. You must sail on,' he concluded, as the last bird left him.

I tried to watch its flight, but it vanished in sun dazzle.

Jason drew a deep breath of relief. Oileus laughed suddenly, a short laugh like a bark. Telamon slapped Tiphys on the back. He was still stroking his throat, and could not speak, but he nodded. We resumed our seat and Melas distributed wine and bread and the remains of the roasted sheep which the Mysians had given us. There were tears running down the boy's face. He feared that the Naiads had indeed taken Hylas, pulling him down to a watery grave, and so did I.

'I apologise, Jason,' said Alabande. 'May the winds blow away my offence against you.'

'You did indeed insult me grievously,' agreed Jason, who was desperately relieved and trying not to show it, 'by accusing me of wronging a loyal friend and hero. But I do not hold grudges, not against a shipmate. This was not a quarrel about property, but about a comrade, and I would like to think that if it had been me left behind, you would have stood up for me as boldly. It is forgotten,' said Jason, and Alabande embraced him.

The wind blew us onward all night, until it failed off another coast, greyish green and unpromising. We landed and lit a fire to roast some of the fish we had netted on the way and I set a pot of sea water to boil dry. We needed salt.

Argos said we were in the territory of a bandit called Amycus—I was evidently not the only one who talked to old fishermen—who had killed his neighbours and was likely to attack us. This robber demanded that every ship which watered on his territory should provide a champion to fight with him, barehanded. If they lost, he took the ship.

'I am the best boxer on this voyage,' said Idas immediately, through a mouthful of fish. 'I demand this honour.'

There was no discussion. Idas was known to be an excellent fighter. He was light, strong and fast, and despite his boasting, his brother Lynkeos had told us that when Idas fought he was cold, dangerous and calculating.

'And if you do not prove my words true, brother,' he warned Idas as he oiled his body carefully and thoroughly, 'I will personally break your neck as a dishonourable rogue. Here he comes,' he observed. 'Now, Idas, no words. Deeds.'

And to my surprise, I saw the twins kiss, rough cheek to rough cheek, and I saw that they loved each other, though I had never heard them exchange anything but insults and they could not even bear to be on the same rowing bench.

A group of warriors were approaching us along the beach. Leading them was a huge naked man. He rippled with muscle and was unarmed. He overtopped Oileus. The newcomer was a young man with a broad jaw and an unpleasant grin. He walked boldly into our midst and challenged, 'No foreigner shall continue his voyage until he has proved worthy against me. I use no weapons, strays from the sea. Only these hands.'

He made them into fists. They were huge, as big as hams, and scarred from many collisions with other people's teeth and bones.

'Very serviceable,' commented Idas quietly. 'I am Idas, and I will meet your terms. I think this place here will do very well for this contest.'

Amycus glared. His eyes rolled and I wondered if he was mad. We separated into groups. The followers of Amycus stood at one side and we stood on the sand at the other. The bandit took two pairs of ox hide gauntlets and threw them at Idas' feet.

'I will make no choice. Pick which pair you like,' he snarled. Idas turned over the gloves, selected two, and Lynkeos and I bound them onto his hands.

I had seen what damage this sort of fighting could do, in the marketplace in Iolkos, and when the heroes sparred with each other in Pelias' palace. It seemed so long ago. Blows struck with clenched fists inside rough leather gloves tear skin, break bones and bruise unmercifully. Most fights end when one fighter can no longer see out of his swollen eyes and submits. I did not think that this fight would end until one of the contestants was dead.

'Keep your weapons to hand,' whispered Jason. 'If we win, I fear we will have to fight these followers. They look used to acting together.'

'Well skilled,' agreed Oileus, dropping his hand onto his sword hilt.

Atalante was sliding unobtrusively toward the rear of our group. One needs room to shoot arrows effectively. Beside her, Clytios sat down, his quiver in his lap.

We sat on the sand and I wondered if the gods were angry with us, despite Idmon's messengers, for leaving Herakles behind; and were about to punish Idas' boasting with defeat, and us with death at the hands of Phrygian bandits.

Idas stretched, bounced on the balls of his feet, and feinted a few times. I was sitting next to Lynkeos, who was as tense as a bowstring. Then Amycus attacked, and Idas began to dance.

Left, left, a step and a leap; each time the great fists slid and missed, and Amycus stumbled, recovered and struck again. It was like watching a bull attempting to gore a gadfly. Idas caught one punch on his forearm, and slipped close to strike, once, twice, the blows thudding home on jaw and chest, then he was out of reach, always just out of reach, taunting, dancing.

A thread of blood was running from Amycus' mouth, and another from his eye. He shook his head like a maddened animal, then roared and dived.

Idas sprang, dodged, and always he punished Amycus, trading blow for blow; on the mouth again, and the giant spat teeth; on the chest, which rang hollow like a drum; and a punch which ripped the skin open along one cheekbone, so that Amycus staggered back, wiping frantically at his face.

It was cruel, cold, merciless. We did not cheer. The bandit was breathless with shame, exhaustion and pain. He decided to finish the fight with one blow. He raised himself to his full height, his face a mask of blood and fury, and both fists together, thudded down like a club.

If Idas had been in the way he would have been killed instantly. But he was not there. As Amycus stumbled, unbalanced, Idas swung with all his weight, pivoting on one foot, and his clenched fist hit the side of Amycus' head.

It was a perfect blow, delivered with all Idas' strength, perfectly timed. It must have crushed the bones of the skull. He was dead before he hit the ground.

The men of Amycus' following attacked us as soon as they found that their champion was dead. There was a scream of fury and a rush of feet on the sand. I heard bows singing and the swish of arrows above me as we fought.

I had never been in a battle before. I was surprised that I was not afraid. A man slashed at me with his sword. I sidestepped and hit him with the pole of my spear, and he fell. Others fell over him. A man in front of me reeled, shrieking, with an arrow through his eye. Another lay begging for death, one leg hacked off below the knee. I did not have time to think. People were trying to kill me, and I may have killed them. I stabbed with my spear at at least one unprotected belly, and saw a following gush of blood and bulging intestines as I retrieved the weapon.

The attack ceased. No one was pressing forward, eager for Nauplios' blood. Then we seemed to have won. The attackers scattered. We raised a ragged cheer to speed them on their way. The warriors ran for the mountain, dragging their wounded and dead after them. The crew clustered together. No one was injured. Atalante lamented her lack of arrows and wondered where she would get more. Jason embraced Telamon and Oileus, laughing with triumph, spattered with someone else's blood.

I went into the bushes to be sick.

When I came back, someone had lit a fire. Lynkeos heated water to wash Idas and then massaged him, using the perfumed oil that his woman on Lemnos had given him. And, oddly enough, we didn't hear a word out of Idas about what a good fighter he was—not a single boast about how he beat the giant Amycus and killed him with a single blow.

And when we departed the next day, well supplied from Amycus' herds, we sailed up the Bosporus with the wind.

For a while it seemed that it was not going to be the dreadful, muscle-wracking struggle which Argos was predicting. I was leaning against the side, discussing music with Philammon and Idas—I did not care for the heroes' gloating talk of their battle the day before—when I saw the bard's sun-tinted skin blanch. I swung around and saw what had produced this reaction in one as brave as Philammon, and yelled for Jason.

A huge wave was poised over us, as big as a mountain, grey green, foaming white at the crest. If we were underneath when that fell, we would be like the kindling boys use to light the kitchen fire. I shouted to Tiphys at the steering oars, and he screamed back, 'Just needs a good hand on the helm, boy!' and leaned his weight into the rudders.

Miraculously, we inched across the face of the great wave. Europe was on one side of us, Asia on the other, formidable cliffs with no landfall for a breakable wooden vessel full of fragile humans. We were a spark, a little lamp, a bundle of limbs and beating hearts in a cloud-topping waste of hostile water. I heard Atalante praying to Poseidon, and Philammon chanting the words.

We moved as warily as mice in a strange kitchen, hardly daring to breathe, keeping pace to the small hand drum. As the wave moved, we moved with it. We kept pace with the monstrous ocean until it picked us up and dropped us onto the coast that faces the Bithinian land.

As we laid down our sweeps, still disbelieving of our good fortune, Idmon raised a hand and said into the silence of the little bay, 'I hear birds. A lot of birds. But what are they? I never heard such bird voices before.'

We were too shocked and exhausted to stop him. He leapt ashore, wading through the surf in his long white robes. After what happened to Hylas, we would not allow anyone to go off alone, so while the others dragged *Argo* out of the water and set up camp, Clytios, Tiphys and I ran after the seer, shouting for him to wait.

He paused at the end of the beach and we caught up with him.

There we saw a very strange sight, so odd that we halted in our tracks, staring.

A table was set up under the sheer fall of a cliff. The rock was dark blue, the hard stone common on this shore, though it was strangely streaked with white. At the table sat an old man. His beard was long and snowy. In front of him was a feast, roasted flesh and bread and olives, but he was clearly starving. His face was gaunt, his eyes hollow, and his bony hands shook as he reached for a loaf and broke it.

From above came a shrieking, which set my teeth on edge. Plunging down through the air and settling onto the table came hundreds of huge birds. I had never seen them before, and from his eagerness, neither had Idmon the bird-diviner. They easily avoided the old man's sweeping arms. His face, as the light caught it, was rugged and strong, but his eyes were open and unseeing, pale as pearls. He was blind. The birds were foul smelling—the cloud of their scent billowed toward us and we choked on the reek. They had green heads and savage hooked beaks, and they tore and befouled the food, gobbling and scattering it. They even wrenched the loaf which he had just broken out of the old man's grasp.

A short time later, they exploded upward in a flurry of verdigris feathers, black beaks and scaly, yellow legs and claws, leaving the old man weeping with rage and then with hunger, spattered with evil smelling droppings, with his ravaged feast on the table before him.

'I have never seen such birds before,' whispered Idmon.

'And I have never seen an old man so starved and mistreated,' I declared. I shook off Tiphys' hand and climbed the tumble of rocks to the table, saying soothingly as I came, 'Lord, I am Nauplios of the ship *Argo*, out of Iolkos, on the quest for the Golden Fleece and the bones of Phrixos; I wish to help you.'

He wiped his face on his sleeve and said in a rich, beautiful voice, 'Well, Nauplios of Iolkos, if you really intend to help me, take my hand and lead me away from this cliff to the sea, where I can wash. And if you have come to slay me, Nauplios of Iolkos, you may then do me that service when I am clean, because I am cursed by the envious gods, and I no longer wish to live if I must live like this.'

I approached the table and took the old man's hand, leading him away from the destroyed dinner. The smell, like rotting flesh, was frightful and I wondered how he bore it. Someone must have set the feast for him, laying a cloth on the table and putting out dishes. Why, if they meant to serve this venerable person, did they continue to set his table under this cliff, where these carrion-eating creatures clearly made their home? It seemed like some sort of torture to me, and I have never approved of torture. I also liked this old man, who reminded me strongly of my own grandfather. He had been blind, also, for two years before he died.

I led him to the sea and helped him to wash, holding his inner garment as he scoured his body and beard in the salt water. I dried him with the inside of his stained and stinking robe and reclothed him in his tunic. It seemed indecent for me to stare at his skeletal nakedness when he was unaware of my gaze. He was cruelly thin. I could count every single bone, from his withered shanks to his knobbed backbone, and his old neck seemed too fragile to hold up the luxuriance of his beard and hair. As with Grandfather, I easily learn to identify and locate people by their voices. Grandfather used to be able to tell me exactly what was happening in the market, just by the sounds.

I was speaking of our mission to regain the fleece when the old man came close to me and touched my face. His hands were thin but still strong, and he traced my mouth, my nose, my eyes, my hair. The spidery fingers crept over my cheek to run along my jaw, then dropped without warning to my chest, where he laid a palm flat over my breast, feeling for my heart.

'A young man, a fine face, and a strong heart,' he commented. 'You are not afraid of me.'

'No, Lord,' I said, touched. 'Why should I be afraid of you?'

'I am Phineas,' he said, the cold hand on my chest feeling for my reaction, an acceleration in my heartbeat. I had heard of Phineas the prophet, of course.

'You have heard of me?' The sightless eyes were turned away, as is the disconcerting habit of the blind.

'Yes, Lord, but I heard no ill of you. Men say that you speak nothing but the truth. But now, lord Phineas, what is your will? My captain would be honoured to meet you, and although our fare is rough it is clean.'

'You are Minyans, are you not? My people have no feud with you. Very well. I will meet your captain. Tell the tall man who is standing behind you to go and warn him that I am coming. For I am Phineas, and speak the truth—which is why the gods blinded me. And I tell all I know, so beware. That is why my food is placed under that cliff, and the harpies come and destroy it. What do they look like? I have often wondered.'

Tiphys, who had been standing behind me, ran off down the beach to warn Jason.

'Their bodies are the size of a newborn kid, Lord Phineas, with a wingspan as broad as my arms, and they are green—a dirty green like unpolished bronze. Their legs are yellow and their beaks are black, and Idmon the seer says he has never seen their like before.'

'Zeus sent them,' said the old man. He leaned more heavily on my arm as we tottered along the beach. When we were in sight of the camp, he suddenly swooned and crumpled. Telamon picked him up in his arms and carried him to the fireside, and Philammon dripped honeyed wine into the open mouth as the old man began to recover.

'It really is Phineas,' breathed the bard, supporting the white head in his lap.

'Why, who's Phineas?' asked Oileus. 'A scrawny old man, almost dead from hunger—I can show you a thousand such.'

'A scrawny old king,' corrected the bard. He stared at Oileus and the hero lowered his eyes. No one, I had noticed, could bear Philammon's direct gaze for long.

'He is the son of Agenor, king of Thrace. He was given the gift of prophecy, Oileus, and then he made a great mistake. He told the truth, and truth is a very dangerous possession. He was exiled here, and someone has arranged this torment for him.'

'The gods,' murmured Phineas, licking his lips.

'Perhaps,' replied Philammon dryly. 'However, it ends today.'

'Jason and the *Argo*,' murmured Phineas. 'Yes, they were the names. You are fated to free me, whether from torture or from life I know not—and neither do I care, greatly. I am to advise you of the way to Colchis, and I will do so.'

'After you have drunk this broth,' said Philammon.

'And eaten some bread,' said Jason. His gentle heart was moved by the old man's condition. Oileus, ashamed, spread his second cloak over Phineas' shoulders and I washed his bespattered robe. The old man ate the broth, bursting into helpless tears as he tasted it. He ate some bread and drank a mouthful of wine.

I saw Atalante and Clytios on guard, bows bent, as I came up from the stream with the wet gown and hung it on a tree to dry. It had been a fine robe, and I had got most of the filth out of it.

'What are you doing?' I asked curiously.

'Nauplios, those birds might be from the gods,' said Artemis' maiden firmly. 'But equally they might just be hungry, and I do not intend to share my dinner with them.'

'They have no courtesy at table,' agreed Phineas, and chuckled.

'Shall we kill the harpies?' asked Clytios. 'It is shameful to so torment you, who was once a king.'

'Do not challenge the gods, archer,' said Phineas. 'Unless you have a single heart and a will which never fails. But you have a diviner with you. What says Idmon the seer?'

'That they will haunt you no more,' said Idmon. 'Your time of suffering is over. The people who bring you offerings in exchange for your prophecies will lay your food in another place, and the harpies will not pursue you.'

'How can you turn them from their purpose, which the gods laid on them?' asked Phineas doubtfully, taking another piece of bread as though he might not taste it again.

'I will speak to them,' said Idmon with perfect confidence.

He went toward the cliff, and we did not see what happened. We heard the harpies arise in a flock, shrieking their ill-omened cry, and Atalante and Clytios readied their bows in case they came to attack us, but they did not. The noise went on until Philammon played the melody of Apollo at sunset. Then Idmon returned. Claws had sliced across his face and there was a set of furrows down his shoulder and chest, which he washed in the sea. He was not smiling.

'They will come no more to torment you, Phineas,' was all he said, and lay down in the sand with his feet to the fire. He was asleep in the time it takes a pot of water to boil, and he did not move all night.

'Listen, heroes,' said Phineas. 'When you leave here, the first thing you will encounter will be the Clashing Rocks, Scylla and Carybdis. Scylla moves, Carybdis is still. Two hundred years ago, the gods struck the island, which was Kalliste the beautiful, with a great convulsion of the sea and the earth. Fire spouted from the sea, blanketing everything in ash, and darkness fell for three nights, and fields burned as the fire fell upon them as far away as Thrace. So the grandfathers of my fathers said, and the story has come through their mouths to mine. A great stone was cast up by that mountain, of a light rock that we call volcano stone—do you know it?'

Jason nodded, remembered that Phineas could not see and said, 'We know it, Lord. It floats on water.'

'A huge piece, as big as a cliff, was washed into the strait. It was lifted by Poseidon to lie in a cradle of rocky teeth. It can move from east to west, but not north or south. And it does move, Jason. Watch, crew of the *Argo*. Time the movement, for it is not always the same. Send a dove through, and see how fast she flies. Then drive your ship through at her fastest pace, and you might survive.'

'We will do as you say,' said Jason. Argos, on the other side of the fire, Melas asleep beside him, drew diagrams in the sand.

'If you come through, you will see other lands. On the fore-land called Carambis, do not land. There the Amazons live and they will massacre you—even a shipload of strong men cannot stand against the armies of those women. After the mouth of Thermodon you will find the Chalybes; the metal workers. After them the sheep farmers, who should welcome you. They are called the Tivareni. The Stymphalian birds may attack; you must find a way of surviving them also.

'Sail on until you come to the farthest corner of the Euxine Sea. There you will find a flat marshy plain and a great river going inland. It is the Phasis, and a little way down the river lies Colchis. In the marshes you will find the bones of Phrixos, and in a wood in the plain of Ares near the city you will find the Golden Fleece. Pray to Artemis, and to Hera your protector. And now I will sleep, heroes, captain. Nauplios? Are you there?'

I kneeled beside him, and he laid his old hand on my head. 'Come home safely and be happy,' he said. 'May you have all the blessing I have to bestow, for because of you, boy, I am clean and filled and before you came I was weary of my life.'

Phineas curled up in Oileus' second-best cloak with a sigh of contentment.

Chapter Fifteen

Medea

I heard dogs baying, but I was loath to wake. I parted from Tyche reluctantly. I had never met a person whom I so instantly trusted and liked. Scylla and Kore had liked her too. I had stayed until the evening of the third day, when I returned alone to the Scyths.

I asked them about her, and they called her 'The Old Woman in the Cave' and said that she was the wisest person in the world. And it was very unlikely that I would see her again. I was going to Colchis to my destiny. And I did not want to go.

Now I heard screams outside Anemone's wagon. The attack had come without warning, but you can't ambush Scyths that way. A Scythian encampment is never without watchers, even if the attackers couldn't see them. Even in their own traditional summer camping place in the heart of their own territory, where we would stay for seven days exchanging without guards. There is even a model guard burned on their pyres, or they wouldn't sleep amongst the dead.

Arrows hummed. I heard one strike the wagon.

This was not some Scythian argument which had got out of hand. Occasional riots ran through the encampment, but none used an arrow against another Scyth. I wondered who could be raiding us, and how bold they were, attacking us. I put on my priestess' robe and took a weapon which Tyche had helped me construct. It was elegant and, I hoped, deadly.

I had a hollow wooden tube made of a reed and a clay pot in which were thin bone darts as long as my hand. This weapon had no other purpose but to kill. Tyche told me that I was welcome to walk through the woods naked, if I liked, but that I must promise to carry the pipe, so I swore. I had practised with it. I could hit a target fairly well at up to ten paces. Now I was about to test it in battle conditions.

I heard a woman scream a name: 'Androphagi!'

I climbed out of the wagon with Kore and Scylla at my side.

The night was as dark as summer nights get, but the watch fires were burning and I could see quite well. A man coated with oil and paint, his head shaved and stained with scarlet, was poised with his back to me. He was preparing to throw a short spear. I could see every muscle in his naked back and buttocks. I could see his target, a Scyth fighting off another painted naked man with a sword.

I broke the seal on my clay pot, inserted one of the darts into the pipe, and blew.

There was a faint 'pfft' and the feathered dart stuck into the middle of that broad back. The spear dropped. The attacker swung about as he fell, and I saw his lips writhe back over teeth which had all been filed to a point; horrible.

I reached him and put a hand to his throat. Dead. The snake venom which we had used to compound this poison was very effective and the Androphagos was quite dead. The Scyth won his contest with the sword, thrusting it through his opponent's chest. He drew out the blade, saw me and the fallen attacker, and shouted, 'My thanks, Sister!'

'How many are there, where did they come from?' I yelled. He was Dianthys' new husband and I did not know his name.

'Don't know how many, they came hunting through the wagons; they slew three guards. What we are taught to do is to fall back on the king's wagon—that way. There we shall stand at the last if we cannot defeat them before. Come,' said the young man. I followed him, creeping through the maze of little camps. One woman, at least, had been carried off sleeping from her bed, for I heard voices shrieking, 'They've taken her! Kill, kill, kill the savages!'

I saw another Androphagos. This one died before he realised what the tiny wound was. I found Iole, clutching at her wounded breast, wielding a bow.

'Get to the king,' she whispered to me. I tucked my shoulder under her arm. Iole, who was so brave and so beautiful, bleeding now and weakening. The camp was deafening with screams and shouts, all in Scythian; the Androphagi hunted in silence, like wolves. I heard bows twanging. As I was about to sink under Iole's weight, someone took her out of my arms. I turned to thank him and looked into another scarlet face with pointed fangs like a dog's. There was no room to use the pipe and he had slung my Iole over his shoulder like a parcel. Kore leapt for his throat. Scylla for his ankles, and he staggered and dropped my friend.

Then I stabbed him with a dart. He looked surprised for the moment it took the venom to penetrate his system. I dragged Iole off his collapsing body and went on through black shadows and grey and the scent of death and burning.

I saw the ring of the Scyths surrounding the king's wagon. Anemone was there, firing a bow. The air stank of blood and Androphagi—they reeked, unwashed skin and oil made from some unthinkable fleshly source. I killed another as I reached the Scythian guard and someone took Iole out of my grasp and laid her in the king's wagon. She would live if I could care for her soon. Kore and Scylla, at my knees, barked and then began to howl.

I did not think we were going to survive, but I would not go down into the dark without taking some sacrifices to please Hekate. I steadied my back against the wagon wheel and searched for a mark. A painted man paused obligingly in my view, and I blew again. I saw the feathery dart take in his hand. He plucked it out and threw it away. It took him longer to die, perhaps because the limb is further from the centre of being than the throat. He raised his spear again, cried some sort of challenge, shook his head, and fell.

I was coldly pleased.

'That's a good weapon!' yelled Anemone. 'The old woman in the cave?'

'Yes,' I yelled. 'How many warriors are there?'

'Hundreds,' she leaned down from her perch on the king's wagon. 'The Scyths have tempted Até, thinking that the Man-killers were defeated. They must have mustered all the tribes. Make sure that you are not taken alive, Scythling. And know that I loved you, that Anemone loved you, Medea.'

The attack began again. I had no time to tell Anemone that I loved her, though I did. I shot four more attackers with my darts. But I only had five left, and there would be no opportunity to make more. I watched a creeping ring of painted men, scarlet heads and oiled bodies, massing just out of bowshot. I knew what I had to do if the Scyths could not hold them off. I would not be taken alive to be defiled and murdered. I would kill my dogs first. The Androphagi also ate dogs. I could use my knife on my dearest friends, but a dart must be saved for me. I doubted I could find my heart with my own knife and a bungled suicide would leave me utterly at the mercy of those who had no mercy. I hoped that my flesh would poison them.

Kore and Scylla were pressed close to me, occasionally barking when an attacker came too close. Their closeness wrung my heart. Their warm bodies had comforted me in all my pain. But they would accompany me on the long path back to the Mother, to play in her fields forever or sleep with me in the warm dark of the Mother's womb.

The night seemed endless. Dawn would bring better light for the archers, but there was no lightening in the sky. I watched as the ring of attackers came closer, many falling to arrows and spears but replaced immediately by those behind. I resolved to keep my last darts until they were very close. Kore and Scylla had stopped howling. I think they knew that we were all going to die.

A painted man broke the ranks and raced toward us, screaming some challenge. He died with my dart in his chest. He plucked it out, scratching as from a mosquito bite, then crashed into our lines, his impetus carrying him on even after he was dead. Then they all began to run. In a moment they would smash through our defences. They were careless of how many would die in that blood-soaked piece of ground between them and us, but enough would get through. The Scyths were defeated and Medea's destiny had arrived earlier than expected. I knelt, and my hounds nuzzled up to me. I drew my knife, weeping, whispering that we would meet again, that they should wait just a little for me, stay on the threshold of the dark cave, and I would come to them, my dearest companions.

Then, as my blade was at Scylla's throat and I wept as I stared into her trusting brown eyes, something came through the camp with a noise like the rumbling of a wagon over a rough path. A thud, a crash, a pause, then thud, crash, again. The Androphagi halted, wavering. Something from behind was felling their ranks like wheat. I could not see what it was, but I heard a name, shouted in Scythian, and the silent attackers broke and began to run.

It did not matter how they fled. A man was visible at the far side of the clearing. He was naked, wearing some sort of skin as a cloak. He swung a club made of most of a tree with silent efficiency, battering the attackers aside. The painted men, who had not made the slightest sound when they were hunting Scythian victims through our camp, cried aloud at the sight of him. '*Kallinikos!*' they screamed, and turned to run.

Which did not do them the slightest good. This *Kallinikos* had no expression that I could see. He did not look angry. He just swung and crushed the skull of every painted man with a terrible inevitability. That was the noise I had heard. Crash of club on skull. Thud as the body hit the ground. Crash, thud. I remained where I was, clutching my hounds, watching in horrified fascination.

Anemone came down from the wagon to join me.

'Who is he?' I demanded. 'Who is this *Kallinikos?*'

'I thought he was just a story,' she said, wiping absently at her mouth, which was bleeding. She had bitten her lip.

'What story?' I put the last of my darts back into the little clay pot. The war appeared to be over. The painted men were herded into a corner between two wagons, and this stranger was going to kill them all. They tried to escape, diving for him, stabbing and scratching and tearing, screaming in their own tongue for what was presumably mercy. It was horrible. He brought each one out and struck and dropped the body and struck again.

'He's an Achaean,' said Anemone. 'Gods of the Scyths, I was sure that we were going to die this night! They call him a hero. He strangled two snakes in his cradle when he was eight months old. He's the strongest man in the world. Are you unhurt, Medea?'

'Yes, not a scratch, but I was preparing to kill Kore and Scylla and then myself. I think I'd like to sit down.'

Anemone gave me a cup of the ice wine which the Scyths use for disinfecting wounds and cleaning tarnished metal. They made it in winter by allowing a tub of wine to freeze, then pouring off the concentrate. I would never ordinarily drink the stuff, but I gulped. It was raw, and I choked and blinked, but the world appeared a little more bearable after I had swallowed a couple of times and passed the cup on. All around the king's wagon, the last-ditch ring of Scythian defenders were staring in fascination at the executioner who had come out of the darkness and saved us. Idanthyrsus ordered his fighters out, to inspect the camp, bring in the wounded, and report.

There were no more painted men. Not alive. I was about to move, to go and thank our rescuer, but Anemone grabbed me.

'Don't approach him,' she warned. 'If the stories are true he is mad. He might kill you as well.'

'What shall we do? He's wounded, see, he's bleeding, and there's an arrow through his leg.'

'Wait,' said the queen of the Scyths. 'The tales say that he'll collapse soon. Then we can tend him.'

I went into the king's wagon to see Iole. The wound proved to be superficial, a long slash which had, however, marred her smooth shoulder and round breast.

'The Amazons cut off that breast so they can shoot better,' she grinned at me. 'Now I shall have a warrior scar. Has *Kallinikos* really come?'

'Yes. He's standing in the clearing amongst heaps of dead painted men, and he hasn't moved for a long time. I'll go out and see what's happening. I just came to see if you were alive, sister.'

'I'm alive and the Androphagi aren't feasting on Scyths,' said Iole, and closed her eyes.

I returned to the clearing in time to see the saviour of the Scyths collapse bonelessly to the ground.

When we reached him he was quite unconscious. The queen ordered him carried to her own wagon, where I could tend him.

He was surprisingly heavy. As the young men laid him on a cloth beside the wagon so I could see to remove the arrows, the sun came up.

It rose in glory, red and gold, and I praised Hekate for allowing us to live another day. I was alive, Kore and Scylla were sitting at my feet, and I was about to try and save a legend's life.

I sang the prayers to Hekate as I washed off the blood to assess the man's injuries. He was not young. His hair was greying, and his face was lined. He was naked apart from what I now recognised as a lion skin. He was dusty and blood soaked and he looked like a peasant. Although someone had plaited his hair carefully with feathers and shells, it had not been tended for a month.

I listened to the Scyths delivering reports to Anemone as I heated more water and then laid my knife in the flames. The arrows of the painted men were barbed and I would have to use great care in extracting them. I could not believe that *Kallinikos* was alive. I removed one arrow from his chest. It was not deep and had not penetrated the cavity where air must not be allowed to go, for Hekate teaches that air runs in the veins, and if the hollow of the torso is penetrated, then blood and air mix and the patient drowns. I cut another out of his forearm, where the muscle was twisted like leather thongs. Then I removed two from his right leg. One was almost through, and I slit a way for it, pulling the broken shaft out. Another was superficial. His hand was cut across the palm, probably from grabbing a sword.

After half an hour, when I was almost sickened by the extra damage I had done to him, I washed the wounds with salt water, then with fresh and then with the ice wine. I stitched the grosser wounds and drank the rest of the spirit myself. At each point when I was inflicting further indignity on his body, I had felt for his heart, which beat strongly under my hand. Whoever this folktale was, he was made of inhumanly strong material.

Finally I bandaged all the injuries. He had stopped bleeding. He had a broad peasant's face with a strong jaw, a wide nose and a broad forehead. I had the young men carry him into Anemone's wagon and rummaged amongst the hanging herbs for feverfew and the disinfectant woundleaf. He would be in a raging fever when he woke. I also wondered about his battle madness. I had been told of a similar condition, perhaps, by the old women in the temple. They said that one should make a *lithos sophronister*, a stone of calm, and they had given me the list of ingredients, most of which I had. I needed the blood of a black dog and a certain mushroom, and I knew where I could get both of those things.

I left *Kallinikos* to sleep and went out to see what damage the Androphagi had done to the Scythians. Anemone was talking to the tenders of the wounded and the heads of families, and she seemed pleased.

'Only five killed, that is wonderful, considering that we were close enough to Death to smell his breath. Three guards died in the initial attack. Several Scyths are so wounded that they may not survive, but we acquitted ourselves well. We would have died in a way of which Ares would approve. But we didn't have to, which is cheering. How is the *Kallinikos*?'

"I can't imagine how he is still alive, but he is. I'm going out to get some herbs, can someone stay with him?'

'He won't wake for days, if the tales are true,' she said.

But he woke only a few hours later. I was compounding my *lithos sophronister* in a mortar. Kore had willingly given me three drops of her blood, as she would willingly have given me her heart or her life. Every time I thought of how close I had come to having to kill the dogs, I felt weak with gratitude to this efficient executioner. He was lying in my own bed, and I glanced across at him and saw that his eyes were open.

I had never seen such beautiful eyes. They were grey, but the actual tint was hard to define; the light in a shallow stream, perhaps, flecked with gold. Clear eyes like water. There was a quality of innocence about this warrior. He looked at me for a while and then said, 'Lady?'

'Lord?' I replied in Achaean, the language he was speaking.

'Where am I?' he asked simply. 'What has happened?'

'You came to rescue the Scythians, Lord, and saved our lives by killing the painted men, the Androphagi. You are in the wagon of the queen of the Scyths. I am Medea, and I will tend you.'

'Am I wounded?' He tried to sit up, grunted, and lay down again. I was reassured. At least this man felt pain.

Not that he would continue to feel it, after I had applied some numbing ointment and administered my willow bark and poppy draught, of course. I did this and he lay peaceably under my hands, though I must have hurt him afresh.

'The leg wound is fairly serious,' he commented, assessing his body as a Scyth assesses a horse she is minded to purchase. 'Arrow, was it?'

'Yes. It was deep and across the bone, and some of the muscle is cut. I have stitched it and if you lie still it may knit.'

'You are young to be so knowledgeable,' he mused, not even flinching as I changed the crusted bandages. I liked his voice. It was deep and clear, like a bell. 'Ah, of course. The lady Medea, eh? You must be princess of Colchis. Why are you here with the Scyths?'

'I am travelling to the shrines, Lord. I am a priestess of Hekate.'

'Someone has taught you well,' he said sleepily. 'Your hands are quick and sure. I am in your debt, Lady, and the debt of all women.'

'Lord, who are you?' I asked. '*Kallinikos* just means 'Beautiful in Victory' in Achaean. But the Scyths say that you are a folktale and I have never seen anyone fight like you did.'

'I am the servant of women, Hera's man. They call me Herakles,' he said simply, and fell asleep.

The Scyths burned their dead on a great pyre. We wailed and tore our hair, chanting the names of the dead. Then the ashes were sifted and pounded for any fragment of bone, and scattered into the air. A wind came up and blew the ash away. The Scythians have no tombs but Scythia itself.

Herakles slept, on and off, for seven days. We talked when he was awake. He told me that he had lost a boy, Hylas, whom he loved and who was under his protection, and that he had run mad for a time—he did not know how long. Around the fire at night, the Scyths had told me tales of this Herakles. The goddess had tested him by sending battle rage, in which he had slain his own children. Then he had undertaken great labours, even descending to the Achaean underworld to haul forth the guardian of the dead, a three-headed dog called Cerberus. I asked him about his labours.

'Eurystheus set me harder and harder tasks,' he told me, lying back in the fleeces and sipping the painkilling infusion. Even after two days, he was sitting up and seemed to have no fever. 'He hoped that each one would kill me, but I could not die. I woke, you see, Princess, in my own house, and piled at my feet were the dead bodies of my sons, and I did not want to live, but the goddess would not let any creature slay me. Wound me, certainly. This,' he traced a long puckered scar down one thigh, 'was the Erimanthean boar. I brought it back alive. This was the Hydra.' Round scars like cupping marks ran down his side. 'One of the Stymphalian birds made this,' he showed me a scar which cut through his hair beside his temple. 'But nothing was allowed to kill me.'

'I am a priestess of the Mother, that same lady who tries you, Herakles,' I said. I had to convince him to try my cure, and therefore needed to explain my credentials, or he would refuse the *lithos,* faithful to his goddess' will. 'In the temple an old woman came to me, and told me of a cure for battle madness. I have compounded it for you.'

'The old woman—did you know her?' he asked. A small light of hope had been lit in the beautiful trout-stream eyes.

'No, Lord, she was a stranger. A bent woman in black robes, with a hood over her hair.' This was perfectly true.

'Hera has approved me,' he murmured. The great hands clasped together. Kore, who was lying with her head on his chest, pricked up her ears.

'Here it is, lord Herakles.' He took the round stone and looked at it. It had a faintly greasy feel, for it was compounded of wax and the correct herbs, melted and poured into a mould.

'How does it work?'

'When you feel the rage coming on you, saviour of the Scyths, put the stone into your mouth and hold it there while you say a prayer to your lady. Then you will feel the madness ebb. Do not swallow it. It can be used again and again; the potency will fade very slowly, and if you need another, come to Colchis and ask for Medea and I will compound it afresh. Put it back into this leather pouch which the grateful Scyths have made for you. There is little we can give you, lord Herakles, for the gift of our lives, since you will not take treasure or women or men, but allow us to give you this.'

'At last,' he whispered. Then he sat up, heedless of his healing wounds, and laid both gnarled hands with wincing delicacy on my shoulders. He drew me forward and kissed me, on the forehead, on both cheeks, and then very gently on my mouth.

Then he lay back and closed his eyes, and I saw that he was weeping.

I left him with Scylla and Kore, who had always comforted me.

◇◇◇

When he had recovered enough to walk, leaning on a staff and my shoulder, he sat down at the Scythian fires and listened to their stories. Sometimes, if they begged, he would tell of his labours and of strange encounters in the world, but he was not really interested in tales of battle and death.

The Scythian children, who sat at his feet, quickly found that they could buy some of his attention with pretty or strange objects; stones shaped like shells, flowers, odd animals or insects.

I came upon Herakles the *Kallinikos* sitting unaffectedly on a rug on the ground, his hands cupped around something which chirped.

'It's hatched untimely, and its parents have abandoned it,' he said, opening his horny palms to show me a featherless bird. It was the ugliest little creature I had ever seen. It consisted of an oversize beak and oversize claws, held together with a little bag of naked yellow skin. It opened the beak and chirped, gaping.

'I can understand that,' I said.

'It will be a beautiful bird when it grows a little and finds some clothing,' he said smiling. 'The children brought it to me.'

And he wove a little basket for the bird and fed it more dotingly than its mother would have. It ate meat, and the children were kept hard at work finding insects to keep up with its ravenous appetite.

Herakles himself healed cleanly and easily. The flesh slid together and knitted, leaving a flat scar, another to join the patchwork leather garment which was his body. I heard the children singing a little song one afternoon, as we lazed in the cool shade and waited for the sun to go down.

> *Red wasp to green wasp said,*
> *'Look, under that bush.*
> *There's a man sleeping,*
> *Careless of wounds.*
> *Come down, brother,*
> *Let's fill our bellies.'*

Green wasp to red wasp said,
'Brother, you are joking.
Do you know who that is
Sleeping in the sun?
That's Herakles, brother,
One they call leather bum.
You'll break your sting
If you try to eat that.'

Herakles heard them and laughed.

By the time the little bird had grown feathers—and it was a fine creature, as he had said, that speckled one the Scyths call sky hawk, and so tame that it took food from his hand—he was healed. He came to me one dawn, walking without a limp, the sky hawk sitting on his shoulder.

'I thank you for your care, Medea, Princess of Colchis,' he said. I took his hand. Kore and Scylla whined.

'I will never see you again, Lord, but I have enjoyed your wisdom and your company,' I said, with perfect truth.

'Yet we may meet again. For your care, Lady, and for your healing, I am your servant. If you need me, Lady Medea, call for me, and if I am still in the world, I will come.'

Then he walked away into the woods, dressed as always in the dusty lion skin, and I was sure I would never see him again.

Chapter Sixteen

Nauplios

There was only one thing more we could do for King Phineas, and Akastos did it. The son of Pelias was an expert herdsman, and took me and Admetos with him as he went to talk to the people of the little village nearest to Phineas' hermitage.

I had not spoken much to Akastos since he came on board against his father's wishes. He was not tall, but stocky and strong, and I had heard his oarmates laughing at his wit. He was dark, as was his cousin Admetos, and now both faces were solemn, indicating that they had come to talk to the *demos* about something very important. I wondered what it was.

'Men of Thynia,' he began. 'I am Akastos of Iolkos, and this is my cousin, Admetos, and our shipmate, Nauplios. You have heard of the terrible curse inflicted on Phineas the prophet?'

Bald heads nodded. The *demos* of this village was composed of ten men, no more. No women, of course, were visible. These men made all the decisions which needed to be made about the fate of the community.

Their spokesman quavered, 'We knew that the harpies were eating his food, good food, too, which we brought him every day. But what could we do, lords? Gods are gods and are not to be disobeyed.'

Akastos nodded, ponderously.

"But now a new prophecy has been made. Phineas' long punishment is over. His table will be set up before his own house. There you will bring his food, for the harpies will no longer molest him. In thanksgiving for the attention of the gods, and to honour him, I am sure that this *demos* will want to make the lord Phineas a present.'

The old men looked resigned. 'Of course, Lords,' they agreed.

'I will not ask for your women,' said Akastos. 'Nor for your oxen or your sheep. I do not ask for your sons, men of Thynia, nor for your horses or donkeys or goats.'

The *demos* looked at each other in relief. Akastos had named all the important possessions of any village.

'But I will ask for one thing, which will make a valuable present,' he said.

Akastos named his wish, and the demos brought out a selection. I sat down as the discussion ranged over birth, parentage, talents, skills and docility. Akastos knew all about his subject, and Admetos rejected several candidates, sipping at terracotta cups of very good local wine as the words flowed. Both of them knew that one cannot hurry peasants, and they must be allowed to proceed at their own pace. A farmer will even bargain with the gods, they say in Iolkos.

About the time of the emptying of the marketplace, one was chosen, the deal concluded and suitable offerings made. And with the fervent and relieved good wishes of the village we carried it back to the beach, where Argo was resupplied and ready to leave as soon as the wind changed.

Telamon, Ancaeas and Oileus had carried the great table between them down to the sea and scoured it clean, scraping off a generation of droppings. Then they had hauled it up the beach to the small stone house in which the old king lived and set it up outside, under his vine. Argos had built him a bench out of driftwood. The house contained some cups and platters, and Melas was serving Phineas roasted meat, white bread and olives, as we came along with our present.

Phineas was superlatively clean. He shone. His beard and hair were as flossy as new wool. His black prophet's robe had dried, and he also wore Oileus' cloak, which that abashed hero had given to the old king. It was a fine, if faded, red.

Phineas ate very slowly, as though he was seated at one of the sacramental meals, when the Orpheans dine with the gods. We sat in the sand and watched him. Melas, who was quick, had learned that he must continue to speak, so that Phineas would feel comfortable with someone behind him. The boy was talking about Iolkos and his father's building of the great ship *Argo,* and Phineas took another mouthful of roasted sheep and smiled.

For some reason his smile made my eyes prick with tears.

When Phineas could not eat any more, Melas collected the dishes and laid them under the cover which Argos had also made, a box-shaped wooden construction which would keep the flies off until Phineas wished to dine again. His wine was kept cool in a big red clay water pot next to the table.

Akastos and Admetos, carrying our gift, knelt at Phineas' feet and put it into his lap.

He recoiled when he touched a live thing, then the old thin hands came down caressingly when he realised that he was touching fur, not feathers.

'Lord, we have brought a companion. We know that you prefer to live alone, nor would we trust any child of that village to stay with you,' said Akastos, grinning.

'But here is a companion who will never leave you. You have no sight, King Phineas, but he will be your eyes, keener than a man's. He will eat from your hand, Lord, but he will not foul your table. This in memory of *Argo* and the quest for the Golden Fleece,' said Admetos, and the puppy scaled the king's chest and licked his neck, wagging its stump of a tail and whimpering with delight.

'He is of the race of the sheepdogs, bred for valour and intelligence,' said Akastos. 'Not a hunting or a war dog, but one who is used to men and has lived close for many generations. He will lie down on your hearth, lord, and his breathing will lull your sleep, for he will watch and bark if any come to you.'

'Blessings uncounted be upon you,' whispered Phineas. 'I shall call him Argo,' he added, and Argo the puppy barked and nibbled at the king's ear, while we went back to *Argo* the ship and clambered aboard.

The last we saw of King Phineas, he was sitting on his bench in front of his house, weeping into Argo's fluffy fur, while the small dog licked his face.

We rowed into the straits. Rugged cliffs hemmed us in on either side, and the sea was behaving strangely. Odd currents thrust us along for a space, then backed as though the sea was draining like a basin or leaking like a cracked pot. There was nothing for Tiphys to do but to keep as straight a course as possible. Trees grew at unnatural angles, twisted and bent, on the cliffs. Sound echoed from either side of the towering cliffs, grey and perilous. Idas kept the beat of the drum and we rowed to the small pipe played by the bard. Idmon sat nursing his dove in his hands, whispering to it.

Then we heard a thudding, like an earthquake, and saw the Clashing Rocks.

They were huge. They rose to perhaps a *stadion* high, though that may have been my eyes, which were still not quite reliable They were, as their name said, *cynaean,* dark blue and sheer.

One side, Carybdis, was flat, overgrown with black streamers as thick as my arm, kelp growing under the sea to ensnare us. The other was somewhat weathered by the continual collision. The top of Carybdis met Scylla as it rocked with a shuddering crash, but the water had worn a curve in the soft stone. Not that it would help us. The gap was not wide enough even for *Argo's* hull to slide through.

'It's like trying to slip between the hammer and the anvil,' breathed my oarmate, Clytios.

Tiphys called, 'Seen worse, shipmates,' which is what he always said; but even Tiphys of the impervious self-confidence did not sound convincing. 'Just needs a good hand on the helm,' he added, his voice dropping to a whisper.

The noise stung our ears, smiting and counter-smiting, like Hephaestos' anvil on which he forged islands. Each time the rocks collided, a burst of spray broke over our heads. We backed oars, attempting to hold our position. Idmon, on Jason's order, stood up and released his dove.

It flew, on his instructions, straight and level through the rocks, as they parted and then crashed together with a sound like thunder. We strained, trying to keep *Argo* where she was, staring after the flash of white.

I had skinned and blistered my hands so often and for so long that I did not notice that I was bleeding on my oar until my grip slipped. I wrapped a scrap of old tunic around the sweep. This was going to require all my strength, and I hoped it would be enough.

The dove returned to Idmon, who cupped it in his hands and stroked it. He looked up and said, 'Just the very last tail-feather clipped.'

'The interval is a count of seven,' said Philammon, who worshipped numbers like all Orpheans.

Idmon spoke to his dove and released her, and she fluttered away. I reflected that the seer did not want the bird to share our death, and tightened my grip on the wooden oar.

Philammon counted as we allowed the current to pick the ship up and carry her toward the rocks as they smashed together again and we were deafened.

'One,' said Philammon as we drove forward with all our strength. The oars bit the water and *Argo* shuddered at this rough handling. 'Two,' said Philammon, and we were inside the Clashing Rocks. 'Three,' he said, and we lurched again, Idas pounding the drum. The cliff was moving inward again at 'four', cutting the blue sky into a patch, and by 'five' it was a slice.

I commended my soul to Poseidon and then all the gods, expecting to see Hermes, guide of souls, walking along the water toward us. The rocks groaned. The sea boiled up around us as the cliff shifted. We were not going to live. The oars dug frantically into the water again. I heard Ancaeas grunt explosively.

The kelp was slowing us. The black arms of Scylla would drag us back until the rocks crushed us and I was glad that Idmon had released his dove. I heard 'six' and the rasping breath expelled from every throat as we dug and dragged and knew that we could not survive.

Then, by direct divine intervention, something like a great hand grasped *Argo* and thrust her forcibly through the narrowing space and into the open sea. I looked back, but I could not see which god had saved us. Philammon said, 'seven,' as the thunder came again and Scylla and Carybdis clashed shut behind us. Only the very last curlicue on our sternpost was missing, clipped off clean.

'Just a tail feather,' said Argos, and sat down rather quickly.

We were out of the Propontis and into the Euxine Sea, and we were through the Clashing Rocks. We were so exhausted that as soon as a harbour opened, we rowed with our last strength into calm water and collapsed over our oars.

My hands were a mess of broken blisters, bleeding freely. Tiphys and Atalante were leaning on the steering oars, breathing like runners at the end of a ten *stadia* race over mountains. I heard the strong men, Telamon and Oileus and Ancaeas, gasping like winded horses. Idas was examining his drum ruefully. He had split the skin. Jason was staring into the sky with utter astonishment. Alabande was embracing Erginos, his grey hair splayed over Alabande's shoulder, and they were laughing helplessly. Melas, pale to the lips, was sitting quietly, clearly striving not to be sick over the side. Akastos was saying to Admetos, 'I don't believe it. Who shoved us forward? Did you see anything?' and Admetos was shaking his head. Lynkeos was begging his oarmate Meleagros, to tell him that he was still alive. Clytios appeared to have fainted. He was leaning on Perithous, who was as white as milk.

Then Philammon began to sing a song of rejoicing which brought the local inhabitants out of their coastal houses to see the marvel; a ship which had rowed through the Clashing Rocks.

Philammon's coppery hair was dark with sea water, but his hands moved on the strings to a light, exultant, ringing tune.

> *Sing and rejoice, for we are alive,*
> *Thanks to all gods who dwell on Olympus,*
> *Children of Oceanos, reprieved from ending,*
> *Men who love the sun and wine,*
> *Free to lie exhausted in the light,*
> *Who might have lain crushed in the cold*
> *Water, food for the Clashing Rocks.*
> *Released from a wet death, rejoice,*
> *Men of Iolkos, heroes of* Argo,
> *Singing praise to the Many-named,*
> *Praise to all the gods.*

I could not sing—I had also, at some time in that monstrous passage, bitten my tongue—but I did rejoice.

Jason didn't. He sat huddled in the bow. When the song had concluded he said, without looking at us, 'I should have stayed in Iolkos. When Pelias laid this upon me, I should have refused the task. I have made bitter errors and we have only just survived.'

'Lord,' said Akastos comfortingly, 'we have passed the worst point. King Phineas told us the rest of the route to Colchis. Nothing as terrible as the Clashing Rocks confronts us now. And now we know how to get through them, we can do it again on the way back.'

'You only have yourself to worry about,' replied my lord. 'I have to be concerned for all of us.'

'Lord and cousin, you are speaking like this to test us,' said Admetos, and Tiphys nodded. 'We have come all this way, faced and conquered many dangers. We will succeed if the gods allow, and clearly someone is helping us. Did we not feel the divine hand, perhaps of Poseidon himself, thrusting *Argo* through the Clashing Rocks?'

'You fill me with confidence,' said Jason, getting to his feet and turning his face toward us at last. 'You warm my heart, comrades. Very well. We will go on.'

A small fleet of fishing boats had set out toward us. Just in case, the heroes laid hands on weapons.

'Are you Jason of Iolkos?' yelled a man, standing up in the lead boat, holding on to the dolphin-carved prow. On receiving our agreement, he flung a bunch of sweet herbs into the ship and called, 'Blessings be upon you, comers from afar! You killed Amycus, who oppressed and robbed us. Come ashore! A feast is being prepared.'

It was a good feast, and a wise woman cleaned and anointed my hands and bound them in soft linen.

We rowed two days against the current. The lands seemed fertile as we trudged past them, green and pleasant. My palms were reblistered within minutes, and every stroke was pain, but I was used to rowing. One drops into a mindless rhythm after a while. The sun rises, soars to noon and then sinks, and the mind is entranced while the body obeys, slide, lift, haul, slide, lift, haul. We would sing to pass the time, old songs which seafarers have always used to while away the tedium of their labour.

But we saw Apollo / Ammon, one morning at sunrise. We were rowing along a flat, green coast of many river mouths when Philammon, who was looking sternwards, cried, 'Phanes!'

We turned to see 'that which is revealed' and we saw, almost all of us, for later Argos said that his eyes had filled, and Admetos told me that he turned too late. But I saw it, on the sea which was as flat as glass: a glowing man, much bigger than a man; and behind him the lightning flashed and forked, behind him the clouds rolled, black thunderheads heavy with storm. But he came with a light step along the water, which was smoothed into a dancing floor for Erikepaios, Lord of Vintage. His light was too bright for mortal eyes. We were blinded.

When we could see again, without rowing or even being aware of moving, we were in a little bay on a green island. We called it *Anaphae*—the revealed place—and stayed the night before we went on.

Philammon sang to us of Ammon, Apollo, The Archer, the Lovely God, Son of Zeus, He Who Drives the Sun, the Hawk in the Horizon, and told us that we had been greatly favoured.

It did not feel like that the next day. We had landed for water in a marsh. Idmon the seer, whistling to hidden birds, was walking through the reeds when we heard him cry out that a snake had bitten him. By the time we hauled him out of the mud, he was dying.

'My fate has come to me,' he whispered. 'Farewell.'

And with complete self-possession, unafraid, Idmon's soul was borne into the light on the wings of white birds. They fluttered down all around the grave where we laid his body—there was nothing in that wet place of which to make a pyre—and they sang all night, a mournful sound, desolate and breathy, not like any bird's voice I had ever heard. At dawn they flew up, aligning themselves like arrows for the north, and were gone.

In that same place Tiphys sickened with some fever which could not be assuaged by any medicines. He did not cry, but shivered as though winter had him in its grip. The marsh held death, it was clear.

We sat with him, Melas and Philammon and I, all through one night; when he cried that he was cold, cold, and we covered him with every cloak we had, and still heard his teeth chattering. In the firelight he was beautiful. His face was a bronze mask, pure of line, like the sculptors of Achaea make as they pour the molten metal into the mould. There were no marks of age on him, no faltering in his slender body, strong arms, deep chest on which the sweat glazed. But the ice had entered his bones.

He could not swallow on the second day, and Philammon played the 'Descent into Hades,' telling us of Orpheus' journey into the underworld. I lay next to Tiphys, holding him in my arms to try and warm him. His body was burning, but he cried always that he was freezing.

> *He came to the cold river*
> *Styx, which no live eyes can see,*

No breathing one can travel.
The old man, Charon, denying him crossing,
Listened to the lyre and the soft voice
And remembered meadows,
And the sound of the wind in grass.
Orpheus crossed the water
Rowed by the old man.

Then Cerberus, the three-headed
Hound of Hades, chained across the portal,
As Achaean husbands chain guard dogs, roared.
The stones echoed with his challenge,
Stinging the ears. Orpheus played
And Cerberus remembered being a puppy,
Lying with his dam in warm lair,
Remembered the taste of bitch's milk,
Slept in the memory, slobbering with joy.

Orpheus passed the threshold
Into the icy dark, and the shades came,
Fluttering grey ghosts, unremembering,
And one came limping, lately come.
Eurydice whom the snake had robbed
Of lover and life.

I realised that the body I was holding as close as a lover was cooling into death, relaxing in my embrace, and I laid my head on our helmsman's silent heart.

We buried him and lay down on the beach to mourn. We lay in our cloaks like wrapped stones, despairing. How would we ever get through this voyage without that voice at the stern saying cheerfully, 'It only needs a good hand on the helm?'

I almost imagined I heard an echo of that voice, 'I've seen worse, shipmate'.

Ancaeas the Strong rose up like a walrus from the beach, shedding sand, and said in a loud voice, 'We cannot stay here. It is true we have lost the best helmsman, but I can steer. You brought me, Jason, because I am a fighter, but I am a son of Poseidon, used to boats, and I've been steering my father's ships since I was eight. Come, friends, lords, we cannot stay longer on this shore, or more of us will die. To join Idmon and Tiphys will not show our grief fittingly. They would want us to go on.'

'The quest is lost,' said Jason dully. 'Even if you can steer, we are weakened by grief, and I fear that we will never reach Aetes' city, nor gain the prizes we seek. No, we are doomed to die in this dreadful place, and the last man will have no memorial.'

'My lord,' I said quickly. 'Do not test us further with these despairing words. It's still light. Let Ancaeas try steering. We can die just as well in the sea as here, and that is a more suitable grave for Nauplios the net-caster's son.'

'And for Telamon,' said Telamon, hauling oarmate, Oileus, out of his sandy nest. 'Come along, old warrior. We aren't dead yet.'

And we weren't, either. Ancaeas was skilled and careful, and several of us relieved him at the rudders. Erginos and I managed it without actually sinking the ship, though Argos said that it would break a serpent's back to follow our trail, and Atalante revealed unexpected talents, as did Philammon, who had sailed an unoared boat on his initiation voyage for the god Ammon.

We passed the land of the Amazons and saw only a few shore guards, who watched us from each prominence to make sure that we kept sailing. Phineas had warned us about them, so we went on, although short of water, passing the metalworkers' island steaming with foul smoke, expecting landfall on the island of the Mossynoeci, who were reputed to be strange people who mated in the street and ate in strict privacy.

Then we heard a rush of wings.

'Look! The Stymphalian birds!' called Lynkeos, who had the keenest sight. 'There are thousands of them.' He pointed to a cloud of pale feathers, like a flight of arrows. They crossed the sea and their shadow followed them underneath. But we seemed to have lost much of our capacity for being afraid. The birds were swooping for us; after Herakles drove them off Lake

Stymphalos, they had come here. Atalante and the other archers bent their bows, but a million arrows could not have brought that flock down.

'Shields,' screamed Akastos, struck by a sudden idea. 'They're just birds, though all moved with one purpose. Put on your helmets and raise your shields above your heads, quickly, lock each shield together, make a shell like a tortoise. When they dive, we will all smite spears on the shields and raise the shout—to Ares, the god of war, the battle shout of the men of Achaea.'

I locked shields with my oarmate, and we sheltered under a bronze lid. When I heard the scrape of claws on the shining metal, I hammered with my spear, and all the crew screamed at the tops of our voices, 'Ares. Evoe! Ares. Evoe! Ares. Evoe!', the triple invocation. There was a massed, startled squawk and a scrabbling of talons, then the weight lifted and I peeped out to see the whole flock airborne and flying away.

Someone was still caring for us.

We picked up some more people that day. Three ragged men ran into our camp, skidding to a halt in the sand. The leader, with Oileus' spear at his breast, said in a cultured tone, 'I am Autolycus, this is Dileon and this Phlogius, lost from Herakles' expedition against the Amazons. Who are you?'

'Jason, son of Aison out of Iolkos, on quest for Colchis,' said Jason. Autolycus, ignoring the spear, took Jason's cup out of his hand and drank it in one draught.

'You may command us in anything,' he said. 'I swore that if anyone would give me real wine again, I would be his slave.'

'I do not need slaves,' said Jason, smiling at this lordly impudence, 'But I need three rowers, so sit down, comrades, and eat.'

So we had a full crew again and the rowing went a little easier the next day, as we passed river mouths, each producing its own strange currents. We avoided the territory of the Scyths, who were supposed to be very fierce. On an island which we thought to be uninhabited, I heard someone crying.

It was raining, a soft soaking rain which rendered vain every attempt to cook in the open and I was looking for an overhang among the sea-cliffs, because if I asked Argos to rig the spare sail as a shelter for my fire, I would have to listen to him grumbling, and I was tired of Argos' complaints. I was tired, too, of the company of my shipmates, and relished an excuse to get away from them for a little while.

I was carrying the firepot, our precious little pot of coals which we kept ever burning, a cauldron and a bundle of kindling. Melas was with me, bearing the salt, herbs and a string of fish. We found a cave and laid and lit a fire, and we were gutting fish and laying them in broth when I heard a child crying.

Somewhere in that cave there were people. I had grown so suspicious that I drew my sword, but Melas, more innocent than I, had already walked into the gloom and called, 'Is anyone there? We mean you no harm.'

It was the kind of innocence that could have got him filled with arrows and I pulled him back angrily, but there was no need to fear. Crawling forth came four men; the eldest perhaps eighteen, down to the youngest who might have been the same age as me. They were soaking wet, miserable and hungry, and even if Melas had not spoken, they would have been drawn out of their cave by the smell of food.

'I am Nauplios and this is Melas, men of Iolkos in Achaea,' I said.

They had been long in the sea, I thought, and I bade Melas give them fresh water, for too long in the salt wave can dessicate a castaway until he pisses blood and so dies. The eldest drank quickly, then the water flask passed speedily from the second to the third, who was supporting his little brother and dripping water into his mouth. The boy had stopped crying. His elder brother stroked his hair.

'We were shipwrecked,' he said. 'I am Cytisoros. These are my brothers, Argeos, Phrontis and Melanion. Two days we floated in the wreck of our boat, clinging to a great beam which had been the keel. We are suppliants and strangers, Nauplios, and belong to Zeus whom we beseech to inspire you to aid us. We have been unjustly exiled by King Aetes of Colchis. Chalkiope the princess is our mother, but our father was an Achaean. They called him Phrixos.'

'Then we are cousins,' I replied. 'We are on a quest to recover the Golden Fleece and the bones of your father, and Jason of the *Argo* will welcome you.'

They were handsome and learned, the sons of Phrixos, though totally unused to the sea. With the lost ones from Herakles' expedition, however, we had enough rowers. We passed the dark shores and the light, and thirteen days after we had found them shivering in their cave, Cytisoros stood up, holding onto a rope, and pointed.

'There, my lord,' he said. We looked. Another river mouth, but much wider than the previous ones. The tide was ebbing, and we could see the dark stain where the river water was flowing into the clean sea. A small wooden town stood at the river mouth, and there was a broad stone quay built on the shore.

'That is Poti,' said the son of Phrixos. 'Brothers, we have come home.'

The quest was not yet achieved, but we had come to the River Phasis, and Colchis lay just down that turbid flood.

◇◇◇

We were sitting in *Argo*, waiting for Jason to speak. All around us reeds rustled. Flocks of mosquitoes had smelt blood and had hummed down to feast. The river gurgled. Other than these noises, the silence was only broken by the slap and curse of Argonauts being eaten alive by stinging hordes of insects.

'What are those bundles hanging from those willow trees, and what is that revolting smell?' asked Telamon.

'They are the corpses of all men who die in the realm of Aetes, and that smell is Colchians rotting,' replied Philammon equably.

'You know, I don't think I like Colchis,' said Telamon after a short pause for thought. 'But if Phrixos is up there, it is going to be easier to carry him home. Someone has already put the bones in a bag for us.' He laughed, and some of the others chuckled.

Jason asked the sons of Phrixos, 'What is our best approach to your grandfather?'

'He's not likely to be pleased to see us,' said Cytisoros. 'He exiled us. However, we have been saved by divine intervention and we should be able to return. Aetes has a strange temper. He is whimsical. But he is old in kingship and subtle. It would be useless to try and cheat him of the fleece.'

'Then we shall not try to defraud him,' decided Jason.

'Well, what shall we do then?' objected Akastos. 'If we can't use tricks, we certainly can't use war. There aren't enough of us to assail the city with arms—not even if Herakles was still with us. And we are tired with travelling and some of us have been injured.'

'Yes. So we shall not use tricks and we shall not use war,' declared Jason.

'What shall we do?' asked Telamon, slapping another mosquito to death. His chest was blotched with bloodspots. He never missed.

'We'll go and ask him to give it to us,' said Jason.

We stared at him. Philammon cleared his throat.

'While that is an approach which, I frankly confess, never occurred to me, Jason, have you a plan of what to do when it doesn't work?'

Atalante nodded. Clytios agreed. Even Idas and Lynkeos protested in one voice, 'That's insane.'

'Has anyone a better idea?' challenged Jason.

'You mean to walk into a king's palace and say, "Greetings, Lord, I am Jason son of Aison, and I want you to give me the greatest treasure of your kingdom because I need it to regain my own father's kingdom of Iolkos?"' asked Nestor, his honey voice rendered a little acid by disbelief. Jason nodded.

'But he's likely to reply, "Greetings, Achaean, nice voyage, wonderful the way you managed to get through the Clashing Rocks, but why should I give you the Golden Fleece?"' protested Authalides.

'That is true,' said Jason. 'Tell me what else to do.'

'Can't we steal it?' asked Nestor. 'Where is it?'

'It's in a wood in the plain of Ares, and it's guarded by a giant serpent,' said Cytisoros.

Idas asked, 'How's giant?' and Cytisoros replied, 'Huge. And deadly. No thief had ever got out of there alive.'

'We have skilled warriors and brave men here,' said Ancaeas the Strong.

'No warrior, however strong and courageous, can get the better of the guardian. Except possibly Herakles. Did he really sail with you?'

'We lost him in Mysia,' said Atalante gloomily. We sat and watched Telamon kill mosquitoes for the time it takes to fill a water amphor from a well. Then Melanion whispered to his brothers, and the sons of Phrixos, for the first time, looked a little brighter.

'No one gets in and out of the grove alive,' repeated Cytisoros.

'You said that,' snapped Nestor.

'Except the priestesses of Hekate,' said Cytisoros, holding up a slim hand.

The well-chewed crew of Argo stared at this overexcited son of Phrixos without much interest.

'My mother's half sister, Medea, is a priestess of Hekate and has twined with the serpent—or so I heard. She is a full priestess now. We were friends once. She might help us.'

'Your mother's half sister? She's your aunt; and a dedicated priestess of the Dark Mother. She must be a virgin then, with no husband or children to hold her to ransom. Why should so venerable a maiden betray her father?' objected Atalante.

'She's the same age as Melanion here, and women have no sense of honour,' said Cytisoros.

Atalante hit back a retort. I thought this a pity. I did not like the sons of Phrixos much—they were lordly and insolent and did no work on board ship, expecting to be waited upon. I would have liked to hear what Artemis' maiden would have replied to this slander of her sex.

'So this aunt of yours might help us?' asked Jason.

'She might—she's fond of our mother, or she was. We haven't seen much of her, even before we were exiled. There we have another brother, you see, Aegialeus. He wants to marry Medea, because he wants the throne. But we used to go fishing together and I thought she liked me then,' said Melanion, doubtfully.

'If you come back to the city with us, then you can speak to your mother, and she can speak to this Medea,' said Jason. 'If she will help us, we might succeed. Or, of course, Aetes might just give me the fleece,' he added.

We all nodded. It was, of course, possible.

In the morning, blanketed in a thick, evil-smelling river mist, we walked into the city of Colchis, a stone-built city with paved streets. I walked beside Nestor. Authalides and Jason walked ahead. Behind us came Telamon, scratching his chest.

I did not think for one moment that this was going to work.

Chapter Seventeen

Medea

I was in Colchis and I did not want to be there.

After the broad plains and forests I had roamed with the Scyths, it seemed narrow and claustrophobic. It was, however, cleaner. The populace were washed and wearing white tunics and the streets did not smell like a Scythian encampment, of smoke, oils, dung, animals, sour milk and dressed leather.

But I had got used to the smells, and I missed them.

I was proud of myself for having returned, driving a Scythian wagon with some skill.

But Trioda seized me by the arm, and hissed 'Medea! Cover yourself!' and dragged me away before I could say farewell to Anemone and Iole. I had long forgotten that I was wearing breeches.

And after that I could not please her. Nothing I did was correct. My account of meeting Tyche in the shrine of Hekate Oldest was not well received.

'Tyche! It has been many years since she left us. Always was a wanderer, an unreliable priestess.'

'But she serves the oldest temple,' I protested.

'And the most remote. There is something wrong with a priestess who lives all alone and enjoys the company of Scyths.

They are barbarians. And I am told that you met the Achaean they call Herakles,' she accused.

'Yes, he saved all our lives. He came into the ring of attackers like a lightning bolt and killed them all.'

'And they say that you tended him.' She came closer to me. I smelled her; sour black dye and unwashed hair. Her eyes were boring into mine.

'Yes,' I said, leaning back, away from her vehemence. 'He was terribly injured.'

'Where was he laid?'

'In the queen's wagon. By her order,' I said, hoping that she would not ask where I slept. I had lain on the skins next to the hero most nights, to keep him warm and attend to his needs. Wounded men get very thirsty; they need fluids to replace the lost blood.

I remembered Herakles with affection, and Trioda must have seen something in my face, for she grabbed my upper arm, digging in her fingers, and hissed, 'Are you still a virgin?'

'Yes, Lady, of course,' I replied, shocked.

'That hero has legendary ability,' she snarled. 'Did he please you, once maiden of Hekate? Was his phallus huge? Did he hurt you? Even after all that riding with the barbarian Scyths, he must have made you bleed. Tell me, Medea. Tell me how you lay down under Herakles the hero. Tell me how you opened your thighs and your virgin mantle broke around the phallus of the Achaean.'

'Mistress, you are hurting me,' I protested. She wasn't just hurting me, she was frightening me. 'I never lay with any man, I swear by the Dark Mother, may she strike me dead this moment if I even looked at a man with lust. Test me as you like, I am virgin. And you might trust me, Mistress. Have I ever shown signs of such blasphemy?'

Her grip did not relax. 'I will test you. He raped the fifty daughters of a king in one night, do you know that, Medea?'

'I don't know what he did to anyone else, but he was far too badly hurt to even think about touching me. He had five arrows in him,' I said coldly. 'But give me the draught and you will see.'

She compounded the potion. I did not speak to her. Certain combinations of herbs used by the priestesses of Hekate produce instant nausea in a woman who is not a virgin, while children can drink them freely. That is why a woman's bodily state must be ascertained before some medicines are administered. I waited, deeply affronted. I was comforted by the thought of the apology she would have to make when I showed no sign of vomiting.

I drank the concoction. It tasted slightly sweet and had a scent like cut grass. Trioda sat down in her chair, and I sat down on the hearth with the dogs and we waited.

Time went on. The marketplace emptied and then filled again. Only when the sun was sinking and I showed no sign of internal distress whatsoever did my mistress say grudgingly, 'Well, perhaps it was not complete penetration.' No apology. She did not say, 'Medea, I was wrong.'

'It was not anything!' I cried. She glared at me.

'Sit down again, Acolyte,' she ordered.

'I am a priestess,' I replied, and walked to the door. I would not stay with this woman any longer. Quite suddenly, I hated her. Her suspicions of unchastity were base and her evil opinion of me entirely unfounded. She should have known me better than that. I stalked out into the street and went through the city to the Scythian encampment. It was late summer.

The mists were rising from the river. I had neglected to apply the lotion of sun daisies and midges hummed up in clouds around me as I walked. My mood was not improved when Anemone, seeing my angry face, laughed, 'Here is our priestess, Iole; and Trioda has scolded her roundly for enjoying the barbarian company of Scythian women.'

'Anemone, did you ever see me even look kindly on a man?' I demanded, sitting down on the platform between the empty shafts.

'No,' she replied promptly. 'But my word would not be good enough for Trioda. She's always been black and bitter, ever since Aetes rejected her advances and she joined the sisterhood out of spite.'

'What?' I gasped. Iole gave a brimming cup into my hands and kissed my cheek. I wondered how I would manage without the matter-of-fact affection which was demonstrated amongst these barbarians. I began, also, to wonder what there was to be said for civilisation, if it meant suspicion and false accusations, midges, river mist and plots. Anemone settled down for a cosy gossip.

'Yes, she wanted the king—he was a prince then, you understand. They say she was a well-looking woman, Trioda, when she was young and still combed her hair. But Aetes knew even then that his seed was lethal. He would not risk her—or so she said—and refused the offered gift of her body. And if she could not be queen she would be a priestess, and so Hekate gained what the king lost. A common story. Does she know you are here?'

'I don't care if she knows or does not know,' I mumbled into the kermiss. 'She accused me of lying with Herakles. And when I swore this was not true, she gave me the draught to test me. I have deserved better of her than that.'

'So you have, but you will not get any better, I fear. But I have some news, Medea. Aegialeus is out of favour, and Aetes has invited the sons of Phrixos back.'

'Someone has dared accuse Aegialeus of treason?' I was amazed.

'No, but he lost his temper and made a scene in the council chamber—or so I am told. He said to Aetes that he had reigned too long, that it was time for a new king to take Colchis, one who was fertile and strong. He said that the fact that Eidyia has not conceived showed that the king's seed was feeble, like his limbs.'

'He said that?' I choked on a mouthful and Iole patted my back.

'He said more, but my informant didn't hear what it was. The king went purple and fell into another fit. When he was brought to himself, he ordered his son out of his presence.'

'So Aegialeus is not an immediate threat, that is good,' I said dully, trying to feel pleased. 'What happened next?'

Anemone was not smiling. 'Then Eupolis, who likes Chalkiope your sister, put in a word about the sons of Phrixos, and the king has sent men out to find them, rescinding their sentence of exile.

'But there is bad news, Medea. I'm sorry to have to tell you. They found the wreckage of their ship, washed up in Scythian territory. Even if they drifted ashore and were not drowned, there is a fair chance that...'

'The Androphagi captured them,' I finished, shivering as I recalled the scarlet, naked heads and the pointed teeth, and how close we had come to both massacre and cannibal feast. Then I was struck with a memory of fishing in the Phasis with Melanion of the curly hair and the brown eyes. He had been merry and deft, extracting hooks for me. I had liked him. And now he and his brothers were dead either in the sea or on land, spitted and roasted by the savages. It was too much for my already lacerated feelings.

I wept, and Iole hugged me and gave me more kermiss.

I stayed with the Scythians that night. They were leaving in the morning, going west toward the mountains. They would be back in autumn, but I did not know if I would see them again. The dogs lay with me, as they always had, one on either side, and we were at least warm and comfortable, as I had been with the Scyths from the first time I had woken in Anemone's wagon.

I climbed out and sat on the driver's seat just after dawn. The sun was rising through mist, like a silver coin, cool and distant, though later in the day Ammon would be too bright for mortal eyes, lord of the sky. I was speaking the prayers to Selene which greet the end of her reign when Kore and Scylla both leapt to their feet and jumped down. I followed them. They were excited, as they would have been to see someone they had missed. I thought resentfully that Trioda was coming for me, and resolved not to be dragged off a wagon again and hauled away to be scolded like a child.

Then through the mist I saw nine men come walking. I thought that they were ghosts. Spirits haunt the marsh, where the men of Colchis hang in their cocoons. We see them often. I raised both hands in the warding gesture which tells them that such a place is not for them, for I did not want them to come in among the wagons. The Scythians do not like spirits, and their exorcising spells are strong. Colchian ghosts are neutral, mindlessly repeating the acts of their natural lives, until they are either sent away or they wear out with the passing of the years. Many people had seen Phrixos, the Achaean, in his bronze armour, fighting the air with his sword. One woman at least had fainted and miscarried at the sight of an armed warrior gleaming in bronze, rushing upon her through the night, flourishing a weapon. He had become such a nuisance that the priestesses had moved his bones to hang from the trees of the sacred grove, where the guardian could also take care that the spirit caused no trouble.

Kore and Scylla always reacted badly to phantoms, so much so that I could not take them with me on nights when the dead were walking. They howled and bristled, despite being experienced temple hounds. Halfway through my invocation, I realised that not only were their ears down and their hackles flat, but they were bouncing up and down in excitement and wagging their tails.

Then I looked more closely at the approaching men, and recognised a curly head of hair and a dark, snub-nosed countenance.

'Melanion!' I screamed, and he stopped, halting the others.

'Princess,' he called. I jumped down from my perch and ran to the path. Kore and Scylla bounded up to Melanion, licked him thoroughly, then leapt for a tall, golden-haired foreigner as though he was the person they had always wanted to meet. They licked his face while he patted their smooth black sides and laughed.

'Melanion, they just told me that you were dead!' I exclaimed. He grinned his old grin at me and put out his hand. I took it. He was warm, had a pulse and appeared to be breathing. He was definitely not a ghost.

Neither were his brothers. Cytisoros, Argeos and Phrontis bowed, and I returned the courtesy.

'You have all four been reprieved from sentence of exile,' I told Cytisoros. 'Aegialeus behaved very badly in council, telling the king that he should give him the throne, and he has been banished from Aetes' sight. The Colchians have been looking for you, but reported that your ship was wrecked and you cast away, somewhere in Scythian land. I thought that you were spirits.'

'We washed up on an island,' said Cytisoros. 'There we were rescued by these noble lords of Achaea. This is Jason, son of Aison of Iolkos; and with him the herald Authalides; Nestor Honey-Voiced; Nauplios, son of Dictys; and Telamon, the hero.'

I bowed. Kore and Scylla were still slobbering over the tall one—Jason, son of Aison. The names meant nothing to me. He was slim, wearing the Achaean tunic and a cloak which I knew was called a chlamys. This left his muscular legs bare. He was shapely, smooth and beautiful. I had never seen a man so fair. His hair spilled down his back, bright as gold thread, and the eyes he turned on me were as blue as the sky. He had been at some hard labour; his hands were blistered.

All of the strangers had mosquito bites marking all their bare skin. The huge one, Telamon the hero, who stood almost double my height, was scratching his torso and looking acutely uncomfortable.

'Take them to the king, Cytisoros,' I advised, 'before they are bitten raw. I believe that he will be pleased to see you.'

'Will you come and see us dine, most beautiful of princesses?' asked the stranger, Jason.

'No, Lord, I may not dine with the king,' I replied, laughing at the idea. 'No women will be at his table.'

I could not take my eyes off Jason. When he shifted his gaze, his eyes were as grey as the mist. But when he looked directly at me, as now, far more directly than I had ever been looked at before, his eyes were as blue as gentians. There was something compelling about him. When he reached out a hand to touch mine, I felt a thump, as though someone had hit me hard in the solar plexus, where the soul resides. Not an arrow such as the Achaean god Eros is reputed to fire, not a sharp pain. Just a thud, which made me clutch my middle.

I evaded contact with him, for no unrelated man may touch a priestess of Hekate, but I said, 'I will come and see your reunion with my sister, Chalkiope, who will be beside herself with joy. Go to the palace, Lords,' I said, retreating in confusion. 'I will see you again.'

I went back to the wagon. Kore and Scylla left the fascinating stranger with reluctance, but they came when I called them. I woke Anemone by poking my head through the curtains and calling, 'The sons of Phrixos have come home, bringing some Achaeans with them, I have to go to the palace.'

'Hmm?' she mumbled. 'Go with your goddess, Scythling.' This was a standard farewell amongst the Scyths. Then she woke fully and looked at me.

She sat up and put both hands on my shoulders.

'We leave today, but you will know where to find us, Princess,' she said solemnly. 'With you you take my blessing, Medea. Do not forget that. And do not forget that if you ever wish to leave your city, you can travel with the Sauromatae. We will give you a wagon, Scythling, and a husband if you can defeat a Pardalatos.'

'I'm a priestess, I'm a maiden, why are you saying this to me?' I asked, anxious to get to Aetes' palace and watch the reception of the sons of Phrixos.

She smiled and said, 'I know, Medea. But things can change and nothing remains the same in the world. Swear that you will remember what I have said.'

'I give you my word,' I said.

She gave me the Scythian double kiss, and woke Iole to kiss me also. Then I was free to leap down and run unnoticed through the mist to the back gate of Aetes' palace, where any women could come and go, as we could not enter through the front. I had momentarily forgotten that I was a priestess of Hekate, and woman, which was odd. I had never forgotten that before. It was a fundamental fact of my life.

I heard a flurry of activity as I came into the courtyard. Three priests of Ammon were skinning and cutting up a bull's carcass, having already made their sacrifice of the outer parts of the thighs, wrapped in fat, to their god. The king was entitled to the rest. The baker's ovens were all red-hot. I could feel the heat from three paces away, and smell both cooking bread and the sour scent of dough being mixed. I avoided a boy carrying a platter piled high with cooked fish, and another with a string of fresh-caught ones. Other slaves were chopping fruit, making sauces, pouring wine, melting honey, cutting cheese and swearing, in about equal proportions. The noise was remarkable.

'What is happening?' I asked a slave woman, who was standing in the middle of the courtyard with an armful of linen towels.

'Oh, Princess, the sons of Phrixos have returned from exile. They were shipwrecked, imagine!' She clutched the towels to her bosom. 'And they have brought some well-looking foreigners, their rescuers, and the king has ordered that they be bathed and tended and then feasted. Go in to your sister, Lady, she was asking for you. Also the priestess Trioda has been here, but we could give her no news of you.'

That was all to the good. I did not want to see Trioda. I remembered Tyche saying that Hekate wants service as a free gift, not as an escape. Trioda had used Hekate as her escape. I was disgusted, and questioned all that she had taught me. How could I have utterly believed in a woman who had herself once wished to be other than a maiden?

Meanwhile, I was being pushed by the crowd toward the entrance to the women's quarters. I would go and visit my sister Chalkiope, whom I had not seen since I went with the Scyths.

And perhaps I might see the stranger, Jason, again. I could not drag my thoughts away from him, though there was no reason why he should remember me. He had called me beautiful, but that was probably a common Achaean courtesy.

I told myself firmly that it meant nothing at all, and fought my way through the preparations for the feast to Chalkiope's chamber.

I almost did not recognise her, she was so full of joy. She was shining. She had Melanion in her arms and the others sitting at her feet, and I could feel her joy from a distance, as I had felt the baker's ovens. She was laughing—I had seldom heard Chalkiope laugh—and weeping, and I had seldom seen her weep.

'Oh, my dears, oh, my loves, my darlings,' she was saying. 'How could you have left me, and oh, the salt sea and the cave, my little Melanion!' Melanion, looking exquisitely embarrassed, embraced his mother and kissed her cheek.

'Oh, Medea, look,' she cried to me, 'I have my children again. The king has relented and the sea has loosed her grip on them. No woman was as fortunate as I,' and she laughed again.

'I rejoice with you,' I told her, sitting on her chair. The sons of Phrixos were tall men and they overfilled the small room. 'They have brought some Achaeans with them. Who are they?'

'Trioda sent you to find out, doubtless,' she commented.

'No, I came on my own. I am a priestess now, sister.'

'So you are, little Medea, and shalt be answered,' said my sister dotingly. 'Cytisoros, talk to your aunt. Melanion, tell me again how you survived the wreck.'

While Melanion spoke about the dreadful strength of the sea and how they had clung to the keel, Cytisoros said to me, 'They are the crew of a ship called *Argo*, which means swift.'

This was something I knew, but I kept silent. If one interrupted Cytisoros he took ages to get back to the subject.

'They have come on quest, from the Aegean to the Propontis to the Bosporus and through the Clashing Rocks—they actually braved Scylla and Carybdid, sister Medea!—to the Euxine Sea, to retrieve the bones of my father, Phrixos.'

'Why do they want the bones of a dead man?' I asked. Achaean customs were obviously strange, though probably not stranger than Scythian.

'Because he's haunting them, saying that he needs to be buried in the earth of his home in Iolkos in Achaea.'

'Buried? A *man*, buried in the womb of the Mother? They're inviting a plague,' I objected. Cytisoros shrugged. 'And they have a request for Aetes,' he added mysteriously, 'of which I may not yet speak.'

I did not enquire further—another thing about the eldest
son of Phrixos was his complete integrity. It would have been of
no use to attempt to tease the secret from Cytisoros. He would
tell me when he could. I asked, 'What do you make of them,
these Achaeans?'

'They are brave and skilled at sea,' he replied. 'They travelled
for a while with Herakles, they say. I thought that he was a story,
not a real man.'

'He's certainly a real man,' I said, warming to the Argonauts.
'I met him when he saved the Sauromatae from massacre by the
Androphagi. He was gravely wounded, but he recovered.'

'Your skill is well known,' said Cytisoros politely.

'No, it wasn't really my skill, he heals like a beast and he's
stronger than any patient I ever had before. And if he is not in
battle fury, he's gentle and kind. These must be the royal children
of Iolkos, then. He told me about them.'

'Yes, Jason is the son of Aison, the rightful king.'

'Tell me of this Jason,' I said, trying to suppress my eagerness. I did not know why the sound of that name was sweet in
my ear, but it was.

'He is the leader of a group of heroes who have passed
unimaginable perils to get here,' interrupted Argeos eagerly.
'Their ship is in the reeds at Poti with the rest of the crew.
Telamon is a mighty man, but there are two others his match
on board: Ancaeas and Oileus.'

My interest in strong men was minimal, and I left the sons
of Phrixos with their mother as I was called into the courtyard
by an urgent voice.

'Lady,' said a boy, plucking at my sleeve.

'Achaean?' I replied.

'You make a lotion, they say, which can repel the mosquitoes. The crew of *Argo* lie in their ship in the reeds, and they are
unused to Colchian insects. Can you make some of your lotion
to relieve the sufferings of my shipmates?'

'Certainly. I shall go and do so. I have forgotten your name,
though, Lord,' I said.

'I am Nauplios, the net-caster's son, lady Medea. I deserve no honorific.'

I liked his modesty. He was good-looking, though much bitten, and he had a shy and charming smile. I gathered up my robes and tiptoed toward the gate through the chaos of shouting bakers and cursing cooks and over-anxious bath slaves, and stopped in my tracks as though Hekate had struck me dead.

Standing naked before me was the Achaean, Jason, and he was the most beautiful man I had ever seen. Slaves were sluicing hot water over his shoulders, to clean off the grime before he was conducted into the bathing chamber to soak in a bath of sweet herbs. There was no reason why he should not stand naked in the king's courtyard—after all, he was a guest, and slaves have no modesty to outrage. He could not have known that a maiden priestess of the Dark Mother would be there to be transfixed by his beauty.

He was like a statue. I let my gaze slide over his wide shoulders, his flat belly, the scribble of hair at his loins, catching the late sunlight and winking golden. I saw that part which a common maiden must never name—the phallus, site of manhood and holder of seed. I saw the neat square buttocks as he twisted, laughing, under the deluge of water and soapy herbs. I saw the ordered propriety of muscle which was his back. And I saw his face, eyes shut, blissful, his chin tipped up to enjoy the water, his hair clinging to his skin, long nose and high cheekbones, utterly alien, utterly captivating.

Then I felt a hard blow across my breast and neck and Trioda was shrieking at me like a black bird, shrieking, 'Traitor! Traitor to the Mother!'

I swung my fist and hit her. The Scythians had trained me in close fighting. I punched her in the belly so that she was doubled over and out of breath.

She staggered back a pace and I followed up the advantage. I have never been so angry or so ashamed. She had caught me. Trioda of all people had caught me staring fascinated at a naked man, and she already thought me fallen and accursed. Well, I might just be fallen and accursed at that. I forced her out of the palace into the street, pinning her with my eyes. When we were in the street, I said through my teeth, 'You will never strike me again, priestess. Do you understand? I am no longer your acolyte and I will not be beaten.'

'Nor are you a priestess of the Mother, Scythian,' she screamed.

'You tested me yourself,' I screamed back. 'I am chaste and virgin. I am a priestess of the Three-Headed One.'

'You were staring at him, at the Achaean.' She lowered her voice a little. 'I saw your eyes riveted to him, to the male body, the phallus.'

'And if you'd let me see one before, perhaps the sight would not be so strange to me.' I seemed unable to regain control of my voice. I was still shouting. 'Leave me, Trioda. You think me unworthy to be a priestess. You wanted to lie with my father, and came to Hekate when he refused you. I believe that you also are unworthy.'

She shrieked and clawed for my arm, but I raised a hand in warning. I was certainly not going to be beaten again, not by this woman who had lusted for my father and had just struck me in the sight of foreigners. I had borne enough bruises from Trioda's hands, and I was resolved not to bear any more.

She hissed, 'Be accursed.' Before I could say anything to placate her, she made the signs in the air and muttered the beginnings of the exorcism ceremony which casts out ghosts and unworthy priestesses.

'No,' I said, horrified. I had never imagined that Trioda would cast me off if I displeased her. And I had not done anything to disqualify myself from the priesthood.

'Yes!' she said.

I stood in the street as my mistress completed the ceremony which made me accursed in the eyes of the sisterhood, and cast me out of the worship of Hekate, the Dark Mother, She Who Meets.

When she had finished, she spat at my feet and went away in a flutter of black garments, like a carrion bird leaving the well-picked bones of a dead beast because there is not even a scrap of meat left upon them.

And I did not know what to do or say, so I went to the temple. I was not struck by lightning as I went in, so I compounded the insect lotion which the Achaean Nauplios had asked of me. That was my last task for Hekate, promised before I had been expelled.

Kore and Scylla, servants of the Black Bitch, who no longer belonged to me, did not appear to have changed their allegiance, and accompanied me back to the palace.

I did not, of course, attend the feast, but I sat in Chalkiope's rooms and listened to the noises. Like all the women, we picked over the remains of the dishes as they were brought out. Our leftovers went to the slaves. If I sat by a certain window, I knew, I could hear without being seen, so I took a plate of broken bread and rich sauces—sometimes I even found a piece of meat or fish—and sat down in the embrasure.

Someone was addressing the king. It was a strong voice, husky, with a foreign accent. I peeped. I would have been executed if I had been caught, for I was no longer a priestess of Hekate, and no woman can look into a men's feast and live. However, no one but Trioda knew I was disgraced, so it was a reasonable risk. And I had to see him, this Jason who would not leave my mind.

'Lord, I have come for the Golden Fleece,' he said simply.

Aetes leapt to his feet and roared at the sons of Phrixos, 'What have you brought to my house? Pirates and thieves!'

They quailed, and Jason moved so that he stood between the sons of Phrixos and the king's wrath.

'Lord, if I was a pirate or a thief, I would not be asking in courtesy. I would have assailed you with war or attempted to steal the fleece. Instead, I am asking for you to demonstrate your royalty by giving it to me. I need it, Lord, to gain my kingdom, to prove my right to my father's realm of Iolkos. I have brought a ship full of heroes on an unprecedented voyage to gain it. For the fleece, I am willing to do anything. Can I fight for you against your enemies? Can I make you a present of gold or any other thing which can be found in the world? Is there a perilous task which you would have me do?'

He was tall and proud, the Achaean, as he stood fearlessly before Aetes my father and put this request. The court was utterly silent. Eupolis had frozen, with a chicken leg raised in the air, dripping with wine sauce onto his snow white tunic. No one knew how the lord of Colchis would react. He might laugh. He might fall into a fit and order Jason's immediate execution.

I thought this and wondered why my stomach dropped. What was happening to me? He was an Achaean and a foreigner and I had more urgent things to worry about—the fact, for instance, that I had just been flung out of the sisterhood of Hekate.

But I could not move from the window until I found out what happened to the long-haired stranger.

'Very well,' said Aetes quietly. 'I will give you a task. If you perform it I will give you both the bones of the stranger, Phrixos, and the Golden Fleece, treasure of Colchis. If you can plough a field with my oxen in yoke, I will do so, and on that you have my word.'

Jason flushed with delight, a delicate rose tinting his skin. I wanted to scream out that he should not accept this task, that these were the bronze-hoofed cattle of the king, which were man-killers for anyone who approached them unprepared.

But he accepted, of course.

And as I left to find a place to sleep amongst the women slaves—for I could not go back to the temple of Hekate which had been my home for all of my life—I resolved that Jason should succeed, if by any skill of mine I could assist him. My father meant to cheat him, meant the bulls to kill him. It was not a fair task.

I lay down on a slave's pallet near the kitchen, with Kore and Scylla beside me, and wished that I had my time again, so that I should never have seen the stranger or quarrelled with Trioda, but at the same time I blessed the day which had given me sight of Jason.

Chapter Eighteen

Nauplios

She was completely beautiful and completely alien, Medea, the priestess of Hekate. Jason was instantly struck with her; so was I. Such a maiden, of course, is not to be thought of in any carnal way, and there was an untouchable quality about her. But as she ran out of the mist toward us, calling the name of the youngest son Phrixos, she seemed unearthly. She was small, a head shorter than I, and I was not tall. She was as slim and fast as a bird, with a bird's delicate bones, revealed for a moment as her speed made her sable draperies fill and billow behind her like a sail. Her hair was as dark as ink and perfectly straight, hanging below her waist in one long, silky curtain, fluid and light-reflecting. Her eyes were very dark and her skin the same olive as the sons of Phrixos, who had inherited none of their father's Achaean colouring.

But the hand which tested Melanion's pulse was deft, strong, and roughened by some hard labour. In fact, I would have said she was a rider. This princess and priestess had clearly not been spending her time like an Achaean woman, out of the sun and spinning in her mother's house.

Her voice was fast, clear and precise, switching from Colchian to Achaean and back without difficulty. She rattled her words out very quickly, like a handful of pebbles dropping onto a shield.

Then she was gone.

We went to the palace and were greeted with acclaim, and preparations for the feast began at once. I stopped the Princess Medea in the courtyard and asked her for some of her insect-defying lotion, and she smiled at me. The smile made me feel quite lightheaded. Her teeth were white and her mouth was red. I thought it a great pity that such a beautiful maiden, and the daughter of a king as well, should remain virgin all her life for the service of the Crone, but it was not my business to say or think such a thing, and I got permission to walk back to *Argo* where she was moored in the reeds, taking a lot of food and wine and the lotion with me.

The crew of the ship doused themselves in the sun daisy infusion, which brought instant relief, not only from further attack but from the intolerable itching, which had driven Oileus to plaster himself with mud so that Meleagros called him a shipping hazard and offered to plant him in the reeds as a mooring rock, and Atalante to threaten either homicide or suicide. She was about to take an axe to Idas, who had challenged her to make very small arrows and shoot all the mosquitoes—through the heart, he insisted.

Once they had stopped scratching, the crew sat down to demolish the feast. It had taken me and two slaves to carry the provisions along that dark and haunted path, and when a damp Oileus demanded more wine I refused to go back for it. I had heard strange noises, whispering and rustling, which the slaves said were the ghosts of dead Colchians, and I had no reason to think that they were lying to scare the foreigner, for they, also, were frightened.

Philammon began to play the long, long tale of our voyage, to which he had added another two verses of heart-felt complaint on the subject of Colchian midges, and Oileus and Perithous went back to Colchis for more supplies.

They arrived out of breath after what must have been a very fast trip. They would not tell us what they had seen on the way, but they did not demand that anyone else make the journey when they had finished the new jugs of wine.

Then we slept, and Jason returned to us with the dawn.

He had agreed to plough with the king's bulls as the price of the Golden Fleece and the bones of Phrixos. He had not, at any time, any idea of what these monsters were. Aetes was playing with us. He had given my lord an impossible task. No human could tame the bulls, said the Colchian slaves. Only once a year were they yoked and used for ploughing the sacred furrow, and no man but the anointed king of Iolkos could handle them. They were twice the size of ordinary cattle. Their horns were sheathed in bronze, as were their hoofs, and they were trained to gore and trample any profane man who approached them.

Jason sat, sunk in gloom. Occasionally someone would offer a suggestion.

'Philammon, can you sing them to sleep?' asked Atalante.

'My master Orpheus could,' he replied regretfully. 'But I do not have that skill.'

There was another heavy silence.

'I say we fight,' said Oileus, and Telamon nodded agreement.

'You always say that,' snarled Clytios. 'There aren't enough of us.'

'Seven men took Thebes,' objected Telamon.

'Seven armies took Thebes,' replied Authalides irritably.

We sat in silence again.

'I shall attempt it,' said Jason. 'I can only fail. You stay here. Be ready to sail, whatever happens. If I win and get the fleece, then that is well. If the bulls kill me, I would not have any of you share my fate.'

We all protested, but he was right. Powerful deities protected Jason, most especially Hera, wife of Zeus. She had spoken when *Argo* was launched. Someone had thrust the ship through the Clashing Rocks. I had a hopeful thought.

'Phineas said that you would succeed,' I offered. 'So did Idmon, when *Argo* was being built, do you remember?'

'Yes,' said several voices.

'That is true,' said Akastos. 'Idmon foresaw that Jason would return with the Golden Fleece.'

'And he was a true prophet, even to the foreseeing of his own death,' agreed Ancaeas.

'And the old man of the island, as you say, Nauplios. Phineas said that I would succeed, a man of truth, a man of such probity that the gods cursed him for it. Well, if I am fated to succeed, I cannot fail no matter what I do. Today I face the bulls. And I will either win or lose,' said Jason. 'It is as Destiny decides.'

Full of misgiving, but saying nothing—there did not seem to be anything more to say—we dressed him for this combat, not in armour, but in a tunic and heavy boots; and we cast a short cloak around him. He looked kingly, indeed, with his hair arrayed on his shoulders. Then he walked alone, as he insisted, to the bulls' field which lay close to the reed bed in which our ship was concealed.

As soon as his straight back had vanished, Atalante said to me, 'Go, Nauplios, follow him. Do not let him see you. But we need to know what happens, whether we should flee or rejoice. Also, you are his oldest friend, and the Achaeans say that a man's back is bare indeed if it is brotherless.'

I looked around the ship. All of the crew were in agreement. It was the first time I had ever seen that happen on the whole voyage. So I took up my dark cloak and followed my lord to the flat space next to the sacred grove. There a plough made of some strange silvery metal—surely not even Colchis, legendary in wealth, would make a plough out of solid silver—lay with yoke and reins on the ground.

Jason halted in a coppice, and I came up behind him carefully. I had watched Atalante and Clytios, and I moved with little noise, stopping whenever Jason stopped. I did not think he knew I was there.

Someone else was in that clump of trees. Someone flitted past me, a wood crafty maiden, moving so lightly that her feet scarcely stirred the leaves. She halted, poised, looking into my face. I gestured toward Jason's back, and she smiled that smile again and went on, leaving me to lean against a trunk to regain my breath.

'Achaean,' she whispered. Jason left off contemplating the soggy expanse of earth and turned swiftly, his hands going to his sword.

'Princess,' he said, astonished.

'My father is unjust, setting you an impossible task,' she said, in her quick, decisive voice. 'Strip and smear this ointment all over your body, then don your tunic again.' She held out a little pot made of white clay, sealed with three seals.

Jason stared at her suspiciously, and her voice sharpened. Her eyes would have bored holes in trees. 'Hurry!' she said. 'They are herding the bulls this way. I have broken my oath and my allegiance and made myself traitor to my family by venturing here. I have put my maiden repute in peril as well, and I do not have time to convince you of my skill. In the name of the Black Mother, do as I order or you will die.'

Jason unpinned the brooch on each shoulder and let the chiton fall. I heard the maiden gasp as she looked at him, but she recovered her wits quickly.

He stood holding the pot, astonished, unmoving, until she took it out of his hand and began applying the ointment to his skin in quick, deft strokes, covering his body from the soles of his feet to the crown of his head. Her hands did not shake as she anointed his intimate part, although I could have sworn she had never touched a man before. Fortunately for her modesty, her touch did not arouse any passion in my lord.

'They will bring the bulls here,' she instructed. 'They are perfectly matched, because they are twins. Have you ploughed before?' Jason inclined his head, still dumbfounded. The priestess continued, 'Do not make sudden movements, do not startle them, and they will be tame and willing under your hands. There. I can hear them.'

An ear-splitting bellow announced that the bronze-hoofed, man-killing beasts were being herded by many men and dogs into the field. It was bounded on one side by the River Phasis, on the east and west by the forest, and toward Colchis by a wooden barrier which was being drawn up behind them.

The bulls were monstrous. I thought that I knew cattle, but these had heads the size of *Argo's* bow-post and were the general size and shape of a small boat. They tossed their heads, crowned with metal horns, and pawed the ground with their shining hoofs, cutting deep gouges in the clay. Those hoofs must have been as sharp as bronze razors. Jason took a deep breath and walked out into the field.

He sloshed through the mud. The surrounding countryside was dry, so I assumed that there was some underground soak in the sacred meadow which kept it perpetually wet. Jason seemed tiny against the bulk of the monsters, two huge red and white bulls as tall as horses. The men of Colchis were watching silently. I heard no jeers, as might have been expected from an Achaean audience.

The bulls saw him coming and wheeled together, lowering their horns and bellowing a challenge. I saw my lord glance around, as though looking for a place to run, but he was a long, slippery distance from any refuge. He stopped, allowing the bulls to approach him.

Standing next to me in the coppice, the priestess Medea, sworn virgin as she was, leaned back against me as though I was a tree, and I put my arm around her as I would my own sister. She accepted this embrace.

She felt very good in my arms. She was not brittle, as her delicacy of bone suggested. She felt warm and rounded as my arm encircled her waist. She was so distracting that I almost forgot to watch as the bulls stamped toward Jason, utterly alone in the middle of a field of mud.

When they were perhaps ten paces away from him, they both stopped and sniffed. I felt the Princess Medea vibrate in my clasp like a lyre when the wind blows through the strings. She was completely alert. She began to sing just under her breath, a prayer, perhaps, in a language I did not know, but which was all gutturals and liquid sounds, like the song of a strange bird.

The bulls walked to Jason and shoved their muzzles into his hands, almost snuffling him off his feet. Medea and I relaxed a little. The ointment had worked.

Now to see if Jason, son of Aison, who had spent most of his life with centaurs who grew no grain, could remember how to plough a field.

He managed to yoke the bulls without making more than three or four mistakes with the reins and harness. Then he walked back five paces, took the strain off the plough, and yelled, 'On!' and the great bulls of Colchis moved forward at his order.

Down the field to the river, up the field to the gate and down again. I knew that my lord was strong, but he was not used to such labour. I was close enough to see Aetes' face. It was set into lines of fury, and my heart misgave me.

'Lady, your father will not give Jason the Golden Fleece, will he?' I asked softly.

'He has sworn, and I have not known him break his word,' she said, never taking her eyes off the field, where more than two thirds of the mud had been cut into wavering furrows.

I would not have liked to sow barley into Jason's seedbeds, but the task was to plough the field, not to plough it well. And my lord Jason, son of Aison, was accomplishing this task. He was tired, but not yet faltering, when he turned the last corner and was approaching the gate again, urging the beasts on with his voice to one last effort.

At this moment Lynkeos and Idas came creeping through the wood, gaped briefly at the sight of Nauplios embracing a priestess in the black robes of Hekate.

'We've had word that Colchis means to play us false,' Idas said. 'Even now an army is massing to attack us—and that at least is true, we've seen them. Even if Jason completes this task, we are lost.'

'He is not lost yet,' snapped the maiden, removing herself from my arms. 'How long will it take for you to gather your crew to defend the ship?'

'Lady, they are already there, except for we three and Jason,' replied Lynkeos.

'I am reluctant to believe that my father means to betray a guest, one who has eaten with him—that is a sacred bond in Colchis. But I am no longer certain of anything. It is all confused which once was secure.' She wrung her hands and I longed to comfort her. 'See, your lord is completing the last furrow. Let us see what the king says.'

We watched from the shadow of the little wood. Jason's bulls finished the last furrow. He lifted the yoke from their sweating backs, patting them. Then, with one arm round the neck of each sacred bull, he said to the king, 'The task is accomplished, my lord of Colchis, and I claim the bones of Phrixos and the Golden Fleece.'

The king rose from his chair of state and smiled. 'I will give them both to you,' he said loudly, and gave a signal. Three warriors seized Jason and bound his hands behind his back.

'Treachery,' said Lynkeos.

'It is proved,' said the maiden in a strange, distant voice.

The king gave an order that we did not hear, and the men moved the fence, allowing the sacred bulls to walk through. The cattle herders came with their dogs to escort the sacred bulls to their own place, and they brought Jason, who was not struggling, across the furrows.

The princess gasped and said, 'They are pushing him into the sacred grove. Nauplios, stay with me. You, Achaeans, gather all the Argonauts and go back to the ship. Only I can rescue your lord, and I may fail. The guardian is Ophis Megale, the great serpent, and she is unpredictable. She may not remember me. Take my hounds. Scylla, Kore, go with the Achaeans and I will come soon or not at all.'

She spoke to two perfectly black dogs which stood almost waist high on the small princess. They did not like it, but they were obedient. They followed as Lynkeos and Idas crept back through the trees toward the reeds.

The least I could do was to be as obedient as the animals. 'What shall I do, Lady, to help you?' I asked.

'I have the infusion with me. I feared this might happen, but I need milk. You will find goats in the field on the other side of this wood. Fill a large dish with milk, and meet me at the sacred grove, where there is a broken, burned tree. Nearer the river, that way. I have preparations of my own to make, Nauplios. If you love your lord, hurry!' She shoved me in the direction of the field, and I ran.

I know nothing of ploughing, but I do know about goats. I found a leather bucket hung on a well coping, and called over a mother goat with the goatherd's calling tune. Luckily the Colchians used it too, and I rewarded the patient lady with a handful of sweet grass as I milked her quickly. The bucket was half full of warm, chalky milk when I carried it away, skirting the dark forest until I came to a burned stump and heard someone hiss, 'In here!'

A naked woman wearing a snakeskin cloak held out her hand for the bucket. She poured into it a flask of some dark fluid, tasted, and added a whole pot of honey, stirring with her hand until the brew was sweet enough.

I could not take my eyes off the Princess Medea, priestess of Hekate.

She was smeared with oil, or perhaps serpent fat. Her brown skin shone, and light fell over her contours; shoulder, breast, belly and hip, and her hair like shadow around her thighs. The snakeskin wrapped her three times, and the thought of how big a snake must be to shed a skin of that size appalled me so much that I took an involuntary step backwards.

'Stand still,' she snapped. 'Haven't you ever seen a naked woman before?'

And despite Lemnos, I really felt that I hadn't. Not like this. The Lemnian women had stripped and lain down for me, for us, with abandon and lust or cold purpose, unaware of being naked as was this priestess of Hekate. She had immense authority, clothed or unclothed, and I was suddenly sure that if anyone could save Jason, and all of us, it would be the Princess of Colchis.

The milk was mixed to her satisfaction.

'Stay here, do not come any further than the edge of the burning,' she told me. 'If this works, you can escort us to the ship. If it does not work, run to *Argo* and tell the others to row out into Phasis and flee. Aetes will pursue them and he has many ships. Thank you for your aid, of which your lord shall know. And the blessings of the Dark Mother, Three-Headed One, She Who Is Met On The Road, be upon you, Nauplios.'

She sketched some signs in the air. I bowed my head, as one does to a bestower of a blessing, and followed her into the wood, halting when I reached the edge of the burned patch. A small fire, perhaps a year ago, had charred the branches and burned the groundcover to ash, which rose in pale dust around my feet. Snakes dislike charcoal; a ring of it will keep them out of a house. Apparently the guardian of the sacred grove was still, in some essentials, a serpent.

I heard the princess calling, 'Jason, Jason, where are you?' into the gloom.

This was not a pleasant forest. It smelled of pines, but also of some deeply unsettling smell, like a rock laden with sleeping vipers on a riverbank at noon; a smell that had been set on the creatures by the gods to warn all men to stay away. An oily, acid smell, like bad vinegar. I wiped my face and drew a fold of my cloak over my nose and mouth so that I should not sneeze. I saw the shiny limbs of the princess as she moved deeper into the trees, walking fearlessly. Then I heard a rustle and a voice.

'I am here,' said Jason, almost fainting with terror. 'And she is here also.'

Rising from the forest floor like a mast, a snake huge beyond all belief was swaying, pinning Jason with its hypnotic gaze. It was mottled like tortoise shell. Jason stood still. Ophis Megale was waiting, with divine, eternal patience, for him to move or fall so that she could bind him in her coils, kill him, and eat him.

Opposed to this monster was a slim girl with a bucket of milk in her hand, which sloshed gentle as she walked toward the snake. The shed skin was over her head and she was singing in a pure, clear voice, '*Ophis Megale, Ophis Megale, Ophis Megale kale,*' over and over again. 'Great Serpent, Great Serpent, Beautiful Great Serpent,' sang the princess.

Despite my terror, which seemed all encompassing, my eyelids drooped. It was a sleepy tune—perfectly pitched, and the singer did not falter as the giant snake turned her cow sized head to regard Medea with those lidless eyes which melted my marrow and made the hair on the back of my neck stand up like quills on the hedgehog.

'*Ophis Megale,*' sang the princess. 'Do not stir, my lord,' she added to Jason. 'Stay quite still.

'Hekate Oldest, Hekate Dark Mother, Hekate be with me, most disgraced of your children,' she said almost to herself, before resuming the somnolent tune.

I held my breath, trying not to move at all, though the dust puffed up at the slightest shift of my feet. The princess held out the bucket, and Ophis Megale slid, rustling, over the pine needles, and dipper her gigantic head to drink, her forked tongue flicking in and out.

I do not know how long I stood in that wood. Jason had frozen. His hands were bound behind his back. Medea sang and held the leather bucket full of milk up to the snake, who must have been twenty paces long. Ophis drank, and the great head drooped, closer and closer to the ground until, with most the milk gone, she subsided into sleep and lay there like a dog, unmoving.

'Now,' said Medea to Jason. She walked carefully away from Ophis, drew her knife, and cut his bonds. My lord stared at her.

'You came for the Golden Fleece,' she reminded him impatiently. 'There it is. Take it. And hanging next to it are the bones of my sister's husband, Phrixos.'

Jason rubbed his wrists, unbelieving, looking first at the princess and then at the serpent. I wanted to shout at him to hurry, but dared not speak. Finally he lifted the Golden Fleece down and slung the leather bag containing Phrixos' bones over his shoulder. Medea gave him her hand, leading him toward where I stood, quivering in the burned trees.

'Give me your sword, Nauplios,' he said, transferring the fleece to me. It was very heavy, being full of gold, and I staggered under the weight.

'Why do you need a sword?' asked the princess, pulling off the snakeskin and dragging on her black robes.

'To kill the serpent,' said Jason, as though this was self-evident. She looked at him aghast.

'You have no need to kill her,' said Medea of Colchis. 'She will sleep for an hour yet and then she will wake. You have what you came for. Your crew is waiting, and my father will be gathering a fleet to pursue you. Come this way.'

Jason followed her out of the grove and into the reeds where, without the princess' guiding hand, we should have been instantly and irrevocably lost.

The reeds were not pathless. On the contrary, they were full of paths, all leading into an evil-smelling, mosquito-loud swamp.

We emerged from cover at the *Argo* and fell aboard. Jason dropped the bones of Phrixos into the ship. I allowed Oileus and Telamon to take the Golden Fleece. They exclaimed over it. The quest was achieved.

Now all we had to do was escape Aetes' vengeance and get home alive.

'Lady,' said Jason to the princess, not releasing her hand, 'we owe all this to you. I plead with you by Hekate and by Zeus and by the power of Aphrodite, come with me. I will make you queen of Iolkos when I return there, bearing the proofs of kingship. I can only repay you by spending the rest of my days singing your praises.'

He was staring into her eyes, and the maiden priestess seemed unable to look away. 'Why would you tempt me from my home, Achaean?' she asked.

'Lady, most beautiful of princesses, dare I leave you alone to face the wrath of your father? He will know that I could never have faced the serpent alone. To what dreadful fate will you be condemned, most beautiful of all women, Princess Medea of the honey skin and soot black hair, when he finds that you have helped the Achaean foreigners to steal the Golden Fleece?'

'He will do nothing to me,' said the princess. 'I will leave him and join the Scyths. I have been cast out of the worship of Hekate by my mistress, Trioda, who believes me, most untruly, to be unchaste. There is no place for me in Colchis, Achaean.'

'Then come with us,' pleaded Jason, sinking down onto his knees. 'My comrades will offer you no insult and neither will I, most learned of women. Songs will be made about you as were made of Ariadne, daughter of Minos and Pasiphae, who helped Theseus through the labyrinth with her thread.'

'And who came to an unfortunate end when Theseus abandoned her on Naxos,' said Princess Medea, sharply.

'That will never happen,' said Jason. 'I swear by our patron, by Hera, goddess of marriage, that I will stay with you as long as I live, that I will always love you and cherish you as I do now. When we return to Iolkos we shall wed. The maidens will escort you to my palace, dancing and singing. But we are married now, if you will so declare. I give my oath before Hestia and Poseidon and all the gods and goddesses that I will never leave you.'

'Someone's coming,' warned Atalante, who had watched this scene with a thoroughly unimpressed countenance.

'Men, along the path,' affirmed Lynkeos. 'Armed men.'

'Medea, I beg you,' Jason pleaded. She paused like a bird alighting on a branch, one foot on the bulwark of the ship and one on the land. The two black hounds rose with their feet on the bench, Jason's other hand was on one black head, and she decided.

She dropped a bundle into the boat and leapt in herself, missed her footing and slipped down in a tangle of garments and hounds, laughing as they licked her face. We released both mooring lines, reefed them, and began to row out into Phasis, heading for the open sea where we belonged.

Chapter Nineteen

Medea

I don't know why I helped them.

I was sorry for the crew of the ship *Argo*. They had travelled a long way with Jason, and had suffered many perils, and it seemed unfair that they should be assailed and slaughtered because my father would not keep his word.

I was also in favour of the sons of Phrixos, of whom I knew no harm, and I was definitely not in favour of my half brother Aegialeus, who wanted to rape me.

I was shocked by Trioda's assault, stung by her unfair suspicions, and utterly taken aback to be cast out of the sisterhood and worship of my mother, Hekate, who had been mine as long as I could remember and who, I thought, would always be my refuge. I felt displaced, confused—as though I had been waylaid and beaten and robbed. Throughout the rescue and the theft of the Golden Fleece, I could not remember that I was no longer a priestess. I had blessed the shy boy, Nauplios, as though he was a Colchian, and I had full authority, and Ophis Megale had responded to my song and my magic and succumbed to the sleeping drug in her milk, just as if I were still Hekate's maiden.

And I was still maiden, but that could be easily amended.

But mostly, I was obsessed with Jason, son of Aison. I did not know myself any more. I did not trust myself. I could not think. I could not bear to have him out of my sight, and I shivered when he touched me as though I had the ague. Whatever this strange state was, it overmastered all the controls on my own emotions that I had learned painfully through ordeal, when Trioda kept me from food or water or sleep for long days, beating me if I wept, so that after the first few times I did not weep. I had thought myself as strong as bronze, and I was as soft as cushion-stuffing. Disgusted at my weakness, I sat on the sterndeck and smiled dotingly on Jason as though I were drunk or drugged. And nothing in the world—neither father nor brothers, nor Colchis, nor even the goddess—seemed to matter, if I could not save this most beautiful of men, whose every movement pleased me, from the vengeance of my treacherous father.

For Jason was mine, sworn and declared and mine, my own love, my promised husband. If I were to marry him, I could lie down in his arms as all women do, and find there, I was convinced, great and abiding joy.

Trioda had suspected me of being unchaste, and now I was: in thought, though not yet in deed. I had fallen. I found myself remembering the mating of the Scyths, and imagined myself as Iole, lying down with her new mate in her arms and crying aloud with delight. Trioda could never have experienced love, I reflected bitterly, or she would never have spoken about it in such crude terms.

I was dragged out of my thoughts by an Argonaut shouting, 'They're coming!'

'How many ships?' demanded Atalante, the only other woman on board.

'Ten, and they're coming up fast with the wind, while we are rowing against it. What are your orders, Jason?'

'Princess Medea?' he asked me. I was honoured by his trust in my counsel. I considered the landscape. We were in Scythian territory, but the Scyths would not be there. The only people to be found would be wandering tribes and the Androphagi, and I did not want to meet them again. There were very few harbours along this stretch of coast. I knew of no place where we could hide.

'We'll have to go on,' I said to my lord Jason. 'No bay along here could conceal a ship this big, until we come to the papyrus beds at the mouth of the Reedy River. There we could hide, if you wish to hide, my lord.'

'No good,' said Argos, the old man at the steering oars. 'They'll catch up within the day.'

'The Brygean Islands,' I suggested. 'We will have to stop for water, and they are within the distance, and perhaps we can parley or give them the slip in the dark. It depends on who is commanding the fleet. I doubt that Aetes would trust the sons of Phrixos with his vengeance. I hope they are not dead already, but they may be.'

'Who, then, would be the likely commander, Princess?' asked Authalides the herald.

'Aegialeus.' I shuddered, and Nauplios noticed and cast his cloak around me. 'It is likely to be my half brother, Aegialeus. I fear that he will not give up, because not only does he need to regain Aetes' favour by slaughtering you and regaining the Golden Fleece, but he wishes to cement his claim to the throne by marrying me.'

'But you're his sister,' objected Atalante.

'Even so,' I rejoiced, and she spat over the side and said, 'Colchian customs are barbaric.'

'It is not a Colchian custom,' I protested, but she was not listening.

The ships gained on us all day. The Brygean Islands loomed, the rowers hauled and swore and hauled, and the boy, Melas, brought watered wine and bread to them when they took short breaks between intervals of muscle-wracking work. The middle of the ship was manned by the biggest men: Telamon, Oileus, Ancaeas the Strong and Nestor, Honey-Voiced. The weaker the muscle, the further away from the middle, so that nearest to me were Philammon, the bard, and Atalante, who told me that she was a dedicated maiden, suckled by the bears of Brauron and devoted to Artemis, the Achaean goddess of hunting. Philammon's god was known to Colchis. Ammon, the sun god, whom the Achaeans call Apollo, though from the stories, our Ammon was pale and weak compared to their plague hurling, dangerously unstable golden god. It was easy to offend Apollo and invariably fatal, and I was alarmed to learn that he had even murdered his favourite, Asclepius the Healer, because he was too learned.

I told no tales of Hekate in return, because they were still sacred to me, and I did not think that they would wish to hear them. The story of how Hekate had designed the serpent, for instance, seemed childish and trifling beside a smith god, called Hephaestos, who forged the bronze pillars of the immortals' palace in a volcano.

The day wore on and the Colchians gained, until we rowed between the two Brygean Islands and into a harbour on the ocean side of the furthest.

The crew shipped oars and cast out an anchor stone, and we drank some more wine. Nauplios and Melas splashed ashore to fill the water skins.

Jason came and sat beside me on the little afterdeck. He took my hand. I felt his hard thigh aligned with mine and my body reacted in a way which I had not experienced. A sharp bolt went through my spine, so that I sat up straight, and then a warming glow crept through my loins. I wriggled a little, trying to lift one buttock and then the other without being noticed. I felt fluid between my thighs, and wondered if my bleeding had begun, though it was not the right phase of the moon.

'What shall we do, my princess, my dearest lady?' he asked.

'We shall talk before we fight,' I replied. 'I am—I was—a priestess of Hekate and, although Trioda has cast me out, I still have some skills. If we can find the right herbs on this island, I can send them to sleep as I did Ophis, or darken the moon in their eyes to cover our escape. But we also need to acquire something which belongs to them.'

'Such as?' asked a gnarled man with a wry grin.

'Something which has lain next their skin, a shift, an amulet; even a sandal would do,' I replied.

'Trust me,' declared the man, 'I am Autolycus, and my father was Hermes, patron of thieves. There is nothing which I cannot obtain for you, Priestess.'

'Without their knowledge?' I asked sceptically.

'Once I was challenged to steal the most closely guarded thing in Libya—a wager for my life and safe passage out of the territory—and I stole the crown of their king.'

'Why was that so hard?' asked Akastos.

'He was wearing it at the time,' said Autolycus simply. 'And he never noticed it was gone until I produced it from his chief counsellor's hat.'

Meleagros scoffed, 'You are a boaster, Autolycus. How could you do such a thing?'

I would have sworn that Autolycus did not move within touching distance of Meleagros, but sat on a rowing bench near me, dangling one hand idly over the thwart of the ship. He grinned and asked Meleagros, 'Haven't you lost something?'

'No,' scowled Meleagros, casting a quick glance around his property.

'What about the Samothrace amulet which preserves you from drowning?' asked Autolycus, with every appearance of concern. 'No sailor should be without such a valuable piece of protection.'

Patting his chest, Meleagros exclaimed, 'It's gone!'

'On the contrary, it's here,' said Autolycus, producing a little purple bag on a leather thong.

Meleagros accepted the amulet, examined it minutely and said, 'Yes, it's mine. How did you do that?'

'Oh, I can't do that sort of thing. I'm just a boaster,' replied Autolycus, straight-faced. 'I just found it here in my hand.'

'Beware, friends,' said Meleagros, relaxing into a huge grin. 'We have on board the very prince of thieves.'

Clearly there were several kinds of magic on the *Argo*, not mine alone.

The Colchian ships moored within spear-throwing range of the ship, and I saw that my detestable half brother was indeed in command.

Aegialeus yelled to Jason, 'You have the Golden Fleece and the bones of Phrixos. My father is willing to allow you to keep Phrixos. He was a stranger in Colchis and belongs, perhaps, to you—also his ghost has been walking and may want to go home. The Golden Fleece you won; the terms are met.'

'Then we have no quarrel, son of Aetes,' responded Jason.

'You have with you my half sister, the Princess Medea, black bitch of Hekate. If you will return her, son of Aison, I will allow you to depart without battle,' called Aegialeus.

I sniffed. What a ludicrous proposal! My lord would not give me up, not after such a profession of love.

'Let us meet,' said Jason, 'to arrange this matter.'

I thought I had misheard at first. But the Argonauts were all looking at me sadly, and I knew that he had said it. I was appalled. I bit back a scream of protest and something inside me turned instantly to ice. Kore and Scylla, sensing my shock as they always did, burrowed through the massed legs of the Argonauts and came to me, sitting one either side.

What had I done? I had abandoned everything dear to me and followed a foreigner without a second thought, and now he was going to hand me back to my half brother. I would lose my maidenhead, not to my chosen husband, but to Aegialeus. He would use me to become king, and then he would kill me. Death did not seem a more dreadful fate. I knew about death. Hekate's priestesses are trained in the dark and are perfectly familiar with death—on friendly, even sisterly terms.

But I knew nothing at all about love. It hurt so much that I was beyond tears. I hugged the hounds and waited to see what this perfidious, this monstrous, beautiful Achaean intended to do with me. I was resolved. I would kill myself before Jason sold me to Aegialeus for his own release; if I could. And if I could not, if I was bound and delivered to my half brother, I would kill both him and myself as soon as I was able.

I was shaking with pain and shock. Scylla leaned closer to me, laying her head on my shoulder, and Kore sprawled half across my lap.

The ship was hauled up the beach. The crew, with the economy of long practice, began to set up camp, light a fire and find shelter for the coming night. Still I sat on the afterdeck, waiting to hear my fate.

Nauplios brought me a dish of mealy porridge, but I could not eat. The dogs enjoyed it, however. The boy smiled nervously at me as he came to collect the empty bowl and said, 'Lady, fate is cruel, but you are strong.'

'Not strong enough, it seems,' I replied, concealing my face from his concerned eyes. I would not cry in front of an Achaean, even this very young and sympathetic one. After a while, he went away.

Dark came, the moon rose. I heard someone picking their way through the tangle of lines and bundles between the rowing benches.

It was Jason. 'Princess,' he said, and took my hand. I snatched it away.

'Traitor,' I replied. 'What are you going to do with me? Are women in Achaea so common that you can afford to waste me? I gave you the ointment for the bulls, Achaean, outraging my oaths to Hekate. I sent Ophis to sleep so that you could take what you came for. I believed your oaths, sworn by your gods, that you honoured me.' I choked, but recovered. I could see his face, silvered in the moon, and he was so beautiful that my heart was moved, despite my horror.

'Lady,' he began, running a hand down my shoulder to my hip. His touch made me shiver with desire, but I pushed him away.

'May your own Furies pursue you, Achaean,' I said as softly as I could. My voice seemed to be failing me, along with my heart and my wits. 'The man to whom you are going to deliver me will rape me and then he will kill me. Have I deserved this of you? But you shall not sell me for your own safety. I will die first. I have a potion here, snake venom and hemlock. Tell me that you are giving me to Aegialeus, Jason, and I will drink it.'

'Medea,' he said softly, and his voice was so musical that I had to listen. 'Lady, there is no other way.'

'And if I find you another way?'

'My own love, any other way and I will take it. I love you, Princess. But I will sacrifice even my own heart to save my shipmates.'

Of course. He would be wounded, hurt, by losing me, but he was so noble that he would bear such injury. Loyalty to his own crew, his relatives and friends who had travelled with him so far and borne so many perils for his sake, must win over love. I drew a breath, the first deep breath since I had heard him reply to Aegialeus.

'Let us meet my half brother,' I said. 'I will call him down from his fellows. He will not want to let any other see this rape. I will lie down for him, and you will kill him.'

'How will that make us safe?'

'I will then make a spell which will cover our escape. They will not be eager to pursue anyway, if Aegialeus is dead. His will was in this, not the king's. In fact, he was probably told just to retrieve the fleece and the bones and possibly me, and kill you all. He is trying to make his own bargain. This makes him vulnerable.'

'We will do as you say,' replied Jason. 'My sweet witch, my most beautiful sorceress.'

'But if you ever betray me, Jason, son of Aison, if you break your most solemn oaths, then you will die.'

I foresaw; which I did very rarely. I have no gift for prophecy. But I saw Jason lying dead under the keel of a ship, crushed by a fallen timber. It was a bright little picture, clear as real life.

He seemed taken aback, even alarmed. He gave me his hand and this time I took it. I summoned Autolycus to me, gave him some instructions, and allowed him to kiss my hand. He was a clever rogue, this son of Hermes, and I trusted him to carry out what he had sworn to do, especially since it would ensure our escape. I sang my spell for sleep. We clambered down from the ship and went, thus linked, along the sand to the camp which the only son of Aetes had established at the other side of the little beach.

'Ah,' said Aegialeus as he saw me held by my Achaen gaoler, 'Hekate's bitch, you are mine.'

'I am captive,' I said, lowering my head so that I should not have to look at his self-satisfied face. 'But I will not lie down under you in the midst of your men, brother. Such an act—such a dreadful act—must not be watched by any.'

'I will make you scream with lust,' he promised, mistaking my shudder for desire. 'Achaean, you are free to leave. I have what I came for,' he said, and his hands grabbed for my breasts. He found a nipple and squeezed hard. I gasped with pain. Jason stepped away from me as Aegialeus dragged me down the beach to a little cove. There he tripped me suddenly, laughing in triumph, and flung himself down on top of me.

No animal likes being turned on its back, its vulnerable belly exposed. I was suddenly terrified that Jason would not come in time, or that he would make another, better, bargain with the others, and I would be violated by the intrusion into my body of the hard thing which butted into my belly. He had both hands on my shoulders, pinning me to the ground, and his weight was cutting off my breath. My legs were parting—he had dug his knees into my thighs—despite my struggle to keep them together. Trioda had lied when she told me in the cave of Hekate that I would never be so frightened again.

The cloth of my robes was torn, my body bared, his tunic cast aside. He had not even searched me. I had the phial of poison, but I could not reach it. My half brother was mad with lust and stronger than me, and I was weakening because I was so desperately afraid.

'I will make you bleed,' he promised, sparing one hand to thrust between my legs, seeking the entrance to the womb. His sandy fingers were thwarted for a moment by my dry, shrinking flesh, then they found an entrance and thrust, hard, and his mouth smothered my scream. His touch hurt in a deep, personal way which mere injury could never even rival. I struggled, feeling for my torn robe and my venomous potion, my only escape.

'Stop fighting, virgin bitch of Hekate,' he said softly. 'In a moment you shall be maiden no longer, and then you will be soft in my arms, conquered, wholly mine.'

'Never,' I spat into his face. 'Never. Hekate will smite you, Aegialeus, for incest and for rape. And for this you will die.'

'Perhaps.' I could not move under his weight. The fingers moved inside me, then he withdrew them. He shifted his weight, still as heavy as the earth, and I felt the phallus positioned at the mouth of my womb; a hard spear with a rounded end. 'But first you will be mine. One thrust,' he gloated. 'I will take your maidenhead with one...'

He fell on me. I screamed. Then I realised that he was not moving. The violation had not taken place. His mouth was on my throat and from it ran a hot sticky fluid. I smelt blood. Not the virgin blood of my sacrifice, but Aegialeus' blood. Jason's voice asked urgently, 'Medea? Medea, my own love, my princess, are you alive?'

'I live,' I groaned under a dead weight. 'Lift him off me, I'm suffocating.'

He rolled the body aside, pulling me up into his embrace. His arms were strong, and I wiped my face against his shoulder. I was shuddering so that my legs would not hold me up. He carried me away from the corpse, holding me close, until he came to the ship. There he laid me down in someone's bedding and sat beside me, stroking my hair. Telamon brought me a terracotta goblet full of wine and Nauplios, who was acute, a bowl of hot water.

In the darkness, I laved my insulted flesh. There was sand inside me, and the edges of the parts which we call the vessel were lacerated by Aegialeus' contaminated touch. My neck and breast were sticky with my half brother's blood, and I tasted it. I have never been so pleased that anyone was dead.

I washed as well as I could, drank neat Achaean wine, which was powerfully sweet, and lay back in the bedding, clutching my torn robes around me and shaking as though I was snowbound. I could not stop shivering. I was as cold as the grave.

The hounds lay close to me, both on one side; for on the other lay Jason, who had rescued me. We waited for the rest of the plan to take effect. I warmed slowly between the animal heat of the dogs and the man, but I could not sleep. The horrible strength of Aegialeus, the nearness of my escape from death and rape, the gloating voice, the intruding fingers, repeated like a vision, until I could have shrieked exorcisms at it.

By dawn we knew that the potion which I had given Autolycus had been included in both the wine and the drinking water of the Colchians. They lay asleep on the beach like seals.

'There is one more thing which will delay them,' I said. 'But it is a horrible thing to do, even to a dead man.'

'I am in your debt, Lady. We are all in your debt. What shall we do?' asked Nauplios, who was now lying at my side to warm me, since my lord was inspecting the fallen Colchians.

'The men of Colchis must be cocooned entire, or they will not reach the afterlife,' I explained. 'Therefore, strike that vile half brother of mine, that rapist Aegialeus, into pieces and scatter the limbs in the ocean. The fleet will not dare return to Aetes without every finger, every toe, and as much as can be found of the king's son.'

Nauplios winced, but nodded. 'I will tell Jason and we will do as you suggest,' he said, getting up and finding a cleaver.

I rose and, with Kore and Scylla flanking me, I stood unmoving, the wind plucking at my torn robes. Jason, Nauplios and Telamon hacked the despised corpse of the monster into quarters and then into pieces and gathered up armfuls of Aegialeus, Aetes' only son, and flung them into the sea. His head rolled almost to my feet with the violence of Telamon's blow, which severed the neck. The face looked surprised, the eyebrows raised, the mouth open.

I spurned it with my foot, still sick with terror and loathing. I noticed that several of the Argonauts made signs of warning at me, and I heard Authalides whisper, 'She is a true Colchian witch, daughter of Hekate the Black Bitch, Mother of Death.'

But I was not—not any more. I was still a virgin, barely. I was fleeing now from my father's wrath, and I was in an Achaean company bound for a foreign land in which I would live as Jason's wife, bear his children, die and be buried in strange earth, all without the protection of Hekate.

I felt that I had lost my mother. My own had died when I was born, Trioda had turned against me without warning, and now the goddess was denied me as a disgraced and fallen daughter. But the potions and spells still worked, even if the divine hand was no longer over Medea, and I did not know why this was so. I dared to hope that perhaps Trioda had been outside her powers, and Hekate was still with her priestess. But I did not think this was possible. Cast out was cast out. I had not only been denied my position, but cursed as well.

Perhaps I was mourning the death of my own mother, Aerope, whom I could not consciously remember ever having seen, or perhaps the loss of the goddess or the brutality of Aegialeus, but something made we weep as we rowed out from the islands. I dressed in Jason's spare tunic and wrapped myself in Nauplios' cloak, sat down to mend my own garments and cried as though my heart was broken as the bone needle moved through the torn cloth of my black robes.

◇◇◇

Ships, I decided six days later, were uncomfortable. In good weather and with a following wind it was fine to perch next to the steersman and watch the Scythian landscape slip past, faster than a galloping horse could run. But most of the time it was work, the groan as the oars were hauled back, the gasp as they were lifted and the rowers moved with precision, like trained warriors advancing on an enemy. There had been no sign of pursuit from Colchis. I vengefully hoped that they were still searching for missing bits of Aegialeus. I sat looking back for two days before Jason told me I could give up my watch.

That, at least, had given me something with which to occupy myself on the way to Circe's isle. His god had spoken to Philammon, saying that Jason and I should be cleansed of blood guilt for my half brother's murder and mutilation before we could marry. The only person—apart from my father—who could conduct this ceremony was the sorceress Circe, my aunt. Her island was, anyway, on the way home to Iolkos.

I was not only bored but I was always damp, if not actually wet, with slapping waves or spray kicked up by the oars and the ocean. There was no task for me. I was not used to being idle and I did not want to think. One night I had woken the whole crew by screaming that Aegialeus was hurting me, and only the presence of Jason and the hounds had reassured me that I was not back on that beach with the scraping, groping hands clawing for my virginity and my life. My dreams were not pleasant, and I did not want to sleep.

I had sewn all my robes back together, with the smallest and most careful stitches. Then I had collected work from the crew. I had mended torn garments, patched tunics and re-cut and soled damaged sandals. I had rethreaded the lacings on Oileus' armour, which was so huge that I had to climb practically inside it to reach, which had made the Achaeans laugh.

There was nothing else I could do and I was as nervous and restless as Kore and Scylla, who were used to running *stadia* a day on the open ground. Fortunately, Phlogius, one of Herakles' expedition, had volunteered to row with Atalante, and Philammon the bard took pity on me. He sat at my side, patting the nearest hound—for they loved him and tried to climb into his lap, staring adoringly up into his face—and talked to me all day, teaching me to play his lyre.

He was exotic to Colchian eyes, with hair like copper and the look which Hekate's maidens call 'goddess gaze'. Possessors of this gift cannot be deceived, and their skill is always to discover truths. I felt that he knew all about me the instant his grey eyes stared into mine, but he was benign and wise, and I did not care. He, at least, knew that I was not unchaste.

It was a clear day with a strong wind, and the men called for a song. Philammon had been talking to me about gods and I had been learning about the divine singer Orpheus, who could tame beasts with his music.

'This is the song of the robe,' he said. Then, with the single strings plucking a simple tune behind the words, he began to sing in a compelling, true, very clear voice.

> *For her garment, the Earth Mother*
> *Wove a green covering. In it are all things made*
> *That ever were made or ever will be made.*
> *We are trees, we are the cold curve of the sea wave,*
> *We are the bright eyes of stars,*
> *We are the precise geometry of salt.*
> *We are as uncounted as the grains of sand,*
> *But she has counted us,*
> *Woven us into her tapestry.*
> *We are part of her garment,*
> *We are designed, have place,*
> *We are part of her pattern.*
> *As her loom was laid out across the heavens,*
> *As her shuffle swung back and forth,*
> *Weaving ants and mountains,*
> *She wove us, and snow, and leaves.*
> *We cannot die*
> *Although we die.*
> *The pattern continues,*
> *We are part of her pattern.*

As I listened I saw the robe flung over Phanes, the revealed one, the blue-sky and white-cloud globe of the Earth, and I saw the fish in the waves and the beasts in the woods, the trees growing and the grass springing. I remembered horses new foaled, running to their dam on wobbling legs, and the feel of new linen and the smell of cold water and blood and pine trees, and it was all one—all one immensely beautiful and intricate pattern, and even I, Medea, was one irreplaceable piece in it, as was my father and the sons of Phrixos, as was the dead Aegialeus and Tyche, the old woman in the cave, and Scylla and Kore and Anemone.

'You are a wondrously skilled bard,' I said to Philammon.

'I am the mouth and hands of my lord Orpheus,' he said. 'But I thought of that song because I have sat here and watched you sew, Princess. Your hands are also wondrously skilled.'

That night I slept without dreams.

We went through the Clashing Rocks without incident. It also seemed the *Argo* was shoved through, though I saw no gods. And we came to Circe, my aunt's island, one morning at dawn, after a god-given wind had blown us for days and nights through the Bosporus and the Propontis without ceasing, dying down to a gentle breeze as we slipped into the arms of the harbour.

Chapter Twenty

Nauplios

There was a strange mist around Circe's island. The path which led to her house was made of pebbles, the house itself was of white stone, like many to be seen in any Achaean city. But there was a pinkish haze, blurring sight which made my eyes water, and no horizon could be seen. This was bound to disconcert any sailor, and we were duly disconcerted.

We followed my lord Jason and the Princess Medea to the house, at a respectful distance. Circe was reputed to be a woman of terrible powers and unknown purposes, and we had already been sobered by the sight of three Achaean vessels and one Libyan ship, all wrecked, which had sunk at their moorings in her harbour. Where had the crews gone, I wondered. Had they died here, or been transformed? Two vessels, at least, had sat waiting for their men until their timbers had rotted. Argos, aghast at the sight of the sunken ships, had stayed behind with *Argo*, keeping Telamon, Oileus, Ancaeas and Nestor as rear guard.

My lord and his affianced bride were clothed only in air, walking barefoot over the stones, as fitted suppliants. The Princess Medea stepped easily. I saw strong muscle moving in her calf, knee, thigh and buttock under her smooth, dark skin, which was as unblemished as the inside of a pearl shell.

I knew that I should not be looking at my lord's wife, especially when she was naked for a religious purpose, and I hoped that the all-seeing Circe could not see me; but my lady was so beautiful, so light and quick and unconscious of her nakedness, that she compelled my gaze.

Then something happened which took even my lecherous mind off my lady. A rabbit hopped past us, pursued by a fox. A common sight, perhaps, except that the rabbit had six legs and the fox had three tails.

I rubbed my face. My eyes were obviously deceived. But then Lynkeos, the most keen sighted of all the Argonauts, exclaimed aloud, and it seemed that he had seen the same thing. Then we saw a flock of birds who called to us, 'Achaeans! Beware Circe, Achaeans!' Under the trees snuffled a herd of swine, and from amongst them a piggish voice grunted, 'Beware.'

'This is a serious place,' remarked Akastos to his cousin. 'We must pay close attention to our behaviour here.'

'What do you mean?' asked Admetos.

'This Circe is a transforming sorceress,' said Akastos. 'And I am afraid that we have just seen those missing ship's crews.'

After that we said nothing and trod very gently as we came to the witch's house.

A woman was standing in the courtyard, washing her very long, silver hair in a deep cauldron. When she saw us she smiled, tossing back her head and spraying water onto us. I tasted one droplet on my lips. It was salt. Who would wash their hair in sea water, when there was a well of sweet water to hand?

'I dreamed of burning and of blood,' she said to the suppliants, who reached her feet and kneeled, heads down. 'I have soaked my hair, my magical hair with which I can spin a cord to draw down the moon, in water as salt as tears, to clean away the threads of my dream. Who comes to Circe's isle, and what do you want of her, suppliants?'

'Purging of blood guilt,' said Medea, then said a phrase in Colchian. The witch sank down on her heels and raised my lady's chin with one sharp forefinger.

'Medea of Colchis, Aetes' child,' she observed, though as far as I knew she had never seen the princess before. 'And this must be Jason, son of Aison. Blood guilt? Have you killed my brother?'

'No, Lady,' replied Medea. 'We have ambushed and killed Aegialeus, my half brother.'

'Wait,' said the witch. She tied up her hair, wringing out the water. She looked down into the cauldron, stirring the water with her hand, then watching as it stilled and cleared. She looked for a long time at whatever vision she saw in the pot. Possibly she was looking at her own reflection.

She was old, Circe, but still beautiful. All the softness which made youth attractive was absent, fined and honed in this witch into a sharp face, such as a sculptor cuts on a grave; one stroke for the line of the nose, two more for the chin, two for the eyes and two for the brows. There was immense intelligence in her eyes, but little there of mercy, or even pity. She hummed distractingly as she watched, biting her lip and curling one tress of the silver hair around her thin brown hand. Then she came to some decision.

'You,' she told the Argonauts. 'Sit where you are. Presently you shall eat, though not with me. Strange transformations have happened after one of Circe's feasts. You may have met some of them on the path. While I am conducting this ceremony, do not move or speak, or I cannot answer for what might happen to you or these bloodstained ones, and I do not need any more animals on my island.'

We sat down abruptly. Most of us hid our faces in our cloaks, that we might not see something which was forbidden. Authalides threw his chlamys over Melas' head, for his father would never forgive us if anything happened to the boy. But I could still not stop looking at the straight back of my lady Medea, and I was concerned for my lord Jason, so I watched as Circe came back with a suckling pig.

It squealed as she raised it high, chanting in a strange tongue, then brought the knife across its throat. Blood flowed down over Jason's bowed head, and my lady's, and fell then upon their upturned hands. The pink mist intensified, like smoke fed by a smouldering pile of wet leaves. Something vast loomed up, much higher than the house, behind the witch and the two suppliants kneeling at her feet. A woman, perhaps, in dark robes, who held out both her arms in blessing. Then a little breeze blew and the smoke dissipated, or the vision was lost.

'You are forgiven,' said Circe in an exhausted tone. She put the carcass down on the ground and raised Jason and the princess to their feet. Blood ran in red lines down the Princess Medea's shoulder, trickling down her belly and down her legs, as straight as a boy's.

'Go down to the sea alone and wash, absolved of the goddess,' ordered Circe. 'You are not mated yet. Do not lie together while you are on my island. There has been enough blood,' she said, and walked back into her house, closing the door. Her shoulders sagged as though she was carrying a heavy weight.

A feast was prepared for us by eleven giggling young women, who were delighted to find a group of men who hadn't been turned into something by their powerful mistress. When my lord and lady came back clean and reclothed from the ocean, we sat down to eat roasted flesh and bread and drink strong, very sweet wine made of honey, and the maidens waited upon us, flirting through the feast, touching and being touched.

I wrapped myself in my blanket and lay down to sleep in the shade of the trees. The fire was still burning, to keep off the deformed animals, and Lynkeos was on watch. I heard Idas promising a maiden that if she lay with him she would never regret, and heard then the unmistakable sounds of someone making love.

All around the fire the Argonauts were being seduced. Circe's maidens were maidens no longer, though I heard no cries of pain, only the laugh and gasp, the sucking slap of flesh in conjunction, and the groan or bird cry of orgasm. Jason and the Princess Medea, I knew, lay under the next tree, but I heard no sound from them. I supposed that they were in sufficient awe of the witch of the island to obey her command.

But I was under no such constraint. When the white-armed girl who had served me with roasted mutton came to me and stroked me, I closed both her bright eyes with kisses, and she put aside my tunic, her long hair splaying across my chest as her mouth moved down my body.

She was smooth and skilled and I pleased her—or perhaps it had just been a long time since she had been allowed to mate with a man. Or men. She had lain with someone else that night, for her sheath was slippery under my questing fingers. But some hunger had built up inside me, some pressure, and instead of slowly pleasuring her with my hands and my lips, as I had learned on Lemnos, I laid her on her back and drove inside her, so that she cried aloud and grasped my hips, digging in her nails. I felt the liquid strength of the female sheath, designed by the gods to raise men to the heights of delight, and thrust again, and the willing sheath embraced my phallus like a mouth, sucking. She bit my neck, curling around me, strong legs locked around my waist, and thrust back, until we sobbed into climax and collapsed.

I did not know her name and she was not the one whom I wanted—I dared not even form the thought about who I really desired—but she was kind, pliable and scented, she took my over-eager seed and sucked out of me some of my pain, and I remember her with gratitude.

When we woke no one was there. As we gathered up our coverings, we called, but no one came. I wondered who we had lain with, beasts perhaps, or phantoms, and every man there was thinking the same, for our progress to the beach went from an orderly walk to a run to a rout, and we threw ourselves into the ship and rowed frantically out of the harbour.

I asked Philammon. 'Who do you think those maidens were?'

'Maidens?' asked the bard, plucking at a string, frowning, and tightening it.

'Last night, at the feast of Circe. You know, the young women who made sacrifice to Aphrodite with us.'

'I saw no young women,' he said, plucking another string.

'What, then, did you see?' demanded several voices anxiously.

'I saw nothing,' replied Philammon. Then he sang, looking at the Princess Medea.

Not the hasty, fleeting, incomplete
Mating of humans and beasts,
But a melting, a fiery loving
Which melded the forms and shapes
Into one creature. In the music,
Male blended with female
And swelled with child.

'What do you mean?' she asked, smiling. 'That they mated with demons or shadows?'

Philammon would not answer, and they began to discuss Orpheus and his death at the hands of the Bacchantes.

'They tore him apart with their bare hands,' said the bard. 'The pieces they threw into the sea. His head, still singing, washed up on the island of Lesbos. The women built a shrine around it, and then a stone temple. Only when the temple was complete did the head complete its song, for the young trees around the building took up his tune. Even now, the Lesbian women allow travellers to sleep a night in that temple, though men are banned from their island as women are banned from Andros. The sleepers listen to the music and become poets or madmen. But then, the women of Lesbos say that all men are poets or madmen.'

It seemed that I had been sailing for all of my life in *Argo*, listening to the same noises. The groan of Ancaeas the Strong as he extracted himself from under his rowing bench—I still could not see how he fitted himself into that space. The incessant quarrelling of Idas and Lynkeos, which began to annoy us so much that we separated them, one at the extreme end of the stern, the other at the furthest point of the bow, and even then they shouted insults at each other until Telamon threatened to tie them into knots and throw them overboard to act as sea anchors. Atalante chanted her prayers to her own goddess, Artemis, at the rising and setting of the moon, and Philammon marked the changes of the planets with music and talked to the princess, who was interested in every facet of Achaean life which he could tell her. Melas was instructed by Argos, his father, in the making and sailing of ships. Nestor, Telamon, Oileus and Ancaeas sang songs from amidships as we heaved through heavy seas. Alabande sewed when we were sailing, long strips of complex embroidery delicate enough for a princess. They were designed for the lady Medea; and she was wrapped in a cloak of immense richness by the time we hove to off Phaeacia.

Meleagros and Perithous exchanged endless reminiscences of women they had known, which were so highly coloured that I did not believe more than one tale in five. Erginos developed a talent for catching sea birds on a long line, so the usual noises of the ship were punctuated by a shout, a frantic flapping, a squawk and a thud. I could smell tarred line, canvas, and wooden planks well seasoned by the ocean. *Argo* was a boat redolent of men and sweat and urine; and of the princess' perfume, a dark, smoky, disturbing female scent.

We had no hint of trouble when we landed on the island of King Alcinous and Queen Arete. They were well known to be hospitable to travellers, and we dragged the ship out of the water and secured her, for a storm was coming. Black clouds scudded in from the east and riding on them came a fleet of ships.

Admetos said to Akastos, 'Here come our lord's royal cousins.'

'They must have picked up all of the bits of Aegialeus,' observed Akastos.

'Holy ground,' said Philammon, leading the way quickly toward a temple which stood on top of a cliff. We had seen it out on Ocean's bosom; the sailors use it as a sighting hark. It was called 'The White Pillars" and was dedicated to Themis, who is Justice.

Slaughtering us in the temple of Justice herself would be unthinkable, even for Colchians.

Then we sent word by the priests that we had arrived, and asked the royal rulers of the island to come to us, as we dared not leave our sanctuary.

The Colchians, grim men and salt stained, climbed the path, but, as Philammon had guessed, they did not dare defy Themis and enter the shrine. They sat down outside and made their camp, and I guessed that they would not be easy to drug again.

They had just lit their cooking fires when King Alcinous and Queen Arete came into the temple.

They were strikingly similar. They were both small and old, with the same long white hair. Alcinous was clean shaven. Both were wearing voluminous purple robes and golden crowns, small circlets set with sea pearls. I wondered, for a moment, whether they were brother and sister. Then I saw that they had been together a long while, and had grown to resemble each other as long-married people do, even when they originally were unlike.

Old goatherds, they say in Iolkos, resemble goats and old sheepmen resemble sheep, and Alcinous and Arete had been ruling for so long that they contained and embodied the concept of royalty.

We all knelt. They sat, in identical thrones which the priests carried forward.

'Who comes to our island?' asked Alcinous.

'Jason, son of Aison, the crew of the ship *Argo*, and the daughter of Aetes, Medea, Princess of Colchis, who is my affianced bride,' replied Jason.

'And who pursues you?' asked Arete, in the same slightly cracked, authoritative tone.

'Men of Colchis,' said a voice from beyond the door. 'To retrieve our stolen fleece, our stolen bones and our stolen princess, and to revenge the death of the king's son, Aegialeus, murdered and then butchered by this Achaean pirate.'

'Will you accept our judgement?' asked Alcinous.

'I will,' declared Jason.

'I will,' said the gruff voice of the Colchian.

'Then there shall be truce,' ordered Arete, or possibly Alcinous. 'Three days. We shall then return and pronounce our verdict. In that time the Achaeans will stay in the palace and the Colchians will stay in the temple. You are forbidden to speak to each other or to come closer to each other than a bowshot. Are these terms understood?'

'Understood,' said Jason and the captain of the Colchians.

We packed up and moved to the palace. The city was like all others on that island where war did not come, a well-maintained, well-built place of stone houses, each with a sleeping dog on the scrubbed step. It was a place where every man had a vine over his courtyard and sat under it when his toil was done, drinking mead from his wooden cup, attended by slaves who had been slaves for ten generations and were content.

The streets were paved and the temples numerous, and every fifth day there seemed to be a festival. The blue-robed priests of Themis were sweeping rose petals from the temple steps as we came into the city, for the island of Alcinous and Arete is famous for its scents. It was clean and comfortable and we were well fed, but I went for long walks with the Princess Medea's hounds, Kore and Scylla, to ease the burning inside me. There was no possibility that Nauplios, the net-caster's son, could achieve his desire, and I strove to push it to the very depths of my mind, to bury it under a thousand other concerns. Her hounds liked me, and that was something I could do for the princess, now secluded like the Achaean woman she would have to become. For women of my country do not walk in the public street unveiled, or talk to unrelated men, not unless they are peasants or market women or whores.

I was bringing the black dogs back on the second day when she called me into the women's quarters. I stood at the door, for my entrance was against all custom, and she said more loudly, 'Come in, Nauplios.'

'Lady, I am your slave,' I replied. 'But you are in the women's quarters and I cannot come in.'

'Then I will come out,' she declared.

'Lady, you must not,' said one of the women within. 'You must not go out into the open street with a man.'

'Let me pass,' said the princess in a dangerous tone, and the woman must have stood aside, for Medea issued forth in no good temper. She was veiled—she had yielded to custom so far. She grabbed my arm and swung me around, so that my back was against the wall, and demanded, "What's happening?'

'The royal ones are still considering our fate, lady Medea.'

'Where is my lord?'

'Lady, he has gone fishing with the men of this island, as there is nothing else we can do but wait.'

'Nauplios, must all women in Achaea live like this?' she asked. 'Confined in the women's quarters, never to see the sun?'

'Lady, that is how women live,' I replied. I trembled at her nearness. I longed to take her into my arms, feel her lay her head on my shoulder, to comfort her, to die defending her—anything, so that she would know how I felt. But she was my lord's affianced wife, and I said nothing and did nothing which might have alerted her to how much I loved Medea, Princess of Colchis.

I felt that if I stood there any longer I must throw myself at her feet and declare my love. I stepped back a pace. She misinterpreted this, laying a hand on my arm to detain me.

'I mean you no harm, Nauplios, son of Dictys,' she said sadly, looking up into my face. 'Only here have I realised how much of a stranger I am to these Achaeans. I am no black witch, no devotee of demons, and I do not use sorcery to gain my ends. I mean no evil.'

'Lady, I never thought that of you, never,' I protested. I loved her so much, this strong, thin woman with the black hair like a waterfall of ebony under her thin veil. She had saved all our lives, even that of Nauplios. She had gained us the Golden Fleece and the bones of Phrixos, and she would obtain Jason his kingdom. I admired her skill and was in awe of her knowledge, and I had told her the truth, which I owed to her; I never thought she was evil. Her touch was warm and I tried not to return it, though I desperately wanted to cover that small hand with my own.

'Find out for me what will be decided,' she begged.

I had never thought that the proud priestess of Hekate would beg, and it hurt me to see her. I took her hand in mine and said hurriedly, 'I will find out, Lady.' Then I walked quickly away, before I could say or do something unfitting.

It was one of the kitchen slaves who told me the decision. He had it from one of the bedchamber slaves, and what bed-chamber slaves do not know about their masters isn't knowledge. I accepted the piece of fresh-baked bread which the fellow insisted on given me, shared a couple of stories about the Lemnian women—the only part of our story which had found universal acceptance—and went to find Jason.

I caught him by the arm when the boat came in. He had netted his own weight in fish and was pleased. 'My lord,' I said. 'I have found out what Alcinous is going to order.'

'You have? Tell me,' ordered my lord.

With the greatest effort of my life, I told him, 'If the Princess Medea is still a maiden, she will have to return to her father, with the fleece and Phrixos. If she is married to you, then we may keep all of them; fleece and Phrixos and the lady Medea.'

'Then we marry tonight,' he decided. 'Tell the women to prepare the bedchamber for us. Lay the Golden Fleece on the bed. I must wash. Hurry, Nauplios!' he said, and ran for the palace, calling for clean linen and hot water.

Into the breeze caused by his departure I asked, 'Shouldn't someone tell the lady Medea?'

In the end, I could not face it. I sent Atalante to tell her that she should prepare to be married, and took myself for a walk all around the island of Arete and Alcinous.

It took me all the rest of the day and all night, and I was so exhausted when I returned that I threw myself down into the nearest bed and slept like a dead man.

Chapter Twenty-one

Medea

They sent Atalante to tell me to prepare for my marriage. The judgement had been made, though not pronounced, and I must surrender my maidenhood to Jason or be sent back to my father. There was no gift I would not give to Jason, my dearest love, more willingly than that.

The women of the palace were delighted. I was stripped of my plain robes and my tunic, plunged into a hot bath, and scrubbed unmercifully. One woman sat at my feet, using a piece of volcano stone to remove tar from my soles. Two others had possession of my hands, paring my nails. More were washing and combing my hair, and the rest of Arete's maidens were rummaging through chests of cloth, seeking wedding garments for a princess.

I was restless and relieved. If I was married to Jason he could not be able to give me to anyone to ensure the safety of his crew. And I wanted him so badly that my knees became unreliable as soon as I pictured his face or remembered his touch.

I had not been much attended before. It was strange to lie back in scented water and be groomed. No wonder Scylla and Kore washed each other so thoroughly. It felt very pleasant.

'My lady has beautiful hands,' observed the slave who was cleaning my nails. 'Has she any jewellery fit for a wedding?'

'The lady has not,' I replied. 'The lady brings nothing to her lord but two hounds and herself.'

'Your lord is fortunate,' said the slave automatically, laying my hand back under the water.

I was lifted from my bath, dried, and laid on a bench while an old woman massaged me with scented oil. The island is famous for its scents, and I did not know this compound; it was sweet and musky, a little like the frankincense which the Scythian women used.

'It is a blend of aromatic herbs,' said the old woman, feeling for knots in my shoulder and back with her knobbed, wise hands. 'It is jasmine and roses, and a scent extracted from the testicles of certain beasts, and it is a soft waxy substance which washes ashore. We call it the gift of Thetis, as our island is the sickle of Cronos. It is the marriage scent, Lady, the essence of the flesh. Here you will know all the joys of love as you lie down with your new husband. He is also being washed and anointed for your sacrifice to Aphrodite.'

'I am a little afraid,' I said truthfully.

'That is to be expected,' she answered, turning me over and smoothing her soft hand down my belly. 'But if you love this man, you will like his touch. You will accept a little pain for greater joy. Here,' she slid her fingers along the inside of my thighs, 'here is the sheath.'

I allowed her to part my legs and she made a sharp tutting noise as she stroked oil into the skin. 'You have been mishandled, Lady. By your lord?'

'By one who tried to rape me,' I replied, remembering Aegialeus and repressing a shudder.

'He did not succeed,' she soothed. 'But there are some small cuts, which I will anoint. In your husband's arms you will forget the cruelty of the other,' she promised, and I drowsed as she stroked me. In Jason's arms, I was convinced, I would forget Aegialeus, Phrixos, Achaea and Colchis.

I bade farewell for the night to Scylla and Kore, bidding them stay with the women. They whined. They had not slept without me before. I kissed each of them on the nose, promising to return. The women brought me into the dark street. I was dressed in a tunic of cobweb thinness and a red robe heavy with gold. I looked through my red veil to the dancers and singers. All the maidens were singing a song to Hymen, the Achaean god of marriage, and they danced around me, their tunics fluttering, as we walked along toward the palace.

The singing and drums and lyres echoed and bounced, and I was suddenly short of breath, my heart thudding like the drums. I leaned on the old woman as the torches blurred. She clucked and bore me up, and she was smiling at me. They were all smiling.

'Maiden, here is your husband,' announced the old woman. And there was Jason—and he was magnificent.

The royal slaves had found him a red robe which matched mine. His hair flowed down, golden as sunrise. The Argonauts flanked him, though I looked for the boy Nauplios and could not see him. Jason held out his arms, and I walked into his embrace.

And then they conducted us into a chamber which was hung with tapestries. In the middle was a bed on which was lain the Golden Fleece of Colchis. Laughing and singing, the attendants laid us down together and gave us wine. I drank thirstily, for my mouth was dry. Then at last they were gone and the door was shut.

The only light came from a small oil lamp. Jason rose on one elbow, and I looked into the face of a god.

His mouth came down on mine. I was naked and he was naked and we lay flank to flank and skin to skin. His hands trailed down, from my hair to my throat, shoulders to breast. He tasted of honey and wine and salt.

'You are so beautiful,' he murmured, kissing my breast. He mouthed the nipple, and a jolt went through me. I reached out for him, caressing his back and his chest. My hands slid down over his flat belly, then faltered. He took my hand in his and laid it on the phallus. It filled my palm, a hard spear, far too big to fit inside me.

But my touch was pleasing him. He gasped, 'Oh, my love, my love, my own princess,' he whispered. 'My wife, my own.'

I opened my legs as his fingers sought the vessel. His touch recalled Aegialeus and I winced, but he was moving slowly, murmuring of my beauty and his desire, and gradually I felt the touch go deep, as though his fingers were sinking into my flesh, as though he was part of me. The scented oil which the old woman had applied to me was easing the way of the clever hands, which found and stroked so gently that I felt the prickling again, an itch which demanded to be scratched.

He was lying with his head on my belly, looking at the sacred place which priestesses of Hekate are forbidden to touch. 'Ah, my beautiful one,' he said, and kissed the place where the hair fails, the mount of Isis, which fitted into his hand as though it had been designed for him.

The kiss sent a shock through me. My back arched. I heard him say, 'Ah, my witch,' and then he was lying between my legs. The weight on me was heavy, but a desired weight. Something inside me was knotted like string, some part of me which I had been unaware was empty, hollow, a void was begging to be filled.

And then I felt the phallus touch, withdraw, touch, and I was filled with fire. I wreathed my legs around his waist and he moved suddenly, and he was inside me.

Oh, strange, oh, beautiful, the closeness, the closeness. There was no rip or tear as he slid inside me, my sheath wet with oil and desire. I felt something stretch and then break without pain. Yet the itch was not relieved, but heightened by this mating; I felt him move within me, forward and back, and each time the fire ran along my limbs and I held him tighter. I saw him reared above me like Poseidon, his hair falling onto my face, his skin bronzed by the light. His face was a mask, holy and worshipful.

I began to move with him, lifting my hips, unbearably stimulated, desperate for some release from the sweet pain, and then I felt the phallus shudder and the world dissolved in bright light. I convulsed, feeling muscles which were not subject to my will wrap the phallus and contract and suck.

I don't know how long it was before I came back to myself. I was lying under my lord. He was heavy, and I wriggled.

He woke and lay beside me. 'Oh, my sweet love,' sighed Jason. I felt down the sheath, and brought my fingers back wet with semen—a new smell, like the herb wormwood—and blood, and he kissed them.

'You have given me a great gift,' he said, and laid his head on my breast. I embraced his body and closed my eyes. I was new made. I was no longer Medea the princess and priestess of Colchis. I was Medea the Achaean, wife of Jason, son of Aison.

We slept a little, then woke and made love again, and slept again. His breath was sweet, his skin smooth, I trembled at his touch, and my caress pleased him. He was my god, my deity, my most beautiful man. I had left the worship of the dark, and fallen in love with the light.

The Argonauts were rowing, I was stitching a new sole for my lord's sandal and we were approaching an island, when there was a dreadful crash and a rock, hurled from the shore, splashed down near us. The boat rocked, the rowers cursed and Philammon commented, 'Ah. Talos' isle.'

'Talos?' I asked. This was a god whose name I did not know.

'The bronze giant. He patrols this place.'

'Well, we can sail around, out of range,' said Nauplios. He was not speaking directly to me, and he did not seem to want to look at me, either. I wondered what I had done to offend him. I liked Nauplios best of all the Argonauts—except for my lord, of course—but he had avoided me since I had been married, and I supposed that his previous good opinion of me had been based on my virgin state.

I was joyfully and entirely no longer virgin. Jason delved into my body with delight, and I wrapped him in my arms. I had never been so happy. I longed for the night, so that I could lie eagerly down with him in his cloak, or naked on soft grass, and open my body to him, drinking in his seed. I was witless, adoring, given over entirely to the service of Isis, whom the Achaeans call Aphrodite.

Queen Arete and King Alcinous had known of my married state as soon as they had seen me—seen us, for my lord also glowed with love. They had dismissed us as blameless and sent the Colchians home, and they had gone, with the judgement of the sweet-scented island to justify their return without fleece or bones or the Princess Medea, or revenge for the death of Aegialeus. It had been two weeks and I was utterly pleased with my marriage, though Scylla and Kore removed themselves in dudgeon when we were making love, and curled up together at a distance. But now it looked as if I would have to gather up what wits love had left me and concentrate. I put down the sandal as another boulder hurtled through the sky and thudded into the sea. The assailant was getting closer to us.

'It may not be possible to navigate around Talos. The sea is intent on carrying us into his realm,' said Argos.

'Tell me of this giant,' I said.

Philammon replied, 'He was made by Hephaestos to guard his smithy. Talos is thirty cubits tall and as strong as the earth, and ships who land on his island never leave, because he bombards them with rocks until they sink.'

'There's a headland,' said Akastos. 'He can't see over there— we'll row for it. The current is strong, but we can do it. And the alternative, shipmates, is to wait until the ocean washes us into the bay, where we will shortly be crushed flatter than an ant under an anvil.'

When it was put like that, the Argonauts were convinced. They bent to the oars, and *Argo* complained in all her timbers. As effortfully as an old woman trudging up a muddy road with an amphora of water, we passed across the mouth of the little bay, with rocks falling all about us, and swung her in behind the headland.

I was thinking, something which I had not done for some time. If this was a real giant, he could surely see us, and could easily follow us and drop his missiles on us from above. But the rocks continued to splash into the bay. This argued that he could not move, and probably could not see. I suspected that Talos was not an earthly monster but a machine such as Daedalus the Cretan made for my father, Aetes. I had examined the fountains which gave the Colchians wine and milk during festivals. They were worked by hydraulics, a technique of great ingenuity which used the pressure of a fluid to raise a stopper up a shaft. That same inventor had made figures which moved and danced, or even sang, as the wine flowed through them.

'My lord,' I called to Jason.

'My lady?'

'Let me go ashore alone,' I said, for if this was a matter of machinery I did not want a lot of strong men distracting me and possibly breaking something important. 'I am a Colchian and a sorceress, and I believe that I can defeat Talos.'

Awe crept into his eyes. 'Medea, can you do this?'

'I will attempt it.' I shed my outer robe and stood up in my tunic. 'While he is still casting those stones, we cannot get out of the harbour, and I am eager to see Iolkos and your kingdom, my lord.' I borrowed a long knife from Clytios, who was near me, and jumped onto the rocks, followed by my hounds.

'Wait for me for one day,' I said, glowing with delight at the idea of being able to do something for my lord in return for the gift of his love and protection. Argos dropped a skin of water into my arms, nearly empty, and a lump of hard bread.

I was alone. It felt very strange. I had become used to living close and lying with my lord. But Kore nosed along the rocks and Scylla and I followed her. Kore was always our pathfinder.

It was a bright day. The island was the usual bare Aegean islet, with a base of limestone and a thin covering of scrubby trees, wild olives on the level and spruces higher up, and thin grass on which some goats grazed. They fled as we approached. They had no bells and no one was attending them, so I assumed that people had once lived on Talos' isle, but lived there no longer.

The reason that the population had fled was explained when I reached the rocky escarpment looking over the bay, and saw him.

He was huge, at least the thirty cubits which Philammon had claimed. He stood in the space between two cliffs. He was indeed bronze, a helmeted man in full armour, standing on legs the size of pillars. His arms never ceased, picking up boulders from the surrounding cliff and hurling them into the sea.

I sat down and watched him. Scylla, who had the most refined nose, sniffed, then whined. The smoothness of his actions, the identical nature of each throw and the fact that he never tired were suggestive; but I had seen a Scythian woman, for a wager, throw a spear twenty times into a tree with the same action. Scylla would probably have howled and fled at the scent of something so alien as this giant must be, if he were flesh and bone. Instead she had seemed worried, but not afraid.

Fling, splash, fling, splash. The interval between movements was always the same, precisely a count of seventy. That decided me. This was a construction, an immense and sophisticated machine, not a reasonable being.

That being so, I climbed down the rocks to the path. I was walking around between the huge legs, attempting to find some way of letting out the fluid which drove it—for it was clear that it was indeed an hydrolos—when a spear whizzed past me and stuck in the sand. I drew my knife. Then a face looked out from behind a rock and I jumped.

'Who are you?' snapped an old, cross voice.

'Medea, wife of Jason, who are you?' I found my voice. The dogs had leapt to my side and were flanking me, fangs bared.

'Talos. Call off the hounds,' he begged.

'Come into view, Talos,' I demanded.

He was a small, bent old man in a stained tunic. The twisting of the bones, which we call rheumatics, had him in its grip. His fingers were like old tree roots. His hair was white and cut short, but he had a very long white beard.

'Well, Medea, wife of Jason, you are a woman of great daring,' he observed. 'No one else would have challenged my giant.'

'I need to get to Iolkos. My husband must be put on the throne,' I explained.

'You are going to Iolkos to depose Pelias?' His eyes lit up. 'Well, that is different. Yes, that is indeed different. You, Lady, you are no Achaean, though you speak it well.'

'I am from Colchis,' I said.

He chuckled. 'Ah, yes, the witches of Colchis, most knowledgeable of women.' He coughed suddenly, putting a hand to his mouth. I knew what the bloodstain meant. I put an arm around his waist.

'Lord, you must sit down,' I urged. 'Let me take you inside.'

I hauled him into his little cave. It was quite comfortable. Scylla and Kore sat down on guard outside, while the bronze giant threw his stones and I brewed an infusion of lungwort and coltsfoot for the old man. The herbs were to hand. He knew that he was dying.

'Thank you,' he whispered. 'I am better, Lady. These fits come on me, and one day I will die in one of them. Pelias exiled me. I have been here for twenty years. I was the best craftsman in Achaea once. Now I will die in a cave, with no company but the sea birds and the goats.'

'Will you come back and watch Pelias' deposition?' I offered. I was sure that Jason would take Talos home. The old man shook his head.

'No, I would not last the voyage.' I had to agree. His lung ailment was smith's disease, got by bending over smelting metal for years and inhaling the toxic fumes. His wasted body was wracked with coughing, and every cough brought blood.

'But I will allow you to pass, Lady. Pull that lever down.'

I did so. There was a shudder in the rock as the giant slowed his movements.

'I have drained the *ichor* from his veins,' said Talos, 'It will take twelve hours to refill. Go, Medea. Bring Pelias down and when he lies at your feet, bid him remember Talos, whom he exiled because he would not make such machines as these for a greedy and cruel king. Machines are for the delight and help of men,' said the old man, blood bubbling to his lips.

'Machines are for fountains, for labour and, perhaps even one day, to fly like a bird through the air. Pelias wanted me to make warriors for him, with which he could conquer cities—and I would not. Here is the only one of his bronze soldiers that I ever made. And once I am dead, no one will be able to use it to kill other men. Farewell, Lady. Come safe home, and revenge me.'

I stoked his fire for him, put an infusion ready to his hand, and left. Pelias would know what had become of Talos.

When I came back to the ship the Argonauts hailed me, but I saw them making the signs to avert evil. Jason kissed me in front of all his crew, and we set a sail because the wind had picked up.

We were within sight of islands which every Argonaut knew. We came down the coast of Phrygia, past Lesbos where only women lived. There Philammon sang the central song of his faith. As he sang, the sun shone on his bright hair, so brightly that I could hardly look at him.

> *As wine mixes, dark wine and clear water,*
> *Spiralling into purple to fill the cup,*
> *The wine in the cup is of grapes not yet grown,*
> *And grapes long dead, and of the drinkers, their clothes,*
>   *and their houses.*
> *The fire built by shepherds to warm their sleep*
> *Among the restless herds, is of tree still in seed and wood*
>   *as ash,*
> *And contains both shepherds, sheep, night and fire.*
> *The nurseling in his mother's arms is live child, dead*
>   *bones, child not yet conceived,*
> *And mother and her mother.*
> *All things are immutable; there live in us and all things*
> *The seed of suns, the matter of night.*

'That song is called the "Krater",' he told me. 'Krater' is Achaean for the large mixing bowl in which they mingle water with their wine.

'But what does it mean?' I asked.

'Ah, Lady, a hundred priests could reply to that question, and all of them would be wrong. And right, of course.'

Which was no answer at all. Was he saying that time, perhaps, is not a straight road down which all must walk from birth to death? Tyche had spoken to me of prophecy, which she called 'a window into another time'. I had little prevision. These matters were too complex for me.

I was beginning to wonder what was happening to my body. I was seasick all the time, even in placid seas, though I had not been sick at first. It had been two months since I lay with my lord for the first time, and I had not bled. I began to think that I was pregnant. I would have been full of joy if I had not felt so ill.

Nauplios found me fruits to eat at some of the islands, though he still would not stay in my company, and that was a pity, for my lord was often busy, and apart from the hounds I was a little lonely.

Atalante's way of living, I had decided, could not be mine. I admired her. She was as skilled and independent as the Scythian women and as strong-minded as a Sauromatae. The Argonauts treated her as though she was a comrade, as they would never treat me, the wife of their commander. She was scornful of me. I had abandoned my maidenhood and my craft. She chided me for my choice, which she considered weak and foolish.

'What will you do, Lady, when you are old, beyond child bearing? The Achaeans have no time for old women, and your lord will take another wife.'

'Take another wife?' I cried. 'But he is married to me.'

'That is so, Lady, but old men need young lovers to keep their bones warm. You were a priestess and a wise woman, a princess in your father's house. Now you will be the drudge of an Achaean man, and no worse fate could befall a woman.'

I did not reply, being taken by a sudden spasm, and when I lifted my head from vomiting over the side, she had turned her back on me. It was a very straight back, Atalante's; bare and smooth. I suppressed the desire to plunge a knife into it. I did not know where these violent images were coming from—perhaps it was the vengeance of Hekate on her faithless one.

Then we sailed into Iolkos.

◇◇◇

We had been sighted as we came around past Skiathos, and all day the crowd on the seafront had been growing. Jason and Nauplios stood beside me.

'There are the cliffs,' said Nauplios softly. 'There is the mountain, where the centaurs fostered us.'

'There is the quay where *Argo* was built,' said Jason. 'And the marketplace where I came, the *monosandalos,* to be given this quest by Pelias Usurper. My quest is achieved,' he said with satisfaction. 'The Golden Fleece lies in this ship, and the bones of restless Phrixos, ancestor of Minyans.

'And we return, who would not have been looked for. But not as we left, alas! Poor Idmon was left in the swamp in Mysia, and Tiphys the beautiful beside him. Herakles we lost on that coast, and Hylas with him.'

'Oh, our lost ones,' whispered Nauplios, and Jason put an arm around his shoulders. The boy was close to tears. He enumerated the names of the dead in a chant, which turned into a song, a wailing of loss shared by all the Argonauts.

Thus *Argo* came back to the city of Pelias as she had left, Nauplios said; in mourning and with weeping. She slipped into the place left for her at the stone waterfront, and the rowers shipped their oars for the last time.

I was lifted ashore with the others, and stood behind Jason in the crowd of well-wishers. The market women hailed the heroes, calling obscene reminiscences at them.

'It's them, sisters,' screamed one fat woman, hands on hips. 'Him with the flagpole phallus and his shipmate with the muscles.'

Oileus and Nestor grinned, recognising themselves. 'Couldn't keep us away from such pretty girls,' they responded, and the fishwife screamed 'Oh, yes? And what about all them Lemnian women?'

'Not a patch on the women of Iolkos,' declared Oileus, and was kissed soundly by three of them. Telamon took the wine cup out of a fisherman's hand and drank it off, smashing the cup on the stones. Nauplios was scanning the people for someone whom he could not find. Alabande and Erginos had taken Clytios and Atalante to the tavern and were calling for wine. Philammon was tuning his lyre, the noise loud enough to hurt the ears.

Did no one in Achaea speak in a normal voice? Scylla and Kore, after being stood on more than once, retreated to my feet and we sat down on the quay on the bundle of our belongings and wondered what would happen when Pelias heard that we had arrived.

We were to know soon enough. The king came from his palace, attended with the *demos* of Iolkos, the old men who were his advisors. He was tall, with a smile I did not like.

'Jason, son of Aison,' he said in a hearty voice. 'Welcome, welcome! You come just in time. The winter gales are beginning.'

'I greet you, Uncle,' said Jason. Then he brought to the king's feet the leather bag containing the bones of Phrixos and the Golden Fleece. Telamon was carrying it, draped over his massive shoulder.

'I have fulfilled my quest,' said Jason loudly. 'Hear, all men of Iolkos! I have brought here what Pelias demanded as the price of my kingship: the Golden Fleece, treasure of Colchis, and the bones of my ancestor Phrixos, who will be buried in his own earth.'

I saw Pelias' face twist with rage. For a moment he could not speak. Jason was looking at him, puzzled. He had done as Pelias had asked. He was expecting Pelias to meekly hand over his sceptre and retire, leaving the kingdom to his nephew.

Jason never expected treachery.

He was staggered and furious when Pelias said, 'You have done well, Nephew. I will think of what we are to do, now that you have so unexpectedly returned. Bring the prizes of such heroism into the palace, and we will feast. You have been long at sea, Nephew. And who is this?'

The crowd had flowed away from me, and the king stared at the sight of a red-robed woman and two hounds, alone amongst the Argonauts.

'This is Medea, Princess of Colchis, my wife,' said Jason.

I knew that I was not supposed to stare directly into a man's face, but I had to know if this king was trustworthy. I judged that he was not.

Pelias' gaze was direct, even rude. He raked me with his eyes for some time before he grunted, 'A Colchian witch.' He turned on his heel and walked back into his palace.

Chapter Twenty-two

Nauplios

I was home. I had thought that I would never see Iolkos again. The journey had been so long, so unlikely, the task so impossible. Yet here I was, standing on the quay again, older, taller, perhaps wiser. I found it hard to remember what he had been like, young Nauplios, the net-caster's son. Since I had last seen the stone pillars of Pelias' palace, soon to be my lord's, I had lain with many women, found out about the secrets of the flesh, watched death and love, and sailed uncounted *stadia* through incredible seas.

And by the blessings of Poseidon and Jason's protector, Hera, we had come back alive, bearing the Golden Fleece and the bones of Phrixos. Most of us had come back alive. We had mourned our lost ones as we came into the harbour.

And soon I had more to mourn.

I wondered that my father was not amongst the crowd, and as soon as Pelias had taken Jason and the lady Medea into the palace I shook off my companions. They were gathered in the tavern on the waterfront and seemed likely to remain there while wine was still made by men. I went searching for my father. I asked the old men, and they stared at me sadly, shaking their heads.

'Go to your mother, Nauplios,' they said and, much worried, I climbed the narrow streets between the whitewashed walls to my father's house.

It is a small place, only one room. On the hearth were a heap of cold ashes. I knew what had happened before I went inside. Only death can extinguish a hearth fire. The bride brings it to her husband's house, and it never goes out while he lives.

'How did he die?' I asked the woman seated on the floor beside the dead fire.

'He went fishing,' she said, without looking up. 'The storm took three boats. He was washed ashore, to lie beside his sons. They are all dead now,' she said in a flat, toneless voice. 'There is nothing left to me.'

'There is me, mother,' I said, kneeling beside her. She looked up into my face. I know she recognised me. She almost smiled. I was looking into the face of an old woman. Her hair was white, clotted with the ashes of her mourning, and her skin was deeply lined, dry and grey, like Colchian parchment.

'Nauplios has come to take his mother to the afterlife,' she said, a little animation creeping into her voice. 'That is kind of you, Son, but where have you left your brothers and your father? This side of Styx, he said, I will wait this side of Styx for you to come, Wife. Has he gone on ahead? That is discourteous. Now he will have forgotten me, who always loved and served him. But I am glad that it is you, Nauplios. You always were my favourite son.' She raised her trembling hand and brushed my hair from my brow, as she had always done when I was a small boy, and the familiar touch brought tears to my eyes. She wiped them briskly away.

'Do not weep, my dearest son,' she said. 'I am ready to die. What life is there for a widow, childless, kinless, wearing away her life on the fading generosity of neighbours until she lies down for weariness and dies at last? Better to die now,' said my mother calmly, leaning her head against my chest and closing her eyes.

And I was holding a body, which sagged into death. Her last breath was breathed almost into my mouth. As she slipped out of my embrace, a little bottle rolled from her unclenching hand. It had contained poison. She must have been sitting on the cold floor alone for hours as it worked. It was hemlock. I knew the smell.

There remained nothing of the family of Dictys, man of Iolkos, but one faithless son, who had gone adventuring with Jason, son of Aison, and returned just in time to watch his own mother leave a life which had become loathsome to her.

I sat by her body until it was dark, holding her hand, trying to explain that I had been under oath; that I had to follow my lord, the lord to whom my father had given me when I was a child. I told her shade, which hovered around me—a loving shade, for my mother was always loving—that I had never forgotten her and that I had returned as I said I would.

And in the end I think she understood and forgave me, because the deep oppression which had compressed my spirit lifted, and I saw a wryneck, the bird which conducts the soul to the river of Hades' realm, flash past the door into the sunset. She was journeying to her other sons and my father, who waited this side of the cold river of forgetfulness for her to come; for my father was a man of his word, and I was sure that he would be there when my mother's shade came down the dark staircase into the underworld.

I would not be long joining them, for all my joy was turned to sorrow.

I called in the neighbours when the darkness came, to prepare the body for burial. Only the bodies of nobles were burned, and I wanted her to share my father's grave, as she had shared his bed all those years. The fishermen took me out of the cold house and into someone's kitchen, where attentive boys gave me wine. They told me that she had been inconsolable when my father was lost. They said that they had sent their daughters and wives to my mother in her despair, and I had no doubt that they had—fishing communities look after each other—but she had refused all help and after a few days, even food.

The women had watched her, fearing suicide, but she had slipped their guard and found, somewhere, a hemlock infusion strong enough to accomplish her purpose. She had asked that she be left alone all day to pray and sacrifice to the gods. That request could not be denied, and she had been cunning. She knew how long it took hemlock to work, and had made sure that no one would intrude on her until it was too late.

The fishermen begged me to absolve them of blame in her death, and truly I did not blame them. I wept and they wept with me.

'You are home now, Nauplios, and although it is a terrible homecoming, it is at least a homecoming. Your quest is achieved, and we welcome you, however sadly,' said Icthyos, the old man who was my father's closest friend. 'You must allow us to care for you, for we will not lose you as well, fisherman of Iolkos.'

They made me eat a hot, strong fish stew and pressed on me honey cakes and more wine, and I ate and drank as they required.

The young men asked about the voyage for the Golden Fleece. I could not talk to them at first, then I imagined in one old face or another that I saw a hint of my father, a spark of his intelligence, or perhaps the cast of his countenance. So I told the tale of the Golden Fleece to my father, Dictys, as though he were alive and listening, while the women washed and shrouded my mother's body, keening their grief, and we carried her out into the street with torches to her funeral.

We accompanied the wrapped bundle which had been my mother, Althea, to the cemetery on the hill, where someone had hacked out a grave beside my father. The priests made the offerings, and I wept and tore my hair and poured ashes on my head, and then someone took me home to sleep by their fire, and I passed out of consciousness.

I awoke with Icthyos' daughter bending over me. I did not remember her well—she had been a little girl when I left with Jason—but she had grown as well as I. She was attempting to reach the hearth without waking me. I had fallen with my feet to the fire, and my soles were almost smouldering. My head, as I found when I tried to lift it, hurt with cold and wine and grief.

'Nauplios,' she said soothingly, helping me to sit up. 'I am sorry about your mother. I hope you do not blame us.'

'I do not blame you,' I said, wrapping someone's cloak around me and moving so that she could get to the fire with her armload of light wood. She threw the kindling on the ashy hearth and it flared up, washing me with heat. She set a pot on the fire, and presently gave me a piece of bread and some warm, heavily watered wine.

'Thank you, maiden,' I said uncertainly. I did not feel altogether real. I knew that as soon as I came wholly back to myself I would be plunged in grief, but at that moment, nothing actually hurt me. 'I have forgotten your name, I am sorry.'

'I am called Amphitrite,' she said. Her voice was low and sympathetic. She was certainly good looking, soft and dark, with long cloudy hair bound up with a white seashell. I drank the wine and stumbled to the door.

The sun was shining. This struck me as unfair and I wept. How could the sun rise callously as if nothing had happened, when my family was gone?

Amphitrite, daughter of Icthyos, gave me a cloth to wipe my face and said nothing, for which I was grateful.

I sat in mourning at my father's hearth for three days, as was fitting. The crew of the *Argo* had heard the news—gossip spreads like wildfire in small seaside towns—and they came, one by one or in small groups, to express their sympathy and bring me gifts and food.

The first was Atalante, who came striding up the steps, scandalously underclad in her short tunic. I heard the wives and the old women clucking with disapproval like a lot of hens as she walked past their windows.

'Nauplios,' she said, sitting down without invitation. Atalante paid no attention to inconvenient customs. 'I mourn with you,' she said, taking a pinch of ash and scattering it over her head. Then she did not speak or try and comfort me, but sat companionably and shared my silence.

Telamon, Oileus, Nestor and Alabande came in a group, bringing bread and oil and precious Kriti honey, but my grief made them uneasy and they did not stay. Argos sent Melas with fish. Erginos, Clytios, Authalides and Ancaeas came and sat with me for a whole day.

As they left, Ancaeas the Strong told me, 'Don't despair. There are gods, you know, shipmate, and they have Tiphys, Hylas and Idmon as well to care for. We have to trust the gods, Nauplios.'

I don't think I replied. I could not get used to my father not being there, not being in the world. I had pictured his pleased face, if I ever got home to tell my tale. I had often thought of how proud he might be of me, and how delighted my mother would be if I had told her that I was never moving from Iolkos again. Now they were gone into the dark, and couldn't hear me. They were all gone into the dark.

Jason never came, nor Akastos or Admetos. None of the royal ones of Iolkos came to sit with Dictys the net-caster's son, in his sorrow. But I should not have expected it. The deaths of a fisherman and his lowly wife were not significant when they were occupied with affairs of state.

Idas told me that Pelias was delaying the transfer of the kingship to Jason; which would have seemed important to me once. All of the other Argonauts came and left some gift or some saying, or sat with me as the dawn grew into noon and then faded into dark.

Even Autolycus came, and his friends Deileon and Phlogius. They brought the most expensive wine, which I could not drink until the third day. It had the seal of Pelias of Iolkos on the jars, and I wondered that the king was so generous.

Then, late on the second day, I heard a lyre, and the noise of a litter being carried up the steps. The bearers were panting and someone was scolding them in inventive but excellent Achaean with a strong Colchian accent.

'Put this litter down and let me walk!' she demanded.

'Lady, you must not walk like a common woman!' protested a bearer.

'I am no common woman, even if I crawl,' said the lady Medea. 'Do as I say. The street is too narrow. Now, stand there and wait for me. You may look inside, if you must, but you will not interrupt or I will stop all your tongues forever, and you will never charm a girl again with your sweet words.'

'What shall we say to your lord, if he asks us why we allowed you to be alone in a room with a man?' wailed the same voice.

'You shall tell him the man is Nauplios, an Argonaut and a comrade, and if he does not trust me in this, he can trust me in nothing,' she spat, evidently seriously displeased. 'Let me pass, or not one of you will be going down this hill with the same number of testicles as he had when he came up.'

This threat worked. She came into my father's house on a gust of wind, accompanied by her hounds. The ashes of mourning puffed up into a cloud. She was clad all in red and her hair was as black as ebony. Kore and Scylla whined and licked at my tears.

'I can do little for you,' the lady said to me. 'I have brought you this potion, which will give you sleep without dreams. I am thinking of you, Nauplios, I grieve with you.'

She did not know our customs, I realise that. She did not know that a man in mourning must not be touched. She knelt beside me and pulled me into her arms, and I was so surprised that I did not withdraw, as I should have.

She smelled so clean. I was sticky with the blood of the funeral sacrifice and streaked with tears and ash. She was fresh from bathing. Strands of her hair fell across my face. Most improperly, I allowed her to stroke my forehead—her fingers were cool and sure—then she traced a sign on my cheek and kissed the centre of it.

'You will recover,' she said seriously. 'You will not die of grief. No one does, not of grief itself. Here is the infusion, it will do you no harm, even if you drink all of it. And I have brought Philammon to you,' she added.

Philammon bent his coppery head to come in under the lintel, and when I looked past him the lady Medea was gone.

The bard was also looking after the retreating red gown. 'She is unique, the daughter of Aetes,' he commented. 'What song can I sing you, Nauplios my friend? Or will you have my silence?'

'Sing,' I said. The lady had done something to me. I had not forgotten my family but the unbearable ache had eased. Not gone. But I no longer felt like a void, a gap in the universe, a nothing. I was Nauplios again, a shaky, incomplete version of him, but Nauplios the Argonaut of Iolkos.

'I will sing you then the song of the net, Dictys net-wielder's son,' Philammon said, tuning the lyre. Then he began to sing. Ash blew at the sound of his voice and the notes of his lyre, and I had a vision.

> *The fisherman casts his net*
> *Across the blue water,*
> *All manner of strange things rise to the surface,*
> *Flatfish and weed and stones and stars,*
> *The net of Phanes ties all things together,*
> *Touch one thread and another vibrates.*
> *A woman groans in childbirth,*
> *And Libyan men get sunstroke.*
> *A man dies of fever in Attica,*
> *And Egyptian palms bear many dates.*
> *A wave moves on Aegeas' ocean,*
> *The stars tremble. Be aware of the net.*
> *Phanes' net, which links all things together.*

I was out in the small boat with my father. My brothers were beside me, and my mother, and my father was saying, 'There, see, boys? There's the harbour.' And we were sailing into a magnificent bay toward a village, golden and white. I did not know the seaport, but I was suddenly flooded with a sense of rightness, of peace.

I drank the potion and slept deeply. Philammon stayed with me for the third day and Atalante, Clytios, Lynkeos, and I got uproariously drunk that night on the wine of Pelias. Nothing hurt me ferociously after that. I felt that nothing could be worse, and a man who has borne the worst, Herakles used to say, can laugh at ordinary pains.

I did not laugh, but I knew what he meant.

I had cleansed my father's house of the ash and blood of mourning. I had washed the step with clean water seven times, to deny entrance to ghosts. Amphitrite, Icthyos' daughter, had brought a flame from her father's hearth to light my fire again. If I prospered, I had agreed with my father's oldest friend to marry his daughter. I was determined that my father's seed should not die utterly, and Amphitrite was a virtuous girl and an excellent housekeeper. She was also his third daughter, so he would not demand too much dowry for her. She liked me well and might grow to love me, and in any case was willing to bear my sons and to care for me and my house. I might, in time, be as happy as I could be.

But when I heard what was happening in the palace of the king, I saw my marriage prospects slipping away like an ebbing tide.

Pelias had broken his word. He would not surrender the kingship to Jason, and there seemed nothing to be done about it. We were not numerous enough to defeat Pelias with arms, and in any case that would not have helped, as Philammon pointed out. It would merely replace one usurper with another. Jason was in despair, and Admetos and Akastos had no advice to offer.

I joined the Argonauts in the waterfront tavern. Some had already gone home. That night we farewelled the strong men, Atalante and Clytios and the twins. My heart was still so tender that I cried like a child, and they all embraced me as they took their leave and went away.

'Come and see us,' begged Idas and Lynkeos, for the first time speaking in harmony with each other. 'We won't forget you,' promised Atalante and Clytios, Meleagros, Perithous and Nestor. His honey voice cracked as he began his speech of parting, and he finished it in a whisper.

My world, which had seemed so solid, was melting again, and I was very glad that Argos and Melas would still be there after this night, as would Admetos, Akastos and Philammon, who said that his god had instructed him to stay until the matter of the kingship of Iolkos was resolved.

The Argonauts went away on the same roads on which they had arrived, shamefully unprovided with treasure or reward for their great courage and skill. The only heavy bundle was that of Autolycus, and I had a suspicion that, witting or unwitting, Pelias had contributed to his travelling expenses.

Atalante's straight back glimmered between Idas and Lynkeos, who were already quarrelling about who had saved whom from the predatory Lemnian women. Clytios was singing a walking song in his clear tenor voice. They were all leaving us, leaving doomed Iolkos, leaving to go home to fame, and to hearths, and parents who would be proud of them. I suddenly remembered Hylas and Herakles coming into the marketplace after dark; the beautiful boy and a great hero who looked like an elderly farmer and who touched a bunch of blue flowers with reverent fingers. All gone; all dead or gone. The darkness was thronged with ghosts, and I shivered.

'He must die,' said Jason suddenly.

'Pelias? But we have just lost most of our comrades, we have no army, and besides, Jason, he is my father and your uncle,' objected Akastos.

'I never forget that he is your father and my uncle,' said Jason hotly. 'Nor that he exiled my father and sits in his chair of state, holding his sceptre unjustly.'

My Lord shook his fist at the sky. 'There are gods. Why do they allow this to go on? They sent us on this impossible quest and we have achieved it, and yet my friends have gone their ways with not so much as a gold coin to sweeten their voyage or reward their labours; and we sit in this tavern, scolding like fishwives because there is nothing we can do.'

'Hera guarded us,' said Argos. 'I heard her voice as the ship was launched. She will contrive. Women always get their way.' 'One way or another, in the end.'

'Women,' said Jason, and poured himself some more wine. 'I have married a witch of Colchis,' he mused. 'There must be something she could do.'

'The people would not accept it,' warned Akastos. 'If she turns him into a frog, they will insist that a frog rules Iolkos, as long as it is a native-born frog. They are suspicious enough of the foreign woman as it is.'

'That is true,' agreed Admetos. 'And she has not taken readily to Achaean customs.'

'They are strange to her,' said Jason. 'She spent some time with the Scyths, where women are allowed to run wild. She will be tamed when her babe is born.'

I had my doubts about that. I did not think the lady Medea was tractable. There are some animals which can never be truly domesticated. Weasels may share a man's house and his fire and hunt and eat his rats, but they act for themselves, not for him, and they own no master. A fox may be caught as a tiny cub, taken from his mother's care, but he will never become a dog, and when he is grown he will leave his master to rove the woods as a free animal. The lady Medea, I judged, was such a creature. But she was none of my concern, and it was not right to allow my mind to dwell on her.

I could not imagine what Jason had in mind. But he went back to the palace, where he lodged, with a satisfied smile. He always had that smile when he was about to win a board game. I did not like it.

◇◇◇

In the morning the streets of Iolkos echoed to the wailing of women. I stumbled out of my bed and leaned out of the doorway, trying to hear what they were crying.

'Pelias, Pelias,' the females keened. 'Pelias, killed by his daughters! Aie! Aie! Pelias is dead! The foreign witch has killed Pelias!'

I feared the worst. I put on my travelling clothes and took a bundle of belongings with me when I descended to the marketplace, thinking that if the people reacted badly to this happening, Jason might have to run.

And that, of course, meant that I would have to go with him, because the oath which I had rashly sworn still held me. I had said I would stay with Jason until he was king of Iolkos, and unless we were all a lot luckier than we had been to date, he would never be king of the place where he was born.

There was a large crowd in the marketplace before the palace. They were armed with cleavers and reaping hooks, and I was shoved and battered as I tried to push through them to reach Jason, who was standing alone at the bronze-bound doors with a drawn sword. He was dangerous, and they had not dared to approach too close. His hair was loose and he was snarling, teeth bared.

'The foreign witch!' shrieked the women, brandishing their razor-sharp oyster knives. 'Bring us the foreign sorceress who killed our king!'

'I am your king,' shouted Jason. There was a moment's silence. I paused behind my lord. The crowd were thinking about this. Then they howled him down. 'Medea, Medea!' they screamed.

I reached Jason and he allowed me to pass him. Behind the door I found the lady Medea, attended by her dogs. She was clad again in red and gold. Jason had been furious, but his furies never lasted. When he had been challenged sufficiently, he would give way as he always did, and then the mob would seize the Colchian witch and tear her to pieces.

She had been listening to the voices, screaming of what they intended to do to her, and she was not confounded. The lady Medea was steadfast and alert. Frightened, but alert.

'What is happening?' she demanded.

'They will come for you,' I said roughly, pushing her further into the room.

'Because the daughters of Pelias killed him?' she protested.

'You caused them to kill him,' I guessed.

She did not waver, agreeing calmly, 'I showed them the cauldron of renewal. They asked their father be allowed to touch it. I said that it was dangerous, they persisted. I said that I would not do it, and they tried it on their own. And failed. Pelias, they found, was just as old as ever when he was cut up and boiled, and dead as well. Why then do the people wish to kill me?'

'Because you are a foreign sorceress. Come, Lady, gather some gowns and food, we will have to leave.'

'Where shall we go?'

'I know not, unless Jason has a plan, but we have to move quickly or we are dead. Jason will not be able to hold them for long.'

'He thought that he would be king of Iolkos by now,' she said, growing pale and grasping for support. She caught at my shoulder. Pregnancy had not deformed her, just added fullness to her breasts and belly. But she was not as strong as she has been. I was worried for her health, and for that of my lord's incipient son, if we had to flee on horseback. Then I recalled that I had a boat.

'I thought it would work,' she murmured. 'But I still do not know enough about Achaean customs. Let me sit down, Nauplios.'

'Can I call your women?'

'They would not come.' She smiled wryly, with a quirk of her red mouth.

'I'll go,' I said. I ran into the princess' apartments, gathered a big armload of cloaks and blankets and tunics, bound them all into a bundle with her bags of herbs and her knife, and brought them to the water gate, where my father's boat, now my own boat, *Good Catch*, was moored. I threw both bundles inside, then returned and led the lady Medea to the back door. She was sick and weak, but she held herself upright with great effort.

'Wait for me here,' I said, and saw her sink down gratefully onto the step between the hounds.

I saw Akastos in the hall. He hailed me. 'Nauplios! Have you heard what that witch has done? There is no chance of Jason being king now. They'll kill him on the steps.'

'Not if I have anything to do with it. I will get him and the lady away, if you will calm the people, Akastos.'

'How can I calm the people?' he asked faintly. 'Gods of Olympus, Nauplios, my sisters killed my father and chopped him into joints and cooked him. I'm going to be sick.'

'No, you aren't,' I yelled, and he blinked at me. He was not used to being addressed so abruptly by a fisherman's son. 'Take hold of yourself, Akastos! Go out there and talk to them. Announce that your father is dead and tell them that they have a new king. Then proclaim three days of mourning so that we can get away.'

'Who can I say is king?' Akastos' eyes were dilated black with shock.

'Why, you,' I said, putting one hand between his shoulder-blades and pushing him through the bronze door into the marketplace. 'You, of course. If you say that you claim the kingship, and that you forbid pursuit of Jason, then you may keep Iolkos forever, and your sons after you, and you have the Golden Fleece as well. Go, now,' I ordered, and he went.

The howling broke over me as the door opened. The wash of fear and hatred left an aftertaste on the tongue like metal. Jason came, and I gave him no time to despair. I took him by the shoulders and marched him through the palace, as the screaming died down in the market.

The lady Medea rose and walked, though I was ready to carry her, and she sat by the steering oars as Jason and I shoved *Good Catch* out into the bay and began to row. Jason was weeping as he rowed. Scylla and Kore howled. The lady Medea stood to guide the boat, dry-eyed, though her face was as white as clay.

We caught a small breeze and hoisted the sail.

'Where are we going?' asked Jason dully.

'Be of good comfort, my lord,' said the Princess Medea. 'I have just remembered something. I am the granddaughter of Helios, and the lordship of Corinth is in my right.'

Chapter Twenty-three

Medea

Corinth was a prosperous city, but I was not in a good state to appreciate it.

It had all gone wrong. I had thought the daughters of Pelias almost too easy to persuade. A little sleight of hand and scented smoke, the old ram's portions in the cauldron and the lamb leaping out of the pot, had worked beautifully. They had been entirely convinced.

There is this to be said for Pelias, he died because his daughters had never been allowed to poke their noses out of their father's house into the world. They were astoundingly credulous, uneducated and superstitious. They instantly believed that a Colchian witch could do anything at all, even raise the dead. At the same time, they were motivated by their love for their father, which I had shamelessly abused to make them kill him.

I had been angry that my lord's right was denied by that old man with sharp teeth in his smile. I remembered also Talos the artificer, coughing out his lungs in the exile which Pelias had imposed upon him. I had listened to the angry Jason, railing into the night about justice as I lay beside him, unable to sleep.

Tyche's plan for outfacing my despised half brother had leapt into my mind, whole and perfect. I would not even need to soil my hands with his blood, for his fools of daughters would kill him. And Jason would love me again, who had drawn away from me. I thought that if I removed the usurper, the traitor Pelias, who had broken his word and was keeping the kingdom when his terms had been fairly met, then my lord, whom I loved and worshipped, would be king as he deserved.

But then it had all gone wrong.

Jason was not king of Iolkos. We were fleeing in Nauplios' little boat to Corinth, and I had compromised my skills and my integrity to no purpose, except that now even Jason was afraid of me.

And I was sick with pregnancy and weak. Corinth, they said, was a stone city with many buildings, but it chiefly interested me at that moment because it was dry land.

The journey took many days. We were able to pick up a couple of sailors, who wanted to go to Athens, to help with navigation as we rowed past Euboea, passing Orchomenus on the edge of a storm. Even Kore and Scylla were sick. It was, as the dead traitor Pelias had said, almost the end of the sailing season.

Jason had little gold, but Nauplios, my most trusted comrade, had wrapped my bag of money and jewellery in the bundle he had brought from the palace of the dismembered king. I broke a gold Scythian necklace into links and sold them one by one as we rowed from little village to little village, buying fish and bread at each stop when the hounds could not hunt for us. And at each place they had heard of the death of Pelias, and several times we were greeted with stones, because *Good Catch* harboured the murderous sorceress, Medea.

I could not eat much, though Nauplios made me swallow the mushy, salty cornmeal porridge that the inhabitants of those parts make with sea water. I was close to despair.

Jason would not speak to me. Even lying close beside him I could feel his distance. I had lost him his heritage and almost cost him his life by my ill-advised action. It seemed like a long, long time before he warmed to me enough to touch me, to kiss me, and even then he was repulsed by my changed state. My belly was swollen, my breasts had grown heavy and tight.

Once, lying in a hut on some Eubocean shore, I had kissed him passionately, trying to bring him back into my embrace and my heart, and he had responded for a moment. I had felt the phallus rise under my touch. His hand caressed me just once, sliding over the altered contours, and then he had patted the curve which contained his child and turned his back on me. He had fallen asleep. I had not.

I estimated that I was two moons from my time of trial when we saw the harbour of Corinth.

Nauplios shouted steering directions to me, and I managed to bring *Good Catch* into the shore without burying her prow in the stone quay. I had learned a little skill with ships on the voyage, for my lord was often so cast down in gloom that he would not help with the boat, caring not where we landed, or if we landed at all. I was pregnant, so I cared.

Jason leapt out and secured the mooring lines, nose and tail. He extended a hand and I clambered out. Kore and Scylla leapt thankfully after me and sniffed at the new scents.

'This is Corinth,' Nauplios commented.

'Do you know anyone here?' asked Jason.

'There is my cousin, Sisyphos, who lives above the market. Come, Lord, the lady is tired and needs rest, and we need to think what to do in order to put her claim before the *demos*. Corinth does not dislike strangers as much as Iolkos. Very many ships come here.'

Leaning on Jason's arm, I surveyed Corinth.

It was a white city, though grey under the lowering skies. It was four times the size of Iolkos, approaching the state of Colchis. It was piled like a child's building blocks, rank on rank of square stone houses from the waterfront to the hill, on which a series of white temples and what was presumably the palace stood. Above the town was a height, which Nauplios told me was the Akrocorinth, where their kings were crowned. The city looked firm, settled, sure of itself. There was no shore guard that I could see, such as small places keep to report on all new arrivals. Corinth had a lot of arrivals.

The stone landing stage was thronged with vessels, even at the end of the season. A shipwright was yelling orders to a group of sweating slaves, who were hauling a galley out of the water and into a cradle dug in the sand. Several fishing boats already lay there, masts dismounted and sails removed, waiting to be careened and stripped of barnacles. A long line of keels stretched from one side of the beach to the other, all cleaned and snugged down for the winter.

A cold wind scoured us with fine sand. The market traders had gone for the day. Night was imminent. The hounds shivered. So did I.

Jason looked at the city and sighed. 'To have come so far, Lady,' he said to me dolefully. 'To have dared so much and borne so many losses, to have done such great deeds in such company, and here we are on the waterfront of Corinth like beggars. I would that Pelias was still alive, and we were in the tavern in Iolkos, drinking Kiti wine.'

'But Pelias is dead, my lord,' I said.

'And whose fault is that?' he snarled, glaring sideways at me.

'Mine, my lord,' I admitted. 'But that cannot now be amended. Do not despair. There is always time to despair, my lord. We can always despair later.'

He seemed to acknowledge this. We stood in silence, looking over the fine city of Corinth, until Nauplios came back and led us to the house of his cousin. The man, it appeared, was nervous of lodging us. He, too, had heard of Medea the sorceress. I wondered whether we were going to be barred from the door. I wondered, too, whether I would give birth to Jason's child in the gutter outside, for it was leaping in the womb and the movement turned me dizzy.

There were two men and a woman in the tiny house. Nauplios held the door open and his cousin Sisyphos said hesitantly, 'I can take you and your lord, Nauplios, in memory of your father, but this foreign woman is another matter. She…'

'Get out of the way, husband,' snapped the large woman, getting ponderously to her feet and shoving the other man out of the way. 'She may be witch or sorceress, but she's a young thing about to become a mother and she will stay with me, or I will never lie here again, and you must give my dowry boat back to my father, for there I shall go and that tonight.'

This statement from an Achaean woman was evidently so surprising that both men stared at her in astonishment. After a long moment, the husband nodded.

'Now out you go, Lords, I must tend her,' she said briskly, and turned her husband and mine out of the room.

I was half carried inside and let down onto a bench, the room's only furnishing. Kore and Scylla threw themselves down in front of the fire, panting in the sudden heat.

'Come now, pretty, sit down here and let Clytie care for you,' she instructed. Her voice was almost rough, but her touch was gentle and sure. She warmed water and washed my face and hands clean of salt, combed my hair, and crouched beside the hearth to heat some soup. I was so touched by this unexpected kindness that tears came into my eyes.

'We women must support each other,' she said in answer to my stammered thanks. 'The world is run by men, and a bad job they make of it, with their pride and their greed. But the real work of the world is done by us, by women. It would never do to let men know that we could manage perfectly well without them, and they are useful for some tasks. In their wisdom, the gods gave them the power to rule us and abuse us, kill us and sell us, put us in jeopardy by every war, murdering our sons. But when I saw you sagging by my doorway, pretty, with my husband about to deny you entry, I knew that I had endured enough from men.'

'But he'll beat you for shaming him in front of strangers,' I protested, sipping at weak, hot soup made of cracked barley grains.

'Then he'll beat me,' she shrugged. 'But meanwhile you are in out of the cold and need not give birth in the street.'

'Mistress, I am in your debt,' I said. The baby had calmed inside me. Perhaps it slept. I was warm and clean and the relief was so great that I began to sob. Clytie wiped my tears away with a work-roughened hand and soothed, 'There, sweeting, there, pretty creature. Your first child?' I nodded. "It took me like that, too.'

'You have many children?' I asked.

She was a big woman, with broad hips and shoulders as wide as an axe handle. Her hair was greying, dragged back under a veil. Her face was generous and bony, with a strong jaw. But she looked for a moment like a girl, a sad maiden, as she replied steadily, 'I had three strong sons; the sea took two and Korinthos the Usurper's border dispute another. My only daughter died in childbirth less than a moon ago. Her son died with her. So when I saw you I knew I could not deny you hospitality. You are the Princess Medea, are you not, Lady?'

'I am Medea, wife of Jason of Iolkos,' I said. 'I am neither princess nor priestess any more.'

'And now you need to sleep. Now, pretty, you lie down in this corner. Wrap yourself in one of these cloaks you have brought and be at peace. Come along, dogs. Lie down with your mistress. Sleep, Lady. No one will molest you, for I will lie here and we will draw the curtain.'

She pulled at a cord which brought a faded piece of old sailcloth across to cut off a third of the room. Achaeans who have only one room cannot seclude their women during the day, but they can make their sleeping place secure. I lay down as ordered, warm in my cloak, and I heard her call in the men.

Clytie bustled them inside, supplied them with watered wine, bread and soup, refreshed the fire, and then sat down between me and the male inhabitants. I heard her grunt as she settled, wrapping her own garment about her. I had never been so generously treated in a place so poor.

As I drifted off to sleep—I seemed to need much more sleep, as though the baby was tiring me—I heard the men discussing what they would do next. The name Creon was mentioned, as the most powerful man in the *demos*, the man who owned the most land and slaves, one who sent a fleet of boats from Corinth to trade all over the sea of Aegeas every spring. He was very rich, they said, and would know what to do about my claim to Corinth.

'She is the granddaughter of Helios,' I heard Nauplios say. 'She has the right.'

'But Korinthos will deny it,' protested Nauplios' cousin.

'What force can we muster?' asked Jason.

'He has the allegiance of many small factions,' explained Clytie's husband. 'This is a city of feud. Apart from Creon and his brother, there are no friends among the demos of Corinth. Each one dislikes one of the others so much that they would rather support Korinthos the Usurper than run the risk of their blood enemy becoming powerful.'

'Korinthos holds Corinth because Helios appointed his grandfather, Bunous, governor of the city,' commented Clytie's brother.

'The only man who could oppose Korinthos and bind together the petty lords is Creon,' decided Nauplios.

My fate was being decided, too, but there seemed nothing I could do to affect it, so I went to sleep. The hounds and Clytie lay next to me, all snoring, and the sound seemed comforting. I had been a long time out of the company of women.

The next day Clytie tended me again, escorting me out into the lanes to find a place to wash and relieve myself. There we met one of her neighbours, a heavily built woman who said affably, 'Who do we have here, sister?'

'A stray from the ocean,' laughed Clytie, pushing me partly behind her. 'My brother brought her in last night. Heavy with child, poor thing.'

'A moon to go, maybe,' observed the woman, poking my belly. She could not see my face under the veil and I had borrowed Clytie's other tunic and stola. My own clothes were too fine for the fisherman's houses of Corinth. 'And so young! She'll have a hard time, unless the goddess is merciful. Her man is here?'

'With mine. They have gone down to the tavern to talk—as men do, the lazy ruffians. How is your daughter, sister?'

'Drooping, poor creature. Her man needs no daughters, and the baby was exposed last night. The midwife should not have let her hold it. She should have taken it right away and not let the mother even see it, for once we hold a babe to the breast our heart is engaged, be it deformed or a despised female. Ah, well, sister, she will recover, and perhaps next time she will bear a son. Better take your stray home, she looks faint.'

And so I was. I had not really realised what being an Achaean wife meant, and it had come home to me all of a sudden, robbing my limbs of strength, so that Clytie had to hold me up with one muscular arm around my thickened waist. This life I nurtured under my breast, this live creature even now dancing in the womb, which drank my blood and shared my breath; when it was born, if it was born alive, and assuming I survived the birth, it could be killed with impunity by my lord if he did not wish to keep it. It could be taken out of my arms and thrown on a cold mountain, and there it would die.

In Colchis we did not treat any animal with such cruelty. A woman could refuse to bear, but no man could kill her child. If she was a slave he could sell it when it was grown, but he could not slaughter it casually as though it was an unwanted puppy.

'Pay no attention to her, pretty,' said Clytie, leading me back to her lord's house. 'Always been as sour as a green plum, that one. That family is descended from sea turtles, it's well known that they have black bile instead of blood.'

And I laughed a little, even in the midst of cold horror. Clytie could always make me laugh.

We ground some corn for the noon meal, tidied the little room and took the mats and blankets outside to beat. All over Corinth the women were doing the same tasks. A child tripped and fell at my feet, and I knelt clumsily to pick him up. His face was distorted with howling, and I did not know what to do. I knew nothing about children.

I was assisted by Kore, who licked his skinned knee, and Scylla, who licked his face. The child was still crying, but the real pain had gone out of him.

'Stop crying,' I ordered, and he was so surprised that he obeyed. I wiped his nose with a corner of my duster. 'There. Now go back to your mother,' I told him. Instead, the child sat down on the cobbles and put one arm around both dog's necks.

'Nice doggies,' he commented. 'Who are you, Lady?'

'I'm Clytie's friend,' I replied.

'Did you come in last night with the men of Iolkos, Nauplios and his friend?' he asked.

'Yes,' I agreed.

'I'm going to be a fisherman,' said the child. 'My father owns a boat. She is called the *Artemis*. She's a goddess,' he informed me.

I was at a loss as to what to say, but luckily at this juncture his mother ran up the steps, all apologies, collected the child and carried him back to her own house. He did not approve of this action, just when he was impressing me with his importance, and he kicked and screamed. 'Foreign witch!' he yelled at his mother, who did not react. 'Stranger! Barbarian!' This insult was apparently too much, for she paused to clip his ears, and the rest of his comments were lost in a scream of rage.

Words which could describe Medea, wife of Jason, were insults in Corinth.

We were summoned to the palace of Creon near dusk. I dressed in the finest clothes which fate and flight had left me. I wore the red and gold gown in which I had left Iolkos and as much jewellery as remained, and I coloured my cheeks with red dye and outlined my eyes with kohl which, in Colchis, denotes royal descent. Clytie stared at me.

'Neither priestess nor princess, eh, pretty?' she chuckled. 'You look both and more. I've brushed the hounds and they match you well.'

Kore and Scylla flanked me. They had a sense of occasion, and adopted the grave demeanour of black stone sculptures. I had no fear that they would have off after a rabbit or respond to the challenge of another dog when they were with me. They were temple bitches of Hekate, and had been well trained. And I hoped that the goddess was still with them, for they were innocent beasts, and not involved in the crimes of the faithless Medea.

Jason wore the red gown of his marriage, and a thin gold crown confined his hair. We were escorted into the street and the houses emptied of people, gaping. It became a progress. I saw some women make sacred signs against evil as I passed.

'Well, I hope this works,' worried Nauplios at Jason's side. 'If Creon does not accept us, there will be no concealing our presence in Corinth now.'

'It will work,' said my lord, confident in his beautiful clothes.

I was not confident at all, but my opinion on the matter was not requested.

We had gathered a train of perhaps a hundred people by the time we climbed the steps to Creon's great house. I was weakening, footsore and over-burdened with the baby, but my training held. A priestess of Hekate could walk until her actual bones failed, long after muscle and tendon had tired beyond breaking point. We sailed across the courtyard and Creon's great doors were opened to admit us.

And there, on something very close to a throne, sat the lord of this place. Creon the most powerful man in Corinth, although it was actually ruled by the usurper Korinthos. He was of middle height, stocky and strong. He was dressed in rich robes embroidered with pearls, but he looked like a fisherman. His skin was weathered, his eyes crinkled at the corners. I knew that he was almost forty years old, a venerable age, and that he had many daughters but no son, despite his Herakles-like efforts with two wives and a houseful of female slaves from all known nations, even Libyans from beyond the temple of Ammon on the shores of Egypt. He stood up immediately and held out both arms. He was smiling a broad, charming smile.

'Jason of Iolkos,' he exclaimed. 'My lady the Princess Medea, granddaughter of Helios! I never thought that I would see this day, and I thank all the gods for it.'

He hurried off the dais and led us to seats on either side of him, then clapped, and music began to play. A garlanded child, a maiden of perhaps eight, carried a plate forward on which were bread and salt. We tasted it, the hospitality gift of Creon, making us *xenoi*, his guests, safe from assault and part of his household while we lived.

'My lord,' said Creon to Jason. 'What brings you to Corinth? Is it, I hope, your intention to take the kingship from the hated usurper Korinthos?'

'It is,' said Jason very impressively. Creon grinned again and rubbed his hands.

'By right of your lady, my lord Jason, and by right of your heroic deeds, we shall have a king again in this city,' he enthused. 'Now, as it is not possible for a woman to share the feast, I will have your wife conducted to my wife Meroe, to be welcomed fittingly. And we shall speak further of political matters, which are not fit for her ears.'

I think Creon was afraid of me. He did not touch my hand as I rose and left the audience chamber, following the little girl through a curtained doorway to the left of the dais and into another dazzling room, lined with fresh-painted frescoes of gods. I bent the knee as I passed Demeter, who is Gaia and the three women, and who contains the Black Mother, the Crone, Hekate, whom I had abandoned. But Hekate's hounds were still with me, preserving their decorous behaviour even amongst the lights and the manifold scents.

'Lady Medea,' said the child. 'My mother waits for you.'

'What is your name, maiden?' I asked. She was a very pretty, attentive child, with pale hair and bright blue eyes, much like her father's. We walked though another corridor. I was unsteady on my feet but she would not see that, and neither would her mother, Creon's wife.

'I am called Creusa, Lady,' said the child, and led me into a room where I could sit down at last. A slave helped me into a decorated, padded chair and immediately brought me a footstall and a mint infusion in a silver cup. Kore and Scylla did not relax, but sat as still as the stone dogs outside a temple.

'Princess,' said a faded, middle-aged woman in the robes of a queen, sinking down at my feet. 'I am Meroe, wife of Creon. Command me and mine anything.'

'Lady,' I replied, as courteously as I could, 'forgive me for not rising. I am advanced in pregnancy and ill. I greet you and I accept your service,' I added, remembering the formula. This released my hostess to rise and sit down at my side.

'They tell me, Princess, that you are the granddaughter of Helios, and hold the kinship of Corinth by that descent.'

'Lady, that is so,' I agreed, as the room swam around me.

'The usurper Korinthos will not give up power easily,' she said.

'What manner of man is he, this grandson of Bounos?'

'Dry and dangerous,' she told me. 'Greedy and cruel. But you are tired, Lady. My lord has told me to lodge you fittingly, and I shall do so. Let Creusa conduct you to your rooms, The dogs can stay in the stables.'

'No, they stay with me,' I said as firmly as I could.

'Shall we provide you with an attendant, Lady?' asked Meroe, not pleased, though my dogs were well trained, and in any case I did not mean to be parted from them. I looked around at the massed, alien faces of the well-cared-for women of Corinth, as soft as new cheese. I was going to need a friend to support me in this new place, someone who knew the world. I needed a strong woman, a shoulder on which I could lean.

I knew just the person. 'Yes. Send for Clytie, Sisyphos the fisherman's wife. My lord's companion, Nauplios, will know where she is to be found. Give her husband this,' I took off a necklace made of linked golden shields, 'and beg Clytie, from me, to come and attend her stray from the sea.'

They did not even blink. Possibly they were used to strange requests, possibly they considered that anything could be expected of a foreigner, a stranger, a Colchian witch. Almost certainly they had heard of the death of Pelias. They were all staring at me, expecting me to turn into something, perhaps, or vanish in a chariot drawn by dragons.

I closed my eyes against their intrusive gaze. When I opened them again, someone was gathering me into strong arms and lifting me. I smelt salt and fish.

'There, sweeting,' said Clytie roughly. ''Tis a brave princess. Just like a man to make you walk all that way in the cold wind, then expect you to entertain the nobility when you are half dead with exhaustion. A plague on all of them. Come along, dogs,' she ordered, and Scylla and Kore fell in obediently at her heels as she carried me away from the court of the Corinthian queen and into soft darkness.

Jason came two days later. I had been settled in soft coverings, provided with delicate scents and warm water, and as Jason arrived I was eating a dish made of eggs and milk, very lightly scented with anise. I tried to rise, but he sat down next to me on the bed.

'My princess,' said Jason, taking my hand.

'My lord,' I said, a little overwhelmed by the attention. He had not looked so kindly at me for moons, and I still loved him more than I could say.

'Lady, we dine tonight with the usurper of Corinth. Before I can be made king, he must be removed. But Creon judges it unwise to begin a war, which would ruin Corinth. He has suggested…' he faltered and fell silent.

I stroked the downcast golden head and prompted my husband, 'Creon suggests?'

'That he might be removed in a quiet way,'

I knew what this meant. I was frightened. The death of Pelias had sent us running from a mob. Occasionally in my sleep I still heard the howling of those people in the Iolkos marketplace, calling for my blood. Would not the suspicious death of Korinthos expose us to the same danger of popular outrage?

I said so, but Jason shook his head. 'No. There is no one group in support of him. If he dies, then I will be king, and I have Creon's support in this, his sworn word. He is my man. He loves Corinth, and says that Korinthos is ruining it, killing the young men in senseless border wars, destroying the trade which is the life of the city. Creon is a man of the polis, devoted to the welfare of Corinth. I trust him.'

'This is a dreadful thing to ask and to do, my lord,' I said.

'But can you do it?' he asked eagerly, so loving and beautiful that my heart shifted and the baby kicked inside me. Was there anything I would not do to secure the love of this most delightful and wonderful of princes?

'My bag of herbs is on the bench,' I said. 'Fetch it.'

Using my despised and abandoned knowledge, I put together a potion which would destroy my lord's enemy. I ground the berries and mushrooms in a mortar and made a powder which could be sprinkled on food or dropped in wine and which would extinguish life like the flame from an oil lamp.

Then I poured it into a little bag and gave it to my lord, who kissed me with great fondness and left me.

I was in the first stages of labour, the next day, when they came to tell me that Korinthos the Usurper was dead, suddenly and mysteriously; and that my lord, Jason, son of Aison, would be crowned on the morrow king of Corinth, in the right of his wife the lady Medea, Princess of Colchis, daughter of Aetes, granddaughter of Helios.

Chapter Twenty-four

Nauplios

The lady Medea was confined while her lord was crowned on the Akrocorinth with great ceremony. I found it hard to keep my mind on the ritual; I was worried about her. I had, of course, not seen her since I had watched her sweep into Creon's palace as though she owned it. I admired her courage more than I can say.

She had been weak and should not have even been able to walk, or so Clytie, my cousin Sisyphos' wife, had said, while scolding the ears off the Corinthian women and tending the lady with great care. According to what the kitchen slaves had whispered, Clytie had made her presence felt. This was to be expected of Sisyphos' wife. She, like my cousin, had great authority.

But the last I had seen of the lady Medea had been her straight back and waterfall of black hair, following the little girl, Creusa, through into the women's quarters. And I was concerned for her, travelling so far in such an advanced state of pregnancy, and she a king's daughter. Her lord, however, had forgotten all about her. He did not even ask the women how the labour was proceeding—she had been in that perilous state for two days!—as we dressed and adorned for the ceremony.

He stood in the royal purple robes of the king of Corinth, crowned with his fleecy hair flowing golden down his shoulders and his bright eyes shining with pride. He was beautiful and kingly, but I could not be wholly pleased with my lord Jason. The priests sprinkled him with oil for luxury and sea water to remind him that Corinth is born of the sea, with grain for increase and milk for prosperity. The chant rose and fell. It was so old that it contained many words which even the priests did not understand. I picked out occasional phrases in Colchian. I think it must have dated from Helios' time. Creon stood at the king's feet, grinning and rubbing his hands.

I turned my gaze away from a scene which ought to have been triumphant but somehow did not satisfy me, and looked out to sea. The ocean has always comforted me. I could see over the whole sweep of the bay, the blocky white houses and the palace on the hill, the boats drawn up on the beach, the few ships still at sea, to the coming storm, the black clouds on the horizon. Unless these priests got through their ancient liturgy fairly soon, we were all going to get very wet. As was the funeral procession of the late and entirely unrevenged lord of Corinth, the usurper Korinthos, which was winding its way to a pyre on the seafront. As I watched, the fire was lit with a sudden flame and smoke, fed by oil, which carried cinders even as high as the Akrocorinth, so that I tasted ashes on my mouth.

The demos of Corinth stood in a group at the bottom of the stairs—the priests and the new king occupied the highest point of the temple—and I scanned them for discontent. They seemed happy, but I noticed a strange shifting amongst them. If one man moved, all his neighbours rearranged themselves to ensure that they were not standing next to a bitter enemy. Surely they had enough fear of the gods to keep the peace in the temple of Apollo, I thought, noticing that the clouds were darkening to the colour of charcoal. Apollo has little patience with blasphemy.

The ceremony concluded with the sacrifice of a goat. We all filed forward to be marked with its blood and then, one by one, we knelt at the feet of the new king. Creon was the first to make obeisance, swearing on all the gods to be faithful to Jason for all of his life; and I followed after the old men. Jason put his hand on my head and I looked up into his strange eyes. He was shining with joy.

'Nauplios, my old friend,' he said.

'My lord Jason,' I replied.

'You are free of your oath,' he told me. 'You swore to stay with me, Nauplios, until I was king of Iolkos. I am king now of an incomparably better city, and I release you from all bonds.'

'Do you wish me to leave you, Lord?' I asked. I don't think my voice trembled.

'No, by all the gods, Nauplios,' he said hastily. 'Stay, stay with me all your life if you wish. I welcome you to my hearth, fellow fosterling. Wouldn't the centaur Cheiron be astounded if he saw us now?'

'Indeed,' I murmured, and he let me go.

I left the gathering as it progressed down the Akrocorinth. Such processions move at the speed of the slowest old man, and I had a religious duty to fulfil.

I went to the temple of the Mother, she who is Demeter and Hera and Persephone and Hekate. This was a fine temple, built on the new pattern, with an enclosed portico made of the stone figures of women, stooping as they hold up the temple roof on their shoulders. They were called caryatids. The temple was made of white marble and floored with cool red stone, highly polished. It smelt clean.

A priestess in loose, homespun robes, crowned with bay, came to attend me as I stood irresolutely on the threshold, not knowing if I was allowed to enter. Every cult is different, and every temple has its own rules.

'Greetings in the name of the Mother,' said the woman amiably. 'What do you seek, Achaean? A fisherman by the look of you, but no—you wear purple. You must be Nauplios, companion of our lord Jason, who by now, I expect, is king.'

'He is, and I am indeed Nauplios,' I answered. 'Lady, can you tell me of your worship here?'

'Certainly. Here we have priestesses of the Mother, in all her forms: Aphrodite, the goddess of love; Hera, the queen of heaven;

the Maiden Persephone; the Crone, Hekate; and Demeter, the mother of the earth. If you seek Persephone, you must leave an offering of flowers and sacrifice a bird; if Demeter, corn or gold and the sacrifice of a lamb; if Hekate, a black dog's blood and precious stones or lead. For Hera you must give a kid or a laurel garland and silver, as for Selene or Artemis.'

'And Aphrodite?' I asked. That was the only goddess she had omitted from her catalogue.

'She seeks nothing but your gold and your seed,' said the priestess, and chuckled. She was a plump, sensible woman. I had not realised that the temple of Corinth housed sacred prostitutes. A sailor's life makes one's ideas about such things flexible. In some places the punishment, even for having lustful thoughts in a temple, is death. In others, the acts of generation is sacred and an act of worship in itself. It is always better to ascertain these things in advance.

'I do not know to whom to give my prayers, Lady.'

'Are they for a woman?' she asked.

'A woman in childbirth. She has lain in labour for days.'

'Is it your child?' she asked matter-of-factly.

'No, indeed.' The priestess nailed me to the temple wall with eyes as sharp as bodkins.

'But you wish it was, eh?' She was very shrewd. 'I think that you should best direct your prayers to Demeter, the Mother, lord Nauplios. I will show you how to make them fittingly. You can purchase corn and a lamb from the traders. Buy them and come back here, and I will conduct you.'

When I had done as she commanded and we stood before the altar of the Mother, the sacrifice drenching the statue's feet with blood, I scattered corn and prayed for Medea, lady of Corinth. The room was heavy with the scent of fruit and the air was so thick with incense that I could hardly breathe. I saw no change in the image's smooth bronze countenance, and the priestess seemed displeased.

'No, that isn't right. There is something you have not told me, Nauplios,' she snapped. 'For whom do you pray?'

I told her and her frown cleared. 'That explains it. Wrong goddess. Come, hurry. Take off that bracelet,' she ordered and I followed her out of the temple of the Mother down a flight of stone steps into the dark, lit by one small flame.

An old woman rose from her seat by the *enagismos,* the altar of the dead, and asked in a creaking voice 'Who comes to Hekate?'

'Nauplios, the Argonaut, to sacrifice for the lady Medea, who lies in childbirth and cannot be delivered,' snapped my guide. 'He has a piece of gold which belonged to her, or I am no judge of these things, and I think the need is urgent, Hekate's Maiden.'

'She left the worship of the Dark Mother,' said the old woman slowly. 'Why should I help her?'

'Because a man petitions you,' I said, now very seriously worried. 'Because she is brave and fair, and because I beg you.'

'And her lord is not here, and you are. Interesting. Well, well, Hekate will know what is acceptable. Give me the bauble. You shall have it again, young lord. Ah, yes,' she turned the band in her old fingers.

It was an arm ring which the lady had given me as a present, to thank me for taking Jason to Corinth. It was the one she wore on her own wrist, and I had been greatly honoured. I do not know how the priestess knew that, but priestesses know things. The old woman took a rope made of something like the tail of a black horse, intermingled with sable sheep's wool. It had nine knots in it. She passed it through my bracelet, muttering charms, then threw a handful of some foul incense on the brazier. It made a reek like a hundred rotting corpses. I squinted through this cloud and watched the old woman untie the knots, one by one, until the line ran smoothly through her fingers. Then she took a comb and drew out strands until there was no roughness in the skein, which flowed and bobbed like black hair.

Then she tossed the golden band back to me and closed her eyes.

My priestess led me up the stairs again. Once in the cool pillared hall, I coughed the noxious stench out of my lungs and thanked her.

'When you find the lady safely delivered, come back,' she told me, refusing my coins. 'Then you may make your own sacrifice, Nauplios, to Aphrodite, who will receive you gladly. But I would have you know that someone makes magic against the lady. Now, go; there is news for you in the town.'

I left the temple and walked down through the town. Nearing the palace, I heard one announcing that the Queen Medea, wife of King Jason, was delivered of a fair son and, almost as an afterthought, that the lady had survived the birth.

I lingered in the kitchen of the palace to hear the news. I managed to catch Clytie as she bustled out of the women's quarters, demanding strong honeyed wine mixed with barley meal, and that instantly.

'My lord?' she asked, not knowing me in my fine garments. 'Oh, it's you, lord and cousin. The king sent you to find out how the lady has borne her ordeal?'

I said nothing, and she went on, filling a large pitcher from the amphora of the best wine. 'She is exhausted, poor sweeting, but she is brave. Such torment would have drawn groans from a sea rock, but not a whimper from the lady. Strange, you know, cousin.'

Clytie re-stoppered the amphora and balanced the full jug on her hip. 'She could not deliver, as though the child was lying across the womb. That is how my daughter died and I feared to watch it again. I passed my hands over my eyes for a moment. I heard both dogs get up, whining and barking, and then all of a sudden the babe appeared and the lady was lighter of her burden. Some deity had a hand in it, I would hazard. If so they took their time. Another few hours and she would have died of exhaustion. However, the baby is thriving and I believe the lady will recover. Ask my lord to wait until tomorrow to see her. She needs to sleep.'

This was not a difficult commission. Jason, much elevated on wine and pomp, called for his son, but did not enquire about his wife. The baby was brought to him on a shield by Creon, and Jason touched the little red hands with wonder.

'See, all his nails intact, so small, so perfect!' he exclaimed, as the baby clutched his finger and bawled a protest at being removed from his mother's breast. 'My son,' said Jason fondly.

Clytie was then allowed to carry the baby away, swaddled and held firmly to her bosom. I heard her talking to Jason's son as she went past me in a flounce of dark red linen.

'I know that this may wound you, little Lord,' she said to the baby, 'But all men are fools. To bring you out into a cold hall when you are so new to the world shows no sense. Come along now, we shall lie you back in your nurse's arms. We've got that Nubian woman of Creon's—she's borne five living children. You'll like her milk.'

'Clytie,' I whispered, and she stopped.

'Cousin?'

'The lady, can you let me see her?' She levelled her eyes at me, as I strove to explain. 'I do not wish her to see me, or greet me, I just need to know that she lives. I made an offering for her to Hekate this day, and…'

She turned on her heel, saying, 'Pull your cloak over your head and follow,' and I did so, keeping my gaze down and watching the red hem as it flicked across the floor. Clytie had the firm, solid walk of a woman used to carrying baskets of fish on her head, but she moved much faster than one would think. I was out of breath when she shoved me into the antechamber of the princess' apartments.

'Stay there. When the door opens for me, shalt see your lady,' she said, and patted me briskly on the arm. 'Don't be alarmed by her appearance. She has been through a great ordeal.'

The door swung open, and Clytie handed the baby to some-one inside. She leaned in the doorway so that I could see over her shoulder.

The lady Medea, still swollen bellied, lay back on linen pillows, swathed in linen sheets, and her face was as white as her wrappings, even to the lips. Her long hair, drawn back and combed, was blacker than shipbuilder's pitch, and there were dark shadowed hollows under her closed eyes. Even the

Argonauts, after a long battle with a storm, had not seemed so tired. It was a face empty of character, perhaps even of life. Scylla and Kore lay together on the floor, one hound's head resting on the other's black back, which reassured me. They would not lie so if their mistress was dead. But somehow I could not leave for the temple until I had seen some sign of life.

Clytie, perhaps, knew this. She called almost gently, 'Sweeting,' and the eyelids flickered. Just for a second the lady Medea opened her eyes. They stared straight into mine, and she smiled at me, a faint quirk on the lips. Then she relaxed again.

Clytie pushed me out and shut the door, and I walked into the slaves' quarters as though I had been seeking a girl for the night, and thence to the temple as I had promised.

The priestess of Aphrodite I lay with was practised and easy to please. I stroked her with scented oil as she stroked me, until our passions were aroused enough to mate. I tried to keep my mind on the goddess. But at the moment of climax, so strong a climax that it almost hurt, I saw the face of Aphrodite, and she had pale cheeks and long, straight, black hair.

When his son, Polyxenius, was one-year-old, barely weaned, my lord sent him to the centaurs, as he himself had been sent. Clytie said that my lady wept, though I had not seen her in that time, except occasionally when she was required at some ceremony. Then she was beautiful, solemn, and always pregnant. She had evolved a stance to support her belly; she leaned back on her heels, a back-saving way of standing which, for some reason, caught at my heart.

And what concerned Nauplios in Corinth? Why was I still in Jason's city? I was free of my oath, loosed from my vows, but I did not want to return to Iolkos. There Akastos ruled; wisely, we heard. Thence I sent a message to Amphitrite's father that I could not marry, because I could not leave Corinth, and I sent her a golden belt set with pearls to assuage her disappointment, which would not have been great.

Jason showed me favour, repeatedly offering me a choice of the daughters of the nobility of Corinth, but I would have made but a distant husband to them, poor girls. I did not marry, because I could not give my heart to anyone except the lady Medea, wife of my lord. There was no hope for me in this love, but it would not be banished. The lady Medea smiled if she saw me at some festival, and she sent gifts 'to lord Nauplios the Argonaut'; such things as wine and honey and sometimes strange company, wandering madmen and bards and singers, for she knew of my fascination with odd things and tales from far countries.

I bought myself a little house near the waterfront and hired a woman to cook for me and keep my house clean. She was a crone, the mother of Clytie, the lady Medea's companion, and she was blessedly silent when I did not wish to speak. If she was cross-grained and sour, I did not need joyful maidens. I went to Aphrodite when the burning became too hot to bear, and the priestesses conceived a kindness for me, treating me well.

I spent my time on my lord's business, though it was not great. I talked to traders in their own tongue, for I had discovered a gift for languages when I sailed with the Argonauts in the quest for the Golden Fleece. But I interpreted for Creon, not Jason. Once all the border disputes had been solved by sending to the oracle at Delphi for solutions, there was little diplomatic business to be done. But there was a great deal of trading and barter, and ships sailed out from Corinth to every port in the world. Creon owned the vessels and Jason had no part in the life of the city, just its ceremonies. This pleased him. He had no gift for making decisions, and he seemed content to allow Creon to run Corinth, which he did very well.

I had been called down to the waterfront to try and puzzle out the speech of a very voluble sailor with rings in his ears and strange garment wrapping his legs, who had tin and jet to sell. He shared no language with any of the sailors, hangers-on and merchants, and we fell back on sign language, the oldest form of communication, which existed before the gods gave men speech. I wondered how far he had sailed his little boat, to have originated beyond the understanding of Libyan, Nubian Egyptian, Colchian, Phrygian, Trojan and Mysian. He was too tall to be a pygmy, and in any case could not understand their clicked speech, for in desperation I tried the few words of it which I knew.

He spread out his cargo. Lumps of jet, perfect for cutting and polishing into seals. Pieces of amber the size of hen's eggs, some with the much-prized insects or grain in them, amulets for a prince. Ingots of crudely smelted tin, essential for making bronze. He had a fortune in trade, the merchants were slavering, and we could not find a common language. I hoped that the trader was not concealing any knowledge of Achaean, for I heard whispers behind me that it might save trouble if we just killed him and stole his treasure.

Then I heard the sound of a lyre, which I had not heard for years. Someone was walking along the quay, cheek to soundbox, tuning the strings. He was tall, barefoot, dressed in a rough green tunic, and his hair was the colour of copper.

The strangely-clad trader cried something in a completely foreign tongue to the approaching bard Philammon who, when he looked up at the voice, ran to me and embraced me, talking all the time in rolling, melodic speech to the sailor.

'He's a Hyperborean,' said Philammon, without greeting me. He always took up his friendships exactly where they had left off. 'He wants golden jewellery, cooking pots and hounds.

'Don't cheat him,' he added severely, looking at the merchants. 'He is the first of his people to pass the Pillars of Herakles and come into Aegeas' sea. If you would have more tin and jet, then you must load him with treasure; and Dike will smite any trader with more greed than morality.'

Dike—Justice, whom the Achaeans also call Themis—would support the most sensible and likely outcome. I impressed on the local merchants how Creon would feel about someone who suppressed a long-term trading advantage for short-term profit, to a general failure of knees, I dragged Philammon to the nearest tavern. I knew that he would not drink wine, but he could at least drink water with me. I was very glad to see him, so glad that I realised I had been lonely for longer than I could recall.

'How fares my dear Nauplios in Corinth?' he asked, accepting a cup of spring water and raising it as in a toast. 'You are older, no longer a boy. It has been—how many years since you came here?'

'Five,' I said, swallowing half a cup of wine. 'Jason has been king for five years. In that time the lady Medea has borne him four children. The last two are twins, they are two years old now. Jason sent the eldest son up to the mountain, to be instructed— and he died there, among the centaurs.'

'There is a sorrow,' said the bard, as he put one finger to my temple and stared into my eyes. 'You have borne it long, too long, perhaps, and it will not let you rest, Nauplios. You should leave this place. You have little status here and here you will never gain your desire. Yearning becomes a habit, and it poisons the blood.'

'You are right,' I agreed.

'I am a bard,' he said.

'Where have you been travelling?'

'On the salt river Ocean, where he bears me,' he said indifferently. 'I have seen some of the other Argonauts. Most prosper, though Ancaeas the Strong is dead.'

'Dead?' I remembered the large modest man, rowing amidships with Herakles. 'How?'

'He returned to Tegea and was sitting in his house. A seer told him that he would never drink the wine of a particular vineyard.' The lyre sang behind his voice as he dropped into a chant.

> *Here is the wine, Lord,*
> *Harvested at your order, the*
> *Grapes pressed from the doomed*
> *Vine. Do not drink, Ancaeas,*
> *Do not challenge their might,*
> *The all-powerful gods.*
> *Plenty of wine, Ancaeas,*
> *Many other vines flourish.*
> *Drink another vintage.*

But he called his slaves
And drank the bitter wine. Then
'My lord' called a slave, 'a wild boar,
Tusked and dangerous, destroys
Your grapes.' He seized his spear,
His boar spear and his sword.
Out hurries Ancaeas the Strong.
Wine still wet on his lips,
The boar charged,
Ancaeas' strength did not prevail.

'He was so strong a man I did not think even the gods could kill him,' I said.

'Alabande is growing fat; he has three sons and spends the day in hard labour like a farmer, but his nights in eating and drinking; he is content,' continued Philammon.

'Idas and Lynkeos are still arguing; now it is about the respective merits of their wives, who are identical twins. Wagers are being taken as to their children. I have not seen Oileus or Telamon, but I hear that they are well, as is Nestor. Do you remember Autolycus? He has made himself a small kingdom on a very poor island called Ithaca. And Hypsipyle, the Lemnian queen, bore Jason a child from that winter. He is called Thoas, a fine son, bright-eyed and sturdy. I know no more. The women of Lemnos are greeting all ships with arrows now.'

'They are stored with enough seed to make their own husbands in future,' I commented, filling my wine cup again.

'And how are matters in Corinth?' he asked.

'Jason is king and the lady Medea queen,' I said carefully. 'Most of the business of the kingdom is done by Creon, the king's adviser. It is by his order that interpreters should attend the docks to translate for the traders, and I am one of them. Teach me some of that strange language, Philammon. I never heard it before, and I thought I had heard all the tongues of men in Ocean.'

'There you ask me a difficult favour, for that tongue took me a shipwrecked year to learn, and even now I speak it very imperfectly,' grinned the bard. He looked older. There were faint strands of grey in his coppery hair, and more lines on his face. But he was alert, alive; Philammon was always more alive than other people. He was drinking in the dockside scene with delight—the arguments of the merchants; a sailor asleep on a prow; a trio of small boys racing the length of the quay, attended by barking dogs; the fishermen coming ashore with the catch and loading it into the baskets of the strong, flat-footed women. I had never lost my love of waterfronts, and now I saw it afresh as the bard saw it: exotic and fascinating, smelling of salt and fish and essence of roses.

The trader had filled his little boat with huge bronze pots and ingots of gold and silver. He had almost vanished under the necklaces, arm bands, rings and belts which the merchants of Corinth had loaded onto him. He grinned at Philammon and waved a jingling, blue-tattooed arm.

Then he leapt into his boat, heaved in after him three water-skins and a basket of bread, dried fish and honeycomb, and set the small sail. It was scarcely larger than a tunic. I was envious and admiring. He had travelled from beyond the north wind to find this port, and now he was going home. I came back to what Philammon was saying.

'And Herakles is married.'

I sat up straight, spilling my wine. 'Herakles? Where is he?'

'In Athens, of course. You know, Athens, little town up from the Isthmus. He has taken the maiden Deianeira to wife. He promised her uncle, they say, when he met him in the underworld. He is cured of battle fury by the Princess Medea's potion, or so he says.'

'Herakles alive?' I wondered.

'Certainly alive, though aging. Even heroes age. I do not like that wife, Nauplios. She has no more sense than would incommode a dormouse. The wife of Herakles needs her wits about her, and Deianeira has no wits whatsoever. What is it?'

I had sprung to my feet. I had sat in this port too long, getting soft, longing and yearning for something I could never have. I had not touched an oar in years and my hands were unmarked. *Argo* was pulled up on the beach. Jason had sent for her and set her there as a monument to his voyage. But I would not need her. My own father's boat, *Good Catch*, was well cared for—out of filial duty, I always told myself.

'I'm leaving,' I told the bard. He did not seem disconcerted, nor even surprised, but it is very hard to surprise a bard.

'Where?'

'Athens, perhaps,' I said. 'But in any case, away from Corinth.'

Chapter Twenty-five

Medea

I had survived the birth of my first child, my little son. Jason had been pleased with him. The training of Hekate's priestess held during my long travail. The revenge of the goddess, I was sure, made my agony protracted.

Clytie stayed with me, her husband Sisyphos resigning her to the care of the palace, though she went home to him occasionally. She was fiercely devoted to me and to my children, and I had not deserved her. Every time I heard her harsh voice comforting a child or felt her roughened hand take mine as I was confined again, I blessed whichever god had sent her to me.

I saw Jason infrequently. He did not sleep in my bed after the first year. But he seemed pleased with me. I had abandoned home and lordship and goddess to follow this beautiful Achaean; and he was still beautiful to me.

I sacrificed to Aphrodite with him and he pleased me, but it seemed that every time I lay with him I conceived. Then I was always sick, though my body had to some extent become used to pregnancy. And I was trapped. By my body, by my children, by my own choice. And life went on. I had made my choice. I tried not to regret it.

The routine of the palace was as set as any religious ritual. At dawn we roused, washed, and ate a light meal of bread and fruit.

Then all the children were woken and washed—although few of the children showed any signs of wanting to sleep through until someone came to wake them, except Eiropis and Alcimedes, the twins. They clung to Morpheus as though he was their father; while Mermerus, my other son, was always awake, not noisy or demanding, but open-eyed on a world he found endlessly interesting. He was always bringing me small discoveries. That water flowed downhill, for instance, or that Kore had two teeth longer than the others, or, memorably, that the bright red coals in a brazier bit the questing finger.

My first-born, Polyxenos, was gone, given away to the centaurs. I dreamed of him sometimes, wondering if he was cold or lost, wondering if he missed his nurse or me. He had been a strong child. The Nubian had complained that he clamped onto her nipple as though they were edible, and she named him 'little Herakles' in memory of the hero, who had bitten the breast of the queen of the gods. When he would have been three, they told me he had died; and I wept, as women weep.

Then we wove or spun, talking as women do. Clytie had no skill at spinning. She had, however, a fund of scandalous stories about Corinth. I think she derived a lot of information from her friends among the kitchen slaves, who had a healthy respect for her. No one crossed Clytie. She was not afraid of anyone, not even Creon.

Meroe, Creon's wife, visited every day and we sat giggling at Clytie's mimicry of him, the rolling seaman's walk, the shrug of the bearlike shoulders, the growl of his deep voice saying, 'Trade is the life-blood of Corinth.'

Meroe was content in her servitude, but I never was. I could not stop remembering the world. Achaean women are secluded, which means that they are imprisoned. I could not walk down to the dockside and talk to the mariners, not even in company with Clytie. I could not move out of my own palace without a veil lest men should lust after my beauty and steal me.

I could go to the temple of the Mother and pray for fertility, but only with an escort of women and guards. I was seen in public only as consort of the king and only at the four ceremonies of the year, in which I had no part but to stand and drop a pinch of incense into the flame on the Akrocorinth, representing the prayers of the women and children and slaves; the powerless of Corinth.

I owned nothing except at the gift of my lord. I breathed by his permission. The jewellery which weighted my neck and wrists and fingers was his. My service was his, and my children were his.

This had been made clear to me when they came to take Polyxenos to the centaurs. I was sitting by a brazier, listening to a slave sing to the lyre the tale of Kadmon and Omonia, when Jason entered and all my women scattered like sparks before a gale. Only Clytie stayed, standing by the wall. Jason did not notice her.

'Lady, I would see my son,' he said, and Clytie went to fetch him, carrying him back screaming under her arm. He had been put down to play in the courtyard, and his face was dirty. I wiped it with a cloth, brushing his tunic down. He screwed up his face as I tried to remove mud from his cheek.

'Lady, my son goes this night to Cheiron, to be taught by the centaurs.'

'But my lord,' I said, surprised, 'He is too young! He has just left the breast. He can't speak yet, and he's only just walking. You cannot take him away from me yet.'

'Lady,' said Jason. 'He is my son, and I say he will go to Cheiron. The bearers wait, and his nurse will travel with him until he is settled on the mountain.'

'Jason, please,' I said, a sense of my own powerlessness washing over me. 'Not yet. He is too small.'

Polyxenos, divining that something was amiss, threw both arms around my neck and started to cry. I can still feel that strong clasp, the child collapsing into sobs and the heave of his small ribs, and the despair which embittered my heart as Jason coldly undid the fingers of his son and handed him to the Nubian.

'This is Creon's idea, is it not?' I cried, stroking the child's head. 'There, my son, there, be brave.' He was too young to understand words, but he knew that something was wrong and cried harder, his face streaked with tears. The black woman looked at me sympathetically, but she had no choice and neither did I.

Jason was offended. 'It is my idea,' he emphasised. 'And you will do as I say, wife.'

They took my little son away, and I did nothing. I stood in the middle of the room, tearing the handkerchief to pieces, until Clytie made me sit down.

'Men,' she spat into the fire. 'The gods must have been drunk when they gave men the ruling of the world.'

We slept in the hot afternoon, then dined at night. Then we were called, perhaps, to our lords to serve their pleasure, and then we were free to sleep. Life fell into seasonal rhythms. Only the food changed, fruit in autumn and dried meat in winter, and each year there was a new child.

I had never been fond of children, but my own were marvellous to me. I bore them in great pain, but when the small, red-faced creature was laid on my breast I felt such a gush of love for this new little animal born into the world, that I did not really notice that my lord's heart was turning from me.

It was clear to me that the real ruler of Corinth was Creon, the bear. Jason had no real power. The women said he had given a few orders in his first week, which were studiously not obeyed, and after that he had been careful not to ask for anything which might be refused. He had respect and the trappings of lordship; he had the title of king of Corinth, and that was all.

But he seemed happy with that, and compared to the lot of most women, I was fortunate. My lord did not beat me, though whenever we argued he taunted me with being a foreigner, a barbarian, a witch of Colchis and a murderer. It always ended with him flinging off into the palace to seek better company amongst the slaves; while I lay with tears soaking my pillow, though what he said was utterly true. I was a witch, a foreigner, a barbarian and a murderer. Pelias was dead, and my brother Aegialeus, and

Korinthos' funeral pyre was long in ashes. But I was also the faithful mother of his children, and they were strong and fine.

The nurse brought them to me every morning. The twins, whose birth had so nearly been fatal that Clytie had ordered my lord to give me a year's respite from his potency, were rising two and curious and bold. There was nothing which had not been examined when they found that a terracotta cup would not endure being dropped to a tiled floor, and had howled over the shards, trying to put them together again.

Mermerus, leaning on my knee, had announced in a superior tone, 'You can't heal a wine cup, it isn't alive. Only live things can heal.'

He was correct, my small son. Only live things can heal. Dead things—lost worship, lost faith, lost lives—cannot be amended.

Eiropis and Alcimedes were inseparable. They screamed when a nurse tried to lay them apart when they were so newborn that the grease and blood were still slicking their bodies, and no one had ever succeeded in parting them. There would be trouble, I envisaged, when they grew up, for Eiropis was destined for the life of an Achaean maiden, and Alcimedes would have to go out in the world. I felt pity for my daughter every time I looked at her. She was so brave—when Scylla, teased beyond endurance, nipped her, she did not even cry—and her courage would be required to live her mother's life. But it would be easier on her, because she had known no other.

Her mother had sailed far seas and walked as Hekate's maiden through free streets, talked with kings, sat unafraid in the dark caverns under the earth. I had looked into the face of death and knew her as a sister. But I needed all my hard-won discipline to reconcile myself to being shut inside all the time.

Sometimes I forgot that I was queen of Corinth and woke thinking that I would walk down to the marketplace or into the woods. I could have wept when I came back to knowledge of my position. Sometimes I dreamed, vivid dreams, of Ophis and the grove, of Trioda and Tyche and the Scyths. One night I was convinced that I lay again in Anemone's wagon, listening to the noises of the camp, and Clytie caught me weeping as I dragged myself out of bed.

'You fret, Lady,' she observed.

'I fret,' I admitted. 'I feel like a caged bird. I would cry to the marketplace, "I cannot get out." But I have made my choice,' I sighed, donning my purple gown.

She did not reply, but patted my shoulder.

The women of the Corinthian court were no companions for me, and I scared them. They were continuously, endlessly concerned with gossip, small doings in kitchen and yard. They were envious of each other, not sisterly; one's good fortune made the others attack her mercilessly when she was not there. What they said about me I could guess: barbarian and witch. But I used no skills or spells, though there was a constant demand for love potions and poisons. Some of them had a devotion to my own goddess, Hekate, but they knew little of her, using the Dark Mother only to attempt curses on a rival in love.

But I had seen things which they could not imagine. Once I spoke of the wide sea, and the Argonauts rowing, and the island of the bronze giant, and they gaped, then commented that it must have been terrible to be looked at by so many men. One coyly asked me how many of the Argonauts I had lain with, and whether my lord measured well against such legendary lovers as Oileus and Telamon. I did not tell them any more about the outside world after that. They did not want to know about it, and I tired of their chatter just as quickly as they tired of my stories.

But my children loved me, and I loved them. Meroe's daughter, Creusa, cared for them also. She was a pretty, polite girl, though always reserved with me. She avoided my gaze, and I had heard her calling me 'sorceress', which did not endear her. Clytie disliked her. 'Sly one' she called Creusa. Clytie suspected her of using magic to damage me, delaying my deliveries. But I could stay away from the presence of Meroe and her children and enjoy my own.

One day I was called from a game of cloth, sword, stone with the children by my lord Jason. He escorted me into my own room and made me sit down, then knelt beside me. He was alight with some scheme, and I was pleased, for he had not come to talk with me since winter began, and now it was nearly spring. I had seen white blossom in the slaves' hair when they came to serve the first meal, which meant that the plum trees in the kitchen garden were in flower.

'Lady, I have concluded a treaty,' he said.

'Indeed, my lord? With Libya?' He looked puzzled, and I explained, 'The women were talking of a trading agreement with Egypt.'

'No, no, nothing like that. Creon has offered me his daughter.'

'Creusa? What do you want with Creon's daughter?' I asked, puzzled in my turn. He touched my thigh, as though he was asking a favour.

'In marriage,' he explained. 'Creon has it all worked out. I shall divorce you—though you shall lose none of your state or position, and my children none of their legitimacy, for I am sure of your fidelity—and I shall marry Creusa, who loves me.'

I did not believe what I was hearing. He looked into my eyes, happy as a dog, and still I didn't believe it.

'You mean to divorce me and marry Creon's daughter,' I said slowly. 'Why?'

'You have never been accepted in the city,' he observed. 'You are still the foreign woman. The rumour is spreading again that you poisoned Korinthos; as indeed, you did. People have not forgotten the fate of Pelias, either. And you have clung to your old ways, even refusing to be parted from Hekate's hounds, which are still with you. People are saying that they are familiars. You look different even under a veil, with your hair and your dark skin.

'Creusa is the daughter of Corinth's most influential citizen. This alliance will cement my hold on Corinth, where I am much respected. You aren't going to be difficult, are you, Medea?'

He must have seen something in my face, for he rose and walked to the doorway. 'Creon said you would weep and scold,' he told me. 'Weep and scold as you wish, Medea. But then you will send your crown to Creusa, for she will be my queen.'

And he was gone before I could say one word of reproach. Clytie found me sitting as he had left me. It was getting dark.

'Lady?' she said into the gloom. 'Sweeting? I have heard of what he intends, this weakling lord of yours. I have been told of Jason's wicked design. But you must not sit here, unspeaking, pretty. See, I have brought some Achaeans who have not betrayed you.'

Mermerus ran into the room and threw himself into my lap. 'Mother,' he cried, burrowing into my embrace. The twins came in, hand in hand as they always did, saw tears on my cheeks and began to howl; and we collapsed into a heap on the smooth floor, injured and rejected Medea and her fatherless children, and wept until we were tired.

But if Jason thought that women can only weep and scold, he was about to be enlightened. I had left my own country for him, killed my own brother. I had betrayed my father and I had become a murderer for his sake, killing Pelias and then giving Jason poison for Korinthos. I had lost the goddess who had been my mother. And the man of Iolkos had sworn a binding oath by all the gods that he would never leave me, or I would not have ventured into that ill-starred boat. I recalled afresh that I had stumbled then, and fallen—a very bad omen. And now it was coming true.

And that sly girl, that pretty blue-eyed, magic-using wanton, had snared Jason and taken him away from me, so that he forgot his vows and his children and my faithfulness, led by his phallus, like all men. She and her father had plotted this divorce. Creon the Corinthian and his daughter had stolen from me everything that I valued—for I had no doubt that a divorced barbarian would lose her children, to be taken away and brought up in civilised company.

I was rejected, abandoned, lost.

Clytie put us all to bed together that first night and sat up by the fire, watching. I think she was afraid that I might kill myself. That crossed my mind, but I rejected the thought instantly. What would my children do without me? As the dark hours wore on I remembered Atalante, the Hunter, saying scornfully, 'Your husband will leave you for another woman. You will live as a drudge, live the life of an Achaean woman, and there could not be a worse fate.'

I could smell sweat and salt as I recalled that scene; see the set, cold face of the maiden of Artemis, her lithe body balanced against the yaw and pitch of Argo. I had thought her a fanatical virgin, deeply prejudiced against the flesh, but she had been telling me the cold truth.

My husband was leaving me for another woman, for a tender, sly, treacherous, young maiden, abandoning the body which was marked with childbearing and no longer attractive to him. He had broken all his most sacred oaths. And he held Corinth in my right, something which both he and Creon had evidently forgotten.

Or perhaps they assumed that I would placidly allow Jason to continue as king and while away the rest of my life in domestic tasks, serving the new queen and tending her children while my own were rejected; for I knew it would come to that when Creusa bore Jason a son.

Perhaps they assumed that I would suicide. Perhaps they did not care what I did. Women, they thought, could only rail at fate, but must accept what men did to them, the arbiters of their destiny.

I was familiar with hot fury, an unreliable emotion, which fades as quickly as it comes. But I was not angry like that. I was chilled, so that even the puppyish bodies of my three children would not warm me.

I would return to my worship, to Hekate, my mother. I would go back to the dark where I had been fostered. I remembered Trioda, who had cursed me—and her curses had worked; all Trioda's curses worked—kneeling down in a forest and talking about power, explaining the contents of my basket.

I had power, as Jason would shortly find. And I could not go back to the Mother until I had made her a sacrifice.

I had just the sacrifice in mind.

The morning dawned wet—spring is chancy in Corinth. I stayed in my own apartments with my children. No wailing or keening came from the cruelly rejected Princess Medea, and the women wondered, I expect, but would have put it down to me being a stranger. There were things I needed, which I sent Clytie to obtain. She frowned.

'Why do you need a file, lady? Sweeting, why do you send me to Hekate's temple, to give this writing which I cannot read to the priestess there?'

'Do as I order,' I said coldly. 'Or leave my service.'

'I have not deserved that of you,' she said slowly. I had hurt her deeply. We were closer than sisters, Medea and the fisherman's wife. She had not deserved that tone from me, she was right and she was faithful, but I dared not trust her with any foreknowledge of what I was going to do, or they would kill her when it was known.

'Go,' I bade her, and she went with her fishwife's waddle, bearing my letter to Hekate's maiden. No one in Corinth except Nauplios could read Colchian, in fact the Achaeans despised writing as a base art, and only used it to list taxes and cargo manifests.

I suddenly wished I could see Nauplios again. But he had left the city, I was told by Clytie's mother; gone in his little boat to Athens where Herakles, the hero, still lived. I had an escape plan, which might not work. Herakles had told me to come to him, if ever there was anything he could do for me, in gratitude for my care and for the *lithos sophronister* I had made for him.

It was not far to Athens, though I would have to steal or buy a boat. I made a careful bundle of my favourite cloaks, the children's clothes, and all my jewellery except the golden crown of the queen of Corinth, which I would dutifully send to Creusa. I wrapped Arktos, Ichthys and Pallas in the bundle. Arktos was a sheepskin bear without which Mermerus could not sleep, Icthys was a carved olive-wood fish, which was my son Alcimedes' dearest possession, and Pallas was Eiropis' doll.

Clytie returned with the instruments and ingredients, and I banished her and the children while I prepared my spell. I took the crown of the queen of Corinth and carefully roughened the inside of the golden band, which fitted closely around the head and was worn across the brow. The gold was pure and very soft, and I managed to make very satisfactory points, like thorns, inside it. Then I coated them with Mycis Kokkinos and venom, which the priestess of Hekate had supplied without question.

If she released my lord and refused to don my crown, of course, then she would live. I did not think this likely. Creusa would never refuse such a gift as Jason, still golden haired and young, so clever and pleasing. I suspected that the girl would not be able to resist trying on the crown as soon as it was delivered. I estimated that it would take perhaps an hour for her to die.

And die she must.

I clapped my hands and a slave entered. I gave her the box and warned her to have it delivered straight to the king's new wife as a token of my submission to Jason's will. The girl must have reported this to Jason, for I soon received a message that he was waiting to see me.

'Lord,' I said.

'Medea,' his voice was gentle. He was pleased with me. He believed that I had accepted his betrayal of all his oaths and my own demotion to drudge without question. I had not realised before that Jason was stupid.

'You have sent the crown to Creusa,' he said. 'That is well. Now, I have arranged that you will remove with the children to the outer wing of the palace. I shall need the royal apartments for my new queen.'

I looked for the last time on his self-satisfied, beautiful face. He had coarsened with good living, but he still made my heart tender. I hardened it.

'It shall be, Lord, as you desire,' I said conventionally. 'I will order it done this day.'

And he patted my cheek as though I was any common slave, and that what he asked was any common favour, and he walked out of my life. I never wished to see Jason, son of Aison, again.

I returned to my apartments, gave orders that all my belongings—my lord's belongings—were to be moved to the old, shabby rooms at the far side of the palace. I ordered Kore and Scylla to accompany me, and they rose obediently. I picked up my own bundle and, carrying Alcimedes and leading Mermerus by the hand, I left the rooms where I had tried, and failed, to become an Achaean woman.

Clytie bore Eiropis in her arms and walked behind me. I could feel her worrying, but she said nothing until we were in the corridor which leads to the kitchen courtyard.

'You are going to leave, Lady?' she asked very quietly.

'Yes. Now.'

'With my lord's children?'

'Indeed,'

'Where are we going?'

'We are not going anywhere. You are staying here and I am going to the Dark Mother, and thence to Herakles, in Athens.'

She said nothing more until we had reached the door. Outside it was raining. I had almost forgotten about weather since I had been imprisoned in my palace. I was almost afraid of going outside. Like a slave, I had grown used to my chains.

I forced my foot over the threshold, and I was out in the street. Mermerus asked, 'Where are we going, Mother?'

'To the temple on the hill,' I replied.

'Have you my father's permission?' he asked, because he knew that I was not allowed to go anywhere unescorted.

'I do not need it now,' I said. 'Hurry. We must get to the Mother. She is calling me.'

'Is that why you're listening so hard?' he asked.

But I was listening for a scream from the house of Creon as we passed it. I heard it. But they were crying not for Creusa, but Creon. Had I managed to kill Creon as well? My spirits rose at the thought. Creusa could never have seduced my lord from his sworn word but with the connivance of her father.

Corinth stared as we passed, the royal witch and her children and the fisherman's wife. We toiled up the hill. I was panting.

I had done no walking since I came to the king's palace. My knees trembled and Alcimedes put on weight with every step.

'Lady,' said Clytie in the rear. 'Let the child walk. Pause for a moment.'

'No, we must get to the temple,' I insisted, hefting my son and forcing my knees to take another step.

'Sweeting,' said Clytie, as we came into the sacred precincts, 'what have you done?'

'A deed fully as dreadful as any which could have been blamed on the Colchian stranger,' I told her. 'Stay here with the children. Stay with Clytie,' I told Mermerus, kissing him. He smelt as the young smell, like new-baked bread and sunshine. 'You cannot come into this temple, my son. But you will be safe here with Clytie and I will come as soon as I can.'

The twins embraced me in their usual way, mirror image kisses on each cheek, and then demanded their toys. I gave Pallas to Eiropis and watched Alcimedes sit down abruptly on the cool stone to play with Icthys, but Mermerus was too old to want to be seen cuddling a shabby sheepskin bear in public, so Arktos remained in the bundle.

With Kore and Scylla at my heels, I went through the cool temple and descended to the cave, where the old woman who had supplied my poisons sat on a bench near the cold hearth.

'Medea,' she said. 'Fallen and abandoned, do you now wish to return to Hekate's embrace, now that your flesh is sated and your lord desires another? Hekate is no second best, Princess.'

'I return to Hekate,' I stated in the ritual words. 'I will wash away my faithlessness with blood, and join with her again in blood, if she will accept me.'

'Take the knife,' said the old woman, handing me a razor-sharp blade socketed in stone.

I heard my children playing outside, above the cavern of Hekate. I heard Eiropis laughing and Mermerus telling Clytie in a worried tone that he was sure that we should not be out in the street without an escort.

Then I cut my wrist, deep. Only my blood would suffice for this sacrifice. The blade stung, being metal. My blood dripped onto the stone altar, and I heard a rustle as of bat wings and smelt the cold smell of stone. I found again the skill which I thought I had lost; I sank into the moment, cutting myself off from every other sound but the drop of my blood and the whisper, if she spoke, of the goddess.

'She Who Meets, Three-Faced One, Black Bitch, hear me,' I said. I smelt blood, my own blood, shed this time in expiation of the murders I had committed and the ones I was intending to commit.

'Lady of Silence, Queen of Phantoms, Blood Drinker, hear me.'

Nothing existed but the darkness, the heavy velvet blackness which blanketed all sense. I heard nothing from the upper temple now, nothing from the outside world at all. I might have imagined it all: the *Argo* and the palace and the traitorous prince.

'Lady of Battles, Lady of the Triple Way, Protector of the Newborn, hear me,' I concluded, and listened.

'Delphi,' said the goddess. A wing touched my mouth, and I felt not anger but pity in the serpent's gaze. I could see her now. Ophis Megale, the sacred snake, guardian of the grove where the Golden Fleece had once hung, before a faithless priestess stole it to win the love of a faithless Achaean.

The vision went, and the next thing I felt was a bandage being tied tightly around my wrist.

'She has sent you to Pythia, the great pythoness in the temple of Apollo,' snapped Hekate's maiden. 'Go, Medea. You have no place here yet.'

I was halfway up the steps when I heard the noise.

I had heard it before. It was the howling of a mob, a deep-throated, hunting howl of men's voices, with the shrill shriek of women over the top. Music for pursuit of some wretched fugitive.

It did not occur to me that they might be hunting me until I came out of the temple into the sacred ground of the mother goddess and saw blood on scattered paving stones and on bundles of cloth lying against the stone wall, under the cool gaze of the caryatids.

Then I ran, though there was no urgency. They were dead. Clytie had tried to protect them with her own body, but a great rock had crushed her head. She was slumped over Mermerus, who must have died last, for his body was still flexible and warm, and I fancied that I felt him respond as I lifted his body into my arms, though the heart in the shattered ribcage did not beat. The twins were broken like dolls, Eiropis still clutching Pallas. Mermerus' neck was broken. He lolled in my embrace.

Scylla and Kore nosed the bodies, howling with distress, but I could not howl.

While I was in the temple, the citizens of Corinth had come and stoned my children to death. And my dearest and most faithful Clytie. How could they have thrown missiles to crush these small bodies, these delicate bones? Why could they not have waited to kill me?

They were screaming at me now, and I managed to decipher some sentences. 'Creon dead,' they were yelling. 'Creon snatched the crown from his daughter's head, and pricked his finger on the poisoned thorns. Die, witch, like your spawn!' they shrieked.

I carried Mermerus to the wall, and they fell silent. I could not put his body down, yet, although he was quite dead.

'Your work,' I said to the suddenly frightened faces. 'The goddess will strike you with plagues for this. She is not lightly defied—I know, who have defied her and been destroyed for my presumption. Will you kill me here, Corinthians, or wait until I come into the street?'

'Lady,' said Clytie's husband Sisyphos. 'I came to prevent this, but I could not.'

'Clytie is murdered,' I said to him. 'Could they not have waited for me?'

'Princess, you have the gift of Corinth,' he said. 'I will take you to the quay and give you a boat. The city will suffer for this slaughter, but we will not kill you.'

'I had not thought you cruel,' I said. 'To take away my only desire.'

'Lady, you must appoint a new king,' he said.

His face was ravaged with grief for his wife. I laid down the body of my dead son and stretched out my right hand, red with my own and my children's blood. I marked Sisyphos the fisherman on the forehead and the breast and declared, 'You are king of Corinth.'

There was a pause. I saw him fill with divine authority. His face shone. He bowed to me, then turned to the mob, shoving them away with his hands as they pressed close, already a little abashed at what they had done.

'Begone,' bellowed Sisyphos to the crowd, his voice loud and harsh. 'To your homes! Pray to the gods against blasphemy, Corinthians, for you will be punished for these blasphemous crimes.' Such was his force of character that they obeyed him, slinking away, dropping the stones which they had retained for me.

'We must bury the children and Clytie my wife,' said the new king of Corinth.

No one touched me or spoke to me as I walked with my hounds down the steep streets to the harbour, as the night came on. I never even thought of Jason, or what might happen to him. I climbed tearlessly onto a Corinthian fishing boat and was borne away on water as dark as death, to Delphi and the Pythoness.

Chapter Twenty-six

Nauplios

Sitting at a tavern table in Khirra, I heard the news from an excited fisherman, who had heard it from a sailor. Medea of Corinth, the sorceress, had slain both Creon the merchant and his daughter Creusa, whom King Jason the Argonaut was intending to marry. Even of Jason, who was always easily influenced, I found this hard to believe, but they said it was true. He had been cast down from his kingship, which had devolved on Medea's choice, to a fisherman called Sisyphos. I bought the fisherman another cup of wine. I was now related to the king of Corinth.

But his voice lowered as he confessed the dreadful sequel to these murders. The people of Corinth, outraged, had flocked to the temple of the Mother, and unable to reach Medea, who was inside with Hekate, they had slaughtered her children and their nurse, a woman called Clytie.

'What happened to the lady Medea?' I asked, horrified.

'Nothing. She has gone to Delphi. She and Sisyphos buried the bodies in the sacred precinct, and then Sisyphos sent the witch away. But the priestesses emerged to denounce the city. They say that all goddesses are outraged, all of them—the Maiden and the Mother and the Crone. Even the gentle women of Aphrodite have prophesied doom, as children are the fruit of love. They say that a terrible plague will fall on Corinth because of these most sacrilegious killings, the murder of children in the temple of the Mother. Corinth trembles.'

'Corinth should tremble,' I said, aghast. 'They killed her children in the temple? And my cousin's wife, Clytie? May all the pestilences in the universe fall on Corinth! May the Earth-Shaker topple the town into the sea!' I leapt to my feet.

'Where are you going?' asked the fisherman, hoping for more wine.

'Nowhere,' I realised. 'I am already in the place where I can be of some use. How long ago, friend, did you hear that the witch left Corinth?'

'Day before yesterday, maybe. The weather has been too dangerous for sailing, but she would not mind that, perhaps. No one has come in from Corinth, if that's what you mean. I've been sitting here all day, waiting for the weather to settle, and it's been dry work.'

I gave him my flask of sour new wine, but I could not sit still. Especially after he asked eagerly, 'Shall we see her, then, this blood-drenched woman? I wonder what erotic spells she used to entrap the son of Aison? Is she beautiful?'

'No spell; she relied on his oaths,' I snarled, and walked the length of the beach and back again, as noon passed and the sun declined.

I was about to return to the tavern and find myself a bed for the night when I saw a fishing boat lurch unsteadily through the heads and sail straight for the beach. There seemed to be only one person on board, and that was unusual; such boats mostly had a crew of three. Someone was steering with one hand and dragging the rope which tautened the sail with the other. They were making a fairly good job of keeping the boat's head into the wind, and I watched, wondering who was out so late and alone.

The boat ran aground broadside—those shore currents are fierce at Khirra. I ran with some other idle men to secure her before the ebb could drag her out to sea again. I reached for the cloaked mariner, saying, 'Heart up, friend! You have reached harbour at last. What misfortune stranded you alone? Shall we search for swimmers?'

Two black dogs climbed over the thwarts and dropped heavily to the sand. I understood, and bid the other helpers away with a sweep of my arm, telling them that I would care for my kinsman. They drifted back to the tavern, and I lifted the lady Medea out of the foundering boat.

She had a heavy bundle with her which she would not release, so I carried both her and the burden up the strand and into the house of a pleasant widow who sold shining shells. I had lain with her sometimes, to ease her loneliness and my own.

'I have a friend,' I said to her. 'She is the witch Medea, so if you do not wish to care for her, I will do so myself. I require your fire and some bedding.'

She replied, 'I dare not touch her, Nauplios, but I would not leave her unattended, so you may have what you require.'

Then she left me the house to myself, and I laid my lady down on the warm floor and stripped off her soaking cloak and sopping gown, hanging the garments to dry, so that the room was quickly full of steam.

I broke bread into fish broth to feed the dogs and they lapped gratefully. Kore and Scylla remembered me, though they were old for hounds, getting stiff, and no longer as enthusiastic as they had been about travel.

The bundle was also wet. It was wrapped in a fine piece of gold-encrusted embroidery, but I did not touch it. The princess, by the time I had finished with the dogs, was sitting up and combing her hair with her fingers.

'Nauplios,' she said wonderingly. 'Nauplios, how came you here? They killed my children.'

'I was on my way to Athens, but I took a side journey to see Idas and Lynkeos,' I replied. 'What happened to your crew?'

'They stayed for a little while, but they were so terrified of travelling with Medea the Witch that they jumped overboard and swam to shore. The goddess has sent me to consult Pythia and therefore I must go to Delphi, so I sailed the boat alone.'

'You will make a mariner yet,' I said. There was a silence. I looked at her. She was still beautiful enough to blur my eyes, but there was a strange distance in her, as though only a small part of her was there, as though a whole chunk of Medea had been broken or destroyed. She ate and drank without further conversation and lay down to sleep, tired out by the journey, which would have tested a grown man in the fullness of his strength.

I lay down before the threshold, so that no one could come in, and looked at her. She seemed very young when she was asleep, scarcely older than the maiden priestess who had stolen the Golden Fleece and saved all of our lives, mine as well. Her hair was still as black as soot, and the hounds lay on either side of her, noses on paws. Under her drying tunic, I could see that her breasts were heavy now and the slim lines of her body blurred with childbearing; those children who had been shamefully murdered by Corinth.

I wished blights and plagues upon them, for I could not see how my lady Medea could ever recover from this wound. The priestesses of Aphrodite, who hear everything, had told me that she loved her children, and loved them even more when her lord had turned away from her.

I could not forgive Jason, once my own lord, for putting such a dreadful insult upon her, but consigned him to the gods, who would arrange some suitable punishment for his cruelty.

I did not care that she had killed Creon, a man whom I had never liked, or his simpering daughter. I had not cared that she had killed Pelias either, or the usurper, Korinthos.

But I cared dearly for my lady, the Colchian princess, and it seemed to me that she was anxious to reach Delphi because she was hoping that the Pythia would demand that she leap from the *Phaedriades*, the shining cliffs, and go back to Hekate.

She did not demur when I appeared the next morning with two horses, bought ironically with one of Jason's gifts to his comrade Nauplios. They were good, for they had cost me a pair of silver earrings. She mounted without comment and sat quietly while I bound her bundle onto the saddle and lifted Kore up before her, and the great dog lay across the horse's neck. I took Scylla on my saddle, for the hounds were too old to follow horses up the hills, and the hills on the road to Delphi were steep. The lady's hand reached for the reins automatically, and we moved through the fishing village of Khirra onto the road.

It was spring. The crocus bloomed in the verges. Sweet scents wafted about us, but the lady Medea did not notice them. She rode, I observed, like a Scyth, sitting high on the horses' shoulders, with Kore lolling before her. Scylla sat up on my saddle, all four feet together like a cat, and watched the landscape alertly, occasionally turning her head to give my face a quick, reassuring lick. Apparently Scylla thought that it would be all right. I did not think so.

Medea did not speak as we threaded the mountain paths. The road is ever rising or falling on the way to Delphi, perhaps to discourage pilgrims who are faint of heart. Another thing which discourages them is the prevalence of bandits, who are numerous and cruel. We turned a corner into a little clearing and were abruptly surrounded.

There were too many of them to fight. I jumped off my horse and stood next to the lady, ready to kill her if we could not talk or buy our way out. I would not see her outraged and sold into slavery.

'Pilgrims, it is time to offer sacrifice,' gloated the captain of the robbers. His men laughed. He had presumably delivered this line before.

'What sacrifice do you require?' I asked.

'Everything you have,' said the captain, drawing out the words. 'You are the first to pass the road since last autumn, and it has been a hard winter and we are hungry and poor. Therefore we will have your offerings, your clothes, your horses, and your lives.'

'That leaves us nothing to bargain with,' I said, drawing my sword. A bow was bent, and they began to close in on us. One slashed at the bundle and a shower of possessions fell out, including a battered sheepskin toy in the shape of a bear. The bandit picked it up, sneered, and threw it down.

Without warning, the lady Medea came to ferocious life. She leapt down, threw off her cloak and cried in a low, dangerous voice, 'I am Medea the Witch, Sorceress, Murderess. If you wish to die, you will touch me or my escort. First your blood will boil,' she said, approaching the knot of frightened men. 'You will be unable to sweat. The heat will strike inward until you tear your own flesh, or plunge into icy water, and yet you will burn until your brains bubble in your burst skull.'

She had no further need for cursing. They had gone, running like rabbits. She picked up the toy from the grass, kissed it, and thrust it into the bosom of her grown.

I strapped up the torn bundle and we remounted and rode on, but she spoke no word to me that day.

I gave her into the care of the priests of Apollo and sat down in a Delphi tavern to worry, I and the hounds. They were sitting at my feet, gnawing bones, when Scylla gave a small yelp. I knelt down and she let me examine her mouth. One of her teeth was rotten, and I busied myself with borrowing a pair of pincers and pulling it out. She bore this operation well, not offering to bite, and was drinking without pain as soon as I had completed it, but I was concerned again. The dogs which had been Medea's constant companions were aging. It was not likely that either Kore or Scylla would live another year. Then what would the lady Medea do, utterly alone in the world?

She would never be utterly alone, I vowed, while I lived.

Medea

I don't remember the ride to Delphi, though I have a vague memory of confronting some bandits who had defiled Arktos with their touch. That toy was all I had of my son Mermerus, who lay cold in his grave in the precinct in Corinth, together with the twins. I had nothing to venture, nothing to lose. Two further gangs had thought about attacking Nauplios and me but had changed their minds, one group even offering to escort us to the road again, provided that I didn't curse them.

Delphi polis is a small but bustling town. It is supported by the temple of Apollo, venerable and famous all over the world for the accuracy of its prophecies. It lies on a hill between the shining cliffs, where the springs of Castalia rise, cold and nourishing, the waters of absolution.

I did not think I would be allowed to drink from them. The Pythia could order a suppliant to pay for her crimes with her death, a thought had encouraged me to bear the sea-voyage and the long ride through the mountains.

There seemed to be nothing left of Medea who had gone with the Achaeans. There was a hollow inside me which the whole of Phanes' creation could not fill. The children, the children were dead, and I had not wailed, I had not mourned. Sisyphos and I had watched the priestesses dig graves for my murdered darlings and my dearest friend, who had died trying to protect them. My Clytie, with her salty tongue now stilled. I had with me the veil she had worn, stained with her blood. I had lain the small bodies of the twins together in one grave, not to be parted in death as they had never been in life; and I gave Eiropis her doll Pallas, and my little son his carved olive wood fish, called Icthys. I had folded the terribly damaged hands of my children over their most treasured possessions without a tear. Mermerus lay curled in the earth without Arktos, because I could not find him. I was so sorry. I hoped that Mermerus would sleep, but he never liked to go to bed in the dark without Arktos. Sometimes I heard him crying, and woke so full of despair that it seemed that the dark could not contain it.

I had not dared to unwrap the bundle of my possessions, so it was not until the bandit had plundered it that I knew that I had my son's bear, and I would certainly have killed to regain it. The soft sheepskin lay against my heart as I climbed the hill toward the three temples. Hekate had sent me to Pythia, and to Pythia I would go.

Then she would release faithless Medea, and I could die.

The first temple was made of laurel branches. There I left my robe and my knife. No one can climb the hill of prophecy bearing marks of rank or weapons. Even a king, the attending priest told me, must leave his crown and sceptre here.

I had no crown. I had used it to kill Creusa and Creon.

The pink dust coated my feet as I climbed again to a circular temple plastered with beeswax and covered with white feathers, where I left my sandals and ascended barefoot to the sanctum. Here was the navel stone, the *omphalosi,* and an altar to Hestia, where I sprinkled incense. It flared up brightly, burning blue, so it must have been resinated. A priest of Apollo—the priests are only Achaean men who wear veils—beckoned me to come into the *oikos,* the outer chamber.

I smelt the presence of gods. A strong, honey-sweet scent, like jasmine on a hot day, filled the chamber, though outside there was a cool clean breeze which bore almost no scent at all. The *adyton,* the inner chamber, was open. I saw a woman straddling a tripod over a crack in the mountain. Her face was perfectly blank. She had no personality at all; the god had stolen her, possessed her, and she was the mouth of Apollo.

The priest brought a kid forward, for which I had paid a handful of gold. He sprinkled it with water and it shivered, which meant that the sacrifice could be made. If it hadn't, I would have had to stay on the mountain until I could get the right omen. This was a black goat. The priest slit the beast's throat and, as bright blood streamed into the channel in the stone, I heard Pythia scream, 'Apollo is here!' I watched the blood move in a sticky stream along the marble, congealing as it flowed.

'*Theoprope,* speak,' she cried, in a voice which must have rasped her throat. 'Oracle seeker, ask.'

'What should Medea do now?' I had thought about my question, always wise when consulting oracles. There was a silence from the *adyton,* so I knelt and waited for Apollo, a god of whom I knew nothing good, to speak my doom.

I wondered what it would be like to fall from those shining cliffs, and how long it would take before I hit the ground and was freed to return to Hekate.

But what I heard from the inner chamber was not the usual prophetic verse, but a child's voice demanding drearily, 'Mother?' as though he had been crying for a long time in the dark and despaired of anyone hearing him.

'Mermerus,' I replied without volition, without thinking or analysing, 'it's all right, my son, there, Mother's here.'

'I want Arktos,' he said. I couldn't see him, though I stared into the gloom. I could only see an elderly priestess grasping a tripod, her eyes shut tight, her knuckles clenched. The child's light voice came strangely from her mouth.

'Mother?' Mermerus' voice rose into panic. 'It's all dark!'

'Oh my son shalt have Arktos, I have him here, it's all right, don't be afraid. Clytie's with you, sweeting. Find Clytie, and Mother will send Arktos to you. You mustn't be afraid, Mermerus. Find Clytie.'

There was a pause. Something clenched inside me, my heart or my womb. I had no doubt that I was speaking to the ghost of my little son. I took Arktos out of my bosom and held him on my lap, stroking the partially bald woolly head, the ears sucked out of shape. Then I kissed his badly embroidered black nose and gave him to the priest, who took him reverently and let him fall into the sulphurous crack in the mountain, to send him to my son.

'Mother?' I heard a moment later. 'Clytie's here, she's holding the twins Mother, she's pulling me away. There's a light. Brighter than the sun. And I've got Arktos,' he said, my solemn little son who always worried about propriety. 'Arktos is here,' he said with deep satisfaction. 'Clytie says to tell you that I love you,' he said after a pause. 'I love you, Mother.'

'I love you, my son. I love all of you. Tell Clytie and the twins. Tell them I love them.' Then, with a tearing wrench, I told him, 'Now go toward the light, little son. Go with Clytie, and I'll see you again, Mermerus.'

I heard Mermerus' voice say crossly, 'I'm coming,' and then, 'Farewell, Mother.'

Still I could not weep, though the silence which followed the last words ripped my heart. Now they were truly gone, my children. But Clytie would look after them. My lap was empty, even of Arktos. I was about to rise when the priestess spoke, this time in the conventional oracular utterance.

> *Medea of Colchis, murderer,*
> *Pelias is ashes, and Aegialeus,*
> *Though Korinthos lies not in your charge.*
> *Creusa is no more, unspotted virgin,*
> *Creon the merchant trades on a different river.*
> *Four dead, Princess, and four dead answer them.*
> *Clytie and Mermerus,*
> *Eiropis and Alcimedes,*
> *Dead by the hand of Corinth,*
> *Who shall also answer for their crimes.*
> *You are freed, Princess, you are balanced,*
> *All paid for and the account closed.*
> *Innocent lives answer innocent lives.*
> *Live, Medea; you may not die.*
> *The dead are happy, being dead,*
> *Not to have lived is better,*
> *But humans must be content.*
> *Another place and another life,*
> *A hero wrapped in flame,*
> *A fisherman with a hero's heart.*
> *Apollo has spoken.*
> *Begone. You are absolved.*

I was disappointed. I did not want absolution. The priest led me down through the temples to the Springs of Castalia and bade me strip and wash, and I did so, for nakedness is no shame on the holy mountain. The water was as cold as ice. I stood in the shallow stone dish which catches the sacred water as he poured dippers of it over me, soaking my hair, the chill penetrating to my bones. Something departed me then. The leaden weight of horror began to lift. I noticed the world, which I had been prepared to leave without a moment's thought. I noticed the priest, a young man with a wrinkled brow, who was trying not to look at my body in case it disturbed his chastity. I ran my hands over it. I was stronger than I had been as a captive, though nothing like the young maiden who had ridden with the Scyths. My body was curved now, though thin as ever, the marks of childbearing were on my belly and my breasts sagged. My hair weighed down my head, stuck to my shoulders, still sooty black. Somehow I had blistered three of my fingers—I thought I recalled picking up a brand to light a fire. The burns stung. The shield of unreality which had protected me from the world had been washed away. The wind was cold on my skin.

When I was clean, the priest gave me three sips from the spring water. I drank obediently. Then he conducted me back to the temple where I had left my clothes, and I found my stained tunic, wrinkling my nose at the smell. I had been wearing it for days, sleeping and riding. It stank of sweat and horse. I could not put that on over my newly cleansed skin.

The keeper of the first temple saw this and chuckled. He was a likeable old man with a bald head and mischievous eyes.

'You're recovering, woman,' he said. He meant no disrespect. Priests of Apollo call all females 'woman', as they call all males 'man'. There is no rank in the temple of Delphi.

'Here, take this. It is overlarge, but it is clean. A woman of Athens left it behind. She was so delighted with the oracle that she ran out of the temple and into the road with not a stitch on her. Still, since she had been told that she would bear a son, she was pleasing to her husband in that state.'

I donned the loose, oatmeal-coloured tunic and he helped me to put on my robe. He even knelt to fasten my sandals, as my hands were shaking so badly that I could not even pin my cloak.

'Spring is a time of hope,' he said gently. 'There is always hope, or what's the point of human life?'

I did not answer, but gave him a coin, and he blessed me in the name of Apollo.

'Go back to Hekate,' he said. 'The Crone waits for you, woman, but you will not go into the light yet. In the name of the Sun-Bright, live long and have joy,' said the priest, and he smiled at me.

I found Nauplios in a tavern with Scylla and Kore. He looked up and scanned my face.

'How is it with you, Lady?' he asked.

'I…do not know,' I said, unable to fathom the strange sense of lightness which the god had given me. The children were gone and the hollow was still there; it would never be wholly filled, and I had yet to mourn them fittingly. But I no longer wanted to die. In fact, I had been forbidden to die.

Nauplios filled a cup and I drank.

I could taste the wine.

Chapter Twenty-seven

Nauplios

It was a slow journey, because we were all tired.

It is not far from Delphi to Athens. A good rider with a strong horse can do it in two days. One of the Achaean message runners can manage it in a day and a night and part of the day, and will come into the marketplace when it is emptying for the noon meal.

But the lady Medea seemed exhausted and always hungry, which I found encouraging, because she would eat enough to feed a ploughman and sleep all night and half the day, which meant that we covered only a few *stadia* before she would say, 'Look for a village, Nauplios,' and I would find us a tavern or a house and tell the owner to prepare a huge meal. This would be consumed as though she had been starving for years, then she would lie down in her cloak and sleep as though stunned.

She did not speak much, but she was noticing the world again. I was content. I was with her, she accepted my company as she accepted that of the dogs—and my devotion, too. Scylla, Kore and I were her faithful followers, and for the moment we were pleased to ride a few hours a day, eat like wolves, and sleep in the new sun.

Spring grew all about us. I gave the lady a sprig of the plum flowers, and she pinned it to her cloak as we rode through the golden blossom and the silver leaves through a landscape so rich and sweet scented that it seemed that we traversed the Elysian Fields, where heroes dwell after death.

Kore and Scylla grew rested and playful, I stopped jumping at every sound, and slept deeply. I was escorting a mourning woman to some unknown fate, and I was happy.

She had opened the bundle which she had carried so devotedly, but even when she saw the little tunics—hardly the length of my forearm—which her children had worn, she did not weep, and that worried me. Until she mourned them she would never recover.

We tended the hurts of the villagers as we passed, and only once did she seem stricken. A child fled almost under my mare's hoofs, crying aloud with fear. I picked him up and asked, 'What, boy, did no one teach you not to run under a horse?' and Princess Medea gasped, though I did not know why. The child told us that he had ruined his tunic with tar and his mother was going to beat him, and the lady reached into her bundle and gave the furious woman a plain, well-woven garment.

The peasant softened instantly, holding the squirming child by the ear, and asked, 'Your own, Lady, are they gone?'

'Gone,' replied the lady Medea. 'Do not beat him. The gods do not give us children, they are lent. A blessing on him,' she added, and the woman made us come inside and fed us new cheese from her own goats, fresh and delicious, while the boy leaned on my knee and demanded to ride my horse.

We reached Athens at last. My lady had gained beauty with every step. She had washed her hair and combed it. Her face was filling out from that skull-like thinness which had frightened me. Her eyes were alert. But there was some part of her which I could not reach, and she still had not wept over her children.

We found the house of Herakles easily. Everyone in the village of Athens knew Herakles. He lived next to the temple of Athene Parthenos, patroness of the city. The Athenians were proud to have such a hero living with them, though they were uneasy about him. He had not been possessed of battle fury for a long time, but he had the potential, and everyone knew if he was in that state he would slaughter all about him without mercy or volition.

We stopped at a tavern to lodge our horses and pick up the gossip. Athens has always been a place buzzing with scandal. I heard many things in that tavern which do not bear repeating, and in any case did not interest me much, for they were about people I had never met. But there was talk of the hero. He had married a maiden called Deianeira, an orphan, whose relative he had met in the underworld. She was supposed to be very beautiful, with pale skin and grey eyes, though her lack of intelligence was something of a byword. However, Achaeans do not like intelligent women, so this was accounted a virtue.

The taverners said that the centaur Nessus, when crossing a river, had assailed this Deianeira from behind, attempting rape.

I remembered Nessus, a thoroughly reprehensible character who could not be trusted within grabbing range of any female creature, even a goat.

Deianeira had shrieked to Herakles for help, who had turned from the other bank and sent a bolt into the centaur. Herakles was always an amazing shot with a bow. He said that the gods directed his arrows. There was, according to the gossip, then some conversation between the dying Nessus and the maiden. She had been observed to collect his blood and semen in a cup; though what use she would have for such a noxious potion was beyond Athens.

The wine was excellent. The vintners of Athens boast rightly of the excellence of their grapes. Herakles was from home, my lady had gone to the kitchen to see what was cooking, so I sat comfortably on a stone bench and listened to the voices. It was a strange, harsh accent, clipped and guttural at the same time.

'Philammon is wandering this way,' observed the owner of the tavern. 'The Orpheans come every year to Athens, stranger,' he informed me, condescendingly. 'There is a festival of singing held on the Acropolis where the new temple is being built in honour of the voluntary suicide of the daughters of Erectheus, our king. All the bards come to Athens, because we feast them well, and we appreciate their music as no other people can. But they will not accept rewards of gold or horses,' he said. 'Philammon performed the Creation last festival and would take only some journey bread and a passage in a fishing boat to Corinth.'

'I know, I saw him there,' I said, nettled by his tone. 'I am a friend of his.'

'Who are you?' asked a man sitting unnoticed in a corner under the vine. 'I have seen your face before, somewhere.'

'Certainly you have,' I answered, recognising a known voice with great pleasure. 'Have I changed so much since we rowed together, Clytios?'

'Nauplios of Iolkos, by all the gods!' he swore. 'What brings you here?'

'I came to see Herakles, but I am delighted to see you.'

'Ah, Nauplios, my comrade.' He came forward into the light, and I saw that he was much scarred. Long stripes marked his face and torso. He had been raked deep, by claws perhaps, though he had healed well and the injuries were a couple of years old. 'A lion,' he explained. 'I missed the first shot and he was on me before I could run.'

Then he announced to the tavern, 'This is Nauplios of Iolkos, companion of Jason, an Argonaut and a brave man. Bring out the best wine,' he ordered the landlord. 'Not that goat's piss you serve to strangers. He is *philos*, my brother.'

Then I was accorded all the respect which I could have wished. Clytios told some highly exaggerated tales of my courage and I told some perfectly truthful ones about his, and we were occupied until the tavern population recollected that it had tasks to do and fields to sow and drifted regretfully away, leaving Clytios and me alone at the table.

'Have you heard of Jason?' he asked quietly.

I had not even thought of Jason in all the time since I had lifted the lady Medea out of the fishing boat. And I did not care what had happened to him, but I felt it politic to ask.

'No, I have not heard. Tell me.'

'He was cast out of his kingship, but he has not left Corinth. Instead, he roams the dockside, telling his tales of the Golden Fleece to the traders. They buy him wine and he drinks until he falls down. And a plague has struck that blasphemous city, sent by the goddesses, by Demeter and Hera and Aphrodite and Artemis. All the men there are struck impotent, and worse.'

'Worse?' I was hoping that something cataclysmic had happened to Corinth.

'They have dreams of blood. Then they burn in fever which cannot be assuaged, until they die. The sufferers tear their own flesh or fling themselves into the sea, but they burn with a fire which cannot be quenched. They are dying by the family. No women are affected, not even those who tend the sick, and very few children.'

I recognised the curse. I had heard the lady Medea applying it to the bandits who had ambushed us. But I did not think that she was responsible for the plague on Corinth. Corinth was responsible for that.

'So they sent to Delphi for advice, and the god told them that the murdered children of Jason and Medea were now demigods, living in the Elysian Fields with the heroes; the three of them and their nurse, a fisherman's wife called Clytie. Or so they say, though how anyone could make a demigod out of a fisherman's wife I cannot imagine.'

I bit my tongue. Clytie would make an excellent, sharp-tongued demigod and would certainly keep the heroes in order.

'She would have been queen of Corinth, if she had lived,' I told him. 'Her husband, Sisyphos, is now king.'

'Oh, well, that makes more sense,' said Clytios, pouring me another cup of wine. 'The god ordered that they be sacrificed to as *myxobarbaroi*, and funeral games should be held for them. And every year, seven Corinthian youths and seven Corinthian maidens of the best families must go and dwell in the temple of the Mother in expiation for the city's sin, and to mourn the victims of their blasphemy. Sisyphos has ordered it, though he has scarcely enough healthy citizens to run a footrace. It should stop the plague if it is divine.'

'That is just,' I agreed.

'But the fate of the lady Medea is unknown. There are those who say that she turned into a raven and flew away, or that she was snatched up by a lustful Zeus. In any case she has been so badly treated, so betrayed by our erstwhile lord, that I expect that she is dead. She left everything for him as you and I know, Nauplios, and I would not have said that he was a cruel man. Is the story true about his demand for a divorce and the exile of his queen?'

'It is true,' I informed him.

'She cured Herakles, you know. He says she made him a stone which wards off *Lyssa*, madness, the goddess who haunted him, sent by the gods. He has been peaceful since he came here and married. His new wife has not conceived yet, but the hero is over seventy. Even heroes get tired, and he must have lain with a thousand women. He must be sick of the sight of them.'

'Can we call on Herakles?' I asked. 'I came to Athens hoping to speak to him.'

'He stays inside, sometimes, for days on end, seeing no one. But we'll go and ask after the noon meal.'

The meal was sumptuous. The landlord, evidently a man who valued heroes, provided the specialities of his village. There was a spicy stew of goat's flesh and herbs, olives bursting with taste, a sweet dish made of dried grapes and honey and breadcrumbs and lamb meat on skewers, roasted over a charcoal fire and wrapped in bread and sauced with *yourti*, a Scythian delicacy lately come to Athens via the seafarers. It tasted like sour cream and was delicious.

Clytios had not spoken to my female companion, as was proper. She was heavily veiled and said nothing, only absorbed food as though she had been fasting. It was only after we sat back, replete, to pick our teeth and sip at the sweet red wine, that he gave her a polite greeting.

She replied as was fitting, but the effect on my shipmate was similar to the time I had seen him grab an electric eel.

'By all the gods, you are the lady Medea!' he whispered, glancing furtively around.

'I am, Clytios,' she answered softly.

'Lady, you must not be seen. The Athenians sympathise, but they will fear to harbour a witch, and one who has killed Creon, the brother of our king. You must leave.'

'Clytios, you have just told me that Corinth is sacrificing to the murder victims as demigods,' I objected.

'Religion is one thing, popular prejudice is another,' he whispered.

I heard the lady sigh and watched her gather up her cloak.

'I will go,' she said, so resignedly that I was saddened.

At that moment, an overpainted, voluptuous slave girl came into the tavern and walked hesitatingly to the lady Medea's chair.

'I am the messenger of Herakles the hero,' said the girl. 'He sends his greetings, and asks you to come with me, Lady.'

'And my companion?'

'Herakles, my master, asks that he stay with Clytios for tonight, and come to our house in the morning,' said the girl. 'He orders me to tell you, lord Nauplios, that he will care for the lady if you will entrust her to him.'

I looked at my lady, and she rose, saying, 'I will see you in the morning, Lord.'

Then they left, the brazen slave girl and the veiled princess. I looked back to find Clytios staring at me, open-mouthed.

'Where did you find her? How do you come to be travelling with her? Are you bespelled?' he demanded.

'Khirra, in a fishing boat which she sailed alone from Corinth. And because she was going to Delphi and I could not let her go alone, though no bandit would have dared come near her after the first. I don't think so.' I answered his questions in turn.

'Come home with me,' said Clytios after a pause in which he clearly debated whether to ask any more questions about my lady and decided against it. 'I have a house, a wife. A child, now. A son. His name was to be Jason, but that is ill omened. I now have a good name, one which will bring him luck,' he said, draping an arm over my shoulder and leading me out of the tavern and into weak sunlight. 'I shall call him Nauplios.'

Medea

The slave girl brought me through the back door of a little house, through a garden bright with rare flowers, under a vine putting on new leaves, and into a cool, dim room. It was simply furnished: one bed and a chair and a cupboard on which stood two wine cups, a jug, and a shallow bowl full of water lilies. They smelt fugitive and sweet. He turned as I came in, and I saw that his hair had thinned. The remaining locks were white. His face was deeply lined.

'Oh, Herakles,' I said.

He made a wry face, as though he knew what I was thinking, then said, 'Lady Medea, they have banished you?'

'Banished me? No, my friend, I left Corinth of my own will, after they…after they killed my children.'

The vision rose again. Flies settled on the eyes of the dead boy, my little son, Mermerus. So many dead, so much blood. All of it on my hands.

'And then?'

I sat down on the bed next to the hero, and he took my hand. 'I went to Delphi.'

'And Pythia told you?' he prompted.

'That I am in balance,' I said, listening to my voice rise out of control. 'That their deaths paid for the deaths I had caused—my brother Aegialeus, Pelias, Creon and Creusa. Four deaths, and my remaining three children and my dearest friend dead. The justice of the gods, ah, Herakles. I have no refuge. I'm hungry again and sleepy; the gods won't let me die.'

I could not weep, but he leaned sideways and gathered me into his arms. He was as strong as ever—a hero's bones are like metal—but the embrace was as delicate as if he were cupping a bird in his hands.

'They are dead, and it is my doing,' I said.

'I know.' The hands ran from my shoulders down my sides like a warrior reassuring himself that his comrade was unbroken. 'Dead,' I said flatly. He raised my chin and forced me to look into the trout-stream eyes. He seemed to contain sorrow.

'Your children are dead because of your deeds,' he said softly. 'My children, Medea, died by my own hand.'

For a moment we were one. I looked into his heart and heard someone weeping; endlessly weeping. Herakles in battle fury had killed his own children. I felt his pain wash against mine like an opposing tide.

'How, then, are we still alive?' I asked drearily, and then the great hero kissed me.

I wore only a chiton and I cast it aside. He lay down beside me, flank to flank, and began to caress me.

He was old, Herakles, not yet the immortal. His skin smelt so sweet to me, but his potency was ebbing; he would no longer be able to deflower the fifty daughters of a king in one night. In its place was skill and understanding, a feeling for my flesh, a soothing balm of sensuality laid over my insulted and abused senses.

Carefully his hands slid, touched, stroked. I turned in his arms, feeling his warmth; not the burning of a young man, like Jason so long ago when I dived into his arms and engulfed the piercing spike which engendered my murdered flesh. Herakles glowed with a banked fire, warm, comforting, and I lay down almost sleepily in his embrace. My breast fitted his hands and the nipples rose between thumb and forefinger.

There was no sharp climax, no spasm in the back and belly, but a mounting heat as his mouth sucked and his hands moved, gentle and inexorable, listening for a response, tasting my kisses.

I had not thought to make love again, destined for death, Medea the outcast. Herakles' phallus slid inside me, gently, letting me feel the strength of his desire, and he moved slowly, each movement of thigh and buttocks bringing more of the buried senses to my skin. Nerves flared on the surface and deep inside me, and I gasped aloud, hearing his breathing roughen, my hands grasping to pull him down close, heavier, twining my legs around his back.

His body anchored me to reality. I was not pierced to the heart as I had been once, and had considered desirable. I was not pinned by one shoulder like a deer beneath a hound. I was close, close—as close to Herakles the hero as his skin, joined along thigh and loins and chest, mouth to mouth.

And as I felt the phallus within me blossom and heard his groan, I glowed with a bright light; we shone in the darkness, and I began to cry and could not stop.

He hauled me across his body as he rolled, so that I was lying on his chest, naked and wet, and my tears rolled down his shoulder. He did not speak or try to comfort me. He pulled a blanket over us, held me as close as a nursing mother holds a newborn, and listened to me weep, drinking my tears so that his mouth was sharp with brine. We lay warm in the scent of tears and semen and sweat, the smell of human love.

I have never loved a man so much as, at that moment, I loved Herakles, the hero; Herakles, servant of women.

◇◇◇

I wept all night. I had not known I contained so many tears. After a while it became spasmodic, and in between we talked. I remembered tending this hero, dreadfully wounded, amongst the Scyths. I was pleased to find that the *lithos sophronister* had worked. Herakles told me that he had retired to Athens to conclude his life without incident. He said that his wife was loving, his sons healthy, his house well run, the wine excellent and the company undemanding.

'But I cannot go to a tavern any more,' he said.

My head was on his chest and his hand was stroking my hair. Something had broken inside me, a knotted cord, and now I could not stop the tears which bathed his chest and soaked his bedclothes.

'Why not? You are a hero,' I said.

'I am a hero, yes, but if I go to a tavern they demand stories. If I tell them I am boasting; if I do not tell them I am too proud to mix with common men. Then some young hothead is likely to challenge me. If I fight him and win, it would be oppression, for everyone knows that Herakles is a great hero. If I fight him and lose, as sooner or later all heroes must, he will gain great notoriety for having defeated the strongest man in the world. So mostly I stay here. I have visitors. Philammon always calls when he is here for the festival. And I have my own courtyard and my own vine and I am content. What else happened at Delphi? There is something which you are not telling me.'

'The children spoke…' I wept again, and when I could speak I told him all that Mermerus, through the priestess, had said.

'They are sacrificing to them as myxobarbaroi, the half strangers, and Corinth has a plague to punish its dreadful deeds,' Herakles said, his voice rumbling in his chest. 'The city will expiate the crime for eternity; unless the gods change their purposes. That can happen, of course—do I not know that all too well? But you know they are safe, Medea. I wish that I knew that.'

I wept again, but with less agony. He rose and gave me wine, mingled with some bitter herbs.

'You will live,' he said, mopping his breast. 'We have to live. I do not mean that you will forget them.' He raised a hand to still my protest. He looked like an elderly farmer reproving a grandson, this hero before whom all the world stood in awe.

'But you will live, now that you have mourned them. They are safe with Clytie and walk in the fields of heaven. You cannot come to them there yet, but you will, in time.'

He lay down with me again and we made love and wept and made love again until dawn. The sun shot beams like arrows through Herakles' window. He was not asleep. He said to me, 'Where will you go?'

'Can't I stay with you?'

'No. The city will not accept you, and my wife will be hurt, and I would not hurt her, poor maiden.'

'I suppose that is so.' I had not even considered that Herakles was married.

'You have rejoined the Dark Mother,' he reminded me.

'Not wholly. My sacrifice was complete, but the priestess said that I could not come back to Hekate yet.'

'I think she will accept you now,' he said slowly. 'When Nauplios comes, what will you say to him?'

'That I will go on alone to the temple of Hekate on the coast.'

'You will not go alone,' said Herakles, rolling over to get to his feet and stretching. I heard his spine crack into place and he scratched his beard unaffectedly.

'I won't?' I asked.

I ran a hand down my body and felt wetness and brought my fingers away bloody. The Mother was asserting her control over me. I had not seen moon blood for some time. I was returning to health, whether I liked it or not.

'Nauplios loves you,' said Herakles simply. 'He always has, from the first time he saw you. But he will offer you no affront, Lady. He wants to care for you, and you should allow him this grace. He has been faithful.'

'Men are not faithful,' I said bitterly.

'Jason was always weak,' said Herakles, catching me in a breath-stopping embrace. 'He had no authority, even on the quest for the Golden Fleece. Nauplios is a fisherman's son, a peasant. He does not share the vices of the nobility, who are effete, cruel, and cowardly. Consider Erystheus, giving me murderous missions from inside his grain emphora. Nauplios has courage and sureness of mind. Go with him to Hekate's temple, at least.'

'If you request this, of course,' I said, dazed with mourning and release.

'It is the last thing I shall ask of you,' said Herakles, and he kissed me very gently.

Chapter Twenty-eight

Nauplios

I drank too much with Clytios, renewing old memories, and rose groaning at sunrise to collect my belongings, saddle the horses and walk out into the sunlight.

Kore and Scylla came from the courtyard where they had been rolling in the dew. Their black coats were sparkling with light, little bright points which made me blink, and they jumped up onto me, happy with the idea of morning and spring.

I was not terribly impressed, but patted them and told them that we were leaving. Clytios would not come with me, but loaded me with presents and food. In return I gave his small son an agate pendant, an amulet of Poseidon, for it had a piece of fringed seaweed trapped inside the stone. The child gummed it instantly and his father just managed to grab it before he swallowed it.

Reminding little Nauplios that amulets were to be worn externally, not internally, I farewelled Clytios affectionately and, following his directions, the lady Medea's faithful followers went through a back lane to Herakles' house, as the hero had requested.

The same bold slave girl let us into a courtyard blooming with beautiful flowers. I bent to sniff, suppressing a spasm as my head reminded me that I was getting too old for late hours and a half emphora of wine between two comrades.

Herakles had managed to make all manner of different flowers grow in his garden, ones that normally would be found in different places. Some were seashore plants, some from the high mountains. Here they all bloomed happily together. There was a theory that Herakles was actually a Dactyl, the demigods born when Rhea the Titan dug her hands into the ground while Zeus All Father was being born. That being so, he might have had green fingers.

The lady Medea came into the garden with the hero, summoned by the girl. Herakles stooped with difficulty and picked some of the dark blue flowers which he had worn when I first saw him. They were stone gentians, which usually only grow just below the snow line. She stood smiling as he plaited them into her straight black hair, an aureole of strong blue around her dark face. She was as beautiful as a goddess. I perceived that she had lain with Herakles, and was struck with an instant and unworthy pang of jealousy so strong that it stirred my already unstable insides and made me feel nauseous.

I felt someone's gaze on me. Out of the window, a set, furious face was staring, watching Herakles kiss my lady very gently on the forehead. A young woman with golden hair and burning grey eyes. She saw me looking at her, grabbed for a veil and vanished. I presumed that this was the maiden Deianeira, the wife of Herakles.

My lady could lie with whomsoever she desired, and who better to comfort her than a hero? It was none of my concern to be jealous of her. She could bestow her body where she wished, and if Herakles had loosed the tears in her, then he had done both of us a great service.

I lost the uncertain feeling in my belly and could appreciate the garden, the vine, and the sight of my lady smiling, which I had not thought to see again.

Then the hero saw me and hailed, 'Nauplios, my dear comrade.' I came to him and he hugged me, the bear hug of Herakles which somehow did not crack the bones as one would expect. He was old. He looked even more like a peasant, which endeared him to me. Even the fame which echoed around the world had not taken his essential earthliness away from Herakles.

'Thank you for entrusting her to me,' he said gravely.

'You have my trust, now and always,' I replied.

He grinned and picked for me a red rose, still a bud.

'Put it in water and when it blooms, so shall your life,' he said. 'Are you well stored for the journey?'

'Indeed,' I said, moving aside so he could see the packhorse which carried our baggage. Clytios had given me the horse and had also contributed largely to its burden, as though he was anxious that I should not take offence at the exile of my lady. 'In any case, today we are only going so far as the temple of Hekate on the coast.'

'This may be useful,' he said, handing me something wrapped in cloth. It was long and heavy. I put back the wrappings and found a sword. It was hilted in gold and encrusted with jewels. It must have been worth a king's ransom.

'Take it,' he ordered over my protest that it was far too valuable for a common sailor to own. 'I need no weapons now. And you are a most uncommon sailor, Nauplios.'

'Farewell. When you hear of my death, remember that I was glad to live, and now I am glad to die. I will be content, I will be happy. Nauplios? Do you understand?'

'I understand, Lord.'

He gazed into my eyes for another moment, then seemed satisfied. He blessed me, then kissed me on both cheeks like a shipmate. The lady Medea preceded me into the lane, where we mounted and rode out of the little village of Athens and into the scrubby countryside, heading for the sea.

The last we saw of Herakles the hero, he was standing in his garden, gently stroking the trunk of a tree.

'I am an exile,' said the lady to me after we had ridden for some time. 'But that does not mean that you need be an exile, too, Nauplios.'

'Lady, I go with you until you are where you wish to be,' I said, shoving down bile. Did she mean to send me away, after we had come so far? Had the hero's love been so sweet that she could not contemplate any other company?

'Nauplios,' she touched me, laying her hand on mine, the horses pacing close together. 'I value you, I do not wish you to lose your future because you are with me. I am witch and sorceress and murderer, remember.'

'I know,' I said.

'And there will be many places where you cannot go if you are with me,' she instructed me gently. 'Most of Achaea, by the look of it. I cannot stay in the land of Pelops, Nauplios. I will have to find another home.'

'Yes,' I agreed. 'And until you find it, you will need company. I have nothing here,' I said, and perhaps a little bitterness crept into my voice, for she took her hand away.

'Since I saw you, Lady, since you came out of the mist in Colchis calling to Melanion, son of Phrixos, I have been your man, wholly. I could not marry in Iolkos, nor in Corinth. Many women were offered to me, but I wanted none of them. If you send me away, Lady, I will go. But there is nothing more in the world I want than to be with you.'

'When we come to the temple, send a messenger to Khirra to bring *Good Catch* to Piraeus,' she said slowly. 'We could buy another boat, but perhaps you would prefer to sail your own vessel.'

'It was my father's ship, and I would prefer it,' I said. 'Especially if we are not coming back to Aegeas' ocean.'

I was hopeful of never hearing the Achaean tongue again. My fellow countrymen were cruel and cowardly, the murderers of children, who could not even refrain from challenging an old hero who only wanted to drink wine in peace. 'Where shall we go?'

'I don't know,' she said. 'But if you wish, you shall come with me. I lay with Herakles,' she told me.

'Yes, Lady.'

'And he taught me that I am still female, and I wept all night for my children. I do not know if I have any love to give to requite your devotion, Nauplios. I would not have you pine for me, if I am fatally crippled.'

'Lady, I will not pine,' I promised. 'But I will go with you,' I insisted, and this time she gave me her hand. I kissed it.

The rose of Herakles was in a slim *lekythos* full of water, carefully fastened to the pack-beast's saddle. I began to hope that it would, indeed, bloom for me.

Medea

I had not noticed that Nauplios loved me, though in retrospect it was obvious and I wondered at my blindness.

He had been always at my side. He had seen that I was cold and given me his cloak on the *Argo* when I was so sunk in love with Jason that I had not even thanked him. He had engineered our escape from Iolkos, had found me fruits when I was sick with pregnancy, had sailed with me when Jason was despondent on the way to Corinth.

He had found me Clytie—oh, my murdered Clytie, I missed her so much!—and when I lay three-quarters dead after Polyxenos' birth, the face I had seen over Clytie's shoulder, coming to see if I lived, had been Nauplios, not Jason.

Nauplios had lifted me out of the foundered boat at Khirra, had cared for me and provided horses, and had accompanied me to Delphi and to Athens without ever importuning me, without even telling me he loved me.

I wondered now if Jason had ever loved me. Or even if the state of insanity in which I had existed for years had been love, or pure self-delusion. I had been very young, stirred by the mating of the Scythians, freed from all vows when Trioda cursed me, angry with the restrictions of life after my freedom amongst the Scyths, shocked by my father breaking his sworn word and by the fraud which debased the worship of the Dark Mother. And I had carried an itch which would not be scratched if I stayed with the maiden.

So I had gone with Jason and done anything he wanted. I had tamed the bulls and doped Ophis. I had murdered Pelias and supplied the poison for Korinthos, though Pythia had said that death was not laid to my charge. I had borne children in agony and loved them beyond measure. Now my life was concluded, and I was not allowed to die. So many dead.

'Lady?' asked Nauplios. 'What did the oracle say?'

'It is too fresh in my heart for me to speak of it,' I said. 'Let us talk of other things. Did I ever tell you about the bronze giant?'

'No, never. Tell me of Talos,' he answered.

And I watched his face as I told him of the dying man and the monstrous bronze machine. I had also not noticed that Nauplios was good to look at. He was not beautiful, not Jason of the golden hair, the pale, cruel eyes and deceitful heart. Nauplios was not tall. He was broad and strong with heavily muscled arms and legs. His hands were big and calloused, like those of a farmer or a fisherman. His hair was dark brown, neither curly nor straight, and was mostly tied back from his tanned forehead by a leather thong. He had a charming smile, very youthful, though experience had carved lines on his face; and his eyes were surrounded with the far-seer's net of lines, which are caused by staring over bright water or through fog. He could always distract me, even now, making me laugh at some waterfront scandal. I could not remember Jason ever making me laugh.

But if I rejoined Hekate I could not lie with a man again.

My body was still languorous with Herakles' love. I still felt his semen flow from my loins along with the moon blood. I would have to give up this pleasure if I went back to Hekate. Even assuming that he would wait until I could bear the idea, I could not take the deserving Nauplios as my lover if I embraced the Dark Mother again.

I was overcome and wept as we rode through the silvery olive groves to the sea. I was confronted continually with choices, and I wanted a straight path. Death had seemed so simple. Life was unbearably complicated.

◇◇◇

The temple of Hekate at Piraeus was very large, very ancient, and most of it was under the ground. I stripped off my fine gown and even my tunic, soaked in Herakles' love, and walked naked down the steps into the blackness beyond, the dogs behind me. Moon blood smeared my inner thighs and I heard the suck and slap of moisture as I walked.

'Medea,' said a voice, and I stood still. It was not the priestess I had been expecting. It was a divine voice, and I hurried down to find a place where I could kneel. The floor of this cavern was carpeted in something which rustled, perhaps pine needles or straw. Scales rubbed against my skin. I was not afraid. If the goddess wished me to die, she need only have not interfered at Delphi. Snakes wreathed around me and the hounds, who crouched at attention on either side of me.

'Medea,' said the voice again, a tone of infinite patience. I felt that she would keep calling me until I replied, if it took forever.

'Lady of Roads, Three-Headed One, Lady of Ghosts, I am here,' I said, almost under my breath. 'I am Medea, once your priestess. I have made the sacrifice of my own blood, of my body and the bodies of my most dearly loved. I am naked, without defence. Drinker of Blood, She Who Is Met On The Road, Snake Lady, speak.'

'Medea, you have always been mine,' she said, and a delicious sleepiness crept over me, as it had so long ago in the grove, when I had been a lonely child.

'Medea, you are mine,' she said, and I strove to force my eyelids open. 'Medea, you will always be mine,' she concluded.

I woke some uncounted time later, curled asleep amongst the hounds. A plump woman in black garments was sitting cross-legged in wheat straw, plaiting it into a band.

'Ah, you have returned,' she commented, her fingers moving without her attention. 'The goddess has spoken. Hekate has accepted you.'

'Yes,' I agreed.

'You do not seem to be as pleased as I would have expected,' she said. She was a young woman with short curly hair and clever hands.

'I am now faced with having to dismiss one who loves me, as I can never lie with him if I rejoin the Crone,' I said, pushing myself wearily upright. Kore nudged me and I shoved her head away.

To my amazement, I heard the priestess laugh. In fact, she did not just laugh, she whooped with merriment and dropped her plait, having to grope for it in the straw.

'Who told you that, sister?' she asked, conquering her mirth. 'What an idea! If the priestesses are barren, where will the acolytes come from?'

'From the populace,' I said.

'That may be the practice in Colchis, a far place where the language is strange and the customs stranger,' she told me. 'Here we prefer to have the daughter of the priestess follow her mother. She can be instructed when she is very young, before she has time to be frightened.'

She finished the plait and wound it around my head, fastening it with a flat knot under Herakles' flowers. I realised that she was not just plump, she was pregnant. This priestess of Hekate had practised what she preached.

'Some women only come to Hekate after they have passed childbearing,' she said, running a finger along my legs. 'But you are still fertile, the moon still rules your tides. You may mate and bear within the goddess' worship, of course, if you wish. And she will be with you, whether you do or not, whether you are chaste or married, whether you are young or old. How else could we trust her, being women, fallible and prone to violence, sin and error?

'Come now, sister. We will say our prayers together to the Dark Mother, and then perhaps you will stay the night. Or several nights, if you wish. For a message has come for you, sent to all the temples of Hekate throughout Achaea, carried on by messengers from the Euxine Sea to the Propontis, from there to the sea of Aegeas, borne on Oceanos.'

'What message?'

'I will tell you later,' she promised.

We came at length out of the dark into a large room, where fifteen women were sitting down to a meal. They had found Nauplios and were clearly pleased with him, for they had seated him at a table by himself and were plying him with tidbits as though he was a performing dog. He rose instantly as I came in, but asked no questions.

'It is all right,' I said. He nodded and relaxed, and the noise rose again.

This was a temple of Hekate, I told myself. It was draped in black, the image was of sable stone, the sanctuary was underground and peopled with serpent folk. The prayers, allowing for a certain freedom of translation, were the same, as were the titles of the goddess. And here I had heard that same divine voice which young Princess Medea had heard and had cried for when it went away.

But there were sixteen women here in one place, which was forbidden in Colchis. They were eating all manner of food, including meat and cheese. They were drinking wine. They were dressed in the black robes over the blue tunic, but they were laughing and chattering like ordinary women.

It was impossible. Dazed, I accepted a seat at the big trestle table and allowed them to feed me soft cheese and green herbs.

'I think the apples will bear well this year, unless the gods send storms,' said one. 'The trees are loaded with blossom like snow.'

'And at least eleven of the goats will deliver. I'm not sure about the old nanny. She could be pregnant, or she could be fat,' commented another.

'Unlike our Nys, who is definitely mated and will definitely bear,' they laughed.

Nyssa, my priestess, grinned and patted her belly. 'I'm sure that the old nanny mated,' she declared. 'That old man goat will mate with anything, as you found when you turned your back on him last spring,' she teased, and a young acolyte blushed and then giggled.

This was not the worship of Hekate as I knew it and I was shocked, but then found myself wondering what was good about the worship of Colchian Hekate as I had known it. It had been gloomy, life denying and cruel, concerned with fear and with power. These chattering girls could probably compound a potion, knew their herbs, relied on Hekate to protect them and prayed to her. What else could a sensible goddess require?

I tasted their stew, at their urgent request, and it was excellent.

After this meal and a cup of their wine, which was rather young and sour, Nyssa sat me on a bench by the temple door and bade me wait for my message.

The scroll was brought by an old woman, the head priestess, who is always called Hekate. She had been sleeping when I arrived, for she was very old. She was conducted to her chair by two deferential acolytes and she stared into my face for a long time. Then she touched the flowers and the plaited band and asked in a whisper, 'Are you Medea of Colchis, sister?'

'Lady Hekate, I am Medea,' I replied.

'Then this message is for you.'

I unwound the scroll. It was written on a parchment in both Colchian and Achaean, with a Phrygian translation underneath. It had passed through Troy, because the mark of the king was on it. His name appeared to be *Priamos,* which means 'one who has been ransomed' and was probably a scribal error. If not, it was a strange name for a king, especially since the next word was *Lykke,* which could only mean 'wolf woman'.

'Strange as Trojan ways' was a proverb in Colchis, but not even Trojans, surely, would be that strange.

On the other hand it was turning into a very peculiar world. Happily pregnant priestesses of Hekate would have seemed unimaginable the day before.

The message began abruptly. 'To the lady Medea, once Princess of Colchis, once Priestess of the Dark Mother, now wife to Jason, son of Aison of Iolkos and King of Corinth in Achaea, your father Aetes' greeting. I am banished by a usurper, who gained my palace with the help of a priestess of your order called Trioda. The sons of Phrixos left to start a colony near Lake Trionis and are not returning. Chalkiope, their mother, died of a spotted fever last summer. If you read this, daughter, return. I repent me of my rash actions, I repent me of my broken oath to the Achaeans, for which the goddess is punishing me by killing my son and taking away my kingdom. The kingdom is still in your gift. The Old Woman in the Cave directed me to send this plea, saying that you are faithful, though to me you were faithless. The Royal Scyths will know where to find me.'

Then there was the royal seal, a square stamp a palm's width, marked in purple dye, the colour of kingship. I let it roll up in my lap and sat thinking for some time. Colchis was in my gift, that was true, if Chalkiope, my sister, was dead. Her sons had left and did not wish to claim it. My half brother Aegialeus was long dead. And now, Trioda, who had cast me out of the worship of Hekate and set my feet firmly on the road to death and unbearable loss, had conspired with a stranger to wrest the lordship from my father and replace him on the throne.

I did not know how long the message had been on its way to find Medea, once wife of Jason, now priestess and princess again. There was no immediate way I could come to the rescue of Aetes. It would take me the rest of the sailing season to get to Colchis, and only if we were lucky with the winds.

I could, however, set out. Nauplios had sent a runner to Khirra to fetch his own boat, and I would wait the days in this strange temple. Kore and Scylla clearly felt completely at home here. They were lying under the big table and graciously accepting the scraps and bits which the priestesses let drop for them. And they were getting old. I would take my most devoted friends home to die in their own country, and see what could be done about the affairs of Colchis.

And I could go with Nauplios for, if it came to that, if I found that I could lie with him and risk another pregnancy—my mind shied off the thought—then I could marry and retain the priesthood of the Mother and the favour of Hekate. But before I did anything of the kind, I would compound some herbs in copper, just in case. My children still occurred to me. Every time I closed my eyes I could see the bundles of bodies lying in the courtyard of the temple, hear Mermerus' voice asking for Arktos. I might risk love, but I could not risk pregnancy again.

And I would not risk love until I had an unequivocal sign. I had felt pleasure with Herakles, but he was a hero on the way to becoming a demigod. I would not insult my friend Nauplios by lying with him just out of gratitude or because I felt I should reward him for his kindness and protection. Those are acceptable motives under ordinary circumstances, but these circumstances were not ordinary.

I gave him the scroll to read.

'We are going to Colchis?' he asked.

'Yes, when the boat arrives. Can the two of us manage it?'

'With luck and care, but it will take months. You will accept my protection, Lady?'

'Yes, I will accept it gladly,' I said, and smiled at him.

'You will make a mariner yet,' he said.

◇◇◇

Three days later, an over-excited sailor brought *Good Catch* into the beach at Piraeus, leapt out and declared to us, 'Have you heard the news?'

'No,' I said, watching a collection of sturdy women load food and water-skins aboard the little red boat. Nauplios had given his three horses to the temple, and they felt that they should make him some return. We had enough food—dried meat and fruit and parched corn—to last most of the way to Colchis, and I had some gold and most of my jewellery. The women of Hekate had plaited wheat-straw collars for the dogs, of which they seemed proud, and had combed and massaged all of us. We were scented with jasmine and so fine that Nauplios declared he did not know us.

'What is the news?' asked Nauplios, taking the mooring line out of the sailor's loosening grasp and leaning back to hold the *Good Catch* against the tide.

'Why, the hero Herakles is dead!' cried the messenger. 'His wife was jealous and thought his affections were waning. He was lying with a slave girl in his house, so she soaked his shirt in the blood of Nessus the centaur. That wicked one had told the gullible maiden to do this, and then Herakles would love her again. He put on the shirt and it burned him, burned him to the bone, and he could not tear it off and he could not die.'

I knew the method. One soaked linen in phosphorus and kept it under oil. Then, when it was expedient, put it on the victim and it burned on contact with the air, with a very hot flame that could not be put out by water. My heart ached for Herakles. This was a dreadful death.

'He ordered his pyre built,' continued the messenger. 'He lay on it and begged the men of Athens to light it. But no one would, afraid of killing the greatest hero in the world; until a passing stranger accepted the hero's bow in payment and thrust a brand into the wood. Then he burned like a torch, so that all within the land of Achaea saw it. But when they came to search the ashes, they found no bones. Nothing of the hero but his empty armour. He is lifted up to heaven to be with the gods,' said the man.

Phosphorus generates kiln-temperature heat. I doubted whether any bones would have been found, without the need for divine intervention.

So a stupid girl had murdered the beloved of Hera, the strongest man in the world, the most delightful of heroes, because she was jealous of a slave. It was revolting. I felt sick, and looked at Nauplios, seeing my disgust reflected in his eyes.

'We leave,' he said, jumping into the boat. I lifted Scylla and Kore and was boosted in myself. Then the sisters of Hekate put their shoulders to the keel and we slid down into the sea.

'Farewell, Achaea,' said Nauplios, spitting over the side. 'I never want to see you again.'

I spat also, and agreed.

Chapter Twenty-nine

Nauplios

The journey to Colchis, as I had expected, occupied months. We took *Good Catch*, slowly and carefully, along the galley route which Jason had followed on the way to Colchis. We sailed when we could, rowed when we had to, and rested each night in a suitable harbour.

We stopped in one temple of Hera to commend Herakles to her attention. Medea mourned the hero, though not excessively, for he had told us that he was about to die and bid us remember that he was happy. I never told my lady of that jealous face I had sighted in Herakles' garden, watching him kiss her on the forehead as he plaited gentians into her straight black hair. It was a thing which she did not need to know.

At first she slept uneasily, waking often, crying that the children were gone, were dead, and I lay beside her to comfort her. But as the time went on, she woke more seldom. We who mourn do not forget, but the pain eases as it wears our hearts into a groove as a turning wheel wears a channel in a millstone, or a worm gnaws a worm chamber in soft fruit. Memory returns, I have found, after a month, when the mind can contemplate it again, and so it was with my lady.

We talked about the children, endlessly rehearsing every moment of their short lives; and about Clytie, her wit and her devotion. We went from Euboea to Andros where no women can land, then to Skiathos, from Skiathos to where we saw Mount Olympus rising into cloud, and finally across to Lesbos, where no men can land. From there, rowing against an adverse current, we sailed into the bay of Troy. Women are seen in public without veils in Troy. An Achaean who tried to imprison one of them would have his work cut out, for they are well-skilled women and make their own terms with their husbands. Achaeans are not favoured amongst the maidens of that city.

It is a prosperous and pleasant place, and their waterfront taverns are better and cleaner than anywhere else. We heard the free-striding female traders speaking Trojan, a form of Phrygian, and we were accosted by a stout woman in a bright red gown and a startling headdress made of feathers and shells. She had a new house, she said, not lived in yet, and she would offer it to us for a small sum. We agreed on a price for a fire and lodging for us and the hounds. She recognised my lady's robes and her pendant of the three-legged cross, requested and got Hekate's blessing on her house, fed us well, and left us alone in a room as clean and pale as the inside of a seashell.

There we spoke, finally, of Jason.

'I don't know what came over me,' she said softly, cupping her chin in her hand and staring into the driftwood fire, which burned blue. 'I was mad, I think.'

'You gave him everything you valued,' I said cautiously.

'Which would have been better given to you, Nauplios,' she said unexpectedly.

'I would have valued it more,' I replied, truthfully.

'Yes,' she sighed. 'You would have. Would you value it now?'

'More than ever,' I replied through numb lips. She laid her hand on mine and I clasped it, unable to believe what I was hearing. Hoping, if this was a dream, that I would not wake. Her hand was warm, calloused and hard with hauling lines.

'I will not ask you to swear me an oath,' she said.

'Yet I will swear it,' I insisted.

'No, all swearing is vain, it is against the gods. I would not hear another man promise never to leave me, and then break his word,' she protested.

'I could not swear that in any case,' I told her. 'No one can swear that. Death will take me, Lady, and I do not know when Thanatos will come for either of us. But I, Nauplios, son of Dictys, fisherman of Iolkos, make oath and say, before all the gods, before Themis and Dike, before Aphrodite, Demeter and Artemis, that I love the lady Medea, and have always loved her. That I will stay with her as long as we live or fate allows.'

These were the words of the marriage oath taken in my own village, simple words not used in sophisticated cities like Corinth. And in the country her word is required of the lady, too, though in rich men's houses no one cares if the bride is pleased or displeased, and no one asks for permission. Poor men cannot afford to give their daughters to unacceptable suitors, for they must live in the same village as the new-married pair, and they can make the unwise father's life a misery if they are mismatched.

I did not know if she understood the significance of the ritual, though my lady understood most things much better than I.

The lady Medea knelt beside me and stared into the fire as she said, very clearly, 'I, Medea, daughter of Aerope, make oath and say before all the gods of both Colchis and Achaea, that I love Nauplios, the fisherman's son, and that I will stay with him as long as we live or fate allows.'

Then she kissed me. Quite deliberately, she unfastened my tunic at the shoulder, and it slid down my body to the floor. I saw her reach behind her neck to free her pendant and her blue tunic followed mine. She was naked and utterly beautiful and I feared to touch her. I had wanted her for so long that I was afraid I would hurt her, disgust her, or somehow turn her away from me.

'I don't know if this will work, Nauplios,' she whispered, leaning her head on my shoulder. 'I waited until I felt desire again, not wishing to give myself to you until I was sure. I have felt the warmth of your body the last moon, lying beside me.'

She sang a little of Philammon's creation hymn: '*Not the hasty fleeting incomplete mating of men and beasts.*'

'Are you afraid, Lady?' I asked.

'Oh, yes, Nauplios, I am afraid.'

'Come and lie down with me,' I said, taking her hand. 'At least we can be afraid together.'

And she chuckled a small chuckle, which gave me hope.

And it was nothing to be afraid of. I had lain with the Lemnian woman and felt as if I was being eaten alive. I had been seduced by the strange, illusory maidens of Circe's isle and felt deeply threatened. After that there had been the priestesses of Aphrodite, the lovely easy women of the temple in Corinth, and the sad Khirra widow who took me into her bed because she was cold. Medea was not like any of them. Her body yielded under my touch, smooth and warm, and I caressed her, using all the skills which I had learned from women all over Aegeas' ocean. Under soft kisses she released her frozen clutch on my shoulders and explored me, seeking to give pleasure and thus receiving it. My skin tingled with the delicate touch of her fingers. She was altogether lovely, strong, female. I would not hurry this mating, this culmination of all my desire. I found the pearl and stroked it, a circular touch which made her body jolt. I felt her begin to glow, I felt the clutch and spasm of her sheath around and under my fingers, then she opened to me by her own desire, guiding my phallus inside her, hungry for my love as I starved for hers.

We tried to be gentle, but we were not. I had wanted her for so long, and she had been without a man for years. As soon as she felt me inside her, she cried aloud and forced my hips against her, grabbing handfuls of flesh and muscle, driving her pelvis against mine until bones should have cracked. Our mouths met and bit and sucked. And I groaned in the rush of fire as her sheath bloomed around my phallus and sucked in my seed.

Then we lay in each other's arms, side by side, still joined, and fell asleep as though we had been drugged.

I woke not altogether sure of who I was or where I was, just that something unimaginably lovely had happened. A woman stirred beside me. My arm was numb, I ascertained, because she had slept in my embrace all night. Her long black hair drifted across my face and made me sneeze, and she laughed sleepily.

It was Medea, my lady, my wife, my sworn love, and she was lying in my bed, in my arms.

It was not the Lemnian woman who had required my semen, nor the generous priestesses who would take any man if he was kind. It was Medea, whom I had loved from the first moment I saw her, and she was content and replete, her head now on my chest.

Few lovers have had such a blissful awakening. I brushed the hair out of my mouth and said, 'Lady, it is morning.'

'So it is,' she replied, interested. 'But it is early, see, just dawn, and we do not need to get up yet. Even the hounds are still asleep.'

I looked. It was true. Kore and Scylla were lying as they always did if someone had banished them from the princess' bed; Kore's chin resting on Scylla's black back. I looked away hurriedly before my gaze brought a black ear up to alert, and lay down again.

And then we made love gently, softly, slowly, as I had never made love before. Time expanded, flesh became infinitely flexible. Touch seemed to sink into skin, as though there would be fingermarks, yet we were as soft as clay. She was responsive, inventive, finding new ways to please me, and I pleased her.

When we climaxed at last and lay back in the disordered bed, she said to me, 'I love you, Nauplios'; and I said, for the first time in my life, 'I love you.' For other women had wanted things from me, but it had never been my love.

When the woman in the red kirtle came with our morning meal, she looked at us and grinned all over her face, commenting, 'Now, that's a good omen for my new building! A house needs lovers in it, so that even when they are gone the walls will repeat their whispers, and those who come will be peaceable and quiet, not quarrelsome. Loving is the best way to complete a new bedchamber, though old friends getting drunk and swapping stories is good as well.'

'Lady,' said Medea, slipping easily into the Trojan tongue. Her Trojan was better than mine, fluent and idiomatic. The princess was naked to the waist and the light gilded her dark skin. I was still not sure that this was real, so I cupped a palm over her shoulder, and she was palpable bone and flesh. 'Did you choose us because you thought we were lovers?' she asked.

'Not lovers yet,' replied the woman in the red kirtle. Her headdress this morning was a relatively undecorated scarlet cloth tied into several interesting knots. 'But I knew you were going to be, this night or soon. And it was the night when you lodged with me, and I am very grateful. I have brought you bread and wine and broth, and the new fruits. The big dish is for the dogs,' she said, and went away, her crimson scarves fluttering.

We looked at each other, and laughed until we got hiccups.

We resumed our slow voyage to Colchis and I was happier than I have ever been. I admired her as she stood to the steering oar, quick and competent, now nearly as strong as she had been before Jason had plundered her love and murdered her children and her faith. We had travelled together for so long that we were friends and shipmates as well as lovers, and this was a union unknown in Achaea, where relations between men and women are always based on a difference in power. Men are strong, women are weak. Men own women and can treat them as they like, although most husbands are kind and most women can stand up for themselves. My lady was stronger than me, and had more courage. And she loved me, lay down with me in delight and rose in joy.

And because we both knew how fragile life was, how a snapped oar blade or a hidden rock could wipe one or both of us out of existence, we were the more precious to each other.

We did not attempt to sail the Clashing Rocks, but landed on the Phrygian side and had the *Good Catch* carried along the ancient portage way, by grumbling men with shoulders like Atlas and an insatiable thirst for the sour, flat beer they make in that country. We supplied a sufficiency of it to encourage their efforts, and they brought us into the Euxine Sea near the end of summer. When we got to Colchis, we would have to stay there, at least until the next spring. But I did not mind where we were, as long as she was with me.

Medea

The Delphic oracle had said that I was absolved. It had said, 'Another place, another life.' Then it mentioned a hero wrapped in flame, then a fisherman with the heart of a hero. I had not understood it until we heard of the death of Herakles in the shirt of Nessus.

I was afraid to believe it. Nauplios, my dear comrade, was a fisherman, and he certainly had the heart of a hero. He had been kind and constant, but I feared that my regard would be a poor return for his constancy and kindness.

I didn't know if I could love anyone ever again. Then I didn't know if I could ever desire anyone again. I had not spoken until we had worked our way almost out of the sea of Aegeas. Even then I only asked him if he still wanted me. He had been living close to me for moons, holding me when I screamed in nightmare or cried for my lost ones. His touch pleased me, and for a week I had been feeling a quiver of desire when I leaned on him to push an oar or touched his hand while tending a cooking pot. My body wanted a man. My mind hoped that it would be all right. It was more than all right. It was wonderful.

I had no right to expect that, after all my sins, I would find a lover again, much less a loving husband. I had not expected to have such pleasure in anyone. It was greater than I had felt with Jason. He had never striven after the first few months, to please me, but I wanted him so much that I was pleased with the most perfunctory attention.

Nauplios was different. He felt my climax in his own bones— I felt his in the same way. We were old friends, comrades, and lovers as well. There was no grabbing, no sense of urgency, to seize the moment before it flew away. After the first night, when I woke covered in bruises, lying on his bruised chest, we had not hurt each other. Even then I had not felt any pain at the time.

And he could still make me laugh; and a man who can make a woman laugh when she is cold, cross and moonstruck, facing a night spent on a wet rock with nothing to eat and no shelter, as we had been one soggy night off Lesbos, is something close to a demigod.

And I relied on him, as he relied on me. 'Back is bare that is brotherless', the proverb said. My back was no longer brotherless. I was rich beyond all deserving.

Kore and Scylla approved, too. It meant that both hounds had a human to rest their chins on, and eliminated their nightly argument about who got to sleep with the princess and who got to sleep on the floor.

We travelled through spring and into summer. I heard the goat bells as we passed Andros; male goats only, of course, which condemned the inhabitants of this gynaephobic isle to a diet of meat and herbs. We were showered with petals as we came into one little bay, where a high wind had stripped the orchards of blossom. It fell all about us, scattering the boat with sweetness. My moon blood continued. I had not conceived. I did not need the little phial of venom which would loose a baby from my womb.

Other mariners hailed us occasionally, telling us news. One said that Jason was much execrated in Corinth, where he still remained. He was always drunk, and the traders were complaining about his demands for wine, saying that he was ruining Corinth's reputation by slobbering over the new arrivals. Nauplios shot me a sharp look when we heard this, wondering how I would react, but I truly no longer even thought of Jason. My love for him, whatever it was, had gone like writing wiped off a Colchian child's slate. The Corinthian plague, it appeared, had been controlled by religious rituals, and the children and Clytie were now the subject of many prayers.

They still had mine, as well. I missed them, and Nauplios' love had not removed their memory. But time was rubbing the edges off the pain. I would never be entirely joyous and carefree again, but that would not be fitting for a woman of my age and a priestess of the Dark Mother, anyway. And although I was still mourning them and would be for all of my life, I was happy.

We reached the portage way and slogged through mud along the well-trodden channel, persuading a very reluctant mule to follow. It was essential, because it bore the refreshment: huge jugs of sticky, sour ale which the carriers consume all the time. I had tasted it out of curiosity, and wondered where they had obtained enough mule urine to compound it. But the porters lived on it and they did carry the boat.

Thus we did not dare the Clashing Rocks, which we had seen at sufficiently close quarters already. As Nauplios remarked, the world required enough of our courage, without our going out of our way to find more dangers.

And somewhere in the Euxine Sea, where a reedy river met the ocean, a black bird came flying; a raven of Hekate. It stooped over us, croaking, and dropped three golden flowers into my lap. There were colchidiums, the princess' flowers. It was summer, and I was going home. As a princess, as a priestess.

I thought vengefully of Trioda. She had, after all, told me that poison was power; and I could still remember fifty-odd, death-dealing potions without straining my memory. I knew nothing of this Perses who had usurped the kingship, but he could not have done it without her help. And she had cursed me with good solid curses which had all come to pass.

'Think, my princess,' Nauplios had urged, after listening to me rail for an afternoon. We were lying under the trees, waiting out the might of the sun, before going on to a safe harbour the other side of the Bynthian Islands. 'Think of what you are saying. Has the use of poison ever done you any good, Medea?'

He was right, of course. I lay down next to him on the pine needles and closed my eyes. I saw the children again. I had lost all of them.

When we enquired in Iolkos for my first-born son, Polyxenos, no one could tell us where his grave was. The centaurs had left Centaurs' Mountain and gone into the hinterland, taking their secrets with them. All of my children were gone.

Nauplios embraced me against his bare shoulder as I wept.

I did not want to take Nauplios, the only human dear to me, into danger; but something had to be done about my father, my only remaining kin.

We brought the boat into a cove where a river ran into the sea, and I hung over the side. I had noticed something.

'Look!' I said excitedly.

Nauplios was unimpressed. 'I see a wash of dirty water, stained with something which kills fish,' said my dear lord. 'It isn't doing the sea much good, either. What is it? Clay?'

'Lye,' I told him. 'We have come to the Washing Place, and with any luck we have found the Sauromatae. They will know where the Royal Scyths are. Let's get *Good Catch* up onto the strand and cover her with branches. If the Sauromatae are here, we can travel with them. They are going back toward Colchis, and they are—or were—my friends.'

'The lizard people?' he translated as we hauled the boat out of the water.

'The lizard clan. The women were Amazons who lost their way and now can't go home. I'll tell you about them as we walk. But if we are ambushed, don't react. They have a tendency to spear first and then not even bother to ask questions afterwards, which they would see as futile, because they never miss.'

'An interesting people,' said Nauplios, taking my hand. 'Hasty, perhaps.'

'No, I wouldn't say they were unduly hasty. They are just quick, that's all,' I smiled. 'All the different clans gather here to sleep out the summer. And this is where Herakles killed the Androphagi.'

Kore and Scylla frisked ahead, delighted to be on land and in familiar forest. I began to sing as we walked through the shrubbery and into the forest, so that a sentry would not leap to any unfortunate conclusions about who we were. I was wearing my priestesses robes, but my companion was identifiable as an Achaean. I sang the lullaby which Anemone had taught me.

Sleep little Scythling,
Thy mother is here.
Shalt be a rider,
Shalt be a fighter,
Shalt be a fine woman
When thou art grown.

A voice growled, 'Stand, woman of Hekate,' and, as we stopped, someone dropped neatly from a tree and roughly dragged back my hood. Nauplios tensed but did not speak.

'It's not her,' shouted the sentry, and was answered from another tree, 'Bring her to the king. Who is she?'

'I am Medea,' I said.

The woman lowered her spear and stared at me, putting back my hair with a hard hand, then suddenly grinned. Nauplios did not relax, but I did.

'Scythling Medea,' said the sentry, then shouted it to the tree-dweller. We heard the message repeated in three more voices, then the noise of hoofs, galloping.

Straight through the forest, avoiding death by inches, a horse ran at its fastest pace. The rider leapt down to land beside me and fold me in a close embrace, so that my face was pressed into a scarred breast and corded shoulder. I could not see the rest of her but I knew the scar.

'Iole,' I said, returning the pressure of her arms as best I could. 'Iole, how good to see you!'

'And you, Scythling! Anemone will be delighted. Not only because we heard that you were dead—or are you?' she demanded, frowning suspiciously. I pushed her fingers into my throat and let her feel the pulse, and her face cleared.

'But also because the king, your father, is a fugitive and there is a usurper in Colchis, one Perses, a tyrant, and one of your order is helping him,' she continued. 'We thought you might be her, and a quick spear would have solved the problem.'

'That's why I have come, to solve the problem of Trioda,' I said. I presented Nauplios, who was far too polite to stare at this painted savage, but who was looking a little bemused. 'This is my lord, Nauplios the fisherman.'

'I thought you ran away with that smooth, pretty one,' said Iole, who had never heard of tact. She punched Nauplios lightly in the upper arm, tapped his chest, and held out her hand for a warrior's salute. Nauplios grasped the offered palm and evidently applied enough pressure to impress Iole, because she punched him amiably again.

'I like this one much better,' she commented. 'This way, Lady. You'll want to speak to the queen.'

We found Anemone sitting on a wagon, shouting at the Scythian king, who was shouting back. Nauplios looked at me, but there was no need to be concerned. Shouting was the standard way of impressing an opponent with your argument in Scythian. I noticed that my lord was managing to follow most of the conversation and his eyebrows were rising. He had some knowledge of Scythian, but his teachers must have been very polite. A Scythian cursing match can curl bark and set fire to forests up to three *stadia* away.

Anemone halted in the middle of advising the king to go and mate with a black pig, and yelled into his wagon, 'Come out, sulking one! Look who's come back to deal with the renegade Hekate's priestess.'

Idanthyrsus poked his head through the curtain, saw me, and grinned his lecherous grin, which I always thought would be more effective if he had been more liberally provided with teeth.

'Princess Medea and the hounds of Hekate. She's not a virgin any more,' he concluded sadly. 'And she's brought her own man. Is not a Scyth good enough for you?'

'One at a time,' I said, and he laughed. I had never liked Idanthyrsus before, finding his sexuality offensive to my modesty. Now he seemed as innocent as a rutting beast, compared to the vice and cruelty of Achaeans. Of course, I no longer had much modesty to be affronted.

'Good. We can send word to your father and plan a campaign. Meanwhile, we can rest. Iole! Bring a jug and some cups.

'Medea, Princess, we heard that you had died, we heard that your children…'

'They are dead and in the Elysian Fields, and the city has been punished for their murder,' I said, finding my voice steady. 'This is Nauplios, who rescued me.'

Anemone sized up Nauplios in one glance and came to the same conclusion as Iole, which was heartening.

'Your man?'

'My man,' I replied.

'Looks like a good fighter,' said Idanthyrsus. 'Probably a good lover, too, so I shall contain my lust. Now, sit down, Lady, and let's talk.

'Aetes your father was deranged after you left with the treasure; and the people murmured, because he had broken his word, and that is bad in a king. But that would have died down, except that the sons of Phrixos left to found their own colony. Then Chalkiope, your sister, died of the spotted fever—though some wondered later if she had been poisoned.

'Then this Perses appeared, a tall man in black armour. He had twenty men with him, but he would never have got through the palace defences if Trioda had not let him in through the back gate. Aetes woke with a knife at his throat and this Perses demanding that he leave; and he obeyed, he and his wife Eidyia and several of the counsellors. They put them out of the city—it is easy to contain a walled city, and this Perses has some military skill, it seems—and into the marsh, where they wandered all night until the Scyths found them and helped them get away.

'Your father consulted The Old Woman in the Cave, and she counselled that he should send for you, saying that you were still a priestess and a child of Hekate, and that Trioda had no right to cast you out.'

I felt a pang. I had been right. I had been a priestess all the time, and a faithless one. The loss of Hekate had been hard to bear, and I had not even lost her.

'So we carried a letter to the scribes on the coast and sent fifty copies of it to the temples of Achaea and Thrace and Mysia, wrapped in wheat straw-like offerings. No one will meddle with a parcel wrapped in sacred straw. But it has been almost a year, Scythling, and we heard that you had died. We are very glad that it is not so.'

'I am glad also,' I agreed.

'And meanwhile your father grows weaker and the tyrant Perses loots Colchis, sending his plunder over the sea to Asia. He won't stay, of course, he will leave when there is nothing more to steal. We heard recently that he is intending to sell the populace as slaves.'

'He must be stopped,' I said firmly. 'We will find a way.'

Chapter Thirty

Nauplios

The Scyths were very hospitable, and clearly very fond of my lady. They are friendly and warlike and they have great strength and stamina. They demonstrate this particularly in their massive consumption of a drink called kermiss; made, I was told, of fermented mare's milk. It is golden brown, foaming, clear, and tastes like nothing else I have ever tasted.

It is also very potent, especially if one is not used to it. I found myself telling an audience of fascinated Scyths the whole tale of the Golden Fleece and all the subsequent history of the Argonauts, from Ancaeas, dead in his vineyard, to Herakles, burning in the shirt of Nessus. They listened with great interest, prompting me when I flagged.

When the tale had meandered to the conclusion—Nauplios and Medea returning to Colchis to put Aetes back on his throne—Idanthyrsus belched and remarked, 'It was all wasted, comrade, all that valour and all that skill. The princess betrayed her family and lost her own children, and the Golden Fleece did not even buy Jason his father's kingdom. Now all that you can do is try and return things to the state they were in before the *Argo* came through the Clashing Rocks.'

He was right, of course.

I was pleased to wake the next morning without the headache I had deserved. Kore and Scylla had lapped some of the kermiss, and were still asleep, paws ridiculously in the air and tongues lolling. I wondered if dogs got hangovers as I sipped the barley broth which a Scythian warrior made for us.

I saw Medea, riding fast across the open glade, high on the horse's shoulders. Her hair blew back from her face and she was urging her steed onto greater efforts.

'She is beautiful, your woman,' said the Scythian.

To Achaean eyes he looked like a barbarian; half naked, scarred and shiny with oil. His hair was braided with feathers and a necklace of what were probably human teeth was strung around his neck. He was the husband of Iole who had first greeted my lady. I knew enough of the world now not to judge by appearances, so I did not take offence but agreed. Medea my lady was indeed beautiful.

'Scythling, they call her,' he said. 'You will not be able to make her live all her life in a stone city, comrade.'

'No,' I said. I wondered where we would live. I doubted that the princess would be content in a fisherman's hut, assuming that they had fishermen on this coast. But the savage was correct. No one who had seen that blue and black figure flying past on a Scythian mount could imagine that Medea would be happy if she were secluded again.

I was leaving it up to the gods, with a certain amount of trepidation.

Two days later a wagon rolled into the Sauromatae camp, to a ritual display of hair-raising insults, and three people were lifted carefully down by a scowling Scythian driver. From what the Sauromatae women were saying, this man's branch of the Scyths did not allow women to ride or hunt or fight, and the reasons which were suggested for this were, I hoped, anatomically impossible.

An old man was conducted to a seat on a bank. He was attended by another old man and a woman in a profusion of veils, loaded down with gold crown, necklace, belt and arm rings. There were even rings around her ankles and she clanked when she moved, like a soldier in full armour.

Medea, beside me, said, 'That is Eidyia, the queen, my father Aetes, and his counsellor Eupolis. Come with me, Nauplios.'

She knelt at the old man's feet and he squinted at her, trying to focus.

'Hekate's child,' he wheezed. 'Medea. So you came. Tyche said you would come. They have banished me, daughter, and my son is dead, and my daughter Chalkiope and her sons are gone.'

'I know,' soothed Medea. 'Take courage, father. I will contrive something.'

'This is my fault,' said the old king. Sudden tears ran down his furrowed face. 'I gave you to that evil woman when you were a baby, because I could not bear to think of you. But how can a child be guilty of the murder of her mother? It was unjust.

'And then I broke my word to the Achaean; that is the root of all this disaster. Why, there is the Achaean,' he looked at me, puzzled. 'No, that is not the man. Who is this, daughter?'

'Nauplios, my husband. You may greet him, father, he is faithful and honourable and he has brought me here to try and repair this mess we have made between us. Can anyone tell me anything about this Perses? Why did Trioda support him?'

'Because she was losing her position,' replied Eidyia. 'She had no right to curse you or cast you out, and she boasted of it. The other priestesses were intending to remove her from the worship of Hekate. They had already sent to Tyche of the shrine of Hekate Oldest for advice. She had told them that Trioda was no longer a fit servant of the Dark Mother.'

Medea

This was a fascinating conversation.

'So she joined Perses to keep her ascendancy. And yet if Hekate has cast her out there are certain immunities which she must lose,' I was thinking aloud. 'Tell me about Perses.'

'He is an Asian adventurer,' Eupolis informed me. He had never approved of me, but now he delivered a report such as a warrior brings to his captain: crisp and unemotional.

'He does not want Colchis, just its goods. He has one ship which is moored at Poti, and there most of his men live, levying taxes on the traders who come there. But he and three of his men are in the palace.'

'Yes, all good. But what do we know about Perses himself?' I asked.

The Scythian wagon driver scowled even more than before and growled, 'He is afraid of the dark. He always has a light burning in his chamber at night. We believe he is afraid of vengeful ghosts. He is brave enough against ordinary terrors, but he is scared of the unseen.'

I reflected that the life led by an Asian pirate would probably gather him a goodly company of phantoms who were not all that happy about being in that state. I could not see how this information would help, but it was interesting.

'How do you know this?' I asked the Scyth.

'He stole a Scythian woman,' he said. 'Although our women are not shameless, like some I could mention, they are not defenceless, either. She stayed with him two nights, long enough to discover a way of escape. She had no knife, or she would have killed him for the insult. But she slipped away, and reported to me all that she had seen.'

'How did she get out?' asked Nauplios. We were, I could see, thinking along the same lines.

'Through the queen's corridor,' said the Scyth, and it made sense. Because women must not enter the great courtyard, a covered way had been constructed so that the queen and her ladies could walk unobserved to feasts and to the king's bedchamber. The Scythian woman had crept out of the king's chamber and into the corridor, which led to the women's quarters but also to the bath, which had a door onto the market. The queen's attendants had used it all the time to meet unsuitable lovers, and when I was a child I had slipped out that way to go fishing with the sons of Phrixos. Unless the pirate had found this bolt-hole and stopped it, we had a way into the palace.

'Also, Trioda is always with him,' said the Scyth. 'The black bitch of Hekate, disgrace of her worship, makes sorceries for Perses, prophesying that he will be a great king and the ruler of a people more numerous than the sands of the desert.'

'Hmm,' I said. 'How many warriors could you take to Poti, to seize that ship?'

'As many as are needed. We could have done it at any time— the strangers are careless and no match for Scyths, even female Scyths—but it seemed pointless while Perses held the palace.'

'We will come to Colchis the day after tomorrow,' I told him. 'When that day dawns or just before, when guards are careless and unsighted by the coming light, seize the vessel. Do not kill the crew unless you have to, but remove all their loot and tie them safely, depositing them in the boat.'

'We will do that or die in the attempt.' He spat to seal his word. 'But what of the palace?'

'Leave the palace to me,' I replied.

I gave my father and his wife and counselor into the care of the Royal Scyths again. Aetes was no longer a figure of power and terror to me. He was a sick old man who needed my help. I kissed his hand and went to choose a horse. I was not altogether sure that my plan was going to work, but it had a better chance than battle. The walls of Colchis are strong, and Scyths have no talent for siege warfare.

Nauplios chose a mount the match of mine—for a fisherman's son he was skilled in the judgment of horses—and asked me worriedly, 'What do you mean to do, Medea?'

I told him. He didn't like it, but he considered it had a fair chance of success, which is as much as can be expected in an imperfect world.

We rode that afternoon; Nauplios, me, Iole and Dianthys. The Scythian women were smarting under the insults laid on them by the Royal Scyth. Until the sun was going down they discussed things which they could do to him which they thought would improve his manners, and Nauplios was shocked. We came into the marshes and the mosquitoes immediately descended. Nauplios remarked that they had missed him on his last visit and were now making up for lost time. He expressed concern for them, starving all that time for Achaean blood. Only Nauplios would express concern for a mosquito.

We rode on, because stopping would have driven the horses wild, until we came to the temple where I had served my apprenticeship. It was the last building at the end of a long street, and the wall was low at that side, because no one could bring an attacking army through the mud. We leapt over, the well-trained Scythian horses taking the barrier in their stride, and rode into the temple.

There was no one there. It was dusty and desolate. Trioda, clearly, had not come back to collect her goods when she had moved to the palace to pour flattery into the ear of a tyrant.

'We stay here for a while,' I ordered. The Scyths dismounted silently and began to groom their beasts. I searched among the scrolls for one which I had read many years ago, and lit a small fire to have light to see by and to take the graveyard chill out of the air. No one was likely to enquire as to who was in the temple of Hekate, but I issued tunics and robes to all of us, even Nauplios. He looked very convincing, as long as he kept his hood up, and I told him that I was glad he had not grown a beard.

Then I searched for the recipe, finally finding it in a scroll written almost a hundred years ago by a priestess with an interest in vapours. The ingredients were mostly ready to hand—I even had fresh horse dung. Then I descended to the underground chamber, to collect some allies and to ask Hekate for her blessing.

The image was covered in spiderwebs, and I wiped it clean and spilled some wine on the statue's feet. I told Hekate what I was intending to do, promising that I would not kill again if it could possibly be avoided. I was done with murder. She must have approved, because her people came gladly when I summoned them.

I cast a very loose, black cloak over my gown and, followed by Nauplios and the Scyths, paced without looking to left or right through the waking streets of Colchis to the marketplace door. I laid a hand on it and it gave.

It swung open. Beyond, all was silent. I stepped inside, followed by Dianthys. She swung and stabbed without warning. I heard a choking gurgle and then the thud of a body hitting the floor.

'He was hiding in the alcove,' she said, examining the corpse and prying a sword from the tight-shut fist.

'Is he a follower of Perses?' I asked.

'He was once,' she chuckled. 'Not now.'

The others came in and we pushed the door shut. The palace was unnaturally silent. There should have been slaves about by now, lighting fires and baking bread and heating wine and water for the first meal. The women's quarters were empty. Where had all the people gone? Had Perses already sold them as slaves? Or were we walking into a trap?

He had known about the door; he had set a guard there. Nauplios was reaching the same conclusion.

'I don't think we are going to come as a terrible surprise to Perses,' he commented in my ear.

'Perhaps not,' I said.

There was a flurry of movement, then another of those choking gurgles. Iole lowered the body onto a bed. She had stabbed him messily through the throat and he was bleeding freely.

'Perses again?' I asked.

'Was,' she said laconically.

I had promised the goddess that I would not kill deliberately again, and my word was being eroded. We passed the corridor without challenge, however, and the king's bed chamber was before us. As the Scyth had said, it was brightly lit by at least three oil lamps, I guessed.

I touched the door and a sword swished past my wrist. The swordsman was silently dispatched. The third man had just died, and there should only be Perses himself in the king's chamber.

I knelt and lit my firepot with a carefully reserved coal, and at once a cold, evil-smelling smoke poured forth. It was heavier than air because it was made of sulphur and herbs and horse dung, and it crept under the bedchamber door. I gave him a few moments to notice.

I heard someone sit up abruptly and exclaim in a language which I did not know. That was something I had not thought of. I needed to speak to this usurper.

Nauplios whispered, 'It's a form of Mysian. I know it, do you?'

'No. You'll have to come with me. Quick. Smear your face with this.' I passed over a pot of the salve which we use against midges. It lends the skin a green cast which is very disconcerting, making even my dear Nauplios' honest countenance look eerie.

I opened the door very slowly. A tall man with black hair was sitting up in bed, wide-eyed. But it was not Perses who held my attention. It was Trioda. She was standing by the wall, her feet hidden in my smoke.

'Medea,' she hissed. 'I thought it might be you, cursed daughter, playing tricks in the night.'

'You were right,' I agreed. I dropped the outer cloak. The three-legged cross shone on my breast. 'I am and always was a priestess of Hekate,' I told her. 'I never left her. She has accepted me again.'

'Why are you here?' she snarled. 'You left this place for another, and abandoned your faith and your father. Are you now here in his cause?'

'I am. Does the tyrant understand Colchian?'

'No,' she snarled.

'Why not just kill him?' suggested Iole, the Scyth, behind me. "Easy. I could do it from here.'

I did not have time to explain that killing one adventurer would only remove him, whereas a terrified pirate fleeing for his life without a coin to show for his efforts would preserve Colchis from similar assaults for some time.

I simply said, 'No,' and she accepted this.

Ignoring Trioda, I walked to the foreigner and spoke to him, while Nauplios' voice made the translation behind me. Instead of being comic, this made the scene more alarming, as though two voices with one mind were in the room.

'Perses, why did you come to Colchis?' I asked.

'For gold,' he answered. He was frightened, but not terrified.

'We are protected by a powerful goddess, Hekate the Black Bitch,' I informed him. He did not reply, but jerked his thumb at Trioda.

'You think that she can protect you?' I laughed softly, and that seemed to alarm him, for he shrank back. 'She has left the goddess to follow you, Perses. She has no power now.'

Something was gathering at the back of my head. It was a pain, as if someone was pinching my brain, or squeezing it in a vice. This had always been Trioda's punishment for inattentive princesses and she would never tell me how she did it. I looked at her. She was smiling in triumph, lips parted over her teeth.

But I knew about pain. I could bear it.

'You will be cursed unless you leave now,' I told Perses. 'Your followers who were in the palace are dead.'

He shouted suddenly, three words which might have been names.

I gave him time to feel the silence, and then said, 'She is a powerful goddess and she gives us certain authorities. One is to command ghosts. Hekate is the queen of phantoms. Ghosts are all about you, Perses. Bloodstained ghosts. You have killed many. One here has a knife in his back—is he yours? And the child with blond hair, how about him?'

The interesting thing was that I could see them, too. They were not vengeful but shadows, quite mindless, and somehow attached to their murderer. The act which had taken their lives had bound them to Perses. I did not have to make them up. I just described them, while the pain in my head grew.

'The woman in the green tunic, her throat is cut—and the other one in red, she was smothered, a rape perhaps? Would you like me to tell her that you didn't mean to kill her, just to silence her screams?'

'Tell her,' he shouted. I spoke to the phantom but she could not hear me, of course. She was what Colchians call the *ba* soul, a mere shape and form, quite harmless, though Perses didn't know that.

'She does not believe you,' I told him. 'What about this man in armour, much like that black armour you wear. Is he your father, Perses, or your brother?'

'Tell him to leave me alone,' he cried.

'They will stay here if you leave Colchis,' I insinuated. He was wavering, almost convinced and very frightened now, when Trioda took a hand.

'Do not believe the witch, Lord,' she said quickly. 'There is nothing she can do to banish your ghosts. And there is much profit to be made of Colchis yet, before we leave for Asia and your destiny.'

'She is powerful,' said Perses, pointing at me.

'She has no power but that of brazen insolence.' Trioda grabbed for my arm, and then laughed.

One of Hekate's people was wrapped around my wrist, and it raised its head and hissed.

'Do you think to frighten me with that?' she demanded. The pain in my head increased.

Trioda smiled a pitying smile at me and seized the viper. Then she watched in great amazement as it turned in her hand and sank its fangs into her arm.

'But I am a priestess of the Dark Mother,' she protested, sinking down into her chair. I was almost sorry for her, this bitter and spiteful woman who had done her best to destroy my life.

'You were her priestess, but when you betrayed her and me, she cast you out,' I explained. Even if I had wanted to save her, there is no cure for the venom of the red viper. 'And she took away from her faithless priestess the ability to handle serpents.'

The pain in my head vanished. Trioda collapsed and died in a few minutes. She tried to speak to me again before her heart ceased to beat, but she could not form words. I do not know whether she meant to ask for my forgiveness or to curse me afresh.

After the removal of his pet priestess, we had little further trouble with the usurper of Colchis. He required no persuasion at all to get out of bed and precede us through the palace, out of the door and down to the river, where we launched a boat in which we also laid the three bodies of his fellow pirates. On the journey he became distressed and shouted at us several times, but all I needed to do was to lean a little closer and let him see the red viper, and he was as clay in our hands.

And when we reached Poti, the town was awake, picking over a huge pile of stolen property on the quay. Three Scyths lolled on the deck of a ship, looking exquisitely self-satisfied and idle, which is a habit of Scyths and an affront to all respectable persons.

I saw into the vessel as we pulled up. The crew were all trussed into neat bundles and laid out in rows. They had been gagged, which explained the silence. We allowed Perses to climb on board, and I spoke to him for the last time.

'We will drag your ship into the middle current, Perses, and it will carry you to Asia, and maybe your destiny. I will keep your ghosts here with me. But if you return, pirate, you will meet all your nightmares here again, and they will haunt you beyond flesh and bone, beyond mind and spirit.'

He nodded. I sprinkled him with certain herbs and made the prayers to my lady Hekate, and saw his phantoms separate, fade and vanish into the Colchian mist. The *ba* soul, once released, sinks back into mist and thence into rain or dew, and re-enters the earth. Perses, who must have had some rudimentary insight, noticed at once that they were gone. Even in his bare skin, about to be thrust into the world with a whole crew to untie and placate because there had been no profit from his capture of a city, he gave me a small bow and thanked me for taking the ghosts away.

I would have liked to know him better. Perhaps. He had a certain brazen, gambler's courage. The sailors towed Perses' ship out into the current and released the lines, and the pirates vanished into the fog.

I returned to the palace to have Trioda's body prepared for burial in the earth. And to my great surprise, I wept.

Nauplios

The restoration of the king was the excuse for a very large feast. Medea and I sat with the Scyths, who ate most delicately and carefully for the most part. The Colchians were loud with complaints about the actions of the tyrant Perses, though any people with a scrap of initiative would not have allowed themselves to be plundered by one shipload of strangers.

Unless, of course, they had inside help. Such as we had received from my lady, or Perses had been given by Trioda. I had accompanied Medea to the funeral of this woman whom she had hated for years. All she said about Trioda was spoken while we were looking down into the wrappings at the corpse.

'All this time I've been thinking of her as a Titaness, a huge, overbearing monster. But she's just a small woman, and old.'

'And now dead and entirely done by her own hand,' I pointed out.

'Just so,' said my lady.

◇◇◇

I walked around Poti and thought it a very nice little town. It was not enclosed, as Colchis was, stranded in the cold marshes halfway up a river. It had a good harbour and a beach for careening ships. Fresh water was always available from Phasis, and there were other springs besides. Plenty of trade went through Poti, in valuable commodities like gold and amber and parchment, so there was a babble of different voices along the dockside; no Achaeans, but Phrygians, Trojans, and a language which I had never heard, spoken on the other shore of the Euxine.

I joined some Colchian fishermen as they went out after the schooling sea bass; and after they had seen for themselves that I could obey an order, secure a line, trim a hip against a wave and haul a net, they accepted me. There were old men amongst them who reminded me of my father, Dictys, and some of their sayings were identical.

'Never assume that a mooring line is secure or an anchor cannot shift,' they warned me solemnly. 'For Oceanos is a god and gods are whimsical.' I felt at home.

I accompanied my lady when she rode with the Sauromatae women the next day. They were returning to Washing Place, and I wanted my boat.

'Lord,' said Medea to me, as we rode knee to knee along the grassy edge of the sea.

'Lady?' I asked.

'Will we stay here?'

'I will take the *Good Catch* down to Poti, and there I will buy or build a house,' I said, smiling into her anxious face. 'I am a fisherman, after all, and the fishing here is good. Will you come with me, Medea?'

'You don't want to live in the palace?' she asked. I could not read her expression, but I owed her the truth. 'Aetes wishes to make you king,' Medea told me.

'I am a simple fisherman, Lady, and I will not be a king.'

'You mean this, Nauplios?'

'Certainly,' I said, fear gripping my heart. I had come from Iolkos by the longest road to Colchis, and I had brought a princess home. She would naturally want to regain her rank and her marble rooms and her slaves. I was about to lose her, who had journeyed so long with me, and whom I loved with all my heart.

Then she grabbed my rein and forced my horse to a halt.

'We must go with the Scyths and collect the hounds and the boat,' she said rapidly. 'Then we will find a house and never, never think of kingship again.' And she flung herself off her horse and into my arms and held me tight, her face pressed against mine.

Medea

I had been so afraid that Nauplios would fall in with the king's wishes and accept the title of prince. I had returned to Colchis, and it was chill and dangerous, full of bloodsucking insects and fog which stank of dead men. I had acquired a taste for waterfronts, and I liked Poti. I thought longingly of a house for a fisherman and a priestess, with a wide bed to lie warm in with room for the dogs, and maybe a small garden and a vine. I would ride with the Scyths, of course, and I had to go and visit Tyche of the shrine of Hekate Oldest. I might bear or I might be barren; I did not care. I wanted a sanctuary, I wanted rest and love and sleep.

But if Nauplios accepted the burden and honour of the title of heir to the throne, I would go with him because I could not bear to leave him. And in that closed stone city our love would be blighted, would sicken and die in the mist, until I would one day wake alone again and forever.

It took me all my courage to ask him, but I should have known; I should have trusted to his integrity and his honest good sense. He knew that he did not want to be king. He had seen enough of kings to last him as many lifetimes as an Orphean. When he told me that he wanted what I wanted, I threw myself into his arms and laughed for joy.

Autumn came. I was sitting on a cask of Achaean wine, watching the unloading of a ship, when I heard a voice singing. It was a clear, beautiful voice, pitched to ring over the sailors swearing and the traders crying prices for their stock, and it was singing my name.

> *Medea, priestess,*
> *Colchis' princess,*
> *Finds her happiness*
> *With a mariner.*
> *Sailors all*
> *Take note of this:*
> *Be kind to your woman,*
> *She might be a princess.*

'Philammon!' exclaimed Nauplios, abandoning his discussion on the respective merits of hemp or hair ropes for nets, a topic on which all sailors had an opinion.

'Greetings and well met! I was looking for you. Ah, you are happy, as the song says,' he said, holding us at arm's length and smiling.

'We are happy, and you? Have you something to tell us?' Nauplios asked.

'Some things, let us sit down,' said the bard. 'I can't stay. That boat over there is taking me back to the portage way. You are settled, that is good. I have bad news for you,' he said.

Nauplios stood behind me, his hands on my shoulders.

The bard said, 'It is about Jason.'

'I care nothing for Jason,' I said, with perfect truth.

'Care then as you would for any human in Phanes' net. He declined, as you might have heard. He drank, and disgraced himself. Then he went down to *Argo*, where she lies rotting on the beach, with a rope, intending to hang himself from the keel. But before he could…'

'The keel fell,' I said, remembering my bright little vision. 'The statue of the goddess Hera fell, and crushed him.'

'Just so. And even I have not been able to make an epic out of the Argosy. It does not end well, not as a story should. The audience would be dissatisfied with Jason's decline and Medea's despair and this small conclusion, a fisherman as a husband and a small house on the shore at Poti.'

'It is not a small thing,' said Nauplios gravely. 'Happiness is not a small thing.'

Philammon shook his coppery hair and laughed. 'You are right. Oh, and here is the other news out of Achaea. Guess who has come from Mysia to defend Herakles' children? Deianeira hanged herself, you know, once she realised what she had done.'

'Who?' I asked.

'Hylas. Nauplios knew him. A very pretty boy, who was, he says, beguiled by the nymphs. Someone clearly beguiled him, and kept him for years, but now he has turned up, a strong young warrior. He fought off one attack on the sons of Herakles, and says he will defend them with his life.

'I'm coming now,' the bard called to the captain of the little boat, who was waving. He leaned down and kissed us both, and the last we saw of Philammon he was running down the quay, red hair flying, green tunic open, then leaping into a boat which would bear him out of the Euxine Sea.

It was the middle of winter. The gales had lashed the sea. Fishing was out of the question, and I came into the house shaking off water from my sodden cloak. Nauplios laid down the carving he was making and told Scylla that she could relax. She had been acting as model and took this seriously, but it was a trial for an aging dog and she collapsed next to Kore with a relieved sigh and went to sleep. The hounds were old, stiff in their joints and disinclined to move, not even to chase birds, though they always accompanied Nauplios on his morning walk down to the quay and back. The house was white and warm. Firelight glittered off Herakles' sword, hung on our wall next to a painting of Hekate on parchment. I was freezing.

Nauplios kissed me and took off my cloak, spreading it over a chair to dry.

'This is threadbare, my love,' he commented. 'Haven't you a better mantle?'

'There's one in the cupboard, I think, in the bundle we brought from Athens,' I answered from the depths of the towel with which I was drying my face and arms. I wrung out my hair on the hearth and rubbed it briskly. I was starting to get warm. A pot of dried-meat stew was simmering on the kitchen fire and the house smelled of cooking and slightly damp dogs, a very pleasant combination.

I heard Nauplios drop something which smashed and I went into the bedchamber with the broom, ready to sweep up the shards.

He was standing as if amazed, staring at something in his hands. I came up to him, walking carefully through a mess of white fragments, and looked over his elbow.

'Herakles gave it to me, on the morning we ran away together,' Nauplios whispered, his brown eyes shining with tears.

'He told me, "when it opens, your lives will bloom". It has been forgotten in this cupboard all this time, more than a year without water or light. But it came true,' said my dear lord, and drew me close to his side.

In his brown hand, impossible, scarlet and scented, a rose was blooming.

Afterword

But we know Medea Killed her children...

No, we don't.

We know that Euripides the playwright came up with the definitive legend in a play so brilliant and effective that all subsequent writers have based their versions on his; from the savage play by the Roman, Seneca, (where Medea throws a blood-covered child at Jason), to the late-nineteenth-century Medea played by Sarah Bernhardt, where she sings lullabies to the babies while she cuts their throats.

Picture the scene. I am sitting in *Le Cafe Francais* having lunch with the most urbane and learned, retired Reader of Classics at Melbourne University, Dennis Pryor. I am nervous. I have been researching for weeks, and I have come to an unbelievable conclusion.

I venture, 'Er, Dennis...I don't think Medea killed her children,' and he does not even put down his wine glass. 'Yes, m'dear?' he asks, waiting for the punch line.

This is so well known amongst classicists that I couldn't even make Dennis Pryor put down his wine glass (which he always does when I float some outrageous theory); and yet *everyone* knows Medea killed her children.

How do we know?

The same way we know that Richard III murdered his nephews. We know it because the best playwright of the age chose to tell us. Shakespeare got his plot from Holinshed, and followed the orthodox Tudor line about the House of York, which was almost certainly innocent of those murders. Euripides took his from Eumoleus and improved it, and according to various sources, was paid five talents to make the sorceress Medea into a child murderer.

Every commentator knew this. Professor Kerenyi of blessed memory knew it. Robert Graves knew it. Dennis Pryor knows it. And yet we still know Medea as the prototype 'bad mother'.

This seems to have been the story, according to such diverse authorities as the travel writer Pausanius, Apollodorus, Kreophylas, Parmeniskos and an anonymous but learned commentator on Pindar.

Medea, granddaughter of Helios (the Sun) held Corinth in her own right. Jason was her consort. He decided to marry Glauke and Medea arranged her murder. Recklessly, she also managed to start a fire which killed Creon, king of Corinth and father of Sisyphos, and possibly a number of other people—but not Jason, regrettably. Medea fled with her children to the temple of Hera on the hill, and either the kin of Creon or the Corinthian women flocked to the temple and stoned her children to death—in the temple.

They either would not or could not touch Medea, and she left Corinth and went to stay with Herakles, thence to Delphi and after that to various other places before she went home to Colchis to put her father back on the throne.

This sacrilegious act—the murder of children in the temple of the Mother herself—brought down the wrath of the gods on Corinth; and there was a plague, which the Corinthians dealt with by sending fourteen of their children every year to that same temple to live in mourning for the crime of the Corinthians in murdering Medea's children. The dead children were honoured with divine rites and were called the *myxobarbaroi*—the half barbarians.

The other group of stories available to Euripides, principally from Eumoleus, say that while carrying out some ritual intended to make them immortal, Medea unintentionally killed her children. Jason refused to forgive her for this.

Either way, none of the ancient writers say that Medea deliberately killed her children.

When the playwright Euripides accepted the Corinthian commission—and playwrights have to live—to write about Medea, they paid him to relieve them of blood guilt by rewriting the story. And it is recorded that Euripides was much censured for changing history. So Medea the sorceress and poisoner was transformed into Medea the child murderess. There is no evidence that she was a bad mother, and the fact that seven of the children she bore in the twelve years she was married to Jason were alive to be murdered indicates, in that time of high-child mortality, that she (or someone) was devoted to their care.

The tale of Philomela, Procne and Tereus—much loved by the Middle Ages—contains the prototype child murderess (and Euripides would have known it). Procne's sister Philomela was carried off, imprisoned and raped by Tereus, Procne's husband. He cut out Philomela's tongue so that she could not tell her sister about this outrage. She wove a tapestry which revealed the story to Procne, who freed her sister by redirecting the Bacchic rout, then Philomela and Procne killed his son, serving him up to his father at dinner. (Shakespeare's *Titus Andronicus*, which adds the gratuitous agony of having Philomela's hands cut off as well, fails in a plot point—how do you weave without hands?) And if this sounds familiar it is also told of the exceptionally doomed House of Atreus, where it happens twice.

Tereus discovered what he was eating, chased the two women, and all three of them were turned into birds. Procne, not her sister Philomela in the earliest stories, becomes the nightingale which mourns her lost child forever.

This story has such strong mythical and magical overtones that it is clearly very old. Procne and Philomela were ensuring that Tereus committed the sin of the Titan Cronos (Saturn)—of eating his own children. It may have been a leftover from the religion which dominated Hellas before the gods came and defeated the Titans. Ritual cannibalism is only mentioned in the most doomed of circumstances; though the playwrights seem to attribute it readily to barbarian cultures.

I have found no modern parallel to the story of Procne. Though I have found several cases where a woman kills a man to avenge or protect another woman who is also in a sexual relationship with him, I have not found one where she kills a child.

The other story available to Euripedes, and actually mentioned in his play, is the story of Ino who, cursed by Hera to wander forever, leapt from a cliff with her children in her arms. Ino follows the pattern of child murderesses in the modern world. She kills the child because she will not leave it behind— because no one will love it like she does, because she is worried about what will happen to the child without her.

Medea's 'murder' of her children so that Jason will not have them has echoes in the modern world too, but it is almost invariablly a non-custodial father who kills his children so that his wife shall not have them.

Euripides' Medea exhibits male characteristics and motivations—which may be why she is so unforgettable—so powerful, as a symbol, that even the all-male Achaean audience listening to that play who *knew* that Medea didn't kill her children, believed it instantly, as we do. Even the Corinthians who certainly *knew* that their children were sent every year to the temple of Hera in expiation for their crime believed it. One could almost wish that Euripides hadn't been such a great playwright.

In 1405 the writer Christine de Pisan, a most learned woman, must have read these different authors and decided to disbelieve everything to Medea's discredit. Medea appears in her *The Book of the City of Ladies* as a wise and stainless soul who was very learned in herbal medicine and who has been unfairly traduced. She wrote:

> *Medea, whom many historical works mention, was no less familiar with science and art than Manto (a diviner mentioned by Virgil). She was the daughter of Aetes, King of Colchis, and*

of Persia, and was very beautiful, with a noble and upright heart and a pleasant face. In learning, however, she surpassed and exceeded all women; she knew the powers of every herb and all the potions which can be concocted, and she was ignorant of no art that can be known. With her spells she could make the air become cloudy or dark, knew how to move winds from the grottoes and caverns of the earth, and how to provoke storms in the air, as well as how to stop the flow of rivers, confect poisons, create fire to burn effortlessly whatever object she chose, and similar arts. It was thanks to the art of her enchantments that Jason won the Golden Fleece...

(*The Book of the City of Ladies*, Christine de Pisan, I 32 I)

Later she concludes the tale of Medea in the companion volume:

For this reason Medea, who would rather have destroyed herself than do anything of this kind [i.e., desert Jason for another lover] turned despondent, nor did her heart ever again feel goodness or joy.

(*The Treasure of the City of Ladies*, Christine de Pisan II 56 I)

The 'fact' that Medea killed her children is so well known that the writer of the introduction to Christine de Pisan's work says:

...It is a trifle peculiar to find [Medea's] story told without a mention of the demented dimension of her despair, the murder of her children, overlooked. Christine actually describes the great prototype of the wronged first wife turning merely 'despondent' after Jason leaves her.[1]

It is quite possible that Christine de Pisan was actually aware of the weight of the evidence in favour of Medea and just didn't mention this slander.

The Argo and the Argonauts

The ships of the time, as I have seen for myself, carried at the absolute most about forty men, and their usual complement was twenty-five. However, what with having to include everyone who was sure that his ancestor was on *Argo* and putting together all sources, there was a cast of thousands on one small ship by the time that Apollonius of Rhodes was writing the compilation album, *Argonautica*. Like the fourteenth-century *Geste of Robin Hood*, it's a collection of all available stories and is quite often inconsistent—there just wasn't room on board for all those well-connected people.

So I have left out the sons of gods; for instance, the sons of Boreas, who could fly; which is going to be tricky for a modern reader to swallow. I omitted people who are archetypes or who already had a representative on board, like Orpheus, who has the Orphic bard Philammon, and Mopsus who has his brother seer, Idmon.

I kept Herakles and Hylas, though they leave the voyage fairly early on, because I have always been fascinated with Herakles. Most of the Argonauts were your basic Ancient Greek hoon—one only has to look at how they behaved. I retained Alabande, in whose persona my dear friend, Susan Tonkin, proudly rowed when she and I were Argonauts on ABC radio. I have also retained Atalante the Hunter, the only woman on board.

The Cauldron of Renewal

Giving support to the Irish statement that they are actually descended from the Danaans—that is, the Greeks—the only other mention of the cauldron is in Irish and Welsh stories; notably *Kilwych and Olwen* from *the Mabinogion*.

I have found it easier to come to the worship of Hekate, the Dark Mother, through Celtic sources than Greek ones (this may be because I have a Welsh background). See entry on Hekate.

Colchis as an Egyptian Colony

After a lot of research and attempts to decide between various Scyths—there are the Royal Scyths, who are nomads, and the ordinary Scyths, who stay in one place, and there are the Scyths whose women were originally Amazons and...

Seconds before I lost what remained of my reason I found that Herodotus clearly states that Colchis was an Egyptian colony. This was a relief to an author who thought she was going to have to re-invent the Scyths, about whom very little is known and not a lot to their credit; though they beat up the Persian army and had a tradition of very tough female rulers indeed. Anyone who doubts this should look up Tomyris and her argument with the king of Persia.

Egyptian colonies were not uncommon; as were colonies of other people in Egypt. The People of the Sea seem to have been Achaeans living on the Nile Delta. But such a colony, isolated on the Black Sea, would tend to become ingrown and traditional, to preserve their autonomy amongst the numberless Scythians. Therefore Medea's Colchis is a lot narrower and more circumscribed than life would have been in Thebes at the same time.

Jason's Claim to the Throne of Iolkos

The father of Pelias—'the usurper king' of Iolkos—was the god Poseidon and his mother was Tyro. Aison—Pelias' half brother and Jason's father—was definitely the offspring of King Kreutheus and Tyro.

This is similar to the argument about the accession of the Persian Xerxes to the throne. He said that when his brother was conceived, their father was only a prince; but when Xerxes was conceived his father was already king, therefore Xerxes should be king. This argument apparently convinced the Persians.

Jason was brought up on Mt Pelion by Cheiron the centaur (which is why he has no tact), and came one sandalled to demand his kingdom from Pelias. He was one sandalled because he lost the other helping an old woman (Hera) across a river.[2] He thus fulfilled the prophecy, made to Pelias, that he would be deposed by a one-sandalled man.

Jason's Family Claim to the Golden Fleece

King Phrixos, grandson of Minyas (therefore 'Minyans') was about to be sacrificed on Mt Laphystios for attempting to ravish his aunt (he hadn't, it was a scenario like the biblical Potiphar's wife) when Herakles appeared, objecting that Zeus does not accept human sacrifice. Then a winged golden ram—made by Hermes and sent by Hera—appeared, and Phrixos climbed aboard and was carried away with his sister Helle (who fell off it into the eponymous Hellespont).

Phrixos went on to Colchis, where he sacrificed the ram to Zeus the deliverer. He and the skin remained in Colchis, where he married Medea's older sister, Chalkiope, and had four sons by her. Aetes banished the four sons. Before all of this, Phrixos had lived in Iolkos and sired Kreutheus, Jason's grandfather.

Herakles

Herakles is Hera's man. The guardian of women, doesn't rape anyone, and spends a lot of his life in expiation of things done during battle fury. One writer suggests that Hera is his enemy, but Professor Kerenyi suggests she is his friend. This has a lot to do with the Argonauts, because Hera is also Jason's friend (and 'Iason', or healer, is also one of Herakles' titles).

Herakles is begotten by Zeus on Alkmene, in the form of her husband. Hermes then tricks Hera into giving him her breast to suck (and he bites her). Jealous Hera sends snakes to his cradle and he strangles them—clearly a sturdy little person. [A recent child in Deer Park (Australia), who was discovered by his horrified mother with a tiger snake's head crushed in his mouth, indicates that this is not impossible. The snake must have been so surprised that it neglected to bite the tot until it was too late.]

Young Herakles is sent out from Tiryns to be a herdsman and kills a lion which is slaughtering the flocks, thus acquiring his trademark lion skin. His club is made of an olive tree with a few branches trimmed off. He roams around until he comes to Tiryns and undertakes the following labours for Eurystheus—each one designed to kill him—in expiation for the murder of Herakles' own children in a battle rage; which sounds like the Norse 'berserk' fury. The 'labours of Herakles' are:

1 The Nemean Lion
2 The Hydra (where Eteocles was killed)
3 Capture the Cerynean Stag
4 Capture the Erimanthean Boar
5 Clean the stables of Augeus
6 Get rid of the Stymphalian Birds
7 Tame the mares of Diomedes
8 Pen the Cretan Bull
9 Seize the girdle of Hippolyte the Amazon
10 Take Geryon's Cattle
11 Fetch the golden apples
12 Lead Cerberus out of Hades

After this he kills his brother, Iphicles; and sells himself into slavery with Queen Omphale who, finding that he is no use whatsoever in spinning and weaving, sensibly employs him to wipe out her bandits. He also murders the children of Laomedon of Troy, because the king tries to cheat him out of his just fee for killing a sea monster.

By the time Herakles goes voyaging with Jason he is an elderly hero and is tired and worried about Hylas. He feels responsible to Hylas because he killed Hylas' father in a fit of that same battle rage. He has yet to find Deianeira and go home to Thebes, where he offers Medea sanctuary because she cured him of his fits of fury.

Some writers put the Jason voyage after the Erimanthean boar—in fact a good story is made of him reading Jason's announcement in a marketplace, dropping the boar and striding off to join the *Argo,* leaving the surprised boar to terrorise the town. I've followed the commentators who put it as his last deed. Herakles then acquires Deianeira, by meeting her relative in Hades; and she causes his death by soaking his shirt in the blood of the centaur, Nessus, because she feels that his affections are wavering.[3]

Hylas as the same person as Hylos

This is just arguable on linguistic grounds, and provides a pretty continuation of the Hylas/Herakles friendship. Hylas, in my version, leaves the nymphs and goes back to find Herakles dying in the shirt of Nessus. Foolish but well-meaning Deianeira kills herself, leaving Hylas to defend Herakles' children with his life.

Orpheus and the Orphic Philosophy

I am not learned enough—or rather, I will never be learned enough—to enter into any arguments about whether the Orphic song cycle (which may or may not be of the right period) is actually Orphean; or whether it was a later invention by scholars who desperately wanted there to have been Orphean Mysteries.

There were Orphean Mysteries and there it is. Orpheus went on the original *Argo*; but I've cut the numbers down, and left Orpheus ashore, taking instead the Orphic bard, Philammon, who is part of the original cast. Orpheans did not eat meat, have sex or shed blood.

Their basic mystery was the net—the belief that all things are connected. A touch on one part of the net will set all the threads vibrating and cause changes on the other side of it. This concept sounds surprisingly modern in these days of Chaos Theory, but it is genuinely ancient.

Their instrument was the lyre, a soundbox made of tortoise shell, a pair of curved arms and a bar across the top. It had between three and seven strings of different thicknesses, stopped with pegs and was strummed or plucked with the fingers. It sounds a bit like a Celtic harp strung with gut strings—soft but thrilling. Its range is that of the human voice and it can be retuned by slackening or tightening the strings.

The Mysteries of Samothrace

This religious ceremony has some Orphean overtones as well, because Philammon takes the Argonauts to the island of

Samothrace. The 'mysteries' appear to be related to the mystic marriage of Kadmos (or Kadmon) and Omonia (Harmony); or Persephone and Hades. This must have been a 'showing'—all mysteries were a showing—but, honourably, all the initiated have refused to reveal their experience. The closest I have found to an exposition of what a mystery was like is in Apuleius, *The Golden Ass*, where the narrator has the most beautiful lyric invocation of Isis—an Egyptian version of Aphrodite with the sterner aspects of Hera. The Argonauts' association with this mystery might explain why Jason ended up with Kadmos' tasks—the dragon's teeth and the earth-born men. I have for that reason omitted them. Jason has enough trouble as it is.

Hekate

Dark Mother, Scylla the Black Bitch, the black aspect of the Mother. But she's not all bad. She was also responsible for the newborn, pigs and journeys.

Women in Ancient Greece

Men must have felt entirely unsafe in Ancient Greece. No wonder homosexuality was so popular. You know where you are with men. But just think of the hazards involved with women; especially if you happen to be Agamemnon, Jason or Herakles. Clytemnestra, the Royal Woman, might—at your most vulnerable moment—bisect you with an axe, just because you sacrificed her daughter (and yours, Agamemnon) for a fair wind to Troy. And perhaps because you killed her first husband and their baby.

Medea, the wise woman, might (if you believe the rewritten texts) wipe out your progeny, attacking your heritage, just because you decided to put her aside and marry another younger, well-connected woman.

And even the dumb blonde of the ancient world, dim little virgin Deianeira, promised to Herakles by her dead relative, might—quite without meaning to hurt you—clothe you in a shirt which will burn your bones to ash.[3]

Perilous creatures, women. The only good one (according to the men who write about such things) is patient Penelope. And all she gets to do is ignore the attentions of freeloading suitors, while waiting forever for Odysseus to return from the Trojan War.

The Middle Ages loved Penelope because they thought she resembled one of the most annoying characters in all folklore or literature: the ever-forgiving patient Griselda, a creature whose self-abnegation was definitely pathological.

Even Chaucer found the story trying. And so did your author; as a folk singer, having to mouth eighteen nauseous verses of *The Forester*—a ballad version of the same thing—or the even longer Scottish version called *Fair Ellen*.

Footnotes

1 Foreword, Picador edition, p.xvi

2 Graves suggests that armies routinely fought with a bare left foot—I can't imagine why and it sounds very unlikely. Even if the other foot is shod for kicking the enemy, both feet shod for the same purpose would surely be more intelligent. Also, what use is an army that limps on one foot, due to thorns, flints, etc? The lack of one sandal therefore has to be unusual or the prophecy could have been fulfilled by any passing soldier and the story would have been sent askew. Of course, the gods were directing it, so I suppose it would have been Jason anyway. It's hard to tell with gods.

3 Any woman who believes that a dying centaur, who has just been shot by her husband with a well-placed arrow— to save her from being raped by said centaur—will tell her the truth about anything is a fool. And to believe that he means to do her a favour when he tells her to collect his blood and semen and soak a shirt in it, to give to her husband to wear when his affection strays is an idiot. Anyone who actually carries this out is a certified moron.

Bibliography

Ancient Sources

Apollonius Rhodios, *Argonautica,* Penguin, London, 1984.

Apuleius, *The Golden Ass,* trans. R. Graves, Penguin Classics, London, 1964.

Euripides, *Medea,* Penguin Classics, London, 1974.

Herodotus, *The Histories,* trans. Aubrey de Selincourt, Penguin Classics, London, 1935.

Pausanius, *Guide to Greece,* Vol. 2, trans. Peter Levi, Penguin Classics, London, 1979.

Secondary Sources

Cavendish, Richard (ed.), *Man, Myth and Magic,* Purnell, London, 1972.

Graves, Robert, *The Greek Myths* (combined edition), Penguin, London, 1992.

Kerenyi, C., *The Heroes of the Greeks,* Thames and Hudson, London, 1978.

Licht, Hans, *Sexual Life in Ancient Greece,* Routledge, London, 1949.

McEvedy, C., *The Penguin Atlas of Ancient History*, Penguin, London, 1983.

Neeson, Eoin, *Irish Myths and Legends*, Mercier, Dublin, 1978.

Page, Denys L., *Euripides' Medea: Introduction and Commentary*, Oxford University Press, London, 1955 (the definitive introduction to the play).

de Pisan, Christine, *The Book of the City of Ladies*, trans. E.J. Richards, introduction by Marion Warner, Picador, London, 1983.

de Pisan, Christine, *The Treasure of the City of Ladies* or *The Book of the Three Virtues*, trans. Sarah Lawson, Penguin, London, 1985

Severin, Tim, *The Jason Voyage*, Hutchinson, London, 1985.

(Contains everything you ever wanted to know about sailing a bronze-age boat, on Jason's course, to what is now Soviet Georgia. Severin is a shining example and a reproach to all who merely theorise. The easiest way to prove or disprove a theory about how something was done or made is to do it. He did it, for which this author is eternally grateful.)

Music Books

Baines, Anthony, *Bagpipes*, Occasional Papers in Technology, Pitt Rivers Museum, Oxford University, 1979.

Horniman Museum Publications, *Musical Instruments*, Inner London Education Authority, London, 1977.

Jenkins, Jean, *Man and Music,* Royal Scottish Museum, Edinburgh, 1983.

Jeankins, Jean, and Olsen, Paul, *Music and Musical Instruments in the World of Islam*, Horniman Museum, London, 1976.

Touma, Habib Hassan, *La Musique Arabe*, Institut International D'Etudes Comparatives de la Musique, Editions Buchet / Chastel, Paris, 1977.

Recordings

Music in the World of Islam, 2. Lutes, 4. Flutes and Trumpets, and *5. Reeds and Bagpipes*. Recordings by Jean Jenkins and Paul Olsen, Tangent Records, London, 1972.

Folktracks, an Anthology of Spanish Folk Music, collected by Alan Lomax and Jeanette Bell, recorded in Spain in 1952 and issued on Folktracks 60-616 (cassette tape), 1981.

Instrumental Families, Folk Instruments From Around The World, collected by Unesco in 1950, Folktracks 90-7000 (cassette tape), 1985.

To receive a free catalog of Poisoned Pen Press titles, please contact us in one of the following ways:

Phone: 1-800-421-3976
Facsimile: 1-480-949-1707
Email: info@poisonedpenpress.com
Website: www.poisonedpenpress.com

Poisoned Pen Press
6962 E. First Ave. Ste 103
Scottsdale, AZ 85251